THE HAND OF MASHYANA

THE EMARI CHRONICLES
BOOK ONE

AMBER HANSFORD

For Dinah, for giving me my love of stories.

For Linda, who showed me that I could tell them.

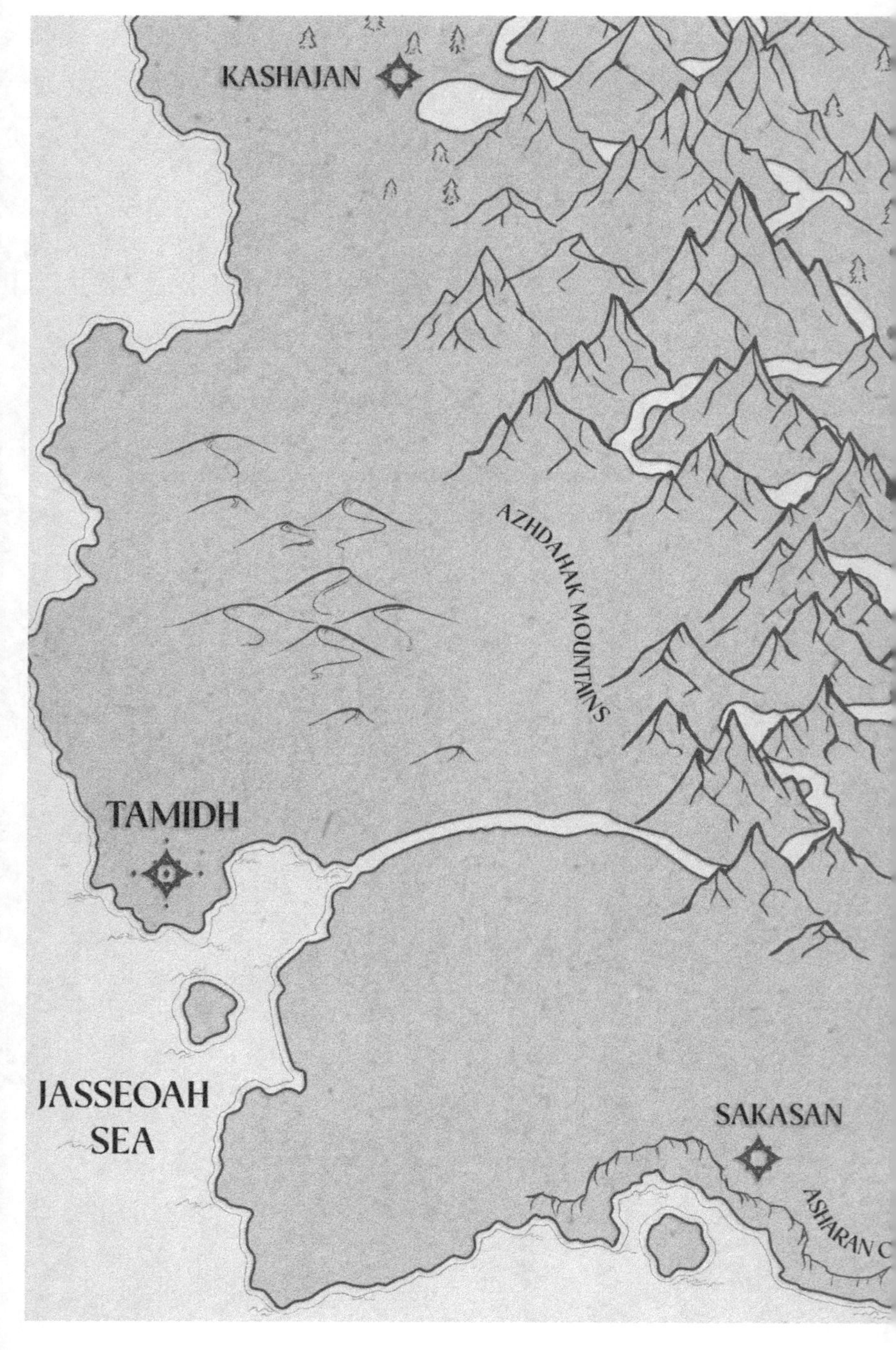

KASHAJAN
AZHDAHAK MOUNTAINS
TAMIDH
JASSEOAH SEA
SAKASAN
ASHARAN C

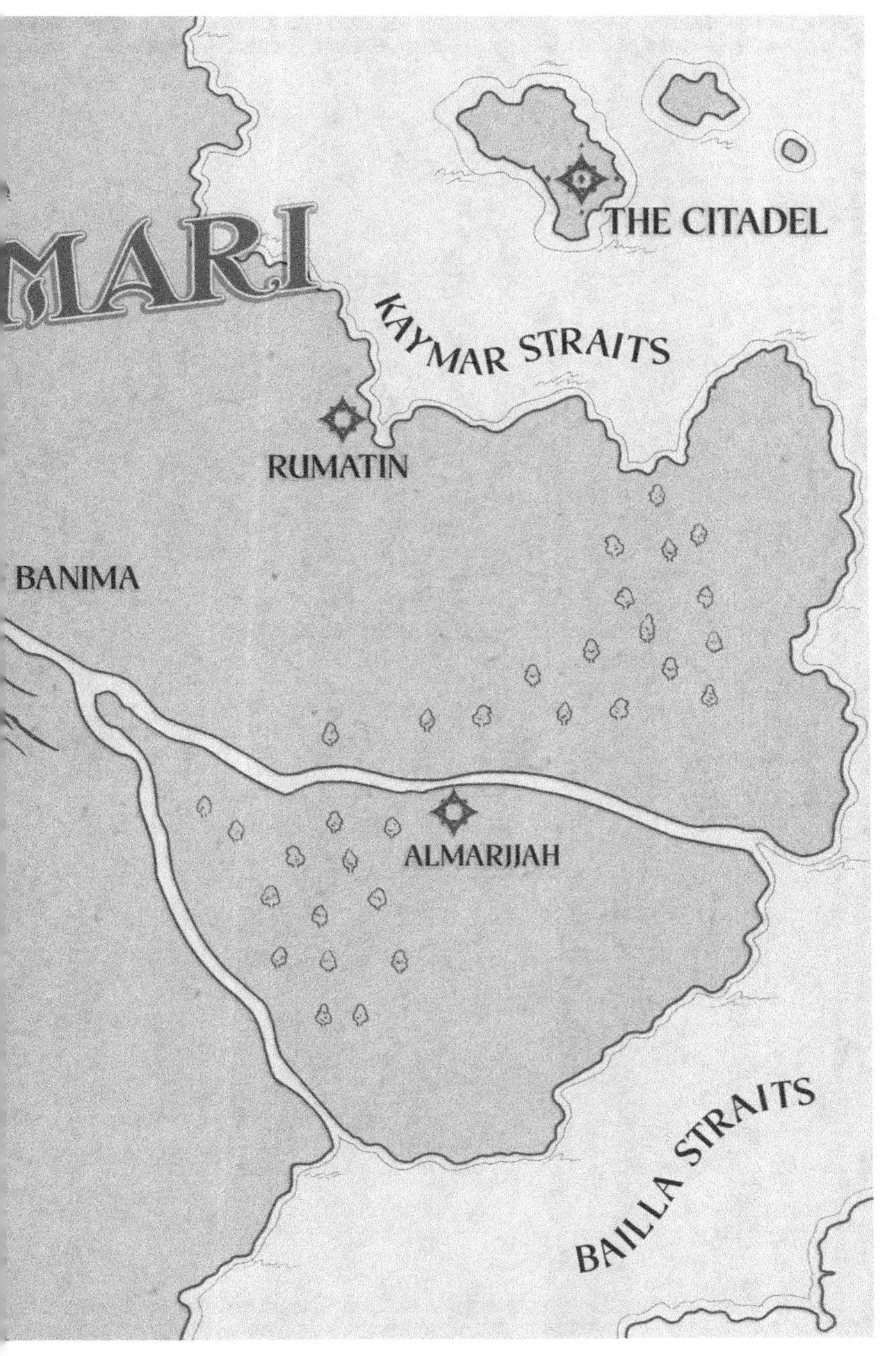
MARI
THE CITADEL
KAYMAR STRAITS
RUMATIN
BANIMA
ALMARIJAH
BAILLA STRAITS

MARKE
THE CITADEL

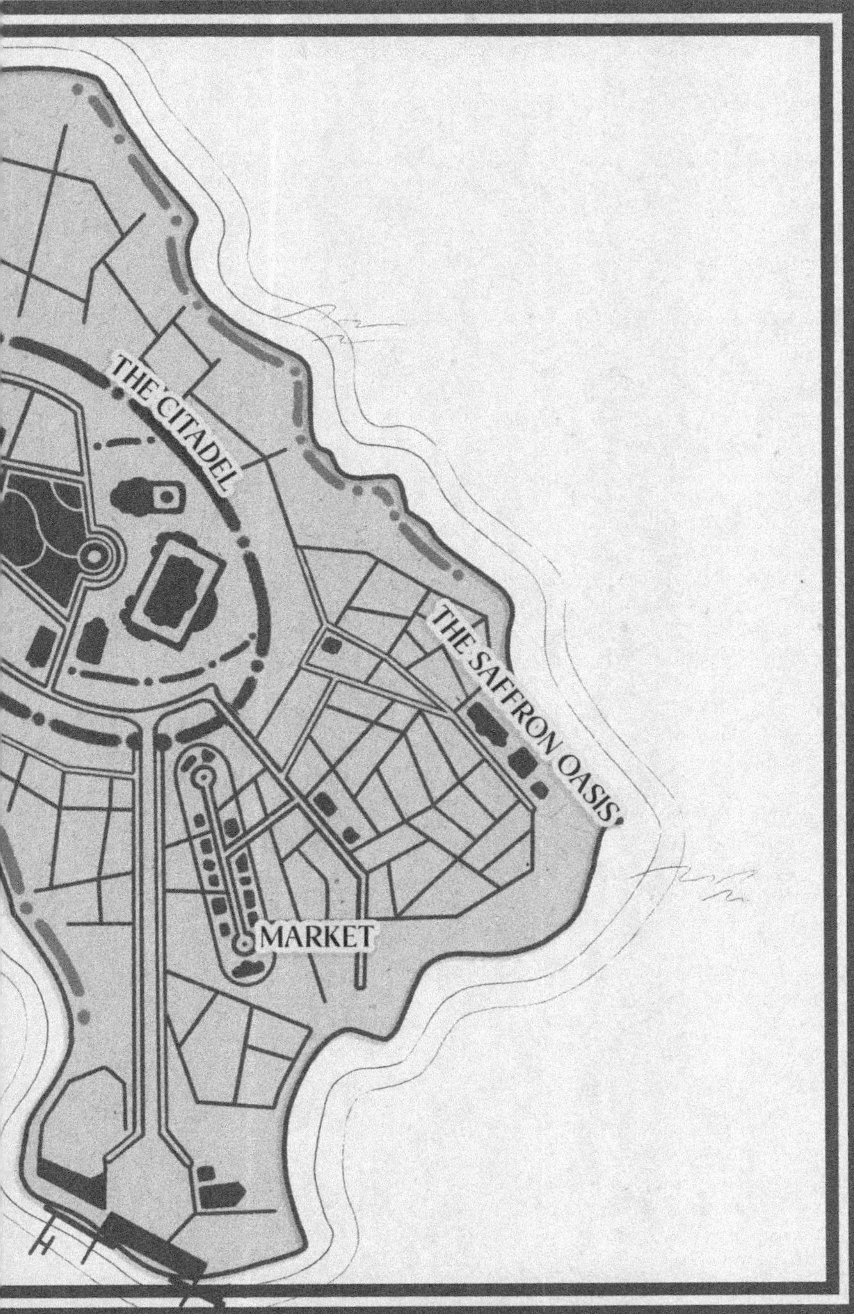

THE CITADEL
THE SAFFRON OASIS
MARKET

CHAPTER I

"Wɪᴛʜ ᴀʟʟ ᴏꜰ the power and rights bestowed to me from the Glorious Radiance of the Unnamed Gods as Mashyana, I name you My Hand."

Farah knelt on the polished floor of the grand throne room, her heart pounding as she looked up at her queen, her Mashyana, Behnaz à Radan. Light streamed through the intricate wooden cutouts high in the dome above, bathing the room in a warm glow as if the gods themselves smiled upon her in this moment of honor. Pride swelled in Farah's chest, floating just above the weight of expectation pooling in her gut.

The queen's thick dark hair gleamed beneath a crown of golden sunbeams and lotus flowers, highlighting her sharp angular face and complementing her dark eyes. She leaned down, her fingers deftly pinning the sigil of the House of Mashyaekhi onto Farah's best crosscoat. The gold brooch stood out starkly against the dull yellow embroidery of her collar, while the five rubies on the winged sun of the brooch glinted in the shafts of light, casting shadows that seemed to mock the fabric's lackluster sheen.

"Rise, Farahnaz Rahnema, and accept your obligation as Hand of Mashyana." With those words, the Queen broke their eye contact and addressed the court. A tremor of excitement coursed through Farah, amplified by the breath of the Mashyana's Talent that filled the sandstone throne room.

"May the Unnamed Gods and their Yazatas show their Grace within My Hand."

As Farah stepped back, she felt the weight of those words—both a blessing and a burden. She was no longer merely one of the Mashyana's Beloveds. She was now the queen's Chosen. Yet, the applause from the court felt like a distant echo, overshadowed by whispers of discontent rippling through the crowd.

Raising her head high, Farah turned at the dismissal nod from the Mashyana releasing her wards before the final prayers and walked to the back of the room. She stopped herself from touching the tight bun she'd wrangled her thick dark curls into before the ceremony, and focused on standing straight as was befitting the Hand. She quickly glanced down the line as they moved towards the back and spotted Arash, his sharp features framed by the flickering light. The noble-born wards walked near him, their disdain scarcely masked behind their pursed lips and narrowed eyes. She turned away from them and walked alone.

"Foundling Farah, look at you." The words slithered into her ear, a whisper laced with venom.

Arash had peeled away from his entourage, his voice dripping with mockery. "A new trinket from Amma Behnaz that you didn't earn?"

Angry heat rose in her chest, but she fixed her gaze on the Mashyana, who was now addressing the court with finality. Arash's presence was a shadow lingering behind her, taunting and insidious. This moment was hers to seize despite the resentful glares of her supposed peers. She steeled herself against it. She had earned this.

His harsh, mirthless laughter echoed in her ears. She didn't need to turn around to see his face twisted in a parody of the Mashyana's, sharp lines and hard edges, his eyes like dull storm clouds. "Just wait, Foundling. That sigil won't be on your collar for long. When you inevitably embarrass Amma Behnaz, it will be stripped from you for all of Emari to see."

"I am not the one who should worry about embarrassing themselves," she countered quietly, matching his whisper and raising her chin and not letting him get the better of her silence. "Your blood ties you to the Mashyana, but they are not as strong as you think. Respect is earned."

He leaned in closer, his breath chilling against her ear. "You speak to one above your station, Foundling. Keep your words in check, or they might bring misfortune upon you."

She felt the weight of his threat, but she refused to turn to face him. She'd already bested him in the Trials, outshining him with a drive he couldn't match. The Mashyana began her final invocation, and Farah steadied her breath. She had nothing to prove to him anymore. She had already won.

The bells rang out, their chimes resonating through the stone hall, marking the end of service as she walked out to the mid-day sun streaming through the stained-glass rotunda above the open area of the citadel. She slowed as the familiar light enveloped her from above. The dome rose like a crown, its vibrant colors casting the polished stone floor in a shifting kaleidoscope of reds, blues, and golds.

The panels told the story of Emari's rise and fall, from the gods' blessings to the chaos of war, and finally to the founding of the Mashya's dynasty. Each panel felt alive, the light breathing movement into their rigid forms. Yet, to those bustling beneath it, the beauty was an afterthought —merely a backdrop to their ambitions. The courtiers broke up into their respective groups, stopping to talk in the open area in the rotunda or heading off to one of the many hallways to their duties.

Farah tilted her head, her eyes drawn as always to the first panel. The gods stood tall and radiant, their hands outstretched as they blessed the land with their gifts. Each figure was rendered with striking precision, their robes flowing like rivers of light, their expressions serene and powerful. She had memorized every detail, the sparks of fire and the swirling waters they commanded, the winds that danced at their feet, the metals gleaming in their hands. It was a vision of what the world could have been, a tapestry of creation and harmony woven by divine hands.

But harmony was fleeting. The next panels shifted, their tones darkening. The seven primary gods stood apart now, their luminous forms marred by sharp lines and jagged fractures that spread across the glass like cracks in a mirror. Their hands, once united in blessing, were now raised against one another in anger. The in-fighting, the pettiness, it had consumed them. Farah traced the path of their destruction with her gaze: the cities set aflame by divine fury, the barren lands they scorched in their wrath, and the broken, hollow faces of the mortals caught in the storm.

Her stomach tightened as her eyes moved to the panels that followed, no matter how many times she looked at them. The gods were gone now, their departure marked by an empty sky, the Talents they had bestowed lingering like echoes in those they had touched. Without the divine, Emari fell into chaos. The once-prosperous lands descended into despair, their people clawing for survival amidst the ruins. These panels were the starkest of all, the flames and shadows rendered in sharp, angular strokes, the colors muted and heavy as though even the glass could feel the weight of the loss.

But then came the final panels. The burned land gave way to the first glimmers of restoration. Farah's gaze swept over the scenes of rebuilding—the strong hands of the Mashya's royal line gripping swords and banners, their faces turned toward the horizon. Each figure radiated purpose, their poses stiff but resolute. The panels moved from one ruler to the next, each carrying the burden of a fractured kingdom, until at last they arrived at the present.

The last panel is the most recent, its colors brighter and its lines more refined than the others. The current Mashyana and Mashya stood side by side, their hands outstretched in an offering of alms. Their faces were serene, noble, their features painstakingly detailed to convey a perfection Farah knew was impossible. The Mashyana's robes seemed to shimmer, the gold threads catching every flicker of the sun streaming through the glass. The image was one of peace and prosperity, a kingdom united under the firm yet benevolent rule of its monarchs.

How could anyone walk through the rotunda and not stop in wonderment as she did? So many things in this city made Farah stop in her tracks with the beauty of it all, and no one else seemed to have seen it. The Mashyana brought her to this island city when she was young enough that memories from before were muddled and removed from solid thoughts. Yet this city, this life that the Mashyana gave her would never be mundane to her when she could look up at things like the beauty and the story in the stained glass above her head every day.

The murmurs behind her told Farah that the Mashyana was leaving the throne room by the main doors. She turned and bowed at her waist as the small group of servants followed behind the queen and the sea of people in the rotunda parted in front of her.

She glanced up after the Mashyana passed by and saw Arash and his followers flowing directly into the wake of the Queen and her servants, smirking down at her. Moving with the rest of the group, she felt a slight but sharp breeze move across her face.

She made a point of brushing past Arash and his followers to stop just behind her queen's left hand, recognizing a summons.

"I am yours, Mashyana."

"Farahnaz, go and celebrate with your friends, but be in my chambers tomorrow morning," she said, still facing away from Farah.

"Yes, Mashyana." Farah dropped her head in deference, and backed away, dismissed by the dropping of the Mashyana's hand.

Friends were in short supply in the Citadel, at least for her. Arash had a grip on the other Beloveds that she never seemed to be able to break through, so she turned to training and becoming someone worthy of the honor she just received, or finding people who cared for her outside of this place, like at the Saffron Oasis. Since Commander Rostam's death, training had become a solitary effort. That wound was still healing even after the grand funeral a few months ago, and since then she spent most of her time alone, preparing for the Trials. Today was the result. The Mashyana's dismissal stung, but she pushed through the small pain to focus on tomorrow. The work begins tomorrow.

Farah smiled, not even letting Arash get under her skin as he passed by her again, a grimace on his face as they looked at one another. She stayed frozen in place, hands behind her back as the entourage followed behind the queen up the grand staircase.

With the queen's departure, the center of the rotunda returned to its regular buzz of movement, with people walking through the area with purpose, unaware of anyone else. The Trials of the Hand had pushed everything to a high level of intensity. It was a kindness to just be still for a moment, and she would take advantage of that.

She moved over to her favorite spot against one of the pillars where she was not in the way of people walking. She touched her hand gently to her sigil, deciding if she would wander to the Saffron Oasis and have a tea with Shirin if she was free. She was surrounded by many people who paid her no notice, even if a few moments ago she stood before them, and would like to celebrate in some fashion.

She was so used to being ignored in this crowd. Now, the strange feeling of being watched disoriented her, pulling at her to find the source of discomfort. She scanned the area, wondering if one of the courtiers had decided to speak with her now that she was the Hand, or if she was in the way of one of them and needed to move.

One little girl stood just inside the main decorative doors from the street side. Her dark hair would be almost invisible if not for the many-colored ribbons that were woven into the two long braids she wore that peeked out from her headscarf. Loose pants were worn under the long, embroidered tunic, and the vest looked worn but service-able, not unique in the island city. She stared at Farah, her dark eyes wide, barely visible in the shadows of open doors that weighed more than three men. Farah couldn't help but stare back in a contest of sorts as she left her spot and moved towards the little girl.

"Hello," Farah said, leaning against the wall, looking away from the little girl and back to the crowd in the rotunda. She propped a leg up and put her hands inside the sleeves of her crosscoat.

"I found you," the little girl said. Farah could feel that she was staring up at her.

"Did you, now? Did you see me in the throne room?"

"I see you in many throne rooms, bright and dark ones. I see you in deep, dark holes, struggling to breathe, and in bright sun-shining colors. I see you smiling, and I see you crying. I see you living a short, painful life, and I see you living a long, fruitful one."

Farah stared back down at the child, a lance of fear running through her as she froze. "What?"

"Rashnu shows me all the paths you are taking or can take. I just had to find you," the girl grinned. "And I found you now."

Farah gathered her thoughts. Was this little girl a part of a prank from Arash and his followers? His pranks were usually more violent and more explosive, like his personality.

She took a deep breath, choosing to play whatever game this was.

"The Yazatas are gone away from us, child. Rashnu can't be showing you my death."

She nodded. "I see you die. Sometimes soon, sometimes

later. But the Justice in Death is what Rashnu rules, so yes, he does show me."

Farah straightened up and dropped her foot to the ground, turning to the little girl.

"Who are you?" The lance of fear returned. There may be no prank, no trick.

"I am Pari. Rashnu wants me to help you not die quite so soon." She looked at the sigil of the Mashyana on Farah's collar and frowned before taking her hand, looking away from her for the first time.

"We need to go. We need to find the Other now." The girl, Pari, pulled at her hand, but Farah didn't budge. "Rashnu says that you and the Other must work together. Without that, all is lost."

Farah struggled to see what the trick could even be at this point. "What could be lost?"

With her free hand, Pari waved all around her, frustrated at Farah as if she was the problem in this conversation.

"All the things." She pulled on Farah's hand again.

"We need to go. I see where the Other is, but he won't be there for very much longer. He has walked into danger that you must help him walk out of."

Farah let the little girl pull her through the main citadel doors, letting the confusion at the whole situation reign over common sense, nudging between the courtiers coming in and out to the main thoroughfare of the city.

Could it be that the Unnamed Gods weren't content with her having a quiet day before beginning her new role, sending her a small adventure, led by a little girl who spoke with angels?

With the sun high above, she let the little girl lead her across the island capital, still trying to work out what was going on. The fine layer of dust that hung in the air from people moving around didn't seem to bother the little girl, though her diminutive height put her at more of a disadvantage as she pulled Farah this way and that, threading through the small crowds of people.

"Where are we going, little girl?" Coming back to her senses, she tried to slow the child down but couldn't seem to stop her. She had sped up, and Farah pulled along from the surprisingly iron grip of the child.

Pari huffed, turning her head around to glance at her for a moment.

"I told you. We need to get the Other before he makes an unfortunate choice. So we're going to get the Other. Rashnu said—"

Farah cut her off. "I know, I know, the Angel of Death speaks and shows you things, child."

"So why does Rashnu want us at the docks?" Frustration seeped into her voice. "Are you going to try and drown me?"

"Too many questions. Keep moving. The Other will be gone soon if we don't hurry. I know you do not like the House of Lies, so please hurry."

Farah almost stumbled hearing her speak of Hell. Divine, this little girl.

Finally, they moved out of the dark alleyways that Pari seemed to prefer. Farah smelled the sea before she heard the birds and voices of the sailors in their rhythmic cadences as they worked to load and unload ships at the docks.

She turned to the boardwalk, walking towards the bawdy houses and taverns. She paused occasionally, looking into the open doorways before moving on. Farah looked in to see what was missing in those that the little girl rejected.

She stopped for nothing, wandering in and around any of the people standing in her way at these doors who were selling their wares, either material or themselves. Farah followed as she could but ended up knocking into a few people.

"So sorry. Yes, pardon us." she would look down in deference. "We're looking for someone. Thank you."

Pari spun around in a doorway and Farah stumbled into one of the men trying to pivot with her, catching his tankard of some foul-smelling brew before it hit her and her court clothes.

"Oi, watch it girl!" he yelled out before looking at her. "Are you one of the new girls? A bit overdressed for work, ain't ya?"

Shame burned through her, her hands forming fists to punch the man before she caught herself. This little girl was making her into a fool. Pari pulled on her arm, away from the drunk.

Pari paused at another tavern door, open to grab the low intercoastal breeze and customers, and her shoulders dropped with a large sigh.

"Good. He's not dead yet," she mumbled, more to herself than Farah.

"Oh, good," Farah replied, over this little girl and whatever trick this whole chase through the docks had taken. She looked into the doorway. "Which one was all this trouble for?"

She scanned the room after Pari had pulled her through the doorway, her eyes adjusting to the darkness that all taverns seemed to breed with their layouts. There were a few men at the bar, either drinking on their own or bartering with the whores, and a few other scattered patrons, all classic sailors with their weather-worn faces at the tables. One of the tables had a card game going, and Farah dropped Pari's hand to move toward them.

A group of sailors sat around a card table, their faces marked by sun and sea, wearing the colors of one of the kingdom's privateer groups. A girl a few years younger than Farah circled the table, replacing the empty tankards with full ones, ignoring the looks and mumbled sailors cant that they shared with one another, and then staring back at the obvious stranger to the city. Farah quickly realized that the tavern girl was trying to signal the gharib as she circled the sailors, the foreigner, with her eyes as she passed behind the sailors. The sailors didn't seem to notice her, either from her job or her gender, but all three were focused on the man that the little girl had sent her to fetch. Two of the sailors looked more confused than anything.

One of them was very, very angry at the Other as he pulled the coins lying in the middle of the table towards himself.

Anger from being dragged through her city flew away from her, replaced with the instinct of something new yet instant recognition. From the back, she couldn't see his face, but his pale skin marked him as not from Emari, and his clothes, though worn and wrinkled as if he'd been sleeping rough, were of good quality. His brown hair cropped just past his chin, didn't hold any real style, as if he had missed a few haircuts while out in the world. She didn't need Pari to tell her who he was.

Her Talent thrummed along her veins, pointing out the metals on his body: a few daggers here and there, a coin pouch, and something she couldn't quite place in his pocket. She shook off the want of her Talent to do something with all the metals around her as another sense pulled at her to protect, to defend, to fight for this man.

One of the sailors — the angry one — shifted suddenly, and the hum grew sharper. Her hand was on her court dagger before she'd realized she moved.

Danger. The same sharp thrill that had flooded her senses when she stepped into the tavern. This gharib was the Other, and he was about to die.

CHAPTER 2

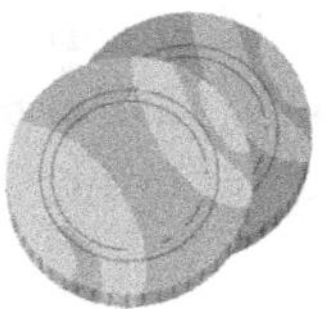

"Many, many thanks, gents," Yasher said, opening his arms wide to shovel the coins from the card game toward him at the table. "I think it's time for me to call it a day, though, if I'm going to make my next appointment."

He knew he shouldn't look at Kambiz as she replaced the sailors' tankards on the table, but he couldn't help but smile a little up at her as he scooped the coins into his road-worn purse. He tossed her a coin. She deftly caught it, but her lips were pressed in a thin line. A silent warning flashed behind her eyes.

"And for our wonderful tavern girl. You brought me luck." He winked at her and saw the sailors around him flinch. He took a little too much joy pushing at her. A blush spread across her tawny face to her dark, almost black hair.

"Not so fast. I believe you should play another round, gharib." One of them said, his hand going to his dagger, sitting on top of the pommel. The other two followed his lead, and Yasher shrugged. Thankfully these three spoke fluent Common, unlike some others he'd played since coming to the city, even if they all sounded as if they were gargling water as they spoke.

"Sorry, gents, but I really do need to get to the other side of the city now." He fixed the ties on his purse and slid it into his inside jacket pocket. "But my thanks for the game. I know I had fun. Another time?" Slapping his thighs, he started to push away from the table.

The first sailor jumped up, his dagger out of the sheath in one hand, his other meaty hand on Yasher's shoulder. He knew without standing that this man could possibly be twice his height and as wide.

"I don't believe that will work for me and my friends. Sit back and play another hand," he growled, gripping Yasher's shoulder tightly.

The big one may be a problem.

"Well, I..." Yasher looked around for Kambiz, who was standing out of the sailor's line of sight, shaking her head.

"You're staying and playing another hand." Yasher couldn't help but stare at the sailor's mouth while he let his mind work up a solution. He wondered how many teeth the big one still had left in his head, and how many he'd try and take from Yasher if he didn't come up with something soon. He felt the slight twitch of his luck changing, swinging like a pendulum between for good or for ill.

"Excuse me," A lyrical voice said from behind him as if it stepped out of a dream he had once. The pull of his luck warmed him, choosing good. "I need a moment with my friend here."

He turned and sucked in a breath as he matched the face to the voice it belonged to. Curly midnight hair, a few tendrils that had pulled out of the bun that captured the rest, highlighting the light freckles that were scattered across her cheeks and nose, and her mahogany eyes that stood out from her light bronze skin. Her formal cross coat was out of place for the tavern, with the obviously expensive jewelry pinned to her collar, the rubies and gold on any other person screaming out to be nicked. But her sheer presence, so out of place, would make any thief pause, even without it being the Royal Crest on her body in this ratty dockside tavern.

Yes, instant attraction to this woman hit him like a brick, but there was a pull to her that went far beyond wanting her, a recognition of something intense and overwhelming to be at her side, fighting off villains like a hero from a campfire story. It's a shame he was nothing like that.

His mouth went dry as she put her hand on her hip, staring down the sailors around him. The big guy, still standing, loosened his grip on his shoulder, staring at her, but didn't let go completely.

"Why would you wanna talk to him?" The big one said, attempting to stare her down.

"That's my business, not yours." Her hand moved to sit on her wide hip sash. Jeweled but well used daggers flashed like freshly mined silver in the dim tavern light, her hand resting gently on them. "Your game with him is done."

The big one laughed. "And when is it the Mashya's business to grab gharibs out of a card game?"

"My work is for the Mashyana, not the Mashya. She is not as kind as he is when her will is questioned."

The big one froze, but he removed his hand from Yasher's shoulder. Not to look a gift away, Yasher pushed back from the table, smiling and nodding at the sailors while standing. He took a large breath in, thanking his lucky stars and his lucky charm for this way out of the predicament.

"Thanks again, gents." He walked back a few steps, not

wanting to break the spell that this woman had put them under, then turned, smiling at his savior, his hand patting the pocket where his lucky charm lived. Another save thanks to it.

"My lady, shall we?" He bowed extravagantly and caught her staring at him with an odd look before the stoic and slightly dangerous face looked back to the sailors.

She nodded curtly to him, then to the sailors. The woman grabbed the hand of a small girl that Yasher hadn't noticed before. The girl was staring at him with an oddly satisfied smile, one that seemed too knowing for someone so young. Yasher gave a quick glance to Kambiz, winking at her to offer reassurance. Her face, however, told him all he needed to know—she would be worrying no matter what he did.

He quickly caught up with the woman and the little girl just outside the tavern doors, shading his eyes against the bright sun. The difference between them was striking. The woman had an air about her that spoke of wealth and status—she moved with the kind of confidence that came from being used to being seen. Her clothes were rich, the fabric soft and expensive, glinting slightly in the sunlight. Everything about her was composed, calculated. In contrast, the little girl at her side was an entirely different presence.

She was small, with dark hair almost entirely hidden under a headscarf, but the brightly colored ribbons woven into her two long braids peeking out gave her a vivid touch, like they were the only bold statement she could make against the otherwise plain, worn clothes. Loose pants under a long tunic, embroidered but faded with time. Her vest was nothing special, serviceable but unremarkable. She looked like one of the kids from the docks, all energy and movement, the kind that darted between the crowds, slipping unnoticed through spaces that others would hesitate to enter. It was odd to see them together—so different in their bearing, yet both somehow fitting into this strange, bright city.

"What I wouldn't give for just one rainy gray day," he mumbled, and the woman stopped and looked at him.

She glared at him, then turned back around, moving further down the boardwalk. The little girl kept turning around to look at him, and then back to the woman, her knowing smile infectious. Yasher smiled back at her and then realized she would steal a glance at his pocket where his lucky charm was before turning back, a shiver running through him that he couldn't quite stop.

"My lady, wait," he said, trying to keep up with her purposeful stride. "I thank you for the assistance back there, but I must be going."

She stopped and spun around to him. "If you'd like to retain your winnings and your life, you'll follow."

She spun back around and started walking away again, hand tight to the little girl. He waited for the twinge of his luck, and it pushed him forward to follow them.

"We need to look as though we're heading back to the Citadel. One of them is following us, more thanks to your extra card that's peeking out of your cuff than your sparkling personality, I'm sure. Using the Mashyana's name in there better not bite me in the ass." She looked down at the little girl at the last part.

"I do not see anything. We have the Other. That's all that matters." The little girl replied, starting to skip a little as the woman nodded once.

Yasher looked down at his left hand and did see the corner of his spare emergency card peeking out from the edge of his slightly dirty linen cuff. He hadn't even had the chance to use it in that game. He tucked it back into his sleeve, and then jogged back up to the two of them, the little girl in between. She grabbed his right hand, and sighed, looking up at him while they walked.

"I am very glad you did not die."

Yasher stumbled a little and looked down at the little girl. Her eyes held a golden sheen that he swore bore straight through him and ran a curl of fear around his chest.

"You know," he shrugged. "So am I."

They cut over and ducked into an alley, the woman taking the lead, and Yasher, still holding the little girl's hand, taking the back.

They walked quickly but silently through a few turns and switchbacks through alleys and busier streets until he could no longer smell the ocean breeze. The dust billowed up from the streets until they came to a market square. The woman pulled them into another alley just off the main square, releasing the child's hand finally.

"You two stay here. I'll see to getting rid of our follower," she said, and then slipped back into the market. Yasher watched her disappear into the crowd with ease, wondering if she'd come back from them at all, or leave them hanging out in the alley. If the big guy was the one following them, it would be best to stay put for a bit.

"So," he knelt to get even with the little girl. "I'm Yasher, and you are?"

The little girl smiled again at him, her face open and innocent, looking at him, and then down to his pocket as if she knew where and what his lucky charm was. This little girl had no business causing him this much anxiety every time she looked at his pocket.

"I'm Pari," she said simply.

"And our friend who seems to work for the Queen of this land?"

"That's Farahnaz." She stared, back and forth, between his pocket and his face. "She prefers Farah, though."

He waited to see what else she'd say, but she looked back at the alley entrance where the woman, Farah, left from. He stood up, looking with a bit of anticipation. Since the girl seemed to know what was going on, at least more than he did, he figured it best to follow her lead.

"Pari," he knelt back down, and she turned to him. "Why are we standing in this alley?"

"We're waiting for Farah to knock the sailor out."

He nodded, solemnly. "And then what are we to do?"

"Then we may have tea and cake. I want that path."

"Cake sounds lovely. But what after cake and tea?"

"Rashnu showed me, but I'm not allowed to say until it's important."

"Rashnu, it is?" he said, hoping that he would have some idea how long to play along. "When is it going to be important?"

"When it is important," she sighed. "Your path is not solid yet. There are still too many choices."

He kept his face as solemn as he could, biting back a grimace at the impatience that was brewing in him. She was not going to give up anything, and he couldn't figure out what grift or trick was needed to get back to his little room above the tavern, maybe even play a few more hands of cards. He tapped his hand against his thigh, wondering what he could do to slip the little girl and her protector without having Farah come after him. He didn't think the little girl would be hard to maneuver away from, but a little part of him knew that there'd be hell to pay from the woman. He reached out to see what his luck would tell him, but it had gone quiet as if it didn't want to get involved. Brilliant.

"Don't leave." Pari broke his train of thought with her small voice. A chill ran through him with how flat her tone was. "I see you dying again."

Yasher whistled. "Well, that's good reason to stay for a bit."

"Both of you are necessary. Rashnu shows me."

"And who is Rashnu?"

Pari giggled. "Rashnu knows you, but you don't him?"

He smiled at her, wondering how long he could keep her talking to figure out the best way to get out of this alleyway and situation in general. "Rashnu is from around these parts, while I, sadly, am not."

"Rashnu is one of our Yazatas - our Angel of Justice in Death."

"Good to know." He kept a smile on his face to placate the little crazy girl. Twelve hells, this day just keeps getting stranger. He needed to get back to his room and make his plans to get off this island if this was a regular day for them.

Pari nodded, then turned away from him, looking back at the entrance of the alley. He glanced over her shoulder and caught sight of the woman moving into the alleyway slowly, her posture straight and composed. There was an intensity in her dark eyes, alert and calculating, as she scanned the surroundings before raising a finger to her lips, signaling for silence. Then, with a fluid, almost predatory grace, she slinked toward a closed doorway, disappearing into the shadows.

After she slid into the shadows, the biggest sailor

stepped into the alley and spotted Yasher, still squatting down with Pari.

"Thought I'd find ya, gharib." His utilitarian knife glinted in the sun as he pulled it out of the sheath at his side. "Time to give back what you stole."

Yasher grabbed Pari around the waist and put her behind him before standing up to face the big man.

"Let's not be too hasty," he said, putting his hands up and taking a step back.

At that moment, Farah came out from the shadows behind the sailor, jumping up on a barrel and wrapping her forearm around his neck with one arm, the other holding that jeweled dagger against his check, a breath away from one of his eyes.

"If you wish to keep your eye, take your leave with his man. He is under my protection," she said softly and calmly. She slid the tip of the blade against his cheek, a drop of blood sliding down the edge of the dagger. A small flash of light ran up and down the blade, as Farah was softly humming.

"He-he stole from us," he whimpered. "Just want what's right."

"Call it a life lesson to not play cards with a gharib. For every one you can steal from, there's one that can steal from you. Now, will you yield?"

He didn't speak, and she moved the dagger closer to his eye.

"Aye, aye," he huffed. "We'll let it lie. Keep the damned coin."

She released him and hopped off the barrel. He slowly turned away from Yasher and Pari to Farah.

She brushed her coat down, sheathing her dagger.

"You should get back to your ship, you and your friends.

The Citadel doesn't hold that much of an appeal to you this evening." She gestured to the street behind him.

Holding his cheek where she'd cut him, he ran out, his heavy footfalls stirring up some of the dust in the alley. Farah watched him go, then turned back to Yasher and Pari, focusing on the little girl.

"Now what?"

Pari moved from behind Yasher, grabbing his hand, pulling him to where Farah was standing, and grabbing her hand with her other.

"Now it is time for tea and cakes. Come along."

He looked over to Farah. Living by instinct had kept him alive thus far and now those instincts told him to fly—get away from this city and the madness this woman and little girl had brought him.

"Pari," she began. "I don't think..."

"My thanks to both of you with the help for my rather... sticky situation. I do appreciate it, but I think I need to be going. More games to play and all that.," he said, releasing the little girl's hand and taking a step back. Pari grabbed for it in a much stronger grip than what he was expecting.

"No," the little girl said, looking at each of them, that odd golden sheen he saw earlier returning to her eyes. "You are both needed to take the Eye of Rashnu to the Chinvat Bridge before he dies."

Yasher choked back a laugh. "Didn't you say that Rashnu is a god or something?"

"The gods are dying."

He looked at Farah, expecting her to share in the joke. Her mahogany eyes were wide, he watched a shiver of fear pass over her face and felt it ripple across to him. Pari, seeming to accept that they were still with her, dropped their hands and skipped away, moving down another alley.

"Come along. Tea and cakes!" she said, exasperated with the two of them for lagging behind.

Lips pursing, Farah followed the child, and he fell into step beside her.

"From the look on your face, I gather that this Rashnu and Chinvat Bridge are all of importance here."

She was silent for a long moment. As she opened her mouth to reply, his luck twisted, as alarming as her words.

"Chinvat Bridge is where your soul is weighed for your deeds," she spoke slowly, not because he wouldn't understand but in obvious disbelief. "And all of our writings say that if the gods die, the world dies."

CHAPTER 3

Every part of Farah was on high alert. It was written in all of the ancient texts that if the gods died, the world would die with them, which was why they departed this plane, leaving only those blessed with Talents behind. Verses and scripture that she'd been raised to believe in but was relegated to stories and threats for children rattled her. But in a way, it also balanced out the shocks of whatever this pull was towards the gharib walking next to her.

She hadn't really gotten a good look at his face when he was at the card table in the tavern, and then her attention was primarily on the sailor following them. She finally looked at the man that Pari had her collect, this very important Other that the little girl had pulled her from the Citadel to save.

She could see his pale blue eyes like aquamarine ringed with a darker sapphire blue that marked him as a gharib as much as the rest of him, from the shade of his pale skin to his brown hair tinged with streaks of auburn, lightened by the sun. His face was dusted with a shadow of a beard, in need of a good shave as much as a haircut, especially in comparison to the pristine courtiers that she was usually surrounded by day in and day out. That pull she felt that was outside of her Talent became more insistent in the back of her mind as if a key had turned in a lock.

He caught her staring at him, and stared back, a quick grin taking over his face.

"Farahnaz, right?" he said, pulling his hair back from his face with his open hand. She startled a bit at her name in his mouth. "Pari and I were chatting while you were stalking the big boy back there."

"Yasher," he said, dipping his head down in greeting. "I suppose we're here to save a god or two after we get tea and cakes?"

Her faith warred with his practical yet dismissive humor. He was attractive, she'd give him that, but she was never pulled towards people who were so glib or reckless.

Pari turned back and moved to grab their hands again to walk together.

"Are you laughing at me?" the little girl asked him. He put his hand on his chest, mock-hurt but his eyes seemed sincere when he looked down at her.

"You believe this," he had a light smile as he looked at the little girl. She nodded vigorously. "And while I may need to be convinced still, I want to hear your story, Little Divine, and share some tea and cakes while I do."

Pari's eyes brightened, and she mirrored his grin.

"I am not a god, silly," she said to him.

"You speak of gods, you speak for a god, and you travel with a Goddess," he said, with a wink to Farah, "I'll call you Little Divine."

Farah ducked her head down, rubbing at her temples to cover the heat that colored her cheeks. She cleared her throat and straightened her coat.

"There's a shop just down the other side of the market square." She looked down at Pari, refusing to look at this irritating gharib.

The sun started to hide behind all the buildings built on top of one another in the island city. They weren't too far away from the Citadel and its stained glass, and every so often she caught a glimpse of the bright colors from an alleyway that showed them the more muddled and muted colors of the merchants.

She tilted her chin in greeting at a few of the merchants scattered throughout the square. Many recognized her and attempted to grab her attention to sell her their wares. The hum of the market, voices raising and lowering like music, soothed her as much as the Citadel's stained glass, but in a different way. She knew so many of the stall owners and would trust them over any of the other Beloveds that she'd grown and trained with, even if they may not see more than the sigil on her coat.

"You're well-known here," he said, startling her, even though Pari still had their hands in each of hers.

"This is my city," she replied, waving again at a merchant who called out her name. "I've been a ward to the Mashyana since I was in swaddling."

A hint of sadness touched his smile. Then he swung Pari's arm until the child giggled.

"I've heard many stories of this country, though this is the first time I've made it here," he said. He gazed ahead toward the square and then turned his blue eyes to her. "I had heard of the beauty and wonders, but today has shown me more than I could have imagined."

Was he flirting with her? She glared at him, irritation taking over the swirl of emotions that looking into his eyes caused her. She wasn't immune to flirtations, but the few that she'd let in were the exact opposite of this insufferable man.

He looked at the ground after a breath and caught him staring at the colors of the rotunda as they reflected on the ground, turning his head to stop and look.

"That is amazing. Is it all glass?" All of the posturing and theatrics that he'd been using since they met dropped, and she could feel the sincerity of the awe as he spoke.

Farah smiled as she looked up. "Yes, it is. It never seems to be less than amazing every time I see it, especially as the light catches it and spreads all the colors to the rest of the city."

He paused, taking a breath in.

"You have a beautiful smile." He walked away before she could respond. Pari stood between the two of them, a satisfied smirk on her face. Divine help her. This day is just one strange, confusing, and annoying moment after another.

She guided them over to a side street, and the air became scented with a hint of jasmine. Once they moved a few meters into it, the colors of greenery seemed to cool the air, and Farah released a breath like she always did when she came to Amma Shirin's tea shop, nestled in the middle of the buildings that lined the street.

Plants, flowering or not, hung down from all the balconies, or vines growing up the bricks, lining the street on both sides, keeping the area cooler than the street under the harsh sun. There were just as many voices as there were in the market, but the tone was hushed.

They walked for a bit, and she couldn't help but look over at him every so often, his mouth open like a fish at the street and people, moving about on their work for the day. He could be silent, praise the Unnamed Gods, though he was right to look around in reverence.

"This is…" he started but couldn't finish his sentence for a beat. "This is beautiful."

"This is Saffron Oasis," she replied, feeling the constant tension that she carried within her slip away with a small smile.

"Farahnaz! It's been too long!" A large woman came out of a doorway, dishtowel thrown over one shoulder, drying her hands on it. Her dark skin shimmered, her plain dress was sturdy but well-worn at the hems and seams. She came up to Farah and embraced her, joy beaming from her face.

"Shirin, I am sorry. I've been busy," she replied, smiling back at her. The woman was always there for Farah when she needed her, at those moments when the Beloveds or a courtier would bring her low.

"Where have you been, My Phoenix? I promised Rostam that I'd always look after you, you know. May the Unnamed Gods protect his soul," the older lady said, then looked down and saw the jewelry adorning her coat. "Oh, my, should I now call you Hand?"

She clapped Farah's upper arms and then looked toward Pari and Yasher for just a moment.

"We shall celebrate, no?" Shirin, her smile getting even bigger. "All friends of our Phoenix are welcome." She released Farah, snatched the towel off her shoulder, and cleaned off one of the few tables just outside of the entrance to the tea shop.

"Sit, sit," she said, pulling a third chair over from one of the other tables and rearranging them a little to make sure it would fit.

"Three cups, coming up." She waved for the three to sit,

and Pari skipped over to one of the chairs, releasing their hands finally.

Farah and Yasher sat after the little girl, taking the two chairs next to one another.

"Will Amma Shirin bring cakes with the tea?" the little girl questioned, looking to the doorway.

Farah smiled. "We will ask."

"Little Divine," he began. "I'm almost afraid to ask, but why are we here?" Yasher dropped his elbows on the table, and knitted his fingers together, resting his chin on them. Farah leaned forward as well, her Talent humming to her as her arms came close to his. She pulled back quickly, crossing her arms across her body instead, not sure if it was her Talent coming unbidden or this unknown pull that seemed separate from it.

"For tea and cakes, silly," the little girl said, copying him by resting her chin on her hands. "More will come in time, but I can't control that."

Shirin came out, three delicate handled mugs in one hand, and a basket of flatbread with oil in the other. She set them down on the table, looking first at Pari.

"Eat up, little one," she said, then looked to Yasher. "And you as well, you're too skinny to keep up with our Phoenix here." She beamed at Farah.

"My thanks, Shirin," Farah said. She bit into the flaky bread and pulled a mug of tea to her place.

"Would you happen to have any of your little cakes at the ready?" She looked down at Pari for a moment. "There is a request."

"Of course! Nothing but the best for the newest Hand of Mashyana and her new friends," Shirin said. "Now, don't let the Mashyana have you running around the kingdom too much that you forget about us here in the Oasis."

Shirin turned as voices called for her inside the shop.

Yasher winked at Farah as he sipped his tea. "Phoenix, huh? Did you set something on fire that you shouldn't have?"

"Shirin just likes nicknames. She decided that I was Phoenix long ago," she said, sipping her tea. "That's all."

"So, what about the business with your sigil and being the Hand of Mashyana? What's that?" he asked her.

"I am the servant of the Mashyana, our Queen," she replied. "I've been given the chance to prove myself as more than a courtier and ward."

"Yes, but..." he grabbed another piece of flatbread, handing a piece to each of them after he tore it in pieces. "What do you do for the Mashyana?"

"She sits at the Mashyana's feet like a rangy feral dog," a voice from behind them said, bitterness seeping into the man's voice. "And pants when she gets attention, or even just a pat on her mangy head."

"Arash," Farah said, her hand going to her dagger. Of course, he and two of his minions had to disturb her here. He'd changed out of his court clothes, which more than likely meant they were out on one of their 'hunts' to harass and bother civilians, hiding behind their privilege as Beloveds.

"Foundling Farahnaz," Arash responded, coming around to look at Pari and Yasher. "Who are your... friends? More urchins from the dirty street where Amma Behnaz found you?" His regal face was pulled into barely disguised disgust at Yasher's road-worn clothes.

"I thought you were banned from Saffron Oasis after you and your friends decided to destroy the shops on a lark?" she replied, taking a drink of tea slowly.

He barked out a laugh, and then spit on the street. "I am

the nephew of the Mashyana, I'd love to see them try and keep me from anywhere in this land."

"Arash à Kamran! Get out of the Oasis, boy!" Shirin came out of the tea shop in force, her towel brought down from her shoulder to shoo the young men away. "You were told by the City Guards not to come round again!"

Arash put his hands on his hips, attempting to stand taller.

"You don't scare me, old woman," he replied. He stepped up to her, his height equal to the older woman. "We go where we want."

The winds around them picked up, turning the soft breeze into something with a hard edge. That bastard was going to knock down the canopy of the Oasis with his Talent.

Farah hummed without thought, as if her Talent was waiting to engage the moment Arash threatened the older woman. Pointing his finger into her face and feeling his own Talent start a gale, she sent the heat from the forges into the rings on his fingers.

It took a moment to sink deep into the thick metal around his index finger, time standing still for her until she saw as well as felt the heat rise.

Arash pulled his hand quickly to his chest as he screamed, spinning to look directly at Farah. The wind died as he sucked in a breath and ripped his rings from his fingers.

"You mongrel!" he cradled his burned hand with his other against his chest.

"Amma will hear of this!" He turned, tilting his head at his boys towards the entrance of the alley.

Farah blanched, and Pari spoke for the first time softly.

"Much worse may happen to you if you do not make

better choices, Arash à Kamran." Farah looked over at her, and seeing a low golden glow wash over her dark eyes felt the promise in those words, but Arash didn't seem to hear the little girl as he and his two boys ran out of the alleyway back to the square.

Farah shuddered, finishing the tea that was left in her cup, deciding not to question the little girl on this new prophecy. Arash would make sure that she was punished for using her talent against another of Behnaz's Beloveds, her supposed family, whether or not the little girl sitting next to her was completely delusional or correct that they were put together to save the gods.

"They were friendly." Yasher broke into her thoughts, grabbing a piece of flatbread from the plate, and smiling at her gently. It also seemed to spur Shirin out of standing where she was threatened. Her eyes softened as she looked to Farah for just a glance, and she shook her towel out as if shaking off the melancholy before putting it back on her shoulder.

"You three need more tea. And those cakes," she said. "I'll be right back."

Yasher rose from his seat, grabbing the mangled ring that Arash dropped from the ground, and started tossing it up in the air, catching it a few times before setting it down in front of Farah on the table.

She hummed just enough to restore the lump of twisted metal into the thick filagreed ring that it was just a few minutes ago on that hateful man's hand.

"Want to share what that was all about, Phoenix?" He smiled, but the edge to his voice betrayed a knowing that the situation wasn't as light as he tried to make it seem.

Farah sighed as he handed her a piece of bread, her fingers brushing his. She didn't meet his gaze. She could feel the nickname *Phoenix* from Shirin hovering between them, but she let it slide. This man was a stranger, despite what Pari might think, and the last thing she needed right now was more questions. Still, there was something about Arash that made it necessary to explain a little, in case their paths crossed again.

"It's nothing," she said, her voice steady as she picked at the bread, keeping her gaze lowered. "I'm one of the Mashyana's Beloveds, chosen as her Hand. We're selected for our Talents, meant to serve the Mashyana's needs. Most of the Beloveds come from noble families, their bloodlines tied to power. My Talent is... useful for keeping people like Arash in line when they start getting carried away."

He didn't say anything at first, but she could feel the pity in the air, his eyes studying her. She quickly glanced down at the bread, tearing off small pieces, focusing on the simple task of eating. She didn't want to explain further. She didn't need anyone's pity, least of all from someone who didn't understand the intricacies of the court. She had earned her place.

Shirin came out, moving smoothly as always, a pot of tea in her grasp. The towel wrapped around the base to protect her hand was a subtle gesture Farah had come to expect. Behind her, a teenager followed with a plate of small cakes, setting them down before retreating, casting a quick glance at Farah's sigil before disappearing into the shop.

"There we are, dears," Shirin said, her voice warm and calming. She poured the tea, her movements slow and deliberate, giving them space. "Stay as long as you'd like now that the trash has been sent off." She placed the teapot on a ceramic trivet and nodded to Farah. "I'll bring out something more filling in a bit if you're wanting something more substantial."

Farah watched Shirin for a moment as she moved back into the shop, but Shirin's words lingered in the air. As she reached the doorway, she added, almost casually, "You're so much better than the Beloveds who run rampant in this place. I'm sure they'll never learn."

The comment was light but sharp, and Farah felt it land more heavily than she expected. Shirin's frustration, carefully veiled, was always there, especially when it came to the Mashyana's other wards. She knew it wasn't meant to make her feel bad, but the weight of it pressed on her. Farah understood the concern. Shirin had always treated her like a daughter, protective and loving. Sometimes though, the old woman's worry felt like another expectation she could never meet.

She shifted uncomfortably but kept her voice steady, "I know, Shirin. I'll manage."

As Shirin disappeared into the shop, Farah let out a slow breath. She trusted the Mashyana, above all else. That was all that mattered.

Farah looked over to Pari. "We do have much to talk about that has nothing to do with the Mashyana's Beloved, like why we needed to save the gharib from his own hubris."

Pari smiled but shook her head.

"We must see how the wind blows before I can share much more," the little girl replied. "My task was to bring the two together and make sure you do not separate."

"That's helpful," Yasher said, sipping his tea. Farah laughed a little.

"So, we may as well enjoy the tea," she said, picking up her own.

"And cakes!" Pari grinned, grabbing one from the plate and stuffing it into her mouth.

———

THE TEA SHOP wrapped around Yasher like a warm blanket, a stark contrast to the chill of the tavern he had escaped earlier today. The aroma of spices and sweet pastries filled the air, making it hard to remember the chaos of the card game. He leaned back in his chair, the tension in his shoulders easing slightly as he watched Pari bound inside, her eyes sparkling with excitement.

"Amma Shirin! Can I help you?" she exclaimed, her voice ringing out like a bell.

Yasher smirked, his attention shifting to Farah, absently stirring her tea. Her gaze drifted toward the door, but Yasher caught the hint of a shadow crossing her features. He leaned in, curiosity piqued.

"Here we are, on the cusp of saving gods," he said, testing the waters of her belief in the whole situation they'd found themselves in. "Or at least drinking tea while we are talked into it by a little girl who speaks for gods."

She offered a weak smile, but he sensed the hesitation still coiling in her chest. "Do you actually believe her?"

He shrugged, leaning back, his fingers tapping against the wooden table. That wasn't a no.

"That little girl believes it. Believes it enough to pull two absolute strangers together." He gestured toward the kitchen, where Pari was helping Shirin with dinner. "Where did she find you?"

"She appeared at the Citadel today," Farah replied, her voice low. "None of the courtiers seemed to pay any attention to her. Then again, she seemed to be waiting for me, not for anyone else." She sighed deeply and leaned back. "She knows the island, and yet, I've never seen her before. While the Citadel does get its fair share of travelers like yourself, she is a child of Emari."

"I am thankful that the two of you showed up when you did," he replied. "But at the end of this lovely meal, we have our own worlds to return to. What about her?"

Farah stopped. "I don't know. I am... I am not well-versed in what a child like her would need, and I don't know who to begin to ask."

He looked around at the calm of the street, this oasis in the city, and for a moment indulged in his own fantasy that this would be a good place to stay a while. He shook it off quickly. No matter how much he would enjoy getting to know this place, this woman, and even the little girl better, this was not for him. It never was. Yet he didn't want to leave the little girl to her own devices when there was something terribly wrong with her.

"Let's see if she'll answer a few questions, and we can see about getting her back to wherever she comes from, or at least somewhere safe tonight. Playing along with this fantasy of hers seems to excite her, at least."

"A part of me wonders if feeding her fantasies will end up harming her, but she may listen to us more if we do." Farah looked towards the door again.

Pari bounced into the room, a flour-covered apron draped around her small frame.

"Look - I helped!" Pari's voice rang out, and Yasher felt a smile tug at the corners of his mouth. Her infectious joy lightened the air, a balm to the tension that lingered.

"Of course you did, Little Divine," he replied, chuckling. "You're a natural."

Pari beamed, and Yasher found himself wishing he had

half her confidence and faith. It's too easy not to believe in something after so many things have let you down.

Did he believe what this little girl said about their path forward? Not in the slightest. But what he said to Farah was the truth. It brings the child a sense of calm, so he was more than happy to play along with whatever it was that the little girl wanted as long as he was here. And if it was something more, he'd let them deal with it, slipping out with the tide to leave them to it.

Farah stood up, walking towards the doorway. "Don't eat my food while I'm gone."

As Pari recounted her experience helping Shirin, Yasher listened, allowing the warmth of the moment to wash over him. But even as laughter filled the space, the knot of unease tightened in his stomach.

"Pari," he said, turning his attention back to the little girl, who was enthusiastically describing the evening meal she had helped make. "What do you think it means to be the voice of a god? Do you really believe you can help them?"

Pari stopped mid-sentence, her brow wrinkling as she considered his question. "It means I have to be brave and listen to what they say. Rashnu shows me many things, both true and not. I just know we're supposed to help bend the better things to be true."

"That's a big responsibility for someone so young," Yasher said, keeping his tone light. "But I guess you have to start somewhere, right?"

"Yes! And you and Farah are here to help." She beamed, her confidence unshakable.

"Pari, you're very special," he said, attempting to reassure her. "But remember, even gods need help sometimes. It's okay to rely on others."

Pari nodded solemnly, her expression serious as if contemplating his words. "I know. But we must trust each other. It's important."

"I do trust you, Little Divine." He grabbed one of the little savory cakes and popped it into his mouth. Even if the little girl was delusional, her work with Shirin was godly.

"You don't," Pari said, grinning and grabbing one of them for herself. "But you will, soon enough."

Yasher chuckled, the lightheartedness of Pari's comment deflecting any lingering unease in his chest. She was bold for a child, brazenly certain in ways he could barely remember being as an adult, let alone as a kid her age. But her words struck a strange chord, lingering in the back of his mind as they finished their meal.

Shirin appeared at that moment, wiping her hands on a towel, her gaze drifting to Pari with a softness that Yasher hadn't expected. Farah followed closely behind her, and took her seat before grabbing one of the cakes for herself.

"Pari, would you like to stay here tonight?" Shirin asked gently, an unspoken kindness in her words. "I could use an extra set of hands in the morning, and it's getting late. I'd feel better knowing you're somewhere warm and safe, unless you have somewhere else to go, of course."

Yasher saw Pari's face light up at the offer, though her eyes held a flicker of hesitation, as if she hadn't expected anyone to consider her well-being. The realization struck him harder than it should have, reminding him that whatever she was—a voice of the gods or just a very imaginative girl—she was still just a child perhaps without a home to return to tonight.

"Really, Amma Shirin?" Pari asked, her voice hopeful but subdued. It tugged at him more than he wanted to admit.

Shirin smiled, nodding. "Really. You can help me with the morning meal. How does that sound?"

Pari nodded eagerly, and he caught the look of relief on Farah's face that the little girl agreed.

With the arrangements settled, Pari disappeared into the back with Shirin, leaving Yasher and Farah alone at the table. A comfortable silence fell between them, the weight of the day finally settling in.

Yasher leaned back, studying Farah, who seemed lost in thought. Her expression softened as she stared at her empty teacup, her fingers tracing an absentminded pattern along its edge. The vulnerability he sensed in her then seemed rare, an unguarded moment that pulled at his curiosity even more.

He broke the silence, his tone casual, trying not to press too hard, "So... you seem to take to the whole protector role pretty naturally."

Farah looked up, meeting his gaze, a flicker of wariness crossing her face before she replied.

"It's part of my job," she said simply, though her tone held a touch of defensiveness. "We are duty bound to help those who need it as an arm of the Crown. The Mashya has cared for and nurtured those in need of charity for his entire reign."

"Is that what this is?" he asked, gesturing toward the back where Pari had gone. "Just another duty for you?"

Farah's eyes narrowed slightly, but she didn't shy away from the question.

"Pari isn't... She's not just a duty," she said, her voice softer, her gaze drifting toward the doorway. "She's... complicated. And if she really is alone..." She shook her head. "I wouldn't feel right leaving her to the world."

Yasher nodded. "You could just... walk away, you know. She'd understand."

Farah's lips curved into a wry smile. "That's not who I am."

"Yeah, I can see that," he replied. "You're one of those people who needs to fix things."

She looked at him sharply, then quickly looked away. "Sometimes people don't have a choice."

Yasher shrugged, feeling a pang of sympathy he hadn't anticipated. "Or maybe you just haven't learned to put yourself first yet."

Farah's gaze snapped back to him, her expression challenging. "And what would you know about that? You strike me as someone who doesn't struggle at all to not put themselves first."

He smirked, not rising to the bait.

"Oh, I know enough. Probably more than you think." He leaned forward, resting his elbows on the table, studying her carefully. "Look, you and I both know this situation with Pari... It's a lot to take on. If you don't want to be part of this grand prophecy of hers, then why not just... let it be?"

She hesitated, and he caught the flicker of conflict in her eyes before she looked away.

"I don't know," she admitted, barely above a whisper. "I think... maybe I want to believe it. That there's something worth fighting for, something bigger than all of this." She looked at him then, her expression open and raw. "But then I think about the cost of running off, away from my duty, my responsibilities and I don't believe it enough to make it worthwhile."

Her words hung in the air, the weight of them pressing down on him. For all her strength, he could see the cracks, the places where she was fraying under the burden. And, for reasons he couldn't quite place, he felt an urge to be the one to ease it, if only a little.

"Look," he said finally, his tone uncharacteristically gentle, "Maybe we're both here because... I don't know, it's a strange twist of fate."

Farah looked at him, surprise flickering in her gaze, but she quickly masked it, her expression closing off again. "And you? What's keeping you here? You seem like the type to vanish before you do anything for someone else."

He chuckled, though it sounded hollow even to his own ears.

"That's usually the plan," he admitted, his gaze dropping to his hands. "But sometimes even a lone wanderer likes a bit of company." He met her gaze again, his tone shifting to something more genuine. "Maybe I just want to understand why someone like you, who could be anywhere else, would choose to stay here, tangled up in this... madness. At least for a day."

Farah hesitated, the vulnerability slipping away as her guard went up once more. "I appreciate your interest, Yasher, but I'm not one for sharing my life story with a stranger."

He grinned, a playful glint in his eyes. "I'm not just any stranger. I'm the one she says is meant to save the gods with you, remember?"

She laughed, a quiet sound that broke some of the tension between them.

"That remains to be seen." Even though he didn't know her at all, he knew that laugh was a rare thing indeed.

They sat in companionable silence for a while, the quiet of the tea shop settling over them. He knew that come morning, he'd likely be back on his own path, leaving this strange girl and her guardian behind. But for tonight, he was content to stay, to let the mystery of it all hang in the air between them.

As they rose to leave, he caught her eye, offering her a small, genuine smile. "Goodnight, Farah. Thanks for saving me from a solid beating earlier, and thank you for... letting me tag along, even if it was only for a night."

She nodded, her own smile faint but warm. "Goodnight, Yasher."

With that, they parted ways. And for the first time in a long while, Yasher found himself wondering what might lie ahead—wondering, and maybe even hoping, that he might cross paths with her again. While a part of him wanted to head back and pack his bags for the mainland, his luck was telling him to stay for a little longer here.

CHAPTER 4

Farah woke, tangled in her meager bedclothes, as the first light of dawn crept through the narrow cracks in her small window. The muted rays spilled onto the rough stone floor, painting the room in shades of gray. She lay still for a moment, her breath steady, while the remnants of a peculiar dream dissolved into the quiet morning. Tea with Yasher, the warmth of his smile, Pari laughing as she held a winning hand of cards—Rashnu watching it all with his impenetrable gaze. It was an odd, vivid tableau, and it left behind a vague sense of apprehension that settled in her chest like a stone.

"Shining Halls," she muttered a curse, pushing herself upright and rubbing the sleep from her eyes. The rough utilitarian blankets slipped from her shoulders, pooling in a crumpled heap on the mattress. She swung her legs over the edge of the bed, the chill of the stone floor biting into her skin and sending a sharp shiver up her spine.

Today was the day. Her first day as the Hand of the Mashyana. Her Chosen.

Rising, she navigated the small space of her cell. The

room was modest and utilitarian, as was fitting for one of the Mashyana's Beloveds. The stone walls were bare, but a woven blanket hung at the foot of her bed—a gift from Shirin, depicting the lush fields of white jasmine outside of Banima. A narrow window, too high for anyone to peer into, let in a stream of soft morning light, illuminating the dust motes that danced in the air. The simple bed took up one corner, its thin mattress barely sufficient, yet it was hers, and she had made this space her own in the years spent as one of the Beloveds. Beside the bed stood a small wooden wardrobe, its surface scratched and worn from years of use, and a rickety desk cluttered with bits of parchment, quills, books, and the occasional piece of fruit that she had forgotten to eat.

Rummaging through her wardrobe, she pulled out a fresh linen tunic and dark felt pants, her hands trembling slightly with anticipation. She dressed quickly with care, adjusting each layer to ensure she presented herself well. As she tucked her tunic into her pants, she glanced at her reflection in the dull glass of the faded mirror. The familiar view showed her dark curls cascading down her back, framing a face speckled with freckles—her distinguishing mark among the other wards. The colors of her simple clothes were practical, yet today she wanted to stand out, to assert her worth in this new role.

Grabbing her favorite green coat, she felt a rush of comfort as she slipped it on. The intricate embroidery made her feel as if she were donning armor. She ran her fingers over the delicate golden thread, the floral motifs woven into the fabric reminding her of her journey to this moment. The rich emerald hue contrasted beautifully with her dark eyes, which gleamed with the weight of expectation.

After fastening her coat, she reached for the scarf gifted

to her by the Mashya and Mashyana on her coming of age. Its silver embroidery and tiny pearl border glimmered in the morning light as she draped it over her shoulders. With one final look in the mirror, she took a deep breath to steady her nerves. Today, she would meet the Mashyana, and she had to be ready for anything.

Perhaps after her assignment from the Mashyana, she'd find a moment to explore the city with Yasher.

Why was he occupying her mind? She shook her head, dismissing the notion. She would not let her focus waver from the work ahead.

As Farah stepped into the hallway, the quiet murmur of the Citadel reached her ears. The distant sound of footsteps, the muted hum of voices—life was stirring, and with it came the weight of expectation. Her boots clicked softly against the stone as she made her way toward the Mashyana's private chambers, her thoughts drifting briefly to Pari.

The little girl's prophecies and strange mannerisms lingered in her mind. Farah hoped she was settling in with Shirin. If nothing else, Pari was safe now. Safer than Farah felt, walking toward the unknown.

The private stairwell leading to the Mashyana's chambers loomed ahead, its spiraling steps dimly lit by flickering torches. Farah ascended slowly, each step echoing in the narrow space. The door at the top stood closed, its heavy wood adorned with carvings of vines and flames.

Two guards stood at attention on either side, their expressions impassive. Farah paused before them, smoothing her coat and willing her hands to steady.

She approached, taking a steadying breath. Although she had never doubted her abilities, the weight of the Mashyana's presence always made her question herself.

The guard nodded to her and knocked on the door, announcing her arrival. "Your Grace, the Hand is here."

"Show her in," the queen's husky voice, regal and commanding, sent a shiver down her spine.

She stepped into the Mashyana's chambers, the heavy door closing behind her with a quiet, final click. The air was thick with the scent of rose oil and incense, the familiar weight of it pressing against her chest. The tension in the room always seemed to coil around Behnaz à Radan like a second skin. The queen stood behind her desk, her figure draped in white silk that shimmered with the soft light of the morning. Gold and crimson embroidery traced intricate designs along the hem, and her tiara caught the light in flashes. Every movement was precise, calculated.

"Ah, Farah," Behnaz said, her voice warm, but there was something in her tone that felt like an assessment, not a greeting. "Precisely on time, as expected."

Farah straightened, meeting Behnaz's sharp gaze. The queen's eyes were always studying, always measuring. It made Farah's pulse race—half from the weight of her gaze, and half from the knowledge that this was no ordinary meeting. Today wasn't just the first time she'd been formally addressed as Hand. It was the day she knew, beyond a doubt, that the work she had already been doing would shift from shadows to the light of open command.

"Congratulations again, my dear," Behnaz continued, her smile faint, but her words calculated. "You have proven yourself worthy of the honor bestowed upon you. Becoming my Hand is no small feat."

"Thank you, Your Grace," Farah replied, her voice steady, though the faint tremor in her hands betrayed her. She had been doing the work of the Hand for months now —breaking into homes, retrieving items for Behnaz, *repatri-*

ating what didn't belong in the wrong hands. And some-times, more than that. Assassinations, done with the same practiced ease as any other task. She had already proven she could be trusted with the darkest of deeds. But now, the title was hers. The weight of it pressed down on her, deeper than before.

Behnaz gestured toward the chair near her desk. "Sit. We have much to discuss."

Farah obeyed, sitting with the careful poise she had perfected over the past months. The weight of Behnaz's gaze didn't shift, didn't soften. Farah could feel the expec-tation thick in the air, could hear the unspoken command —*prove yourself.*

"As my Hand," Behnaz began, her tone sharpening, "you will carry out tasks essential to Emari's future. This is not a role of ceremony. It is one of action, of purpose. And it requires skill, discretion, and absolute loyalty. Are you prepared for that?"

Farah nodded. She had already been tested. "I am, Your Grace."

Behnaz studied her for a long moment, as though weighing her words, before continuing. "Good. Then let us begin." She opened a leather-bound book, its pages filled with detailed illustrations and elegant script. The faded ink, the delicate sketches, spoke of time long passed, of scribes whose work would last long after their deaths. She turned the book toward Farah, and her finger traced an image—an ancient, filigreed sphere.

"This relic," Behnaz said, voice laced with a quiet inten-sity, "has resurfaced in Emari after centuries. It was thought lost to the sands of the Forgotten Temple, buried deep within its ruins. Yet now, it rests in the hands of a gharib. My informants tell me they've recently arrived in the city."

Farah leaned forward, her focus shifting from Behnaz's words to the image on the page. The relic's delicate filigree caught her eye, its beauty almost impossible to fathom for something so old.

"A gharib?" she asked, her tone neutral, though her mind already raced with questions. "What do we know about them?"

Behnaz's expression darkened. "Very little. They came to the city not long ago, and like most foreigners, they likely have no idea what they're carrying. But others will. This relic must not fall into the wrong hands."

Farah nodded, mentally noting the details. "What is it capable of?"

Behnaz's voice dropped, the words heavy with meaning. "It is said to hold the essence of the Divine, taken from the Forgotten Temple before the Wastes claimed it. Its power is something I would never trust in the hands of outsiders—or anyone outside this court. Not now, not when our enemies grow bolder by the day."

Farah's mind churned, but she kept her questions to herself. She had seen the price of asking too much. Behnaz's trust was absolute, but her tolerance for doubt was nonexistent.

"The world around us grows more unstable," Behnaz continued, her voice tightening. "Enemies gather in the shadows, rebellions stir in the provinces, and even within our walls, cracks begin to form. Emari must be strong—stronger than it has ever been. And strength requires power."

Farah's breath hitched at the weight of those words.

She had already seen the cracks, in the city and the court, felt the tremors that rippled beneath the surface. The Mashyana's expectations were clear. *Strength through power.*

"And you believe this relic will provide that power?" Farah asked carefully.

"It is not a belief, Farah," Behnaz said, her voice sharp, though her expression softened as she continued. "It is a necessity. This relic is a tool—a weapon, if need be. It is something that can tip the balance in our favor. We cannot afford to leave it in the hands of the ignorant or the unworthy."

Farah nodded, her mind already locking the details away. She could feel the weight of Behnaz's gaze pressing down on her, an unspoken challenge to prove her loyalty, her capability. It was never just about following orders. It was about doing so in a way that showed she understood the stakes.

The queen's gaze softened for the briefest moment.

"Farah," she said, her tone unexpectedly gentle, "We have not spoken privately since Commander Rostam's funeral. I know you were close, and your pain is mine."

Farah's heart stuttered at the mention of Rostam. She kept her face neutral, though his death still gnawed at her, a wound she hadn't let herself acknowledge fully. Rostam had been more than just a commander—he had been a guide, a mentor, someone who had always known what needed to be done, even when Farah had no idea. She had learned to trust him implicitly. But he was gone now.

Behnaz continued, her voice steady, "His death was a blow, not just to the Mashya and myself, but to Emari as a whole."

Farah swallowed, fighting the lump in her throat. "I owe much of what I am to him."

Behnaz's eyes narrowed, studying her. "And that is why I chose you, Farah. Rostam saw something in you that cannot be taught. His death was a reminder of what we stand to lose if we falter. Do you understand?"

Farah nodded, the tightness in her chest only growing. "I do, Your Grace."

Behnaz straightened, her voice returning to its usual sharpness, "Then you understand why this relic must be secured."

Farah's thoughts flickered briefly, drawn to the silence from the Mashya and Tamidh. Tamidh was a city of great strategic importance, sitting at the crossroads between the Citadel and the rebel territories. It was where the Mashya, Enayat à Mashayekhi, had sent Rostam, his most trusted Commander, to negotiate with the rebels. Rostam had gone first, the negotiation meant to secure peace, or at least a temporary truce. But it had gone horribly wrong, he'd been killed during the talks—an outcome that sent shockwaves through the kingdom.

After Rostam's death, Enayat himself had gone to Tamidh to continue the negotiations. But since his arrival, no word had come back. The absence of communication, the lack of resolution, was suffocating.

Farah hesitated, her voice softer than usual. "Has there been any word from Tamidh, Your Grace?"

Behnaz's jaw tightened, but her face remained composed.

"No," she said, her voice clipped and controlled. "The Mashya went to negotiate with the rebels after Rostam's death. I expected his presence to yield results. Instead, we have heard nothing. It is... troubling."

Farah didn't press. She had already learned the limits of speaking out of turn.

"You have your orders," Behnaz said, her voice firm again. "Find the relic. Bring it back to me. Do not let anyone or anything stand in your way."

Farah bowed deeply. "Your will is mine, Your Grace."

Behnaz's gaze softened for a brief moment, the briefest of touches brushing Farah's cheek. "You are my Hand, my dear. Do not disappoint me."

As Farah exited the chamber, the weight of the task ahead settled fully on her shoulders. The halls of the Citadel felt alive with the bustle of the court, but the noise seemed distant, muffled. The Mashyana's trust was a double-edged sword, but Farah had no choice but to carry it. Her first true task as Hand was already upon her, and failure wasn't an option. She would prove herself, or risk losing everything she had worked for.

IF IT WERE any other day, or any other task from the Mashyana, Farah would start her search at the market but given that the voice of a god connected her to a foreigner, who hadn't been in the Capital all that long, she couldn't overlook the symmetry that this Yasher may be the one to hold the relic her Mashyana needed. So, instead, she headed for the docks to track down the charming rogue.

She paused after turning down one of the many short-cuts to the docks. It had to be coincidence that that annoying man was here as she was given this task, and nothing more.

There were a few new merchants from the North who'd gained access to stalls recently, likely a better place to begin the search. She twisted her rings around her fingers with her Talent to let off a little bit of power she could feel just like an itch beneath her skin as she changed course to the market, humming softly.

There were a few new faces in the stalls, and not all of them looked as though they had been in Emari long, especially those who hadn't yet learned their skin would burn in the noonday sun.

The merchants who recognized Farah waved and occasionally called to her, but she focused on an obvious gharib with pale straw hair and even paler skin, his stall wares a series of trinkets and statuary from the Northern kingdoms mixed in with pieces that were obviously Emari-made on prominent display.

"Hail, my lady," the ruddy-faced man fanned himself from under one of the shades that dotted the market stalls. "Anything of interest?"

She scanned through all the pieces in his stall, her eyes landing on a flat piece with a similar filagree pattern as the relic in the illustration from the Mashyana's book.

"How much?" She asked, picking it up. The man looked over at it intensely, then at her face.

"I can make you a deal on that, as it's just a piece I was traded."

She pulled out a few coins and handed them over, nodding to the man before walking away, down the next row of stalls.

"You paid too much for that, it's broken." A voice said from behind her as she moved away. She didn't bother turning around as she felt Yasher behind her. She wandered through the stalls, humming under her breath for a moment as she worked the flat metal with her talent, turning her hands around and around the piece.

"I paid what was fair." She stopped to look at a stall filled with fruits from the mainland, waiting for him to catch up to her. She palmed the new form she'd created and slipped it into her pocket.

She spared a glance at him and couldn't help but catch his slightly crooked smile that lit up his whole face, even behind the chin-length hair that kept falling into it. She realized she started to mirror his smile and dropped her face into nonchalance that she wore throughout the Citadel.

"I see you've found your way back to the square," she said. "I recommend the pears here." She nodded at the woman in the stall, who beamed at her.

"Good to know." He held up two fingers, pointing to the pears before handing over a few coins.

Farah walked on, looking for the other Northern market stall she saw a few days prior, leaving him standing there. A pear appeared in front of her, suspended by its stem which he dangled. She took it from his hand, careful not to touch him. Still, she felt that pull that she had written off as a trick of the mind from the evening prior.

She paused, holding the fruit up to her mouth, and tilted just her eyes over to him.

"My thanks." She looked away and took a bite, starting to walk again. She caught his quick grin as he walked in stride with her, eating his own pear.

She moved through the rows of stalls, the familiar chaos of the market buzzing around her. At first, she didn't notice how many Northerns were there, but as soon as she did, she couldn't stop seeing them. Their pale skin stood out, and despite the warm sun, they still wore clothing that seemed too heavy for Emari's climate—simple but well-made tunics and trousers, not quite as light and flowing as the locals. It was odd to see so many of them at once, though she supposed it wasn't uncommon for people from colder lands to come south during the winter. She hadn't traveled that far north herself, but she'd heard enough about the harsh winters up there to know why they might seek warmth here.

Other than the flat panel she purchased at the beginning though, no one seemed to have any potential relics from her land and country, let alone her gods. She began humming softly, twisting her rings around her fingers with her Talent again, letting her frustration get the better of her.

"So," Yasher broke her attention from her talent. "What exactly are we shopping for today?" He picked up a piece of pottery from the stall they'd stopped at, then put it back down after she shook her head.

She began humming again, but didn't answer him, instead pulling out the filagree piece, rolling it between her hands as she left the stall to wander down the last aisle.

He followed next to her, and she caught his glance down to her hands as they reached the last stall. She stopped humming to mutter a small curse.

"Of course it's not going to be that simple." She mumbled to herself, turning around to head out of the market square. He stopped and stood in her way, his hand up as if to touch her shoulder, but pausing as she slid her shoulder out of his range.

"I did not say you could touch me." She stared at him, her talent automatically looking for anything metal on his body to manipulate. "And I did not ask for your help in my task."

"Oh, so this is part of your job, to shop?" he said, putting his hand down and brushing imaginary wrinkles from his vest. He kept his head down, but snuck a glance at her face and she couldn't escape that grin reappearing, distracting her.

She held out the sphere that she'd created from the flat piece of filagree as they walked, holding it in her open palm and sighed.

"Have you ever seen one of these on your travels?" She said to him. "Or at least a close approximation?"

He froze in front of her, staring at the filagree ball. His pale blue eyes, normally sly and playful, were wide and fearful as he reached to an interior pocket, searching for something. He relaxed after a moment, with just a painful twinge wrinkling around his eyes, patting his coat.

"May I see that?" he held out his hand, and Farah turned hers to drop it into his without touching him.

"I've been tasked to find the original," she said as he ran his fingers across the filagree, as if comparing it to something else. He seemed to weigh it, and then look at the seam, looking for an opening.

"Can't say that I have," he said, tossing it gently back to her. "Sorry."

She played with the filagree stand-in relic, watching him as he took a step back from her. For living by his ability to bluff, he was failing spectacularly now. The false relic she'd created had startled him, and he could not hide it at all.

"Well, I should be on my way," he said, raising two fingers and walking backwards another step or two. "Games to play, money to be made."

"Games to rig, you mean?" she replied, taking a single step forward as he kept walking backwards away and raising her voice a little. "Trouble follows those that do not keep to the honest path, you know."

"Mayhaps, my dear Phoenix," he said, finally turning to walk away from her and waving. "Mayhaps."

"Of course. The Divine always has trials to give to the faithful," Farah mumbled to herself, looking around a moment before shimmying up the side of the wall to follow along via the rooftops behind him.

CHAPTER 5

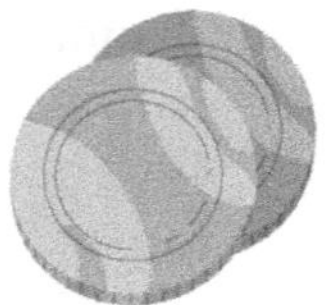

Yasher darted through the twisting alleys of the dockside district, the sharp tang of salt air mingling with the stench of stale beer and unwashed bodies. His boots struck the cobblestones with muted thuds as he zigzagged through narrow passages, sweat dripping down his temple despite the cool breeze. He didn't need to look back to know she was following him—he could feel it, the weight of her presence pressing on him like a drawn bowstring.

Farah.

That woman put him off his game without even trying. The moment he saw the glint in her eyes, he knew he was made. She'd seen through his facade and copied his lucky charm with that infernal Talent of hers. The memory of her hands shaping the fake right in front of him, showing it to him, sent a fresh wave of anxiety through his chest. He touched the inside of his coat pocket, feeling the reassuring weight of the relic hidden there. The one thing that had been guiding him ever since he'd stowed away on a traveler's vardo to escape the men who'd once owned it.

If Farah got her hands on it, he was finished. Utterly and completely screwed.

His thoughts churned as he slipped into an alley, the shadows swallowing him whole. He leaned against a brick wall, his chest heaving, and scanned the rooftops above. The sense of being watched hadn't left him, though he couldn't pinpoint where she might be. He wanted to pull out the relic, to let its strange luck guide him, but showing his hand now would only bring her swooping in faster than a hawk on a hare.

No, he had to rely on his wits. At least for now.

He pushed off the wall and headed toward the dockside tavern where he'd been staying. The hum of voices and the clinking of mugs grew louder as he approached. Lantern light spilled from the windows, casting long, flickering shadows across the cobblestones. He quickened his pace, already calculating how much coin he'd need to secure passage to the mainland. If he could reach a caravan heading south to Tamidh, he'd be safe within a week. A fortnight, at worst.

The thought of games and grifts along the way, of winning enough coin to live comfortably for months, briefly lifted his spirits. Then he thought of Farah's sharp eyes, her relentless determination, and the heavy shadow of the Citadel looming behind her.

He grimaced. No amount of tricks can outrun a woman like her.

The moment he entered the tavern, his name rang out like a challenge.

"Yasher!"

His hand flew to the hilt of his dagger before he could stop himself, his body tensing as he scanned the crowded room. A sailor shot him a dirty look but turned back to his drink. Then he spotted the source of the voice—Kambiz.

She wove through the throng of patrons, ignoring a drunken sailor who tried to catch her attention. Her dark braid swayed behind her, and her long tunic and breeches, though plain, fit her as comfortably as her easy smile.

"Did you get caught running a game again?" she asked, planting her hands on her hips. "You look even paler than normal."

Yasher forced a grin, trying to shake off the tension in his muscles.

"Nothing to worry about," he said, dropping his hand from his dagger. "Just a busy day."

Her brow furrowed, her dark eyes searching his face. "You're lying."

"Since when do I lie?" He flashed her his most charming smile, but her expression didn't soften.

She crossed her arms. "Since always."

Yasher sighed, running a hand through his hair. "Kambiz, I just need to grab something from my room. I'll be down in a bit, I swear."

"Uh-huh," she said, following him as he headed for the stairs.

Her presence was both comforting and disquieting. Kambiz had been one of the few people in this gods-forsaken city who had shown him genuine kindness and care, and he appreciated her for it. But her attention often lingered a beat too long, her smiles a shade too warm. He knew she cared for him in a way he would never be able to return.

As they reached the top of the stairs, she grabbed his arm, forcing him to stop.

"I don't know what you've gotten yourself into, Yash,

but you're not acting right," she said. "If this has anything to do with those new friends of yours at the Citadel—"

He plastered on another quick smile, cutting her off, "Everything's fine. I promise."

She didn't look convinced, but she let go of his arm. He opened the door to his room and stepped inside, turning back to flash her a wink before shutting the door in her face.

The moment the door clicked shut, Yasher let out a long breath and leaned his forehead against the wood. Her footsteps receded down the stairs, leaving him alone in the quiet room.

"Twelve holy hells," he muttered, her warning ringing in his ears.

He turned, his eyes scanning the small, cluttered space. His pack was slumped in the corner, half-packed, but before he could move toward it, the hairs on the back of his neck prickled.

Someone was here.

Perched on the sill of the open window, her green coat trailing like a predator's shadow, was Farah. The late morning light cast her features in sharp relief—her dark curls tumbling in loose waves, her sharp eyes gleaming with purpose, and the jeweled dagger in her hand catching the faint light like a promise of danger.

"Your friend isn't wrong, you know," she said, her voice smooth as silk, her lips curving into a smile that sent both shivers and heat racing through him. She toyed with the dagger in her hand, humming, her Talent sparking faintly along the blade in a low, rhythmic hum.

"Which part?" Yasher asked, already backing toward the far wall. His hands stayed loose at his sides, ready to act, though he kept his tone as light as possible.

"I am no one's friend," she said, stepping through the window with a predator's grace. Her boots hit the floor soundlessly, and her coat flared slightly as she moved. "Now, hand over the relic."

He sighed dramatically, running a hand through his dark hair. "Why would you think I have this relic? What is it about me that screams 'divine artifact smuggler'? Is it the smile?" He flashed her his best grin, all teeth and charm, hoping to disarm her—or at least buy himself time.

Farah's eyes flickered with faint amusement, though her stance remained deadly.

"Oh, gharib," she purred, the word rolling off her tongue like a curse and a compliment all at once. "You can drop the act. We both know you're hiding something, and I'm here to collect it."

"Your bedside manner could use some work," Yasher replied, sidestepping toward the pack in the corner of the room. "Maybe a little charm, a little soft persuasion? Instead, you jump straight to threats and daggers. Is this your idea of flirting, or are you just bad at conversation?"

Farah raised an eyebrow, her lips twitching in something that wasn't quite a smile. "I don't need charm to deal with someone like you."

"Someone like me?" Yasher feigned offense, placing a hand over his chest. "I'm wounded, Phoenix."

Her eyes narrowed at the nickname, and the dagger in her hand sparked brighter. She took another step closer, the gap between them closing. "Call me that again, and I'll give you something to be wounded about."

He held up his hands in mock surrender. "Fine, fine. Let's not get ahead of ourselves. I'd rather this stay playful, you know?" He grinned, his voice dropping just enough to make the word suggestive, "Wouldn't want things to get... complicated."

Farah stopped a breath away from him, her dagger pointed toward the ground but humming with barely contained energy. "You think this is playful?"

He tilted his head, his grin widening. "Isn't it? You, me, alone in a room, the tension thick enough to cut with that very sharp dagger of yours... Admit it, you're enjoying this."

Her eyes flicked over his face, her expression unreadable. "You're insufferable."

"True," he said, leaning slightly against the wall. "But you're still here, not stabbing me. Makes me think you don't hate me as much as you claim."

Farah's blade rose, just enough to remind him of the power she wielded, but she didn't strike. Instead, she tilted her head, studying him like a puzzle she was debating whether to solve or smash.

"You're stalling," she said finally, her voice low and steady. "I wonder why. Do you think I'll let you walk out of here if you keep talking? Or are you just hoping I'll get bored and leave you with the relic?"

"Neither," he replied, his tone light. "I'm just trying to figure out what makes you tick. You're a puzzle, Farah, and I do love a good mystery."

Her lips curved into a faint smile, but the edge in her eyes remained sharp. "Then let me make this simple for you. I'm not interested in games, Yasher. Hand over the relic, or I'll take it myself."

He sighed again, as if the weight of her demands were too much to bear.

"You're so quick to violence. What if we talked about this instead? Had a drink, maybe?" He gestured vaguely toward the pack in the corner. "I think I still have a bottle of wine in there somewhere. We could share it, get to know each other better. Who knows? You might even find me charming."

Farah's dagger hummed brighter, the sparks dancing along its edge. "You're lucky I find you more annoying than dangerous. Otherwise, you'd already be bleeding."

"Lucky is my middle name," he said, winking.

She took another step, pressing into his space, her blade rising until it hovered just beneath his chin. The warmth of her Talent radiated through the air, prickling against his skin.

"You think this is a joke?" she asked, her voice barely above a whisper. "I'm not here to play with you, Yasher. Hand it over. Now."

His grin didn't falter, though his pulse quickened.

"And here I thought we were having a moment. But fine." He lifted his hands slowly, his fingers brushing against her cheek as he reached up, his other hand reaching for his hidden punch dagger. She stiffened at the unexpected touch, her eyes widening slightly.

"What are you—"

Before she could finish, a loud squawk shattered the tension. Both of them froze, their heads snapping toward the window.

A white hawk perched on the sill, its golden eyes gleaming in the dim light. Blood stained one of its wings, a dark streak vivid against its pristine feathers. The hawk's sharp beak opened as it let out another piercing cry, its talons tapping against the wood.

Farah stepped back slightly, her dagger lowering as her gaze locked on the bird.

"Great Divine," she whispered.

Yasher blinked, his grin fading as he took in the sight.

"Another friend of yours?" he asked, his voice a mix of humor and unease.

The hawk cocked its head, its golden eyes flicking between them. Then, with a burst of energy that seemed impossible for its wounded state, it flapped its wings and took off, soaring into the sky. Its shadow streaked across the floor, vanishing as quickly as it had appeared.

Farah turned back to Yasher, her expression unreadable. For a moment, neither of them spoke.

"Well," Yasher said finally, straightening and brushing off his coat. "That was dramatic."

Farah sheathed her dagger, her gaze lingering on the empty window.

"A harbinger," she said, almost to herself.

"A harbinger?" Yasher echoed, raising an eyebrow. "Looked more like an angry bird to me."

She shot him a sharp look, but her focus quickly shifted back to the window. "We follow it."

"We follow it?" He gestured toward the door. "What about—oh, I don't know—the part where you're trying to stab me?"

Farah stepped toward the door, her expression hardening. "The relic can wait. The harbinger can't. You follow them when they appear, or you ignore it at your peril."

Yasher sighed, slipping his dagger back into its sheath. "Fine. But for the record, I thought we were having a moment."

"Keep up, gharib," Farah said as she opened the door and waved him through. "Or I'll drag you along myself. You don't leave my sight or my side as long as you hold that relic."

He walked out the door and down the creaky stairs,

Farah close behind. He swore she was muttering to herself, instead of her humming to draw her power.

He stopped just before the stairs opened, looking over his shoulder.

"What's that, Phoenix?" he smirked.

Her eyes narrowed and she leaned close.

"I'm just composing your eulogy."

"Write it well, then."

He winked, then continued down the stairs, Farah moving behind him like a shadow as they walked down the narrow corridor that the stairs made.

The tavern's common room was alive with noise—shouted orders, the clinking of mugs, and the occasional burst of raucous laughter from a table of sailors. Yasher descended the stairs with a confidence that didn't quite match the turmoil in his chest. Behind him, Farah's presence loomed like a shadow, her silence weighted with authority that could cut through the din of the room.

His heart hadn't stopped racing since the confrontation in his room. The memory of her blade sparking with her Talent, the banter, and her cool, calculating gaze still burned in his mind.

Focus. He tugged at his coat, willing his charm to carry him through the next hurdle: Kambiz.

She was waiting for him. Of course she was.

"Kambiz," he muttered under his breath as her sharp eyes locked onto him the moment he stepped off the last stair. She moved toward him, her braid swinging and her steps purposeful. Her gaze flicked to Farah trailing behind him, and Yasher saw her expression falter—first with recognition, then with fear.

"Khānum," Kambiz said quickly, her voice shifting to

one of deference as she bowed her head slightly. "Forgive me. I didn't realize…"

Farah inclined her head a fraction, her expression unreadable, though her gaze flicked briefly to Yasher before settling on Kambiz.

Kambiz straightened, her hands wringing at her sides. She glanced back at Yasher, her tone low and urgent, "What have you done?"

Yasher flashed her a grin, though his pulse quickened at the weight of her words. "Nothing to worry about, Kambiz. Everything's under control."

"Control?" she repeated, her disbelief clear. She darted another glance at Farah, lowering her voice even further, "Yasher, do you even realize who she is?"

"Of course," he said lightly. "Farah. We've met."

Kambiz looked like she wanted to shake him.

"She's not just 'Farah.' She's one of the Mashyana's Beloveds." Her voice dropped to a whisper. "Do you have any idea what kind of trouble you're in?"

Yasher shrugged, slipping his hands into his pockets. "Trouble's just part of the charm, isn't it?"

Kambiz's expression darkened, her eyes flicking between him and Farah. "This isn't a game, Yasher. This isn't some sailor you can bluff or some merchant you can sweet-talk. She's… she's dangerous. All of Emari knows the Mashyana's Beloveds."

"I'm right here, you know," Farah said, her voice bored but carrying enough weight to make Kambiz flinch.

"My apologies, Khānum," Kambiz said quickly, bowing her head again. "I didn't mean any offense."

Farah tilted her head slightly, her lips curving into the faintest hint of a smile. "None taken."

Yasher cleared his throat, stepping slightly closer to Kambiz. "Relax. Everything's fine."

She turned on him, her fear morphing into frustration. "Fine? Do you even hear yourself? She's one of the Mashyana's Beloveds. They don't just... accompany people like you."

Farah said nothing, but he could feel her gaze on him, sharp and assessing. He resisted the urge to fidget, instead focusing on Kambiz.

"You don't have to worry about me," he said softly, his grin softening into something almost sincere. "I've got this."

Kambiz's lips pressed into a thin line. "You always say that. And every time, it's me or someone else cleaning up after you."

"Kambiz," he began, but she cut him off with a sharp shake of her head.

"I mean it, Yasher," she said, her voice low and urgent. "Whatever this is, it's bigger than you. You're going to get yourself hurt—or worse. And this time, I won't be able to help you."

Her words landed harder than he wanted to admit, but he shrugged them off, forcing his grin back into place. "You're always underestimating me."

"No," she said firmly. "You're underestimating her."

Farah's voice cut through the tension, calm and steady. "You're protective of him."

Kambiz blinked, clearly startled. "I... he's my friend, Khānum. And he doesn't always think things through."

"That much is obvious," Farah replied, her tone faintly amused.

Yasher let out a nervous chuckle, glancing between the

two women. "See? Everyone agrees. I'm an idiot. Can we move on now?"

Kambiz ignored him, her gaze shifting back to Farah. "If he's caused you trouble, Khānum, I apologize on his behalf. He doesn't mean harm—he's just reckless."

Farah inclined her head slightly, her expression unreadable. "I've noticed."

The quiet in her voice seemed to unsettle Kambiz further. She glanced at him one last time, her eyes filled with worry. "Please. Just... be careful."

He reached out, brushing her arm gently. "I always am."

Kambiz gave him a look that said she didn't believe him for a second, but she stepped back, bowing her head once more to Farah before turning away.

As they stepped out onto the dockside boardwalk, Yasher let out a long breath, the tension in his chest easing slightly.

"Well," he said lightly, glancing at Farah. "That wasn't awkward at all."

Farah raised an eyebrow, her lips curving into a faint smirk. "Your friend worries too much."

"She worries just the right amount," he replied, though his voice lacked its usual humor.

Farah studied him for a moment, her gaze sharp. "She's right about one thing, though. You don't think things through."

"Maybe not," Yasher said, slipping his hands into his pockets. "But it makes life interesting."

Her expression unreadable as she turned her head to look to the sky. "Interesting won't save you, gharib."

Yasher chuckled, though the sound was hollow. "Maybe not. But it's gotten me this far."

The silence between them lingered, broken only by the faint hum of activity drifting up from the docks. Yasher's thoughts were a tangled mess, cycling between Kambiz's words, the weight of Farah's presence beside him, and the sharp edge of their earlier confrontation.

You're underestimating her.

Maybe Kambiz was right. Maybe he didn't fully understand what he'd gotten himself into. But as he glanced at Farah, her steps steady and deliberate, her coat catching the midday sun in faint glimmers of gold-threaded embroidery, he knew one thing for certain. He wasn't ready to walk away.

A piercing cry cut through the bustle of the docks, sharp and commanding. Yasher's head snapped up, his gaze darting toward the sound. A shadow passed overhead, its wings stark against the clear blue sky.

It was the white hawk again.

Farah froze beside him, her gaze tracking the bird as it swooped low over the street, its golden eyes flashing in the sunlight. It circled once, then dove toward a narrow alley just ahead, disappearing into the shadows between the buildings.

"There it is," she said simply, her tone as steady as ever. She started toward the alley without hesitation, her movements fluid and purposeful.

"A harbinger," he muttered, falling into step behind her. "Of what? Trouble? Because I'm pretty sure we've already got enough of that."

Farah glanced back at him with a glare.

He groaned, though the corners of his mouth twitched upward despite himself. He quickened his pace to keep up with her, his boots scuffing against the uneven cobblestones as they approached the alley.

The hawk was perched atop a stack of crates, its feathers gleaming in the sunlight. A streak of dark blood marred one of its wings, the red vivid against the pristine white. It tilted its head, its golden eyes fixed on them with an almost unnatural intensity.

Farah slowed, her gaze locked on the bird. Her hand drifted toward the hilt of her dagger, though she didn't draw it. "A harbinger of something, all right."

"Yeah, of bad decisions," Yasher muttered, eyeing the bird warily. "It's broad daylight, Farah. This feels like one of those moments where sane people walk away."

Farah didn't respond. She stepped into the alley, her movements careful but unhesitant. The shadows from the surrounding buildings stretched across the narrow space, but the sunlight filtering in through the gaps caught the gleam of her blade as her fingers tightened briefly around the hilt.

Yasher hesitated at the edge of the alley, his gaze darting between the hawk and the relative safety of the street. He could hear the faint murmur of voices and clattering carts in the distance, a reminder that the world beyond this moment still existed. But then the hawk let out another sharp cry, and Farah moved deeper into the alley without a backward glance.

"Twelve hells," Yasher muttered, running a hand through his hair. "This is a terrible idea."

Still, he stepped into the alley after her, his footsteps softer now as the shadows swallowed them. The hawk ruffled its feathers and hopped to another perch farther down the passage, its gaze never leaving them.

"You seriously trust a bird to lead us somewhere?" Yasher asked, his voice low.

"It's not about trust," Farah replied, her tone clipped.

"It's about paying attention. Harbingers don't appear without reason."

"Oh, great," Yasher said, rolling his eyes. "So, we're following a prophetic bird, instead of a prophetic little girl. You realize that doing the same thing over and over again doesn't really bode well for your sanity."

The hawk let out another piercing cry and took off, its bloodstained wing beating unevenly as it disappeared deeper into the alley.

Farah turned to him, her expression unreadable. "Are you coming willingly, or do you plan to complain the whole way?"

Yasher hesitated, his hand brushing against the relic hidden in his pocket. He could feel the weight of it, the way it seemed to pulse faintly, like it was calling for him to follow, though he'd rather sneak back to grab his bag and be off.

"Fine," he said finally, his voice tinged with resignation. "But if this bird turns out to be leading us into a trap, I'm blaming you."

She raised an eyebrow, her lips curving into that faint, knowing smile. "Blame doesn't matter if you're dead due to ignoring a harbinger."

"Comforting," he muttered, though he couldn't help the grin that tugged at his lips.

They moved deeper into the alley, the sounds of the bustling docks fading into the distance. The air grew cooler in the shadows, carrying the faint scent of salt and damp stone.

Yasher kept his eyes on the hawk, which perched briefly on a wooden beam overhead before taking flight again. The blood on its wing caught the sunlight in a brief, vivid streak as it soared ahead.

"This feels ominous," he said under his breath, glancing at Farah. "Doesn't this feel ominous to you?"

She didn't answer. Her focus remained on the bird, her steps steady and deliberate as she followed its flight path.

"Of course it doesn't," Yasher muttered to himself. "Because you're Farah. And ominous is your comfort zone."

Her lips twitched, though she didn't look at him. "Keep talking, gharib. It's not running the harbinger off at all."

"I think the bird would appreciate my wit more than you," he shot back, his grin widening despite the tension coiling in his chest.

The hawk let out another cry, its wings beating heavily as it disappeared around a corner. Farah quickened her pace, and Yasher followed, his hand brushing against the hilt of his dagger as they moved deeper into the shadows.

The sun bore down on the alley, but the shadows stretched unnaturally, swallowing the light in defiance of the midday glow. Yasher's skin prickled as they stepped deeper into the passage, the air cooling unnaturally. He drew his dagger, the familiar weight grounding him as his eyes darted around the space. Farah moved beside him, her daggers already in hand, the soft hum of her Talent vibrating faintly in the air.

"Do you know any birdcalls?" Yasher whispered, his voice barely breaking the silence.

Farah's gaze remained focused ahead, scanning the dim alley.

"It's a harbinger," she replied, her tone low and sharp. "It calls you, not the other way around. Keep quiet and look."

Yasher stifled a retort, though his fingers tightened around his blade. His heartbeat thudded in his ears as they crept forward. The shadows pooled around their feet, darker than they should have been, and even the distant sounds of the docks seemed muted here. He felt the faint tug of unease, like a thread being pulled taut in his chest.

Farah tilted her head slightly, nodding toward the end of the alley. He followed her gaze, his pulse quickening as they moved deeper into the gloom. The unnatural shadows wrapped around them, pressing close as the light faded further with every step.

The faint hum of voices drifted toward them from deeper in the alley. Yasher leaned toward Farah, his breath brushing against her ear as he whispered, "Do you hear that?"

"Yes." Her reply was soft but carried a note of disappointment. "I think..."

She trailed off, her gaze snapping to a movement in the corner of the alley. Yasher followed her line of sight, spotting the white hawk perched atop a pile of lumber. Its talons tapped rhythmically against the wood, the sound strangely precise.

Farah took a step toward the hawk, her focus narrowing. Her daggers remained in her hands, but her grip loosened slightly, as if she were gauging the situation. Yasher moved instinctively, angling himself between her and the distant voices that seemed to be growing louder.

"Farah," he whispered, his tone urgent, though he didn't know why. The hawk's golden eyes bore into them, its head tilting slightly as if measuring their intentions.

The voices drew closer, indistinct but unmistakably Emarian. Yasher's chest tightened as his mind raced. He'd trusted his Luck to guide him before, but this was different. This wasn't a game or a casual con—this was real, and the stakes felt higher than ever.

He stepped beside Farah, his fingers brushing against the relic in his pocket. Her focus remained on the hawk, and he took the chance. In a single, fluid motion, he slipped the real relic into her pocket and pulled out the fake she'd created.

The once distant voices became clearer, and one of them sounded very familiar.

"Grapple me," he hissed, leaning close enough to see the faint flicker of confusion in her eyes. "Now."

Before she could react, he pulled her close to him in a movement that made it look like she'd forced him. Their faces were suddenly inches apart, and for a moment, neither moved. He adjusted, making sure to accommodate her smaller frame, feeling the difference in height between them as her body pressed against his. He could see the sharp lines of her features—her high cheekbones, her jawline both delicate and defined—and the faint sheen of sweat on her temple. The calculating look in her eyes told him she was already analyzing the situation, her mind working quickly.

Then, a sudden gust of wind howled through the alley, sharp and unexpected. Yasher stumbled, instinctively pulling Farah closer as the hawk let out a piercing cry. Another gust hit them, scattering debris from the ground and sending a plume of dust into the air. Farah stiffened, her dagger shifting to a defensive grip.

"Arash," she muttered under her breath, her voice tinged with irritation. Times like this, he really did hate being right.

As if on cue, three figures emerged from the swirling dust, their silhouettes sharp against the alley's entrance. At the forefront was Arash, his hand raised, the air around him shimmering faintly with movement. The two young men flanking him stood ready, their weapons drawn but unnecessary with his control of the wind.

Arash's slingshot hung loosely at his side, forgotten in favor of his Talent. His eyes swept the alley before settling on Farah and Yasher. His lips curved into a smirk, though his gaze was cold.

"Foundling," he said, his voice carrying easily despite the wind's howl. "Didn't expect to see you here. What's this?" His gaze flicked to Yasher, disdain flickering in his expression. "A lover's quarrel with your gharib?"

Farah's grip on Yasher's arm tightened, turning him to face the other Beloveds and pulling it higher against his back. He winced, leaning into the movement to sell the act.

"While you hunt birds throughout the city?" she countered, her tone sharp. "The Mashyana must have you on such important business. Wouldn't seabirds be more your speed to kill?"

Arash's smirk faltered, and the wind surged around them, tugging at Farah's scarf and Yasher's coat. He placed a hand on the hilt of his dagger, though he didn't draw it.

"I have a task," he said coldly. "And you didn't answer my question. What are you doing with him?"

Farah's stance didn't waver, though the wind whipped her curls around her face.

"I also have a task," she replied smoothly. "Leave me to mine, and I'll leave you to yours."

Arash's eyes narrowed, his hand twitching slightly. The wind shifted, swirling in a tight spiral around Farah's feet. Yasher felt her stiffen beside him, though her expression remained calm.

"Careful, Arash," she said softly, her tone cutting

through the wind like a blade. "I'd hate to report to the Mashyana that you wasted her time chasing birds and harassing her Hand."

The air stilled suddenly, the wind dying as quickly as it had risen. Arash's jaw tightened, but he stepped back, his gaze flicking to the rooftops as if searching for the hawk.

"Have fun with your task, Foundling," he said, his voice laced with contempt. "But don't think you can outplay me."

Farah didn't respond. She shoved Yasher forward, using him to create space between her and the group. He stumbled, cringing as the movement pulled at his shoulder.

"You're taking this a little too seriously," he muttered under his breath.

Her lips barely moved as she replied, "Do you have a better plan?"

The tension hung thick in the air as they walked away, the weight of the wards' gazes pressing on Yasher's back. They didn't speak until they reached the end of the alley and stepped into the sunlit side street.

Yasher exhaled sharply, glancing over his shoulder.

"You can let go now," he said, his arm starting to cramp where she held it tight against his back.

Farah leaned close, her breath warm against his ear.

"They're following us," she whispered. "To the Citadel. Unless, of course, you're ready to give me the relic."

He laughed softly, the sound more for himself than her. "You'll get your relic when you introduce me to this Mashyana."

"Be careful what you wish for," she replied, her voice carrying a note of warning. She released his arm but stayed close enough that her presence felt like a tether.

"Always careful," Yasher said, grinning despite the tension knotting in his chest. He gestured toward the road ahead with his free hand. "Introduce me, Phoenix."

Her glare could have stopped his heart, but she said nothing, leading the way toward the Citadel.

CHAPTER 6

THIS IS A HORRIBLE IDEA. Horrible. And I don't know how to get out of it.

Farah lead Yasher through the streets of the Citadel. Each step closer built into a steady mantra in her mind.

Turn out his pockets, take the relic, leave him behind.

But no, she wasn't doing that. Instead, she was taking him to face the Mashyana—her Mashyana. The queen she served with every fiber of her being, the woman whose faith in her had shaped her life.

Her fingers tightened on Yasher's arm, as if holding him in place might somehow steady her thoughts. Behind them, the faint shuffle of footsteps and the sense of the metals they wore told her that Arash and his friends were still trailing them, keeping a careful distance but ready to pounce the moment her ruse faltered.

You should just end this now, she told herself. *Take the relic and be done with him.*

But then Yasher's arm tensed beneath her grip, and she glanced at him, catching the faint smirk on his lips. His banter, his ridiculous confidence—it should have gotten him killed in four different ways before breakfast. And yet, for some Divine-forsaken reason, she found it... endearing.

That realization nearly made her stumble. Divine's sake, focus.

The weight of what she was doing pressed harder on her chest with every step. The audacity of this man may get them both killed if she didn't think of something fast.

She stopped abruptly on the other side of the main street from the gates to the Citadel, her mind racing. Another idea bloomed—just as bad as the last one, but maybe it could work.

Yasher turned to her, his brows furrowed in question. "Why are we stopping?"

Farah leaned close, keeping her voice low. "They're blind to us at the moment, but only for a moment longer. Punch me, then disappear into the crowd."

Yasher blinked, clearly taken aback. "What?"

"Make it a good hit," she said, her voice firm despite the trembling in her chest. "Do it now, or we're both dead."

For a moment, his expression flickered—indecision, hesitation. Then he nodded, his jaw tightening as he prepared himself. Farah released his arm, closing her eyes to brace for the blow. If she saw it coming, her instincts would take over, and he'd be the one in pain instead of her.

"Divine, help me," she whispered.

The punch landed square on her jaw, snapping her head to the side and sending a burst of pain radiating through her face. She stumbled back, her hand flying to her dagger as if by reflex, her balance faltering for just a moment.

"Apologies, Phoenix," Yasher murmured. His hand hovered near her face for a heartbeat before he stepped back.

Farah touched her jaw, wincing at the sharp ache

already blooming into what would surely be a spectacular bruise. At least he could throw a punch. She glared at him, watching as he began to back away, his movements fluid and deliberate.

Out of the corner of her eye, she saw Arash and his friends closing in, their pace quickening. She cradled her jaw, stumbling again for effect, and cast a look toward Yasher as he darted into a nearby alley.

"Catch him!" Arash's voice rang out, sharp and commanding.

The three young men took off after Yasher, one of them sparing her a glance filled with disdain. She met his gaze evenly, her hand still pressed to her face as if nursing her injury.

The moment they passed her, Farah bolted after them, her boots pounding against the cobblestones. Her heart raced, her mind scrambling for a solution.

Think of something, she urged herself. *Anything.*

When she turned the corner, her stomach twisted at the sight before her. Yasher stood at the far end of the alley, his back pressed against the wall, his expression carefully composed despite the tension radiating from him.

Arash was on him in an instant, his fist driving into Yasher's gut with a sickening thud. Yasher doubled over, gasping, but Arash didn't let up. He yanked Yasher upright by his arm, twisting it behind his back with enough force that Farah thought she heard the seam of his coat tear.

One of the other wards produced a length of chain, its surface faintly glinting with Talent. Farah's chest tightened as they wrapped it around Yasher's wrists, binding him securely.

"I caught him," Arash said, his gray eyes gleaming with triumph. "And I won't let him get away. Unlike you."

He shoved Yasher forward, his shoulder slamming into Farah's. For a moment, their eyes met, and she caught the faintest glimmer of malice in Arash's expression.

Farah reached out, steadying Yasher as he stumbled. His lips curved into a grin—sharp-edged, infuriatingly cocky, and entirely out of place.

"Worth a shot, aye, gents?" Yasher said, his voice light despite the strain in it. He leaned closer, lowering his voice to a whisper. "New plan?"

Farah shook her head, her jaw tightening. There's no way out of this now.

She grabbed Yasher's arm, pushing him toward the Citadel gates with enough force to make it look convincing.

"Move, gharib," she growled, wishing she could direct her anger at Arash instead.

The gates to the Citadel stood open, flanked by guards in polished armor. As they approached, the captain of the guard, Hajir, stepped forward to meet them.

"Is the Mashyana in the throne room today?" Farah asked, her voice steady despite the turmoil churning inside her. "I have a task to complete for her."

"The Mashyana is in her personal chambers, Hand," Hajir replied, his tone respectful.

"Thank you." Farah gave Yasher another shove toward the stairs.

Hajir's gaze flicked to Arash and his companions, his expression hardening.

"Aqa à Kamran," he said, addressing Arash, "the Mashyana has instructed that only her Hand is to meet with her today. You and the Beloveds are dismissed to your own tasks."

Farah fought to keep her expression neutral as Hajir and

another guard moved to block Arash's path. She could feel his glare burning into her back as she led Yasher up the sandstone stairs, her heart pounding with a mixture of relief and dread.

"Now what?" Yasher murmured, his voice barely audible over the murmur of courtiers passing by.

She sighed, reaching for the chains around his wrists. She undid them quickly, letting the length of chain fall into her hands. "Now," she began, but the words faltered on her tongue.

She took a deep breath, trying again. "Now you give me the relic, and I'll get you out of here. Past the Mashyana's chambers and through the servant's passages."

He stopped at the top of the stairs, turning to face her. He rubbed his wrists, his eyes catching hers with an intensity that made her chest tighten. The faint curve of a grin played on his lips, but she didn't have the patience for his games.

"Well?" she prompted, her voice sharper than she intended.

Yasher tilted his head, the grin spreading into something infuriatingly smug. "What if I were to say—"

"Hand," a guard called, cutting him off. "The Mashyana is waiting for you."

Farah froze, her blood turning cold. The guard's words were final, there was no escaping now.

"I'm sorry," she whispered, leaning close to Yasher. Her voice cracked despite her effort to keep it steady. "I'll do what I can, but we have to go through with this."

She pushed him toward the open door of the Mashyana's private chambers, her hand resting lightly on his shoulder. As they entered, the Mashyana's voice greeted them, warm and commanding.

"Farahnaz, my dear."

The Mashyana's voice wrapped around her like a silken cord. Soft, warm, but impossible to escape. Farah's back straightened automatically, her hand resting lightly on Yasher's shoulder as she guided him into the room. The scent of rose oil and incense hung heavy in the air, a constant reminder of the Mashyana's presence.

The queen stood at her desk, her court garb shimmering in the faint light streaming through the arched windows. The robes were immaculate with layers of white and gold, with rich red accents along the hemline, regal and commanding. Her crown, a delicate piece of filigree adorned with ruby and emerald, caught the light like fire, reflecting her authority. Her dark hair was styled elegantly up, soft curls framing her sharp features, and her high cheekbones and strong jawline added to the severity of her presence. Every inch of her was a study in power, poised and unwavering.

"Leave us," the Mashyana said without turning, her voice calm but absolute.

The guard who had followed them inside gave a curt bow and exited, the heavy door closing with a muffled thud behind him. The silence that followed was oppressive, punctuated only by the faint rustle of Behnaz smoothing her skirts as she seated herself in the chair beside her desk.

Farah forced herself to focus on the crown instead of the woman wearing it. Yasher, however, seemed unfazed. His stance was relaxed, his hands at his sides, though she could sense the tension simmering beneath the surface.

"And who have you brought me?" Behnaz's gaze shifted to Yasher, her sharp eyes assessing him with the precision of a blade. She raised an elegant brow, her attention flicking briefly to Farah's hand still resting on his shoulder.

Farah's cheeks burned. She dropped her hand quickly, clasping both behind her back as she stepped away.

"Your Grace," she began, keeping her voice steady, "I believe this gharib has information pertaining to the task you assigned me this morning. I thought it best to present him directly to you."

"So soon?" The Mashyana chuckled softly, a sound that sent a chill racing down Farah's spine. "I should have made you my Hand ages ago if you're this efficient, my Beloved."

She rose from her chair, her movements deliberate and graceful. Farah watched as Behnaz approached Yasher, her gaze sweeping over him like a predator sizing up its prey.

"I am Mashyana Behnaz à Radan," she said, her voice soft but commanding. "You are welcome to the kingdom of Emari, Aqa. What are you known by?"

Yasher inclined his head, his lips curving into a smile that Farah recognized all too well even with such a short time knowing him. It was the same charm-laden grin he used to disarm, to deflect, to win over whoever stood in his way.

"I am Yasher of Gavrilov, Your Majesty," he said smoothly. His voice was warm, confident—too confident. "And while I'd love to say my time here in your kingdom has been entirely pleasant, I find myself wondering about the purpose of this meeting."

Her stomach twisted. She wanted to shake him, to remind him that this was not the time for his games. But then Behnaz smiled—a slow, calculated expression that made her blood run cold.

"Bold," the Mashyana said, her tone carrying the faintest hint of amusement. "I like that. Tell me, Aqa Yasher, what do you know of this?"

She gestured to the book on the small table beside her

chair, lifting it and turning it so he could see the illustration of the relic.

Farah held her breath, her eyes flicking to him. He leaned forward, squinting dramatically as if trying to make out the details.

"Oh, yes," he said, drawing the words out as he reached into his inner pocket. Farah's pulse quickened, her Talent humming faintly in her bones.

He wouldn't.

Yasher pulled out the relic and tossed it lightly in the air before catching it in his palm.

"That's my lucky charm," he said, holding it up between his fingers as if it were a trinket he'd picked up at a market stall.

Her breath caught. Every muscle in her body tensed as she watched him hold it out toward the Mashyana. Her mind raced.

What is he doing?

Behnaz stepped closer, her eyes locked on the relic.

"May I look at it?" she asked, her voice soft but filled with an intensity that made Farah's skin prickle.

Her gaze darted to him, willing him to refuse as he had to her over and over today. But instead, he inclined his head, his grin widening.

"I would be honored to return such a valuable relic to your keeping, Your Majesty," he said, his tone smooth as silk. "I found it along my travels, thought it a beautiful piece of ephemera. To learn it's a holy relic of your people... Well, that makes this encounter all the more fortuitous."

Behnaz's hands closed around the relic the moment he offered it, cradling it against her chest as if it were the most precious thing in the world.

"My kingdom, and I, thank you, Yasher of Gavrilov," she

said, her voice regaining its usual poise. She moved to her desk, unlocking the small ornate box that sat there and placing the relic inside.

Farah exhaled slowly, her tension easing just enough for her to feel the ache in her jaw from Yasher's earlier punch. This should have been a relief. The relic was in Behnaz's hands, and Yasher had avoided the worst—for now.

But something felt wrong.

Behnaz turned back to them, her regal mask firmly in place.

"Farahnaz, my dear," she said, her tone warm. "You have done well. More than I could have hoped for. You have proven yourself beyond measure."

Farah dipped into a deep bow. "I serve only Your Grace, Mashyana."

Behnaz's smile softened as she gestured toward Yasher. "And you, young man. You have shown respect and grace in returning this relic to its rightful place. I believe a reward is in order."

Yasher raised an eyebrow, his grin returning. "A reward, Your Majesty? I'm intrigued."

Behnaz chuckled, the sound like the ring of a distant bell. "Come. Before the evening service, I shall grant you a private tour of the rotunda and royal gardens. Farahnaz will join us and ensure you are safely returned to your lodgings afterward."

Farah stiffened, her Talent humming faintly again. She cast a sideways glance at Yasher, who seemed unfazed—amused, even. She resisted the urge to roll her eyes.

Behnaz swept toward the door, her presence commanding as she led the way out of her chambers. Yasher followed, his steps light and confident. Farah trailed behind, her mind a storm of questions and doubts.

Her Talent pulsed faintly, a reminder of its connection to the relic. But it was back in the Mashyana's chamber, locked away, protected.

Wasn't it?

Her hand drifted to her pocket, her fingers brushing against the surface of the fake relic she'd created earlier. A faint jolt of energy buzzed through her fingertips, and her heart sank.

He didn't.

She looked ahead at Yasher, his stride easy, his grin infuriating.

He did.

The realization settled in her chest like a stone. He'd swapped the relic, right under her nose.

Farah's jaw tightened, her steps slowing as she fought to keep her expression neutral. But as the three of them descended the staircase toward the royal gardens, one thought burned in her mind.

I'm going to kill him.

WHO WOULD HAVE GUESSED Yasher would find himself being guided through the Citadel of Emari by none other than the Mashyana herself? Yasher certainly hadn't. Not from any fortune-teller in a smoke-filled tent, not from a whispered rumor over cards, and certainly not from any plan he'd concocted in his own mind.

The Mashyana had led them first through the royal gardens, a lush and fragrant maze of citrus trees, flowering vines, and meticulously trimmed hedges. The air was thick with the scent of jasmine and orange blossoms, the beauty of the space almost enough to distract Yasher from the tension simmering beneath the surface. The Mashyana walked with unhurried grace, her flowing robes brushing the cobblestones as she paused occasionally to point out rare blooms or comment on the significance of a particular tree planted by a past ruler.

"Every plant here has its place," she remarked, her voice carrying just enough weight to feel like a lesson. "Just as every subject in my kingdom does. Order sustains us all."

Yasher kept his mouth shut, nodding politely while his thoughts churned. It was a beautiful prison, this garden. And the more she spoke, the more her words felt like veiled reminders of control.

Finally, she led them into the grand rotunda, the air cooling instantly as they stepped beneath its domed roof. The sudden change in atmosphere felt like stepping into a temple.

The rotunda was a masterpiece. Light streamed through the stained glass above, spilling a kaleidoscope of colors onto the polished stone floor. Yasher craned his neck, his breath catching as his gaze swept over the intricate panels. Each one was a story unto itself, a vivid depiction of the kingdom's history and its gods.

Yasher's eyes lingered on the final panels, which transitioned into a vision of peace. The founding of the Mashya's dynasty was rendered in exquisite detail, each ruler's face etched with reverence. But it was the very last panel that held his attention.

Unlike the others, it showed the current Mashyana standing beside the Mashya. They were depicted handing alms to their people, their faces serene and noble. It was too perfect, too recent, too deliberate.

That's new, his lips quirking in amusement. He'd bet his lucky charm that panel was added to solidify the Mashyana's image, a seamless addition to history. Talent-made or not, it was clever.

"The Mashya recently brought in artisans from across the kingdom," the Mashyana said, her voice a smooth counterpoint to the echoing space, "to confirm the structural soundness of the rotunda and to restore the stories etched into the columns."

She gestured to one of the towering sandstone columns, where spiraling text in Emari's script wrapped around the surface. Yasher squinted at the intricate carvings, but his attention drifted back to the stained glass.

"The rotunda tells us everything we need to know about who we are," she continued, her tone softening as she looked upward. "It reminds me daily of my duty to this kingdom and my role as its servant."

Yasher's brow arched as he studied her. The Mashyana's serene expression radiated piety, her hands spread wide as if to embrace the stories of her ancestors. It was a performance, of course, but a masterful one. The small cluster of servants and courtiers nearby seemed enraptured, their admiration evident in their gazes.

She plays the part well, I'll give her that.

One of the servants made a small noise, stepping forward hesitantly with hands clasped behind his back.

"Your Grace," he said quietly, inclining his head.

The Mashyana's sharp glance snapped to the servant before she turned to Yasher, her smile softening instantly.

"The Crown's work is never done," she said. Her gaze shifted to Farah, who stood a few feet away, her expression unreadable.

"Hand, return the Aqa to his lodgings safely."

Farah bowed low, her movements precise, and gestured for Yasher to follow her toward the massive wooden doors at the entrance. The Mashyana swept away without another word, her skirts swirling around her as she disappeared into the corridors.

As soon as they stepped into the beating sun and swirling dust of the main road, Yasher's pace faltered, the abrupt brightness forcing him to squint against the glare. The bustling sounds of the city struck him like a wave—vendors calling out their wares, carts creaking under heavy loads, and the faint clink of coins changing hands. Farah's grip on his arm was unrelenting, her fingers digging into his sleeve with a strength that felt more like a warning than a guide. Her face was a storm, shadows of frustration and something deeper flickering across her features, too quick for him to fully catch. He opened his mouth to speak, to crack some joke that might break the tension, but before he could get a word out, she yanked him sharply to the side.

The movement was sudden, forceful, and entirely uncompromising. Yasher stumbled slightly as she pulled him into the first alley they passed, the cacophony of the main road fading abruptly into a quieter, shadowed space that felt stifling despite the midday heat. The scent of dust and dried herbs mingled with the faint tang of iron in the air, making him wonder just how often this alley saw confrontations like the one he was about to endure.

Before he could regain his balance, Farah shoved him roughly against the wall, the sandstone cool against his back despite the sun's relentless glare. The impact knocked the breath out of him for a moment, and he barely had time to register the intensity in her gaze before she stepped closer, her presence as sharp and commanding as the blade she undoubtedly carried. Somehow, despite the fact that she was half a head shorter than him, her dominance made her feel far taller. Yasher forced himself to grin, though the edge of it was more defensive than charming, his mind racing to figure out how to spin this in his favor.

"I don't know how you did it," she growled, her voice low and dangerous. "But you will hand over the real relic to the Mashyana, Divine help you."

Yasher barely had time to raise his hands in mock surrender before she pressed her dagger to his throat. The blade was warm, her Talent thrumming faintly through the metal.

"Now wait a moment," he said, his voice light despite the pressure against his neck. "Your queen seemed perfectly satisfied with the—"

"You are not allowed to speak about her, or really anything," Farah interrupted, her tone icy. The dagger nicked his skin, a bead of blood sliding down his neck.

"Now, Phoenix," he murmured, placing his fingers gently on the flat of her blade to push it away just a hair. His other hand dipped into her coat pocket with practiced ease, retrieving the real relic while her rage blinded her. It was still his lucky charm, not hers.

Before he could step back, a small voice rang out behind him, clear and unwavering.

"Stop."

Yasher froze, his hand holding the relic almost to his own coat. Pari stepped into view, her small frame seeming impossibly steady for a child her age. Her wide, dark eyes met Farah's, and there was an undeniable weight to her presence.

"You are both needed for this journey," she said, her voice carrying an authority that made even Farah hesitate.

Farah's grip on the dagger tightened, her gaze flicking between Yasher, the relic, and Pari.

"He does not respect the Mashyana or the gods," she said, her tone defensive.

"The gods see what we cannot," Pari replied calmly. She stepped closer, her small hand reaching up to rest on Farah's chest. "You are bound to the Mashyana, yes, but this path is not yours alone. Trust me."

Farah's breath hitched, her expression flickering with conflict. "He is reckless. Selfish."

"And necessary," Pari said simply. She turned her gaze to Yasher, her expression softening. "You carry more than you know, Yasher. Hold onto it."

Yasher blinked, caught off guard by her certainty. "Uh… thanks, Little Divine?"

Pari's hand guided Farah's arm down, the dagger finally sheathed with a faint click.

"The Eye of Rashnu needs to stay with Yasher," Pari said firmly, that golden sheen crossing her eyes, bringing to mind the hawk from earlier. "The relic is important, vital."

Farah's jaw tightened, her eyes narrowing as they locked onto him. "Don't even think of hopping on the next boat off this island," she growled. "The second she even briefly thinks about questioning what you handed her, I'll track you down and finish this."

"I wouldn't expect anything else, Phoenix." Yasher forced a grin, though his heart sank at the wall now firmly between them.

Without another glance, Farah brushed past him, her strides purposeful as she headed back toward the Citadel. Pari lingered, watching her go before turning back to Yasher.

"Well, that could have gone better," he muttered,

rubbing the nick on his neck before looking down at Pari with a smile. "What do you say we find our way back to Shirin's tea shop? I could use a little peace and quiet after all of that."

"Do you think Amma Shirin will have cakes ready?" Pari's smile was bright, unshaken by the tension that had just passed.

"We can hope, Little Divine," he said, his grin finally reaching his eyes as she slipped her small hand into his.

CHAPTER 7

FARAH'S RAGE simmered as she strode through the sunlit halls of the Citadel. Each step back to her quarters felt heavier than the last, her frustration at Yasher gnawing at her. Yet, beneath the anger, a flicker of doubt stirred. She couldn't shake the way Pari had intervened, the child's soft voice threading through her thoughts like an unwanted reminder that Yasher's survival was somehow entwined with a greater purpose. She pushed it away, there was no time to dwell on riddles when her anger demanded release.

Her feet carried her to the private block set aside for the Beloved, her sanctuary from the chaos of the Citadel. There, the opulence of the public halls gave way to sparse simplicity. She went directly to her cell, determined to shed her embroidered coat and scarf before heading to the training area to burn off her fury. The ritual of preparation always helped her focus, and she needed clarity now more than ever.

Inside her small room, Farah removed her coat with care, smoothing the rich fabric and hanging it on the hook by the door. The golden embroidery glinted faintly in the soft light from the narrow window, a reminder of her position and the responsibilities that weighed on her. She straightened the scarf draped nearby, the delicate silver embroidery a stark contrast to the coarse training gear she now donned.

Once dressed, she gently latched the door behind her and paused in the hallway. The stillness here was comforting, a sharp contrast to the bustling activity of the main Citadel. But as she turned toward the stairwell, a faint sound stopped her in her tracks—a low, ragged moan coming from the direction of Mozhde's cell down the hall.

Farah frowned, her hand tightening on the edge of her sleeve. Mozhde wasn't a close friend, but she was one of the few Beloved who treated Farah with something resembling kindness—or at least indifference. To hear her in distress sent a chill of unease through Farah's anger.

"Mozhde?" she called softly, stepping closer. Her voice echoed faintly in the quiet corridor as she knocked on the door. "Are you well?"

There was no answer, only another faint groan. Farah hesitated, her stomach tightening. Slowly, she pushed the door open just a crack.

The sight inside froze her blood.

Mozhde lay crumpled on her cot, her once-pristine appearance now ravaged by an unseen enemy. Sweat slicked her pallid skin, soaking her hair, which hung in matted tangles around her face. Her lips were cracked and stained with flecks of blood, and her sunken cheeks revealed sharp bones beneath. Her hands trembled as they clutched the edge of her blanket, her nails discolored and brittle.

"Mozhde!" Farah stepped back instinctively, lifting her sleeve to cover her mouth and nose. The faint scent of decay lingered in the room, mixing with the sour tang of sweat. Her pulse thundered in her ears as the words *wasting sickness* rose unbidden in her mind.

"Stay back," Mozhde rasped, her voice barely above a whisper. Her glassy eyes flickered toward Farah, clouded with pain. "I'm afraid... I've caught it."

The wasting sickness. Farah's stomach churned. She'd heard the whispered rumors around the Citadel—of a disease that consumed its victims from within, leaving them frail and hollow until their bodies simply gave out. It spread quickly, silently, sparing no one. Once the sickness took hold, no amount of Talent or skill could stop it.

Farah swallowed hard, her voice trembling. "I'll fetch the healer."

Mozhde coughed violently, her body convulsing with the effort. Blood stained her teeth, and the sound of her labored breathing filled the small cell. "Don't..." she managed, her words broken by shallow gasps. "It's too late. I am already... dead."

"You don't know that," Farah insisted, her feet rooted to the spot. She wanted to step forward, to help, but the fear of infection held her back.

Mozhde's lips twitched in a faint, bitter smile. "They'll... give me the blessing. That's all... they can do."

Her thin hand fluttered weakly, gesturing toward the door. "Go," she whispered. "I served... the Mashyana's pleasure. May Rashnu judge me kindly."

Mozhde's chest rose and fell in slow, uneven movements, her breaths barely audible now. Farah stared, her heart hammering against her ribs. She wanted to say something, anything, but the words wouldn't come. Instead, she backed away, gently pulling the door closed behind her.

The moment the latch clicked into place, Farah turned and ran. Her boots echoed against the stone floor as she raced toward the healers' floor, her mind a tangled mess of fear and urgency.

Farah took the stairs two at a time, the pounding of her feet on the stone drowned out by the thrum of her thoughts.

The wasting sickness was in the Citadel. No Talented was safe. Not the guards, not the courtiers, especially not the Mashyana's Beloved. If Mozhde, one of the queen's favored wards, could fall ill so swiftly, how much longer would it be before others followed?

She reached the healers' floor, breathless not from exertion but from the dread curling in her chest. The cool air of the infirmary hall felt oppressive, and the faint scent of herbs and disinfectant did little to calm her racing mind. Shadows moved behind the narrow curtains of smaller cells, their occupants speaking in low, hushed voices. Farah focused on the larger infirmary at the end of the hall, where figures in pristine white robes moved purposefully.

Farah pushed through the doors, grabbing the arm of the nearest healer. The woman turned, startled, her hood slipping back to reveal a face barely older than Farah's. Her irritation was immediate, evident in the way her lips thinned.

"We need help for one of the Beloveds," Farah said, her grip tight on the healer's arm.

The woman sighed, clearly expecting another minor injury. "Another broken bone? You wards need to learn discipline, not constant—"

"No," Farah interrupted sharply, her voice cutting through the healer's complaint with an edge that left no room for argument, staring the healer down. "It's the wasting sickness."

The healer froze. Her eyes widened, and her body stiffened as though Farah had struck her.

"That's not possible," she said quietly. "The wasting sickness hasn't reached the Citadel."

"It has," Farah insisted, her voice tight. "Mozhde is dying in her cell. You need to help her."

The healer pulled her arm free, taking a step back. The stark fear in her expression sent a pang of frustration through Farah's chest.

"There's nothing we can do," the healer whispered. Her hands clutched the front of her robes as though seeking reassurance. "No Talent in the world can stop it. Once it takes hold, it's... just death."

Farah's jaw clenched. "You're saying Mozhde is already gone? That you won't even try?"

The healer's shoulders straightened, her fear giving way to grim resolve. "We can offer her the blessing to ease her passing, but that is all. Anything more would be false hope."

Farah opened her mouth to argue, but the healer cut her off with a sharp question. "Did you go into her cell? Touch her?"

"No." Farah shook her head vehemently. "I opened the door, but I left the moment I realized what was wrong."

The healer's shoulders relaxed slightly, though her expression remained tense. "Thank you for informing us, Hand. We'll see to it."

With a quick gesture, the healer summoned two

apprentices. The young women moved swiftly, donning masks and gloves as they followed the healer toward the stairwell. Farah watched as they disappeared, her stomach twisting with helplessness. She hated feeling like this—useless, dismissed.

The infirmary buzzed with renewed urgency as the remaining staff moved with brisk efficiency. With all their precision, Farah felt like an outsider, a bystander to something larger than her.

Swallowing her frustration, Farah turned away, her feet carrying her toward the training area. She needed to clear her head, to push away the image of Mozhde's gaunt face and cracked lips. The anger she'd felt toward Yasher seemed distant now, replaced by a gnawing sense of dread that she couldn't quite shake.

As she descended the stairs, her thoughts drifted to the Mashyana. The queen needed to know. She would want to know.

Farah's steps slowed as she approached the private door leading to the Mashyana's chambers. Her hand hovered over the latch, her mind racing. Would the healers inform the queen? Or would they try to contain the news, fearing the panic it might cause?

No. This wasn't something that could be kept quiet. The Mashyana deserved the truth.

Squaring her shoulders, Farah pushed through the door and made her way down the hall to the Mashyana's private chambers. The guards stationed outside straightened at her approach, their gazes sharp.

"The Hand requests an audience with the Mashyana," she said firmly, pushing down the panic she'd felt moments before.

One of the guards nodded and knocked on the door. "Your Grace, the Hand is here."

A moment of silence passed before the Mashyana's voice drifted through the door, calm and composed. "Show her in."

Farah stepped inside, the rich scents of rose oil and incense washing over her. The Mashyana stood before a gilded mirror, her reflection serene as a servant adjusted the intricate jewelry adorning her. The light caught the edges of her crown, making it gleam like captured sunlight.

"You are not dressed for service, Hand," the Mashyana remarked, her voice even but tinged with curiosity.

Farah bowed her head deeply, the weight of her news pressing heavily on her shoulders. "Your Grace, one of the Beloved is... ill."

The Mashyana's hands paused, her eyes meeting Farah's in the mirror. "Which one?"

"Mozhde," Farah said softly. She paused before saying more, looking at the servant.

For a moment, the Mashyana didn't move. Then, with deliberate calm, she dismissed the maid with a wave of her hand. As the door clicked shut behind the servant, the queen turned to face Farah fully.

"What is it?"

"The wasting sickness." Her stomach went sour, saying it out loud to her queen as if it was her fault.

"You are certain?" the Mashyana asked, her tone sharper now, though her expression remained composed.

Farah nodded. "I've informed the healers, but they... They don't believe they can do anything."

The Mashyana's gaze shifted, her expression distant, calculating the implications of Farah's words. After a long moment, she sighed and smoothed the fabric of her skirts.

"We shall pray to Rashnu during evening services. May he find her soul pure and welcome her to the House of Song."

Farah dipped her head, unsure how to respond. The Mashyana's calm in the face of such news was both reassuring and unsettling.

The queen stepped closer, her tone softening. "I know you and Mozhde were close. Go to the training room, my dear. Work off your sadness. I will inform the others."

Farah bowed again, her movements stiff with emotion. As she turned to leave, the Mashyana's voice stopped her.

"Farah," the queen said quietly, her gaze heavy with meaning. "Let us keep the details of her passing to ourselves for now. There's no need to cause undue fear in the court."

"Yes, Your Grace," Farah murmured, nodding before retreating from the room.

As she descended toward the training area, her thoughts churned. The Mashyana's request made sense, but it did little to ease the weight in her chest. Mozhde was gone, and the wasting sickness had reached the heart of the kingdom. How long before it spread further?

THE RAIN HAMMERED RELENTLESSLY against the high, narrow windows of the Citadel, the sound a constant drumbeat that seemed to reverberate through Farah's bones. Each droplet streaked down the glass like tears, distorting the faint glow of lanterns outside and casting flickering, fluid shadows across the damp stone walls of the training area. The humid air was thick with the mingling scents of sweat and wet stone, a heady, oppressive reminder of the storm raging outside—and the storm within her.

Farah stood in the center of the room, her fists clenched tightly. Her body moved through a series of forms, each strike and block a release of pent-up energy. Her movements were fluid yet sharp, her bare feet sliding and pivoting across the slick training mat as though she could physically fight the thoughts that hounded her.

Mozhde's gaunt face flashed in her mind—sunken cheeks, cracked lips, the hopelessness in her eyes. The sight had etched itself into Farah's memory like a scar. She struck harder, her breath coming faster.

The stories of the wasting sickness still gnawed at her. She had heard whispers from the mainland of the Talented succumbing to a sickness that drained them until they were nothing but shells. It started with a fever that no medicine could touch, followed by the slow withering of flesh, muscle, and spirit. Only the Talented seemed to fall victim to it, even if they didn't know that they held a spark of the Unnamed Gods' last gift.

The Mashyana's response to it lingered in Farah's mind. Her calm, measured demeanor struck Farah as wrong. She had spoken of the sickness as though it were just another inconvenience to manage. She couldn't help but wonder why the queen was keeping her thoughts to herself, guarding them as she always did, even when it came to something so... devastating. Farah's fists tightened again, the movement almost involuntary. There was a sharpness in her chest that she couldn't quite shake, a small, unsettling doubt.

Farah gritted her teeth, pivoting sharply and striking out at an invisible opponent. The fury that had simmered within her since her encounter with Yasher now boiled over. Her Talent stirred faintly in her blood, a subtle hum in the back of her mind, but she pushed it down. This wasn't about power—it was about control. About focus.

And that infuriating gharib.

Yasher's image drifted into her mind. His lopsided grin, his piercing blue eyes glinting with a maddening mix of arrogance and charm. He'd swindled her, swindled the Mashyana, and walked away with that smug smirk on his face, as if he'd won the greatest game of his life. And what had she done? Let him.

She struck out again, her knuckles grazing the edge of the wooden training post. Pain flared through her hand, sharp and grounding, a welcome distraction from the storm in her mind.

She grabbed a towel from a nearby peg and pressed it to her damp face. The scent of her sweat mingled with the earthy musk of the training room. She wiped her brow, trying to calm the tumult within her. Every step she took as the Hand seemed to tighten the noose of expectations and betrayals around her neck.

What had she truly expected when she became the Hand of the Mashyana? Prestige? Purpose? Instead, the title weighed on her like a shackle, binding her to the Mashyana's whims and the tangled mess of courtly intrigues. She'd lied to her queen, traded the real relic for a counterfeit, and now every step forward felt like balancing on the edge of a blade.

The sound of voices echoing down the hallway snapped her out of her spiraling thoughts. Farah turned, dropping the towel as the door to the training area opened. The Mashyana entered, her regal figure cutting through the shadows like a blade. Her crown glinted faintly in the lantern light, and her skirts swirled around her as the air bent to her Talent. Behind her trailed Arash, his sharp eyes darting around the room, and a single guard.

"Hand," the queen called, her voice smooth and commanding.

Farah immediately dropped into a deep bow, her damp curls falling forward as she straightened. "Your Grace."

The Mashyana waved Arash and the guard toward the door.

"Leave us," she said, her tone leaving no room for argument. The two men nodded and stepped outside, closing the door behind them.

Farah straightened as the queen moved to the side of the room, her movements as fluid and deliberate as Farah's training forms. She followed quickly, clasping her hands in front of her, her heart pounding in her chest.

"Yes, Your Grace?"

Before Behnaz could speak, Farah took a tentative step closer, her voice wavering slightly. "Your Grace... I beg your pardon, but... has Mozhde—has she...?"

Behnaz paused, her head tilting ever so slightly. "Mozhde?"

Farah's throat tightened. "Yes, Your Grace. Has she survived? Or... is she gone?"

The queen's expression was unreadable, her gaze steady and sharp.

"She has been seen to," Behnaz said after a moment. Her tone was soft but distant, as though the matter were already a memory. "Rashnu will weigh her soul as he sees fit."

Farah's heart clenched, the weight of the unspoken words falling heavy between them. Mozhde was gone. The healers hadn't saved her, and now all that remained was the hope of mercy in the afterlife. She wanted to press further, to demand to know why nothing more had been done, but the calm finality in Behnaz's voice left no room for argument.

The Mashyana's expression shifted, a faint smile gracing her lips as she gestured for Farah to follow.

"You have other duties now, Hand. Pack your things."

Farah blinked, momentarily caught off guard. "You... Your Grace?"

"You heard me," Behnaz said, her tone patient but firm. "Since you were so quickly successful in finding a relic, I require your skills again. You will leave for the mainland at first light."

Farah felt a rush of conflicting emotions. Relief at the chance to escape the Citadel, but also a nagging fear. The Mashyana trusted her now, and yet Farah's success had been built on lies.

"Yes, Your Grace," Farah said, keeping her voice steady despite the surge of questions rising in her mind.

Behnaz's expression softened slightly. "I have heard of a relic outside Banima, the Shard of Ameretat," she explained, her voice calm and measured. "A merchant there holds information about it, unaware of its true value. You must procure it."

Farah nodded, her mind already turning to logistics, but the Mashyana wasn't finished.

"The second relic," Behnaz continued, "is rumored to be near Tamidh, where negotiations with the rebels are faltering. The Mashya's authority is at stake."

Farah's brow furrowed. "Rumors? What about the Mashya's negotiations?"

Behnaz's gaze hardened. "The Mashya attempts to broker peace, but the rebels see an opportunity to demand more than the Crown can offer. The tension grows by the hour."

Farah hesitated, weighing her next question carefully. "Is the Mashya in danger?"

Behnaz's eyes flickered, a faint hint of something unreadable passing through her expression before she answered.

"The Mashya is protected by his guard and by the Unnamed Gods. But the traitors are cunning, and they may seek to use this opportunity to strike."

Farah nodded, though her mind churned with unease. The rebels were no fools, and the rumors she'd heard in the Citadel painted a picture of a group growing more desperate and more dangerous.

Behnaz's voice broke through her thoughts.

"Be ready to leave on the first barge tomorrow morning. You have served me well, Farah. Continue to do so, and you will ensure the future of this kingdom."

Farah bowed deeply. "Yes, Your Grace."

The Mashyana turned, her skirts swirling as she exited the training area. Farah watched her go, the weight of the queen's words settling heavily on her shoulders. She stood there for a long moment, the faint echo of Behnaz's steps fading into silence.

The storm outside continued to rage, the pounding rain matching the tumult in Farah's mind. She clenched her fists, her nails digging into her palms as her anger surged once more. She stepped back onto the training mat, the damp fabric squelching beneath her feet. Her movements became sharper, more aggressive, each strike a way to channel her frustration. Rostam would have been annoyed at her letting her emotions dictate her forms.

The queen trusted her. Mozhde was dead. Yasher had stolen the real relic. She had helped him.

With every punch, every kick, Farah felt the storm inside her rise and fall, ebb and flow, an unrelenting tide mirroring that of the one raging just outside. Her breath came in short bursts, her muscles burning with exertion. She didn't stop until her limbs ached and her chest heaved.

She wouldn't still be here if the Mashyana had discovered the deception. That was her only comfort as the rain continued to fall, unyielding and merciless.

CHAPTER 8

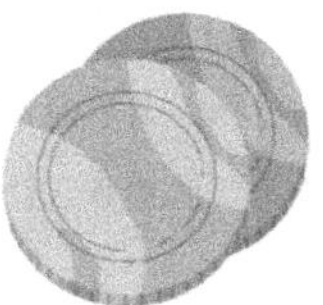

TIME TO LEAVE, *time to leave, time to leave.*

The thought echoed relentlessly in Yasher's mind, like a steady drumbeat urging him forward. He kept a smile plastered on his face as he and Pari sat outside the Saffron Oasis, the warmth of the day ending mixing with the sweet scent of saffron wafting through the air. Shirin appeared as if by magic whenever the tea began to dwindle or the plate of delicate cakes approached crumbs.

Threatening clouds crept across the moon as it began to peek over the rooftops, casting ominous shadows on the cobblestones below. Yasher slapped his thighs and turned to Pari, adopting his best grown-up expression.

"Little Divine, it's time for me to go." He brushed crumbs from her cheeks, unable to resist the fondness that welled within him. "I'm afraid I'll need to embark on my own journey soon."

Pari's face fell momentarily before a small smile replaced it.

"I know," she said quietly, her eyes shining with something deeper than mere innocence. "You will leave the

Citadel in the morning. Rashnu told me that this was to come for you both, on a barge with blue sails."

"Indeed," he said, feeling a flicker of uncertainty. "But I doubt Farah will be eager to speak with me again, unless I'm on the verge of death at her hand."

She looked at him with a seriousness that belied her small stature. "You and she have many things to accomplish together before you must choose your path at the Bridge."

Yasher found himself torn between amusement and concern. Was the girl truly attuned to the divine, or was her mind wandering the realms of childlike fantasy? He nodded along, a grin creeping back onto his face as she beamed up at him.

"We will see you again," she said, placing her tiny hand atop his. "Don't worry."

He covered her hand with his other, feeling a warmth that anchored him amid the storm brewing in his heart.

"You are a wonder, Little Divine."

Shirin came to their table, clearing the remnants of their feast. "Another cup before the storm rolls in, my lovelies?"

"I need to head out, Shirin," Yasher replied, the bittersweetness of leaving hanging in the air. "Thank you for everything. You've created a special place here."

She laughed, her presence brightening the dim light of the evening. "The Saffron Oasis is a community commitment, dear. It's a place where we preserve the old ways and nourish the spirit, even in the midst of turmoil."

"Little Divine," he looked to Pari. "Would you take the cups into the shop for Shirin as a thank you?"

The little girl grinned and grabbed their dishes, leaving the older woman with him.

"I appreciate your hospitality," his voice dropped low. "If you would keep an eye out for the little girl, I'd owe you a debt."

She stopped cleaning up and threw the towel over one shoulder.

"Of course." A sad smile crossed her face as she looked directly at him.

She walked up to him, reaching up and placing her gentle, calloused hands on either side of his face.

"You are always welcome here. May the Unnamed Gods keep you safe, young man."

He was warmed by her care, placing his hands over hers, still on his face. "You are a wonder, Shirin. May your Gods keep you."

As she released him, a soft blush colored her cheeks.

"You should leave now, before she comes back out." She said, wiping down the table again with her ever-present towel. "It would be a kindness to the little one."

Nodding, Yasher turned, battling his cowardice at not wanting to say goodbye to Pari. Better to walk away now, before she noticed he was leaving.

The chill of the evening air bit at his skin as he left the comfort of warmth and the scent of freshly brewed tea that the Saffron Oasis contained. Dark clouds loomed overhead, and he could hear the distant rumble of thunder, a prelude to the storm that seemed to mirror the tumult within him.

The streets of the Citadel were alive with movement, merchants packing their wares and citizens bustling about before the storm came in. It was a dance of life that Yasher had grown accustomed to regardless of where he was in the world, but tonight, the atmosphere felt different. More tension was in the air, along with the first drops of rain.

Thoughts of Farah lingered in his mind. Her anger had

been palpable, and despite their brief connection, he felt the distance between them stretching wider. How could he have let her think he was so callous? The lingering image of her narrowed gaze sent a flicker of unease through him. Her fierce determination, a fire that had ignited something in him, now felt like a weight he couldn't shake off.

As he neared the docks, the salty air filled his lungs, invigorating him and reminding him of the freedom that awaited him on the mainland. There, he would escape the tangled web of the Citadel, its politics, and even that woman, free to make his own choices.

The rain started as a light drizzle, softening the edges of the Citadel's cobblestones, but it carried a promise of the storm looming above. Yasher's boots splashed lightly in shallow puddles as he threaded through the increasingly busy streets. The docks were always alive at this hour, the scent of salt mingling with fish and damp wood, but tonight carried an undercurrent of urgency.

He tugged his coat tighter around himself, fingers brushing the inner pocket where the relic lay hidden. It felt heavier now, as though it could sense his mood and choices ahead. He quickened his pace, keeping his head down, avoiding the watchful eyes of passersby.

This is your chance. Get on a boat and leave all of this behind.

He reached the edge of the docks, where lanterns swung precariously in the growing wind, their light casting distorted shadows over the bustling chaos. Sailors barked orders, ropes creaked, and crates clattered as they were hurriedly loaded onto ships. The storm was clearly chasing them all.

A vessel with pale blue sails stood out among the others, its crew working frantically to secure cargo and prepare for departure. Yasher's heart skipped. Pari's words echoed in his mind—*a barge with blue sails*. Was this his way out?

He approached a grizzled sailor standing near the gangplank, a man whose scarred face and weary eyes suggested years spent battling more than just the sea.

"Any chance you're leaving tonight?" Yasher asked, keeping his tone light, casual.

The sailor gave him a once-over and shook his head. "Not in this storm, mate. Cap'n don't take risks with lightning overhead. You'll have to wait till morning, if it clears."

Yasher's stomach sank, though he forced a grin. "Figures. Always the way with my luck."

The sailor grunted something unintelligible, turning back to his work. Yasher lingered for a moment, staring at the barge and the dark clouds gathering on the horizon. Rain splattered harder now, fat droplets that soaked into his coat.

He let out a slow breath, frustration mingling with a creeping sense of inevitability.

"Of course," he muttered, turning away from the docks. "The one time I actually want to run, and the gods decide to cage me."

The streets were quieter now, most of the vendors gone and only the occasional hooded figure darting between awnings to escape the downpour. Yasher trudged onward, each step feeling heavier as the storm intensified.

THE SUN HADN'T QUITE RISEN when Yasher woke, the pale gray light of early dawn seeping through the narrow window of his rented room. He splashed cold water onto his face from the basin, the chill shocking him into full alertness. His rucksack was packed—had been since the restless hours of the night when sleep refused to claim him. He checked it again anyway, fingers brushing over the worn leather straps, ensuring he hadn't left behind anything vital. Not that he owned much worth leaving behind.

Every second he lingered on this island seemed to stretch taut, the risk of discovery sharpening with each heartbeat. The Citadel was no place to remain, certainly not with Farah prowling around. She was a storm he had no desire to weather any longer.

For a moment, he hesitated, standing in the center of the small room. Should he say goodbye to Kambiz? She'd been kind to him, and for once he hated leaving threads untied. But he shook the thought off quickly. No. A clean break is best.

This wasn't the first time he'd disappeared without warning, and it wouldn't be the last.

His eyes strayed to the window sill, where sunlight had once caught the curve of Farah's chin as she'd confronted him. He could almost see her again, her hair wild, dagger humming with her Talent, her eyes fierce and unyielding. And, somehow, in that moment of mortal peril, all he wanted to do was kiss her, to bed her. Why had he not kissed her when he'd had his chance?

Twelve hells, he did love to play with fire.

Enough. He pulled himself out of the memory. There was no time for regrets or reflection. He shouldered his rucksack, casting a final glance around the room. It was as if he'd never been there, and that was precisely how he wanted it.

The stairs creaked beneath his boots as he descended, each step slow and deliberate. He knew the loose boards by now but still managed to misstep, one groaning loudly under his weight. He winced, freezing in place, and listened. The tavern was quiet. Just a few more steps and he'd be out.

But as his foot touched the ground floor, a soft voice stopped him.

"Yash? Where are you going?"

Kambiz stood in the doorway to her room beneath the stairs, her dark hair loose around her shoulders, her night-shift rumpled from sleep. She blinked at him, her eyes immediately locking on the rucksack slung over his shoulder. The light of the lanterns outside cast long shadows over her face, but he didn't need to see her clearly to know what was coming.

He turned to her, plastering a warm, apologetic smile on his face. "Kambiz, I didn't mean to wake you."

Her gaze didn't waver. "You're leaving."

"Just for a bit, dearheart," he said, walking toward her with easy steps. "There's a whole mainland out there waiting for me to explore."

She shrugged off his charm like it was nothing, her arms crossing over her chest. "You're running."

"Kambiz," he said softly, reaching out to touch her shoulder. "I'm sorry. My choices—well, let's just say they've been made for me."

Her eyes searched his face for a moment, and he saw the flicker of hope that remained in her.

"I could come with you," she offered suddenly, her voice brightening. "Sohrab can find another girl for the tavern. You'd be safer with someone watching your back."

Yasher felt a pang of guilt twist in his chest.

"Kambiz…" He said her name with as much care as he could muster, his hand falling away from her shoulder. His voice carried the weight of regret he rarely allowed himself to feel.

Her expression hardened, and she straightened her posture, brushing past him with a forced calm.

"Well, then," she said, her tone cool. She adjusted her shawl over her shoulders, pulling it tight as though it were armor. "May the Unnamed Gods keep you, Yasher of Gavrilov."

She disappeared into her small room, the door clicking shut behind her. Yasher stood there, hand still half-raised as though he could stop her. But his feet remained rooted to the floor.

"Twelve hells," he muttered under his breath. His shoulders slumped, and for a moment, he allowed himself to stare at the worn floorboards beneath his boots, scuffing them lightly. He glanced once more toward her door but knew better than to knock. Better to leave it this way.

Turning, he made his way out of the tavern and into the waking world of the Citadel.

The air was heavy with the scent of brine and rain, the remnants of the storm hanging in the dissipating dark clouds moving off overhead. Lanterns swayed in the early morning breeze, casting their flickering light over the cobbled streets and the bustling figures of merchants preparing for the day.

Yasher pulled his coat tighter around him as he reached the boardwalk. His boots echoed faintly against the worn wood, mingling with the murmurs of fishermen and sailors readying their vessels. The Kamyar Strait stretched out before him, its waters dark and restless. Somewhere beyond that expanse lay Rumatin, the mainland, and a fresh start.

He scanned the docks, his eyes catching on the barge with blue sails near the end of the pier he'd spotted last night. Pari's words from the night before echoed in his mind, and though he wasn't one to put too much stock in divine portents, he wasn't about to ignore one either.

A man in slightly better clothing than the sailors stood by the barge, a ledger in hand and a stick of charcoal tucked behind his ear. Yasher approached him with his best charming smile.

"Hail," he said, tipping an imaginary hat. "Might you be heading to the mainland?"

The man barely glanced up, his attention fixed on his ledger.

"Three crowns to Rumatin," he said briskly, striking through an entry.

Yasher's grin faltered slightly. Three crowns? Blatant robbery. But he shrugged it off, pulling the coins from his pocket and handing them over. "You drive a hard bargain, my friend."

The man grunted, gesturing toward the barge with a jerk of his thumb. "The hold's off-limits. Stay out of my sailors' way, and no sick on my deck."

"Wouldn't dream of it," Yasher replied, slipping past him and finding a quiet spot near the bow of the barge.

He dropped his rucksack, using it as a makeshift pillow, and leaned back against the railing. The low murmur of the crew's voices, the creak of ropes, and the rhythmic thud of boots on wood lulled him into a state of near-relaxation.

As the crew prepared to cast off, a disturbance on the dock drew Yasher's attention. Voices, sharp and urgent, rose above the morning hum. His eyes snapped open, and his heart skipped a beat as he caught sight of a familiar figure striding toward the barge, her presence unmistakable even in the half-light.

Farah.

Her voice carried, clear and commanding.

"The Mashyana is grateful."

Every fiber of his being screamed at him to move, to hide, to escape. But instead, he remained frozen, heart pounding as her shadow loomed over him.

"Twelve holy hells," he whispered again, and this time, he meant it.

CHAPTER 9

FARAH STARED down at the gharib leaning lazily against the bow wall, his legs crisscrossed to stay out of the way of the sailors as they prepared the barge for its journey. Her fingers twitched toward the hilt of her dagger, her anger rising like a tide.

"You," she growled, her voice low and sharp, vibrating with the storm of emotions she had tried and failed to suppress.

Her hand slid to her blade, the cool metal grounding her fury for just a moment. Two sailors froze mid-task, glancing nervously between her and Yasher. One of them slipped away, vanishing to get help, sensing trouble on the horizon.

"Now, now, Phoenix," Yasher said, scrambling to his feet. His grin was infuriatingly intact, even as he raised one hand in mock surrender, the other gripping the strap of his rucksack. "Let's not be hasty."

"Hasty?" Her voice edged higher, incredulity slicing through her rage. She pulled her dagger halfway from its sheath, her Talent humming faintly in her blood. "You arrogant—"

"No trouble on my barge, Hand." The captain's voice cut through her fury like a whip. The solid clap of his ledger echoed in the tense silence as he strode toward them, his weathered face impassive.

Farah turned, caught between fury and embarrassment. "The Mashyana—" she began, her words clipped.

"The Mashya and Mashyana rule the land," the captain interrupted, his tone firm but even. "I rule this barge. Do we have a problem, then?"

He stood between them now, his broad frame a wall of authority. The sailors stilled, waiting. Yasher remained where he was, hands raised in a performative gesture of peace. The decision was hers. Farah's teeth clenched against the tide of her emotions.

"Fine," she spat, her voice low and dangerous. She drew in a deep breath, the exhalation doing little to cool her temper. Her gaze pinned Yasher where he stood, though he was still grinning, damn him. "We will finish this conversation on the mainland, gharib."

She turned sharply, stomping to the opposite side of the barge. The sailors, who had been watching with open curiosity, resumed their work with a studied effort to avoid her path. Her boots clanged against the wooden deck as she reached the rail, gripping it tightly to anchor herself against the roiling storm inside her.

The final call and response echoed from the dock as the barge lurched forward, the sails catching the early morning breeze as they pushed off from the dock. Farah forced herself to focus on the rhythm of her breathing, matching it to the sway of the waves. She leaned into the railing, the briny air cooling the heat in her cheeks.

Control, Farah. Focus. Rostam's voice that she carried with her said.

But she couldn't stop the hum of the relic, faint yet persistent, brushing against the edge of her consciousness. Now that she knew its signature, she could feel it even without Yasher waving it around like a trinket. It called to her, teasing, taunting. Her fingers tightened on the rail as she tried to block it out, her mind instead turning to the sun's warm rays at her back and the horizon that stretched endlessly ahead.

She could still feel his eyes on her. Even with her back turned, she knew Yasher wasn't asleep. He was watching, waiting, and that maddening smirk was likely plastered across his face. She turned her head slightly, just enough to catch him out of the corner of her eye.

He grinned, a slow, deliberate expression that sent her rage roaring back to life. The arrogance. The audacity. The absolute nerve of that man.

Her fingers curled around the hilt of her dagger, but before she could take a step, a sailor glanced up, his eyes wide with alarm. She exhaled sharply, forcing herself to release her grip. Yasher chuckled before shrugging and closing his eyes again, his hands folding neatly over his stomach.

That little shit.

She turned back to the railing, her knuckles whitening as she gripped the wood. The relic's hum grew louder, an incessant reminder of her failure, of the deception she'd let slip past the Mashyana. That Yasher, with his infuriating charm, had bested her. She refused to let him see her seethe, refused to let him win again.

The low, steady hum of her Talent buzzed and she released a low hum as she began to work her frustration into something useful. She focused on the simple ring on her finger, willing it to shift. Slowly, the smooth metal twisted and curled, forming into a serpent chasing its own tail. The motion was soothing, repetitive, and as the barge cut through the water, an idea began to take shape in her mind.

Farah smiled faintly to herself, her grip on the railing loosening. *Let him think he's won. Let him think he's safe.*

She glanced back at him, his still form a picture of smug satisfaction as he settled in, closing his eyes without a care for the world. Her smile grew sharper, colder.

We'll see who's laughing when this is over, gharib.

Farah's mind churned with schemes as the barge glided over the Kamyar Strait. The waves slapped against the hull in a steady rhythm, but it did little to calm her racing anger. She leaned against the railing, letting the wind cool the heat still radiating from her skin, though the sight of Yasher lounging like a lazy cat on the opposite side of the barge kept her simmering.

She glanced over her shoulder again, her eyes narrowing. Yasher's effort in feigning his relaxation was obvious—his grin was a little too fixed, his posture too still. He was waiting, watching, likely planning his next move. The thought twisted in her chest, a mix of anger and a begrudging admiration for his confidence.

Turning back to the water, she forced herself to breathe deeply, letting the salty air fill her lungs. She needed to keep her focus on what mattered. The Mashyana's task loomed ahead, and her failure to retrieve the relic in its entirety weighed heavily on her. The idea of the queen discovering her deception with this first relic gnawed at her insides.

The fake will hold for now, she told herself, gripping the railing tightly. *But for how long? And what happens when she realizes what I've done?*

A sharp gust of wind whipped her curls into her face, and she brushed them back impatiently. The relic. That damned relic. Its presence was unrelenting, like a faint itch she couldn't quite scratch. Yasher carried it casually, as if it were a bauble, oblivious—or indifferent—to its true power.

Her hand drifted to the snake-ring on her finger, its endless loop a comfort in the chaos of her thoughts. She twisted it absently, the metal warm beneath her touch. She could take it from him, here and now. It wouldn't take much—a distraction, a slight of hand, and it would be hers. But the sailors, and the captain's sharp eye, were obstacles she couldn't ignore.

And then there was the promise she'd made to Pari. The little girl's words echoed in her mind.

The gods need both of you.

Farah sighed, her fingers stilling on the ring. Pari's faith in Yasher felt misplaced, but the girl's conviction had been unshakable. The weight of it pressed against Farah's own doubts, enough to stay her hand—at least for now.

A low chuckle broke through her thoughts, and she turned sharply. Yasher was watching her again, his blue eyes glinting in the morning light. He didn't say a word, just tilted his head slightly, as if daring her to speak.

She scowled, giving in. "What are you grinning at?"

He stretched lazily, his grin widening. "You, Phoenix. You're rather mesmerizing when you're plotting my untimely demise."

"Keep talking, and you'll find out just how untimely it can be," she snapped, her hand brushing her dagger. The sailors nearby exchanged nervous glances but wisely kept their distance.

Yasher laughed, the sound low and warm, grating against her nerves. "I do appreciate your creativity. But perhaps we could call a truce for the duration of this journey? I'd rather not end up overboard, and you don't seem the type to swim."

Her jaw tightened, but she forced herself to take a calming breath.

"A truce?" she repeated, her tone dripping with skepticism. "You expect me to trust you?"

"I'd settle for tolerance," he said, his tone infuriatingly light. "At least until we're off this boat. After that, I assume you'll resume your plans to stab me in some dramatic fashion."

"Assume correctly," she said, turning back to the railing. The waves churned below, mirroring the tumult within her. She didn't trust him, not for a second, but for now, the captain's rules—and her own reluctance to cause a scene— would have to suffice as a truce.

"Farah," Yasher said softly, and she stiffened at the sound of her name on his lips. When she turned, his grin was gone, replaced by something quieter, more serious. "I know I've given you little reason to believe me, but I'm not your enemy."

Her lips parted in surprise, but she quickly masked it with a scowl. "You stole from me."

"It was mine first," he corrected, his voice calm.

Their gazes locked, the tension between them crackling like the air before a storm.

Yasher broke the silence first, a small grin teasing. "For what it's worth, Phoenix, I don't envy your position. But this relic is mine."

"For the moment," she said coldly.

He nodded, stepping back to lean against the bow wall again. "Duly noted."

Farah turned away, her chest tight with emotions she couldn't name. The relic hummed faintly in her senses, a reminder of the tangled web she now found herself in. She stared out at the horizon, the mainland just beginning to take shape in the distance.

Focus on the task ahead. The relics. The Mashyana. The task. Nothing else matters.

THE BARGE DOCKED without ceremony hours later, its creaking timbers blending into the noise of Rumatin's bustling port. Farah stood motionless for a moment, her travel bag slung over one shoulder as the crew disembarked and dockworkers began the chaotic ballet of unloading cargo. The salt-scented air was heavy with shouted orders and the rhythmic groan of pulleys.

Her gaze snapped to Yasher, who hopped off the barge with a grace that belied the burden of his rucksack. He spared her a fleeting glance before melting into the crowd, his movements deliberate yet casual, as if she wouldn't notice him weaving toward the largest throng of people.

Farah clenched her jaw. He thinks he can lose me here? He's underestimated me once too often.

Sliding her hood over her curls, she stepped lightly onto the dock and joined the flow of bodies spilling into the port city. Rumatin's streets were a sharp contrast to the ordered layout of the Citadel. Here, alleys twisted and turned without rhyme or reason, splitting into narrow lanes and dead ends, as if the city had grown organically around the whims of its residents. The low mud-brick and timber buildings leaned into one another, their wooden balconies sagging under the weight of laundry strung between them.

Farah moved with purpose, her senses attuned to the tug of the relic and the faint glint of Yasher's brown hair, lighter than most among the crowd. Even without the pull of the relic, he stood out. A foreigner in both bearing and manner, like a peacock among sparrows. She allowed herself a small, satisfied smile. *He doesn't realize how obvious he is.*

As he made his way toward the heart of the city, Farah followed at a steady pace, careful to remain unnoticed. Her anger tempered by a cold determination. The relic was her priority. Yasher was just an obstacle—or a means to an end, depending on her strategy.

When he slipped into a covered alley leading to the market square, she quickened her pace, weaving through the throng until she was close enough to see him pause at a stall. His eyes scanned the crowd, his jaw tight, betraying his awareness of being followed. Farah pressed forward, closing the distance until she was within arm's reach. She let her shoulder collide with his, using the momentum to shove him into a shadowed alcove off the main thoroughfare.

Yasher stumbled, his hand darting toward the hilt of his punch dagger. Before he could draw, Farah hummed under her breath, slipping a bracelet from her wrist and clasping it around his. The metal tightened instantly, the subtle heat of her Talent ensuring he felt her control. His weapon clattered to the ground, and he winced as the bracelet constricted further.

"That's enough, *gharib*," she hissed, her voice low and dangerous. With another hum, she transformed a second bracelet into a delicate but unbreakable chain, linking herself to him.

Yasher raised his hands in mock surrender.

"May I at least pick that up?" He gestured to his fallen dagger.

Farah scoffed and stooped to retrieve it herself, slipping it into her belt. "I know you've got at least two more hidden. Give them to me."

"I don't—" he began, but her glare silenced him.

"Now," she said, the threat in her tone enough to make him sigh dramatically.

With exaggerated slowness, Yasher handed over a second dagger from his belt. When Farah's gaze dropped to his boots, he rolled his eyes before crouching to remove yet another blade from the side of his calf.

"Satisfied?" he asked, his voice dripping with sarcasm.

Farah's lip curled in disdain as she pocketed the weapons. "Do you think this is a game?"

"I'm beginning to suspect you don't share my sense of humor," he replied, flashing her a sheepish grin.

"Walk," she snapped, tugging the chain and pulling him toward the city center.

Yasher stumbled slightly but fell in step beside her, uncharacteristically silent. She didn't loosen her grip on the chain, heating it just enough to remind him of the consequences of resistance. Her anger burned as fiercely as the heat in the metal. She was furious with him, furious with herself, and furious with the Gods that seemed determined to entangle her fate with his.

As they neared the Commons House, the imposing sandstone building loomed over the chaotic sprawl of Rumatin like a sentinel. Unlike the rest of the city, its design was deliberate, its clean lines and three-story height a testament to its importance as an arm of the Citadel in this town. But something was wrong.

The usual hum of activity around the building was absent, replaced by a tension that pricked at Farah's senses. Guards stood at stiff attention, their gazes darting nervously toward anyone who coughed or moved too slowly.

Yasher stopped abruptly, his eyes narrowing as he took in the scene.

"I'm beginning to think this isn't a friendly visit," he said.

Farah tightened her grip and yanked the chain, forcing him forward. "Keep moving."

At the entrance, a guard stepped forward, his stance stiff, one hand resting lightly on the hilt of his sword.

"No entry," he barked, his voice clipped and firm.

Farah drew herself up, pulling her medallion from beneath her coat and holding it aloft.

"I am the Hand of the Mashyana," she declared in Emari. "I demand entry. Bring me the Commander."

The guard's eyes flicked to the medallion, then to her face. His hesitation was telling. "The Commander is indisposed."

Farah's brows furrowed. "What do you mean, indisposed? He was hale and present at court not two days ago."

The guard's mouth tightened, his gaze darting to the doorway behind him.

"He has taken ill," he said softly, lowering his voice.

Before the guard could respond, the door creaked open, and an official stepped out. He was a small man with a thin, sharp face, his scarf pulled up over his mouth and nose. He paused a moment, lowering it slightly when he saw Farah.

"Hand," he greeted her, bowing his head briefly. "Congratulations on your elevation." His tone was polite but subdued, and he glanced nervously at the chain connecting her to Yasher. "What brings you to Rumatin?"

Farah inclined her head, her voice steady. "I require the assistance of the Commander. This man is to be placed in confinement under orders from the Mashyana."

The official's expression darkened. "I am sorry, but that will not be possible."

Farah's eyes narrowed. "Explain."

The official exchanged a glance with the guard before stepping closer to Farah. "The Commander is gravely ill, Hand. We suspect... the wasting sickness."

Farah's stomach turned.

"That is impossible," she said, though her voice lacked conviction.

"It is fast, Hand." The official nodded grimly. "He fell ill upon his return from the Citadel. We have taken every precaution, but..." He trailed off, his eyes darting back toward the partially open door.

A low, ragged cough sounded from within, harsh and phlegmy. Farah's heart sank.

The official pulled the door closed behind him, his movements deliberate.

"We are doing all we can to keep it contained," he said quietly. "I hope you understand why we cannot house your prisoner."

Farah's throat tightened. The words felt heavy as she forced them out. "And the Commander?"

The official shook his head. "We can only make him comfortable. The rest lies in the hands of the Unnamed Gods."

A prayer rose unbidden to Farah's lips. "May the Unnamed Gods guide his soul to the Bridge."

The official echoed her sentiment, lowering his head in respect. For a moment, there was only the sound of the fountain and the distant hum of the port.

Behind her, Yasher coughed softly, a sound that jolted Farah back to the present. She turned to him sharply, the weight of the relic, the sickness, and his continued insolence bearing down on her all at once.

"Come," she snapped, yanking the chain and pulling him away from the Commons House.

"Where are we going now?" Yasher asked, his voice tinged with unease.

She didn't answer immediately, her mind racing. The wasting sickness here in Rumatin was more than a tragedy —it was a disaster waiting to happen, even if it explained how the disease had made it to the Citadel.

They reached a narrow alleyway, she stopped abruptly, spinning to face him.

"Give me the relic, and you can go on your way."

Yasher hesitated, reaching into his pocket only to come up empty.

"It's... not here," he said, confusion flashing across his face.

Her frustration erupted like a storm breaking over a dry plain.

"Not here? Don't lie to me, Yasher." Her voice was a low growl, her hand tightening on the chain that bound them.

She shoved him against the rough wall of the alley, her other hand already reaching for the pocket where the relic should have been.

"I'm not lying!" he snapped, raising his hands defensively as she rummaged through his coat. "I don't understand—"

"Of course you don't," she hissed, cutting him off. The

relic's pull was undeniable, thrumming like a heartbeat, but her fingers brushed against nothing but fabric. It was there—she could feel it—but somehow just out of reach. She shoved him again, her anger boiling over. "You're playing games, gharib. I will not be made a fool of."

"I swear, Phoenix, it's not me!" Yasher's voice cracked, a rare hint of genuine alarm breaking through his usual charm. He patted his own pocket frantically, his brow furrowing as his hand met the same resistance. "I can feel it, but—why can't I grab it?"

Farah froze, her fingers still hovering near his coat. The buzzing in her blood from the relic felt wrong, unstable. How could it be present and yet untouchable? Before she could voice her thoughts, a soft, familiar voice echoed from behind them.

"It is his until Rashnu deems it not."

Farah spun around, her heart lurching as Pari stepped out from the shadows of the alley. The little girl looked completely at ease, as though appearing unbidden in the middle of Rumatin's chaos was the most natural thing in the world.

"Pari?" Farah's voice came out sharper than intended, laced with disbelief. Her mind scrambled to make sense of the sight before her.

How had Pari gotten here? They'd left her safely at the Saffron Oasis in Shirin's care. Hadn't they?

Yasher blinked, his mouth hanging open slightly. "Little Divine, how... How did you—?"

Pari smiled serenely, her small hands clasped in front of her. "Rashnu guided me."

Farah stared at the child, her anger momentarily overtaken by bewilderment. "You were in the Citadel yesterday. This—this isn't possible."

"Nothing is impossible for the gods," Pari said, her tone so calm it bordered on maddening.

Farah's hand fell from Yasher's coat as she turned fully to Pari, her body rigid with a mix of tension and confusion.

"This isn't the time for riddles, Pari. Explain. How are you here?"

The little girl stepped closer, her gaze unwavering. "I was needed here, with you."

Farah's disbelief warred with her anger. This wasn't the first time Pari had seemed to defy explanation, but here, in the sprawling, chaotic streets of Rumatin? It felt different. More intrusive. The little girl's presence chipped away at Farah's carefully constructed control, leaving her exposed to a torrent of emotions she didn't want to face.

Yasher, for once, seemed equally disoriented.

"Right. Needed. That explains everything," he muttered, running a hand through his hair. His usual sarcasm lacked its bite, overshadowed by his clear discomfort.

Pari ignored him, turning her attention to Farah.

"The relic belongs to him for now," she said firmly. "Rashnu requires it."

Farah's temper flared again, her hands balling into fists.

"I don't care what Rashnu requires," she snapped. "That relic is the only thing keeping me alive right now. The Mashyana holds a forgery. If she finds out, I'll be executed."

"You will not be executed," Pari said, her voice soft but resolute. "You are needed. The relic stays with him because it balances the scales. Rashnu has spoken."

"Enough of this!" Farah turned away, wanting to pace the narrow alley but she was still attached to the gharib. The pull of the relic taunted her with its nearness, yet it was out of reach. Protected, apparently, by divine decree. She couldn't reconcile the practicality of her situation with the mysticism Pari seemed to embody.

Yasher leaned back against the wall, watching the exchange with a mixture of fascination and exasperation.

"So what you're saying," he began, addressing Pari, "is that my lucky charm isn't just lucky?"

Pari smiled at him. "It brings you balance."

"Well, I'll take that over curses, I suppose," he quipped, though his expression betrayed unease.

Farah whirled on him, pointing a finger at his chest. "You are not helping."

Yasher raised his hands, a half-smile tugging at his lips. "I wasn't trying to."

Pari stepped between them, her small hand resting on the chain that linked them.

"You need each other," she said simply. "The scales have tipped. Balance can only be restored if you walk together."

Farah opened her mouth to argue, but no words came. There was something in the child's presence, something steady and unyielding that made resistance feel futile. She turned away, pressing a hand to her temple as she tried to gather her thoughts.

"This is madness," she muttered.

"It's destiny," Pari corrected.

Farah shot a glare over her shoulder but said nothing. Her gaze shifted to Yasher, who had the audacity to look smug despite the absurdity of their situation. She groaned, rubbing her temples.

"Fine," she said at last, her voice tight with anger as she destroyed the chain connecting the two, recreating it into one of her bracelets. "But your bracelet stays. If you even think about running—"

"I know, I know." Yasher rubbed his wrist pointedly. "I like my hands where they are."

Pari beamed up at them, as though the matter had been settled entirely to her satisfaction.

"This is a good choice," she said, slipping past them and out of the alley, her hum light and carefree.

Farah followed her reluctantly, pulling on the bracelet with her Talent to ensure Yasher kept up. This is a disaster. A complete, maddening disaster.

CHAPTER 10

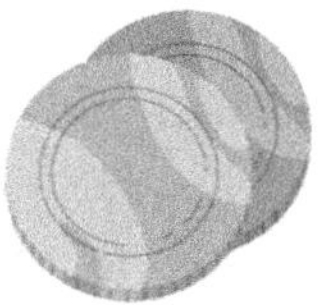

WHAT TO DO. **What to do.**

Yasher's thoughts churned as he trudged behind the two people who had inexplicably taken charge of his fate. The muddy streets of Rumatin sprawled out before him, slick with the remnants of last night's storm. His boots squelched in the muck, the sound muffled by the constant hum of activity that filled the port town.

Pari, led the way, her small frame radiating purpose as she darted ahead, avoiding puddles with uncanny precision. Farah followed close behind her, her steps measured and deliberate, as though the mud dared not cling to her boots.

Yasher frowned, his gaze flicking between the two. This morning, he had been certain he'd slipped away from Farah for good. He'd felt a spark of victory as he boarded the barge, the blue sails promising freedom from the chaos she embodied. But here he was, shackled—metaphorically and literally—to a mission he neither understood nor wanted any part of.

He tried again, slipping his hand into the interior

pocket of his coat. His lucky charm should have been there, nestled snugly against the fabric. But every time he reached for it, the charm seemed to evade his grasp, like trying to catch smoke in his palm. A soft hum in the air made him glance sideways at Farah. He didn't trust her not to notice and smirk.

He fell behind, his frustration bubbling over, until a sharp heat encircled his left wrist. The metallic band Farah had forged tightened like a living thing, biting into his skin until he yelped and jogged back up beside her.

"You were joking about taking my hand earlier, right?" he asked, forcing a grin to cover the unease gnawing at him.

"I don't joke," she said coolly, not bothering to look at him.

The heat dissipated, but the bracelet remained snug against his wrist, a constant reminder of his precarious position. Yasher gently slid a finger underneath the metal, wincing as his wrist throbbed.

"That'll leave a bruise," he muttered, keeping his tone light. If Farah cared, she didn't show it.

Rumatin unfolded around them, a labyrinth of low, squat buildings that seemed to lean into each other for support. The walls were streaked with mud and salt, their surfaces worn smooth by years of wind and rain.

The air smelled of the sea, but not in the bracing way Yasher had experienced in other ports. Here, it was thick and cloying, mingled with the faint, unpleasant tang of marshland decay.

He couldn't help but compare it to the Citadel. The capital had a sharpness to its design, its sandstone buildings standing tall and proud, a testament to Emari's might. Rumatin, by contrast, felt like it had grown haphazardly, sprouting wherever people found space. The streets twisted unpredictably, some ending abruptly at walls that seemed to have materialized overnight.

The odd smell brought back memories of his first visit to Rumatin, back when his journey had been a carefree one. He'd been so eager to see the fabled Citadel, to stand beneath its towering gates and marvel at the city that was the beating heart of Emari. Now, he couldn't help but curse himself for that decision. What had started as an adventure had turned into a quagmire, one he wasn't sure he could escape from.

They reached the far side of town, where the merchant caravans had set up camp. The scene was one of organized chaos. Large tents of faded fabric flapped in the breeze, their colors dulled by years of travel. Oxen and pack mules shuffled restlessly, their breath steaming in the cool morning air. Merchants shouted orders, their voices rising above the clatter of crates being loaded onto carts.

Pari stopped abruptly, her small hand rising to point toward a group of travelers near the town gates. Farah followed the motion and nodded once, her sharp gaze locking onto the most ostentatiously dressed member of the group. Without a word to Yasher, she marched off, leaving him and Pari standing awkwardly in the middle of the bustling camp.

"Well, Little Divine," Yasher said, bending slightly to take Pari's hand and guide her out of the way of a passing cart. "Thank you for convincing her to leave me with my lucky charm. That was very thoughtful of you."

"She would give it to the queen," Pari said matter-of-factly, her gaze fixed somewhere far beyond the camp. "Or not give it to her at all. But you'd be dead either way, and that would make me sad."

Yasher blinked, caught off guard by her bluntness.

"G-Good?" he stammered, unsure how to respond. Shaking his head, he turned his attention back to Farah who was locked in what appeared to be a heated negotiation. The man gestured animatedly, his hands slicing through the air as he made his point. Farah countered with sharp, deliberate movements, her voice too low for Yasher to hear.

He couldn't help but stare. Farah was a puzzle, one he wasn't sure he wanted to solve. She moved through the world with the confidence of someone who knew exactly what they wanted and how to get it. Yet there was a fire in her, one that could scorch anyone who got too close, as if she wanted to protect herself from the world. Yasher wasn't sure whether he was drawn to it or terrified of being burned.

"Well," he muttered, "if the gods I was raised with are correct, you only live once. May as well spend it teetering on the edge of a cliff."

Pari looked up at him, her expression unreadable.

"You and Farah will be important to each other," she said softly. "You will understand when it matters."

Yasher frowned. "What do you mean by that, Little Divine?"

Pari didn't answer, her gaze shifting back to Farah. His eyes followed her line of sight just in time to see the caravan leader throw up his hands in surrender. Farah reached into her coat, pulling out a coin purse and depositing a sizable amount into the man's outstretched palm.

She stalked back toward them, her rucksack slung over one shoulder. Yasher hastily leaned against a fencepost, doing his best to look casual and unconcerned.

"We have transportation and board to Banima with this caravan," she said, her tone clipped. "Come along."

Farah turned and strode off without looking back to see if he followed, her boots kicking up small puffs of dust. Yasher sighed, grabbing his own bag and taking Pari's hand.

"Where is Banima?" he called after her, though he doubted she'd answer.

The caravan's carts were varied in design, some covered with well-maintained canopies, others little more than wooden frames stacked high with goods.

Farah led them to one of the simpler carts near the back of the line. Its sides were made of weathered slats, and four reedy poles held up a patched sail that provided a modicum of shade from the scorching rays of the too-hot sun. A few crates and barrels were already loaded into the cart, their surfaces scuffed from years of use.

Farah climbed in and began rearranging the cargo, her movements efficient. Yasher followed, lifting Pari up and settling her onto a folded piece of sailcloth.

"Here, Little Divine," he said, grabbing another scrap of fabric and folding it into a makeshift cushion. "The road will be bumpy."

Pari smiled up at him, her eyes bright. "Thank you."

After she was satisfied with her organization, Farah jumped down, her gaze scanning the bustling camp.

"Stay here," she ordered before disappearing into the crowd.

Yasher sighed and leaned against the side of the cart, watching as the younger caravan workers led the oxen into place. The animals snorted and huffed, their massive frames shifting as they were strapped into their harnesses.

Yasher turned his attention to the horizon. Beyond the

edges of the town, the land stretched out in endless waves of golden grass, the breeze rippling through it like the surface of a lake. Farther out, small clusters of trees broke up the monotony, their green canopies stark against the pale sky. The sight was both calming and disquieting—a reminder of just how far he was from anything familiar.

Farah returned, tossing a pair of large water skins and a few bags into the cart. She vaulted over the slats with ease, her rucksack hitting the floor with a dull thud.

"We'll be moving soon," she said, sliding into a seated position against one of the crates. "I'd recommend sitting before you fall out, gharib."

As if on cue, the oxen huffed and the cart jolted forward, nearly knocking Yasher into a barrel. He recovered quickly and settled next to Pari, ignoring the smirk on Farah's face. He adjusted his rucksack, using it as a makeshift cushion, and wrapped an arm around Pari as she curled up beside him.

The cart creaked and swayed as it joined the caravan's slow march out of the camp. Yasher leaned his head back, letting the steady rhythm of the wheels on the dirt road lull him into a semblance of calm. He wasn't sure where this path would lead, but for now, he had no choice but to follow it.

YASHER LEANED against the side of the cart, one arm resting on his knee while Pari sat cross-legged beside him. Farah sat across from them, her back resting against a crate, her gaze fixed somewhere beyond the horizon, anger still radiating from her. She looked like she wanted to ignore the world, and he wasn't about to disturb her. Not when he had more immediate questions on his mind.

He glanced down at Pari, who was fiddling with the edge of her tunic, humming softly to herself as if the dusty road, the strangers surrounding them, and their strange predicament were all perfectly normal. Yasher tilted his head, studying the little girl. Her calm demeanor unnerved him. She acted far too composed for a child her age. The way she had spoken earlier, the certainty in her tone—it lingered like an itch in the back of his mind.

"How did you even get to Rumatin, Little Divine?" he asked, keeping his voice light but firm enough to demand an answer. "You were with us on the Citadel, and then suddenly you show up here, in the middle of all this madness."

Pari looked up at him, her dark eyes calm, as if the question was of no consequence. "I was meant to find you."

Yasher sighed, rubbing his forehead as if it would stop his irritation from seeping into his voice.

"That's not really what I asked, is it? You were with us on the Citadel, on an island. I'd love to know how you managed to cross the strait on your own, let alone figure out where to find us in this mess of a town."

Pari tilted her head, her expression serene, though there was a glimmer of something deeper in her gaze. "Rashnu guided me. It was his will that I be here."

Yasher blinked, caught off guard by the matter-of-fact way she said it. Her words carried a weight that didn't match her small stature.

"Rashnu, huh? The big death bird with all the answers, is that it?" He leaned closer, lowering his voice conspiratorially. "Does he tell you everything, or just the bits that leave people like me scratching their heads?"

Pari giggled softly, her hand rising to cover her mouth, as though she were sharing a secret only she could understand. "Rashnu doesn't tell everything. He shows me pieces. Paths. Choices."

Yasher's brow furrowed, his curiosity piqued despite himself.

"Choices? Like what kind of choices?"

Pari paused, her small fingers tracing invisible patterns on the wooden plank beneath her.

"Everything is a choice. You choose where you go, who you trust, what you believe." She looked up at him, her gaze steady. "Rashnu shows the paths, but they are always changing. What you do shapes the outcome."

"That's a lot for a kid to carry, isn't it? Seeing paths, making choices. It sounds exhausting." Yasher leaned back, letting out a low whistle.

Pari smiled faintly, tilting her head to the side. "It's not exhausting. It's... like breathing. It's just there."

"Okay," He ran a hand through his hair, feeling a mix of frustration and fascination. "Let's go back to the beginning. Did Rashnu put you on a boat? Did he whisper in someone's ear to give you a lift? I need something a little more solid than 'it's his will.'"

Pari didn't answer immediately. Instead, she looked down at her lap, her hands resting lightly against her knees. "The how doesn't matter. What matters is that I'm here."

"Oh, it absolutely matters," Yasher raised an eyebrow. "To me, at least. Because as far as I'm concerned, you've done something impossible, and impossible things tend to come with a price."

Pari's gaze snapped up, and for the first time, there was a flicker of intensity in her expression. "Rashnu ensures that the price is fair."

He blinked, startled by the sudden shift in her tone.

"Fair? That's comforting, I guess." He studied her, the gears in his mind turning. "But fair for whom? For you? For me? For Farah? Or are we just pawns in some celestial game?"

She shook her head, her expression softening again. "You're not pawns. You're people. Your choices matter. They shape the world."

"That's a lovely sentiment," he said dryly, leaning back against the cart. "But you didn't really answer my question."

She shrugged, a small, almost playful smile tugging at the corners of her lips. "I answered the question you needed, not the one you asked."

"You sound like one of those traveling mystics, you know that?" he groaned, rubbing his temples. "Always speaking in riddles, leaving people more confused than enlightened."

"Maybe confusion is part of the path," Pari said lightly, her gaze shifting to the horizon. "Sometimes, you have to walk forward without knowing where you'll end up."

Yasher let out a short laugh, shaking his head.

"You're something else, Little Divine."

She beamed at the nickname, clearly pleased. "And you, Yasher, are important."

"Important? To who?" he asked, raising an eyebrow.

"To the world," she said simply. "To Farah. To yourself."

Yasher glanced over at Farah, who was still seated against the crate, her eyes closed as if she were tuning out the entire conversation.

He frowned, turning his attention back to Pari.

"What do you mean, 'to Farah'? She doesn't seem particularly thrilled about having me around."

"She doesn't see everything yet," Pari said softly. "But she will."

"And what about me?" Yasher pressed. "What am I supposed to see?"

Pari's smile widened, and she reached out to pat his hand. "You'll see. All will be clear when it is needed."

He stared at her, half-exasperated, half-amused. "You really don't make this easy, do you?"

Pari giggled again, her laughter light and carefree. "It's not supposed to be easy. It's supposed to be right."

He let out a sigh, leaning his head back against the cart's side. "Right. Whatever that means."

The cart hit a bump, jolting them slightly, and Yasher instinctively tightened his arm around Pari to keep her steady. She settled back against him, her humming resuming as though their conversation had never happened. Yasher glanced at Farah one last time, her face impassive, and let his thoughts wander.

This child, this woman, this whole situation was impossible. But somewhere in the back of his mind, a small, unwelcome voice whispered that maybe, just maybe, Pari was onto something.

***

The jolt of the cart stopping woke Yasher before Farah's boot connected with his thigh.

"We're stopping," she said brusquely, already unloading her rucksack without sparing him a glance. "We need to set up our tent."

He groaned and rubbed his leg, blinking against the

bright sunlight filtering through the sparse cover of the trees. His back ached from the uneven floor of the cart, and his limbs felt heavy with stiffness.

"Our tent?" he muttered, hauling himself to his feet. A sharp wave of pins and needles shot up his leg, and he grimaced, hopping down from the cart.

Pari stood, balancing on the edge of the cart like a tightrope walker.

"Come along, Little Divine," he said, opening his arms to her. She giggled as he wrapped his hands around her waist and lowered her gently to the ground.

He straightened and looked around. The caravan had stopped in a small clearing near the road.

A cluster of trees provided a modest patch of shade, their leaves rustling softly in the dry breeze. Beyond that, the landscape stretched out in vast plains, dotted with scraggly bushes and tufts of grass. On one side, Yasher glimpsed the glint of water through the trees—an oasis, maybe. The air carried a faint tang of moisture, a brief respite from the dryness that clung to his throat and skin.

The other travelers bustled around, unloading crates and bundles from their carts and moving toward the larger stand of trees. Some shade pavilions were already going up, their colorful fabrics a striking contrast to the muted browns and greens of the landscape. A few people had begun gathering wood, preparing to start cooking fires.

Pari tugged on his hand, and Yasher allowed her to lead him toward Farah. She was already hammering stakes into the ground at the edge of the clearing, her movements precise and efficient, of course.

The tent was weathered and patched in places, and sat in a heap nearby, ready to be raised. She worked with single-minded focus, ignoring the activity around her.

Yasher dropped the water skins and his rucksack beside the tent, releasing Pari's hand to help Farah.

"So," he said lightly, trying to coax a response from her, "where are we?"

"Oasis," she replied curtly, her attention on the stakes.

Helpful as ever. Yasher sighed and crouched to assist, holding one of the poles steady while she tied it in place.

The silence between them stretched uncomfortably, punctuated only by the distant hum of conversation and the occasional snort of oxen. He tried a few more times to engage her, tossing out questions and remarks that earned nothing more than a grunt or a withering look.

By the fifth attempt, he gave up. Instead, he focused on the task, watching the way her mahogany eyes flicked to him when he slipped up or moved too slowly. It was almost worth it, just to see her react, even if it meant enduring another glare.

When the tent was finally up, Yasher stepped back, brushing his hands against his trousers. Farah left without a word, gathering Pari and heading toward the stand of trees, presumably to collect kindling. Yasher lingered by the tent, fussing with the stakes to make himself look busy.

The crunch of footsteps on dry grass made him turn. An older woman approached, carrying a basket in her arms, her dark hair streaked with gray strands peeking out from under her headscarf. Her clothes, though worn from the road, didn't diminish the way she carried herself, straight-backed, with quiet confidence. Her dark eyes were sharp, alert, as though she took in everything around her without effort.

Silver chains and bangles, each set with colorful stones, caught the light, marking her as someone of status within the caravan. Still, the smile she gave Yasher was steady, calm. One that conveyed quiet authority without needing to say a word.

"Hail, gharib," she greeted him, her voice smooth. Thank the gods she spoke Common.

"Hail, Khānum," he replied, slipping effortlessly into charm mode despite his road-worn appearance. He inclined his head in a polite bow and was thankful to have picked up enough Emari to remember the word for lady.

"I've brought you some things to supplement your hasty departure from Rumatin," she said, pulling back the edges of the blankets that topped the basket. Inside were neatly packed bundles of travel-ready food, small personal items, and other essentials. "The plains, like the Unnamed Gods, are not always kind to the unprepared."

"Many thanks, Khānum," Yasher said, dipping into another bow. The woman chuckled softly, shaking her head.

"No need to bow to me, gharib. You may call me Pouri." Her smile widened slightly. "My husband is the one who bartered with your companion to join our caravan."

"Ah," Yasher said, straightening. "Farah isn't—" He paused, realizing he didn't have the right words to explain their current arrangement. She studied him for a moment as he stood in silence, her gaze steady and unyielding. He shifted under her scrutiny, rubbing the back of his neck.

"Well," he said finally, attempting to fill the silence, "thank you for the supplies. They're greatly appreciated."

"You are welcome," Pouri replied. "We invite you to join our evening service and meal. It will be good for your group to share in our company."

Before he could respond, Pouri's gaze shifted over his shoulder.

"Your companions return. I shall leave you to it." She nodded once and walked away, her steps unhurried.

He turned to see Pari skipping toward him, a bundle of twigs cradled in her arms. Farah followed close behind, her hands full of larger sticks and branches.

"What do you have there? Cakes?" Pari asked, her eyes lighting up as she eyed the basket.

He laughed, setting the basket on the ground and taking the kindling from her.

"While I'd love some of Shirin's cakes right now, Little Divine, this is just travel fare. And blankets," he added, pulling one out and shaking it slightly. "To keep us cozy when the sun sets."

Pari beamed, clapping her hands together. "Perfect!"

Farah dropped her bundle of wood next to the tent, dusting her hands off.

"How much did you pay her?" she asked, her tone sharp.

"Nothing," Yasher replied, keeping his smile in check. It was nice to hear her talk to him, even if she sounded suspicious. "She said it was a gift. She also invited us to their evening meal."

Farah grunted in response, her attention already on arranging the stones for their fire. She didn't look at him, her movements deliberate.

He tugged at the bracelet on his wrist, the cool metal a constant reminder of his predicament. The road stretched ahead, uncertain and unyielding, and Yasher couldn't shake the feeling that he was being pulled along by forces far beyond his control, and he really didn't like it.

CHAPTER 11

Farah woke to voices just outside the tent. The muted
sounds of conversation outside the tent tugged her from
sleep, taking a moment to remind her where she was. The
fog in her head cleared slowly, memories returning in fragments. The relentless heat of the day, the caravan's bustling
stop at the oasis, and her eventual retreat from the incessant visitors who flocked to meet the foreigner.

The gharib had charmed them all—one by one. Farah
grimaced, the memory of the fourth young woman giggling
over Yasher's apparent sweetness grating on her nerves.

She had taken herself to the tent for a nap rather than
endure more of the spectacle. Yet now, as she stretched and
rolled her shoulders to dispel the stiffness, she realized it
had only delayed the inevitable.

The tent flap snapped open, flooding the interior with
the warm glow of the setting sun. Yasher stepped inside,
his silhouette outlined by the light. His grin was as insufferable as ever.

"Oh good, you're up,' he said, arms laden with an
assortment of items. Water skins, blankets, and even a

brightly colored headscarf that dangled precariously over his shoulder. "Pari wanted to wake you every time we had a new visitor. I managed to hold her off, but barely."

Farah raised an eyebrow and reached out, snatching the headscarf from the pile. It was simple but beautiful, a natural linen base embroidered with vivid blue and green vines that trailed gracefully along its hem.

"All of these are gifts?" she asked, running her fingers over the delicate stitching.

"Such a lovely group of people," Yasher mumbled as he set the trove down on a crate Farah had dragged into the tent earlier. "Very generous."

"It's customary to give gifts to strangers," Farah said, wrapping the scarf around her head and shoulders. "And you, gharib, are a novelty."

Yasher turned to her, mouth half-open as if preparing to retort, but he stopped. His gaze lingered, his expression shifting as he took her in. Farah glanced down at herself, realizing she had removed her vest before her nap. Her simple tunic and pants hung tighter, though still modest, and they lacked the formal polish from the clothes she wore at the Citadel. She tugged the scarf loose, letting it pool around her shoulders.

"What?" she said, narrowing her eyes. "Does it not suit me?"

"No," he said quickly, his voice softer than usual. "It suits you well."

He took a single step toward her, and the tent flap opened again, cutting the moment short. Pari darted in, her bright energy filling the small space.

"I told the Yeganeh I'd help serve tonight," Pari announced, then paused, her eyes lighting up as she noticed the scarf. "Oh! That's the one I saw on you. This is good."

Farah sighed, the sound carrying more weariness than words. Pari's ability to shift seamlessly between an ordinary child and Rashnu's prophet never failed to unsettle her. One moment, she was chattering about cakes. The next, she was delivering cryptic proclamations about choices and fates.

Even now, Farah felt an odd weight in the girl's observation, as though wearing the scarf was a step on some unseen path. She itched to yank it off and throw it to the corner of the tent, proclaiming her path was her own, but knew that it would just upset the little girl.

The rhythmic beat of drums began outside, accompanied by voices raised in song. The sound grew louder, passing near their tent in a procession.

"We should follow them for the invocation," Farah said, turning her attention to the pile of gifts. "Is there a lantern in there?"

Yasher rummaged through the items, pulling out a small lantern. He handed it to her without a word, his hand brushing hers briefly. Pari had already darted outside, her excitement evident in the quick patter of her footsteps.

Farah adjusted the scarf over her head and stepped into the golden light of the setting sun. Yasher followed close behind, his proximity a constant reminder of the bracelet she had forged around his wrist, and the relic in his pocket that remained tantalizingly out of reach.

The sight that greeted her was breathtaking, pulling her back from wanting to try again to retrieve the relic.

The sun's rays stretched across the endless plains, turning the dry grasses into a sea of molten gold. Each blade seemed to catch the light, shimmering as if kissed by the divine. The sparse trees that dotted the landscape cast long shadows that stretched toward the horizon, their dark forms softening the brilliance of the scene.

The oasis, nestled at the edge of the caravan's encampment, shimmered like a jewel. Its still waters reflected the azure sky and streaks of orange and pink from the setting sun, creating a perfect mirror that made the world feel doubled, as though Farah stood on the edge of another realm.

The caravan moved as one toward the water's edge, their voices harmonizing in an ancient song that seemed to rise from the very earth beneath their feet.

The melody was haunting, its rhythm slow and deliberate, like the steady beat of a heart.

The words, though simple, carried an almost sacred resonance, the cadence blending with the gentle rustle of the grasses and the occasional call of birds overhead.

The drums accompanied the singers, their deep, resonant tones vibrating through Farah's chest, grounding her in the moment.

She took a slow breath, the air heavy with the mingling scents of dust and the faint tang of the oasis. The warmth of the sun on her cheeks was a contrast to the cool breeze that swept across the plains, carrying with it the faint but distinct aroma of spices from the cooking tents. It was a stark reminder of how different this place was from the Citadel. Here, the land itself seemed to breathe, its spirit palpable and unburdened by the weight of walls and courts.

Pari's small hand slipped into hers, the girl's presence grounding her as much as the music. Farah glanced down to see her expression, calm and serene, her dark eyes fixed on the horizon as if she could see something no one else could.

Following her line of sight, Farah let the vibrant colors of the sunset wash over her. The light seemed to stretch infinitely, wrapping the world in a warm, golden embrace.

The procession moved closer to the oasis, the grass underfoot giving way to soft, sandy earth, then glistening water, its surface broken only by the faintest ripple from a gentle breeze.

The caravan members lined the edges of the water, their movements deliberate and reverent as they prepared for the evening invocation. Lanterns were lit, their soft glow adding another layer of warmth to the fading sunlight, creating a delicate interplay of light and shadow that danced across the gathered faces.

At the forefront of the procession stood the caravan leader and his wife. Their long coats, richly adorned with embroidery, trailed into the shallow water, the fabric darkening as it absorbed the moisture.

They looked like they belonged here, as much a part of the land as the oasis itself. The leader raised his hands, his voice ringing out in welcome, the tone steady and grounding, much like the drums.

Farah closed her eyes for a moment, letting the sounds of the invocation wash over her. This wasn't the performative ritual of the Citadel, where gold and opulence took precedence over sincerity. This was raw, heartfelt, and intimate. The words weren't just recited, they were felt, offered up to the Unnamed Gods with a quiet desperation and hope that resonated deep within her.

When she opened her eyes again, her chest ached with a bittersweet longing she hadn't felt in years. The Citadel had always been her home, but it had never filled her with this sense of connection. Here, standing among strangers in the waning light of day, she felt a closeness to the world she hadn't realized she was missing.

As Pouri began the invocation, her melodic voice carried the prayers to the heavens. The words, though familiar, felt different here—infused with a raw power that made Farah's throat tighten. She blinked rapidly, refusing to let tears fall, even as the sun dipped lower, its final rays caressing the land before disappearing below the horizon.

Pari squeezed her hand, her small fingers surprisingly strong. Farah glanced down again, finding the little girl's gaze fixed on her. Her expression held a knowing, almost otherworldly calm.

"Your choice is here," Pari whispered, her voice barely audible over the fading song. She placed her free hand over her heart, the gesture simple but profound. "It's always here."

Farah knelt without thinking, lowering herself to Pari's level. The weight of those words pressed against her chest, and for a moment, she felt vulnerable, exposed. She wanted to ask what the girl meant, to demand clarity, but something stopped her. Instead, she nodded, her throat tight as if the words she needed were caught there.

Pari's solemn expression softened into a gentle smile. The little girl reached out, brushing her fingers against Farah's cheek.

"You should go help them set for the evening meal, little one," Farah said, her voice hoarse with emotion as she tried to swallow them down. She wiped at her cheek, brushing away a single traitorous tear that had escaped. "I'll keep the gharib out of trouble."

Pari giggled, the sound light and pure, before skipping

off toward the cooking tents. Farah straightened, taking a deep breath to steady herself before turning to face Yasher. He stood just behind her, his expression unreadable.

"I can remove that if you'd prefer," she said, gesturing toward the bracelet encircling his wrist.

Yasher glanced down at it as if he'd forgotten it was there. His lips quirked into a grin, and he shook his head.

"I'll keep it," he said, raising his arm slightly so the metal caught the torchlight. "It suits me. But I have to say, it's almost too fitting. You do have a way of picking out accessories that match my... charm."

Farah's patience snapped. A small pulse of heat traveled through the bracelet, and Yasher yelped, jerking his arm back.

"That was not called for." He glared at her, his grin replaced by a scowl.

Before she could retort, Pouri appeared, her serene presence cutting through the tension like a balm. The older woman approached with the same quiet grace she had exhibited throughout the day, her eyes warm as they settled on Farah.

"I trust the invocation was to your standards, Hand?" Pouri asked, bowing slightly.

Farah returned the bow, slipping back into the practiced poise she had learned in the Citadel. "It was beautiful, Khānum Yeganeh. I felt at peace."

Pouri inclined her head, a small smile gracing her lips. "We are simple folk, but we strive to honor the road and all who travel it."

Farah nodded. "Your hospitality has been beyond measure. May the Unnamed Gods keep you and yours."

Pouri's smile widened, and she placed a hand on each of

their arms, gently guiding them toward the growing bonfire. "Come," she said, her voice as warm as the flames ahead. "Let us break bread together."

CHAPTER 12

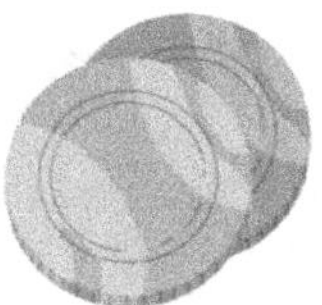

YASHER WAS CAUGHT off guard as Pouri took his arm with ease, her touch light but firm. She guided the two of them toward the bonfire, her warmth and calm demeanor a stark contrast to the simmering tension between him and his erstwhile captor. The fire crackled ahead, its golden glow spreading outward to touch the faces of the gathered caravan members. Shadows danced along the edges of the gathering, flickering across the worn canvas tents and weathered carts.

Pouri gestured to a pair of stools near the fire, her gaze lingering on Yasher with an almost grandmotherly fondness.

"Please, sit," she said. "You've had a long journey, and the road to Banima will not be kinder tomorrow."

Farah hesitated for a heartbeat before lowering herself gracefully onto one of the stools. Yasher followed, looking around at the crowd of people. Pari had already joined a cluster of children near the fire, her animated chatter blending into the lively hum of the gathering.

Yasher found himself transfixed by the scene before

him. The caravan members moved with practiced ease, serving food and passing around platters piled high with bread, roasted meats, and dried fruits. The aromas were intoxicating, a heady mix of spices and smoke that made his stomach growl audibly.

"The road is hungry work, gharib." Pouri smiled. "Eat your fill."

He nodded, accepting a wooden plate from one of the younger caravan members who beamed at him before hurrying away. The food was simple but hearty, and Yasher didn't realize how famished he was until he took his first bite. The spiced lamb melted in his mouth, its flavor rich and warming.

Farah ate with a quiet efficiency that made him smirk. He wondered if she ever let herself enjoy anything.

"Good, isn't it?" he ventured, earning a sharp glance in response.

Pouri took a seat beside them, her posture regal despite the rustic setting.

"Do you travel often on the mainland?"

Farah paused mid-bite, carefully setting her plate on her lap before answering.

"When the Mashyana requires it. My duties often take me far from the Citadel."

"A Beloved must carry many burdens, I imagine," Pouri inclined her head. "And yet you bear them with such grace."

Farah's expression softened slightly, though her reply was guarded. "The Mashyana's will is mine to serve."

Yasher bit back a chuckle, earning a subtle glare from Farah. He leaned back on his stool, his fingers absently toying with the bracelet around his wrist.

"She's modest, isn't she?" he said, directing the

comment to Pouri. "You wouldn't guess how terrifyingly efficient she is with a dagger."

Farah's eyes narrowed, and Yasher braced for another pulse of heat from the bracelet. Instead, she simply shook her head and resumed eating, muttering something under her breath that he didn't quite catch.

Pouri laughed softly, her gaze shifting between the two of them.

"It's good to see companions who can challenge one another. The road is long, and shared burdens make it easier to bear."

Yasher frowned slightly at the word companions. Farah's expression was unreadable, her focus seemingly fixed on her plate, but he knew better.

The bonfire crackled, sending a spray of embers spiraling into the night sky. The conversations around them grew louder, laughter mixing with the rhythmic beat of a drum someone had produced.

A few of the caravan members began clapping, their hands keeping time as a young man started to sing. His voice was soulful, weaving a melody that spoke of distant lands and the hope of home.

Yasher leaned into the moment, the camaraderie and warmth of the gathering soothing the unease that had followed him since Rumatin. It felt strange, almost unnatural, to be part of something so simple and genuine. He caught himself glancing at Farah again, wondering if she felt it too.

Pari darted back to their side, her cheeks flushed and her eyes alight with excitement.

"The children are learning a new dance!" she announced, tugging at Farah's hand. "Come see!"

Farah sighed but allowed the girl to pull her to her feet.

Yasher followed suit, grinning at Pari's boundless energy. The girl led them closer to the fire, where a group of children was attempting to mimic the intricate steps of an older dancer. The movements were swift and fluid, the rhythm demanding but joyous.

Pari joined in without hesitation, her small feet moving with surprising precision. She laughed as she stumbled, catching herself before jumping back into the dance. Yasher watched, his grin softening into something more genuine. There was something infectious about her joy, something that made the heavy weight of the world feel a little lighter.

Farah stood beside him, her arms crossed but her expression less guarded than usual. The firelight caught the edges of her scarf, the bright blues and greens vivid against the warm glow. For a moment, he thought she might smile.

"You should try it," he said, nudging her lightly with his elbow.

Farah raised a brow, her tone dry. "I think not."

"Oh, come on. Even you can't be all work and no play."

Farah's gaze flicked to him, a hint of amusement in her eyes. "And you think you'd fare better?"

"I've been known to possess a few... skills," he said with a mock-serious nod.

Farah scoffed but didn't respond, her attention shifting back to Pari. The girl was now teaching one of the smaller children, her hands moving in exaggerated gestures as she demonstrated a step. Yasher couldn't help but admire her determination.

The song ended with a flourish, the dancers collapsing into laughter and applause. Pari returned to their side, slightly out of breath but beaming.

"You should have danced!" she scolded Yasher, poking him in the side.

"Next time," he promised, ruffling her hair.

Farah's gaze lingered on Pari for a moment before she spoke. "It's getting late. We should prepare for tomorrow."

Pari nodded, her energy finally showing signs of waning. Yasher bent to scoop her up, carrying her back toward their tent as Farah walked ahead. The bonfire and the laughter faded behind them, replaced by the quiet hum of the night.

By the time they reached the tent, the little girl was already half-asleep in his arms. He set her down gently, tucking a blanket around her before stepping back. Farah was crouched near the tent flap, her expression thoughtful as she adjusted the lantern's wick.

"Good night, Farah," he said softly, not expecting a reply.

To his surprise, she glanced at him, her eyes meeting his for a brief moment. "Good night, Yasher."

It wasn't much, but it felt like a small step. He settled onto his pallet, the bracelet on his wrist cool against his skin. As he closed his eyes, the warmth of the fire and the sound of Pari's laughter lingered in his mind, a fragile but comforting memory to carry forward.

YASHER WOKE ABRUPTLY, his body instinctively alert in the deep silence of the night. The faint sounds of the caravan, so lively earlier, had fallen to a hushed stillness, broken only by the occasional soft shuffle of animals in the distance. His eyes adjusted to the dim light, and he noticed the faint flicker of flames through the thin walls of the tent.

He glanced to his side and saw Pari, curled up and breathing softly. Her small face, peaceful in sleep, was illuminated by the faint glow of the lantern. A protective warmth stirred in his chest at the sight of her innocence. But his attention was drawn to the empty pallet across from him.

He rubbed his eyes, sitting up quietly to avoid waking the child, and moved to the tent flap. Pushing it aside, he stepped into the cool night air. The small firepit outside their tent still glowed with embers, its faint warmth seeping into the otherwise chilly atmosphere.

Farah was there, seated on a flat stone beside the fire with a cup cradled in her hands, her posture tense but contemplative. The scarf she'd worn earlier had been removed, and her hair tumbled loosely around her shoulders, catching the faint orange glow. She didn't look up as he approached, her focus fixed on the flames, but there was no doubt in his mind that she was aware of his movements.

Her gaze flicked to him, and for a moment, her expression was guarded.

"If you're going to hover, you may as well sit," she sighed, gesturing to the spot across from her.

Yasher smirked, dropping onto a log near the fire. The warmth was welcome, but he didn't miss the faint lines of weariness etched into her face. She poured from a small flask into a spare cup and slid it across the stone toward him.

He held her gaze as he lifted the cup to his nose. A sharp, bitter smell invaded his senses and a slow, approving smile graced his lips. "Strong stuff."

Farah shrugged, cradling her own cup. "It helps clear the mind."

Yasher leaned back slightly, stretching his legs out toward the fire. The silence stretched between them, heavy but not oppressive. While she stared into the fire, he let himself look at her. The tension she carried during the day was still there, just different, more reflective.

"Noticed your pallet was empty," he said, breaking the quiet. "Thought maybe you were off sharpening your daggers."

Her lips twitched in the faintest ghost of a smile. "Not tonight."

He tilted his head, watching her carefully. "What's on your mind?"

Farah stared into the fire for a long moment, before taking a deep breath.

"Everything," she said finally, her voice quiet but steady. "The relics. The Mashyana. The state of this kingdom."

Yasher took another sip, waiting for her to continue. When she didn't, he leaned forward, resting his elbows on his knees. "You've been angry with me since the moment we met. And while I'll admit I've given you a few reasons—"

"A few?" she interrupted, raising a brow.

He chuckled, holding up a hand in mock surrender. "Fine. More than a few. But I'd like to think I'm not entirely without charm."

Farah shook her head, a sigh escaping her. "This isn't about charm. This is about trust—or the lack of it."

Her words carried a weight that made him pause. She looked at him then, her expression uncharacteristically vulnerable.

"You swapped the relic," she said, her voice even but tinged with frustration. "You gave the Mashyana a fake and didn't think about the consequences because they wouldn't touch you."

Yasher frowned, sitting back. "I did what I had to. The real relic... it felt wrong to hand it over."

"To her?" Farah pressed, her gaze sharp. "Or to anyone?"

He hesitated, the memory of the relic's weight in his pocket vivid in his mind. "To her. Something about the way she looked at it... like it wasn't a tool for restoration but a prize."

Farah's expression softened slightly, but her tone remained firm. "You might think you've done the right thing, but you've put me and this kingdom in a dangerous position. Those relics are supposed to help stabilize Emari. To ease the suffering of our people."

"The rebels in Tamidh are growing bolder," she paused, staring back into the fire. "People have died, people that I care about. The Mashya himself went to negotiate with them, but I doubt words will be enough. And then there's the wasting sickness spreading across the mainland. The relics are supposed to be part of the solution."

Yasher studied her, his earlier bravado fading. He hadn't considered the broader implications of his actions, the ripples they might create. "So, you're saying you need the relics to fix all of this?"

"I don't know if they'll fix everything," she admitted. "But they're part of the balance, part of the old ways that held this land together. And now, when we need them most, they're scattered and hoarded, their power wasted on greed."

Her voice cracked slightly, and she took a long drink from her cup, as if to steady herself. Yasher's chest tightened at the raw emotion in her words.

"I didn't realize..." he began, but she held up a hand to stop him.

"I'm not asking for your pity or your guilt. I'm asking you to understand why this matters."

The fire crackled between them, filling the silence as Yasher considered her words. He wasn't used to thinking beyond the immediate, beyond his own survival. But Farah's conviction stirred something unfamiliar in him.

"I can't change what I've done," he said finally, his tone quieter than usual. "But I can see this through. I can help you find the other relics."

Farah regarded him carefully, her expression unreadable. "When we reach Banima, you're free to go. I'll figure out the rest."

"And if I don't want to go?" he asked, surprising even himself with the question.

Her lips parted slightly, but she closed them again, clearly caught off guard. She turned her gaze back to the fire.

"That's your choice."

Yasher leaned back, letting her words sink in. The fire's warmth seeped into his skin, and for the first time in days, the tension between them seemed to ease.

"I'll stick around," he said softly, drawing her attention. "At least to help make up for what trouble I've brought you."

She studied him for a moment, her dark eyes searching his face. Then she nodded, the faintest hint of a smile tugging at her lips. "Very well."

It wasn't much—a truce, fragile and unspoken—but it was a start. As they sat together, the fire casting long shadows across the plains, Yasher felt a flicker of something

unexpected. Not forgiveness, not yet, but the possibility
of it.

CHAPTER 13

THE GENTLE RUSTLE of the tent's fabric stirred Farah awake. She blinked into the dim light, the familiar smell of dry grass and dust reminding her where she was. A faint chill clung to the air, though the rising sun promised warmth soon enough. Her body ached from the restless sleep, but she ignored it, stretching as quietly as she could to avoid waking Yasher or Pari.

The sounds of the caravan stirring to life filtered in, the low murmur of voices and the occasional clatter of pots pulling her fully from the haze of sleep. She glanced over to the pallets.

Pari looked to have gotten up earlier, her pallet folded up and ready to be packed away. Yasher, sprawled on his side, looked less foreign in the soft light, his usual smirk absent in his unconscious state.

Farah hesitated, the urge to let him sleep a little longer tugging at her. But practicality won out.

She nudged Yasher's leg with her foot—firmly, but not unkindly. "Up, gharib. The caravan won't wait for us."

Yasher stirred, groaning softly before rolling onto his back.

"Good and gracious morning to you too, Phoenix." He squinted up at her, his voice thick with sleep.

Farah ignored the barb, stepping over to the crate she'd used as a makeshift table the night before. She picked it up and carried it outside, the morning air cool against her skin.

The oxen were already being yoked to their cart, the rest of the caravan moving with quiet efficiency to break camp. Farah dropped the crate near the cart, turning back toward the tent.

She found Yasher emerging, bundled pallet and blanket in hand, stomping his feet into his boots as he came. He set the bedding on the crate before looking around.

"Where's Pari?" he asked, his voice light but edged with concern.

"With Khānum Yeganeh more than likely," Farah replied, moving to dismantle the tent. She pulled at one of the stakes, the damp ground giving way easily beneath her hands. Folding the fabric with practiced movements, she tried to focus on the task rather than Yasher's lingering gaze. He grabbed one corner of the tent to help, his usual chatter subdued.

The silence between them wasn't uncomfortable, but it carried the weight of unfinished conversations from the night prior. Farah found herself grateful for it. Words felt too fragile to use so carelessly, and she wasn't ready to trust him—or herself—with them just yet.

By the time they finished, Pari had returned, hand-in-hand with Pouri. The caravan leader's wife exuded the same calm authority she seemed to always carry, her smile warm as she approached.

"Little Divine," Yasher said, his smile could have lit up the night. He turned to Pouri, bowing his head slightly. "And Khānum Pouri. My thanks again for the hospitality last evening."

"No thanks are needed," Pouri replied, releasing Pari's hand. "You are always welcome among us. I came to let you know we won't reach Banima until tomorrow. A storm blocks the way, so we'll stop early at a smaller oasis along the route."

Farah frowned, wiping her hands on her trousers. "Should we wait here for the storm to pass?"

Pouri shook her head gently. "There is no need. The storm will not reach us until evening, but we must make haste to camp safely before it arrives."

She nodded, the tension in her shoulders easing. "Thank you, Khānum Pouri. We're ready to join the line."

She lifted Pari into the cart, settling her securely before climbing in herself.

"Come along, gharib," she said, glancing at Yasher. Her voice held no malice, only the weariness of someone resigned to his company.

Yasher smiled faintly at Pouri before climbing in beside Pari. The little girl leaned against him, her small hand tapping lightly against his chest.

"Hold tight," she murmured, tucking her head into his shoulder as the cart lurched into motion.

Farah watched the two of them for a moment before turning her gaze to the horizon. The road stretched endlessly ahead, the golden plains bathed in the soft light of morning.

The storm that Pouri had spoken of wasn't yet visible, but Farah trusted the caravan leader's instincts. The Yeganeh had been keeping caravans safe for decades, and their reputation for navigating the harsh Emari landscape was unmatched.

Yasher's quiet movements drew her attention back to the cart. He had pulled out a deck of cards, shuffling them with the deftness of a seasoned traveler. His hands moved with practiced ease, the faint rustle of the cards blending with the creak of the cart's wheels.

Pari stirred, her voice cutting through the stillness. "Will you show me a game?"

Yasher's smile widened, and he nodded. "Of course, Little Divine. It's better if you sit across from me, though."

The little girl stretched and crawled to the other side of the cart. Farah watched as Yasher explained the rules, his voice patient and kind. Pari nodded along, her small hands reaching for the cards as she absorbed his instructions.

She tried to focus on the horizon, but her gaze kept drifting back to them. The gharib's ease with Pari was disarming, his usual charm softened into something genuine. He coaxed laughter from the little girl with his antics, crossing his eyes whenever she caught him trying to cheat.

Though the people and the circumstances were so different, her memories of Rostam training her as a little girl, bringing her to the Saffron Oasis after those training sessions, flooded to her mind.

Farah smiled despite herself, the sound of Pari's laughter tugging at something she'd buried long ago. She quickly schooled her features, turning her attention back to the road, but the warmth lingered.

After several rounds, Pari threw up her hands in mock frustration, her eyes bright with laughter.

"You should play," she said, tugging at her sleeve. "I'm tired now."

She hesitated, glancing at Yasher before shaking her head. "I don't know how."

Pari frowned, her tone firm. "You watched us. You know."

With a resigned sigh, she moved to sit across from him.

"I wasn't paying enough attention," she admitted quietly, avoiding his gaze. "Will you show me again?"

His smile was soft, lacking the usual teasing edge.

"As you wish," he said, shuffling the cards with a flourish.

He laid the cards out carefully, his instructions clear and patient. Farah nodded along, her fingers brushing against the cards as she tried to commit the rules to memory. When she finally looked up, her tentative smile was met with one of his own, a moment of understanding passing between them.

Before they could begin a proper game, a shout rippled through the caravan, signaling a halt. The cart slowed, and Farah rose to peer over the side. The small oasis ahead was modest compared to the one they'd left that morning, but its trees and water offered a welcome respite from the endless plains.

"We'd better set up quickly," she said, handing Pari down from the cart before jumping down herself. She turned to Yasher, who was already lifting their supplies. "The storm won't wait."

They worked in silence, the rhythm of their movements steady and efficient. The dark line on the horizon loomed closer with each passing moment, a stark reminder of the storm's approach.

Farah glanced at the swirling clouds, a deep unease settling in her chest. But for now, the tent was secure, and Pari's laughter echoed faintly in her mind, a small comfort.

This storm looked to be dangerous, and the tent would provide little support.

THE STORM RAGED ON, a relentless force battering the tent as though it sought to test their every preparation. The walls quivered with each gust, the fabric pulling taut before ballooning back, creating a rhythmic, unsettling cadence.

Farah sat stiffly on her pallet, arms crossed over her chest as she stared at the shifting shadows cast by the lantern's flickering light. Every breath felt heavy, her chest tight with the weight of her thoughts. She pulled out her whetstone, taking care of her knives to have something to do as a distraction.

The tent was solid, as she had ensured it would be. Yasher might have helped set the stays, but she'd gone back over his work, tightening knots and checking anchors, knowing he hadn't fully grasped the ferocity of Emari's storms.

She had learned the hard way, years ago, how brutal the winds could be—tearing through even the most fortified camps. Yet tonight, the storm outside wasn't the real threat. The tempest within her mind dwarfed it entirely.

She couldn't shake the doubt gnawing at her. She could hear the Mashyana's voice in her mind, the expectation in her words when she'd sent Farah on these tasks. It was meant to be simple—retrieve the relics and return. But now, with gharib saying he'd help her as an apology, she found herself questioning everything. Was it the right choice to trust him? How much did she really know about him, beyond what he showed her? What if he wasn't as neutral as he claimed, or worse, what if the Mashyana had already realized the deception?

Had she made a mistake in bringing him and Pari along, even though her hand had been forced?

She had no room for error. If the Mashyana had learned of the false relic, it would be more than just failure, it would be a betrayal.

Farah couldn't afford that. Not now. Not when everything had already been set into motion. She had to hold it together, for the Mashyana, for herself, and for the mission. No one could know.

A faint creak of the tent's structure pulled her attention briefly, and she glanced toward Yasher. He sat cross-legged near the center of the tent, his hands moving deftly as he shuffled his ever-present deck of cards. The motions were methodical, almost hypnotic, but she didn't miss the slight jump in his shoulders whenever the wind pushed particularly hard against the walls.

It took effort to keep the smirk off her face. Let the gharib jump at shadows. It was small penance for the chaos he had brought into her life.

Pari sat nearby, carefully working her small bundle of fibers with the focus only a child could muster. Her tiny fingers tugged and twisted the threads into a pattern Farah didn't recognize. Pari's head was bowed, her face serene despite the howling winds outside. That little girl had an uncanny ability to tune out the world when she chose, an enviable skill Farah wished she could master.

"Pouri gave it to me," Pari said suddenly, her voice soft but firm, breaking the silence. She didn't look up from her work. "She said I needed something to occupy my time, to practice stillness. You have your knives, and he has his cards. This is mine."

Farah felt a flicker of warmth at the girl's words, but before she could respond, Yasher let out a muffled laugh, quickly dropping several cards as he tried to cover his mouth. The sound was sudden, absurd, and disarming. Farah glanced at him, catching the way his face split into a grin despite his efforts to stifle it.

Against her better judgment, Farah felt a small laugh bubble up in her own chest. It escaped before she could stop it, and she turned her head slightly to hide the smile tugging at her lips. She hated how easily this gharib could break through her defenses.

Yasher, emboldened by her reaction, laughed openly now, his voice a warm counterpoint to the cold, howling wind. Pari huffed in mock annoyance and bent closer to her work, but Farah noticed the faint smile tugging at the girl's lips.

The moment passed too quickly, and the storm's roar returned to fill the silence. Yasher coughed lightly, as though to reset the atmosphere, and began shuffling his cards again. Farah's eyes drifted to his hands, watching the smooth, practiced motions.

There was a grace to the way he handled the cards, the kind of precision that spoke of years of practice. She could see how those same hands could have so deftly swapped the relic without her noticing.

"Fancy a game?" Yasher's voice broke through her thoughts.

Farah hesitated, her instincts warring against her curiosity. Finally, she sighed and set her whetstone and dagger aside, twisting to face him. "Why not?"

He grinned, his confidence infuriatingly unshaken. "Primer or straight to play?"

"I remember the rules," she said curtly, keeping her

gaze fixed on the cards rather than his face. She didn't like looking at him. Every time she did, she felt an uncomfortable pull, as if the storm outside wasn't the only force trying to tear her apart.

Yasher dealt the cards with a practiced flair, the deck snapping crisply in his hands. The first hand was played in silence, the only sounds the occasional scrape of Pari's fiber work and the relentless wind outside.

Farah focused on the game, though her mind wandered back to the deeper implications of their journey. The relics were supposed to be a means of salvation for Emari, tools to heal a fractured land. Yet here she was, chasing the next one while an actual relic sat in Yasher's pocket, not with her queen as it should be.

The way he seemed so nonchalant about the weight of his actions bloomed anger as she thought about it. His recklessness would blow back on her, no matter how much he said that he wanted to make it right.

The storm outside intensified as her anger and fear did, the tent shuddering with each gust. Farah glanced up at the fabric walls, her pulse quickening with the storm's ferocity. They would hold—she was certain of it—but the memories of past storms surged in her mind. She could still hear the tearing fabric, the panicked shouts, the frantic scramble to salvage what could be saved.

"Farah?" Yasher's voice pulled her back to the present, and she realized she had frozen mid-play, her fingers gripping a card too tightly. He raised an eyebrow, his tone teasing. "Did the discard offend you somehow?"

Her jaw tightened. She threw her cards onto the pile and stood abruptly, the motion more forceful than she intended. "I'm done."

The words hung in the air, heavy with unspoken

tension. Farah turned, facing away from them, the wind pressing against her through the tent's flap. The wind pressed against her, the force of it reminding her there was no escape. Not from the storm outside, nor from the storm within.

She hesitated, then dropped her hand and turned back. Yasher was watching her, his expression unreadable, but she refused to meet his gaze. Instead, she stepped around him and returned to her pallet, sinking onto the blankets with a quiet exhale. She pulled her knees up to her chest and wrapped her arms around them, closing her eyes against the storm's howling.

The air inside the tent felt thick, oppressive. Farah tried to focus on the familiar sensation of her dagger's hilt against her thigh, the steady rhythm of her breathing, anything to anchor herself. But her thoughts kept circling back to Yasher—his infuriating grin, his deft hands, the way he could pull a laugh from her despite everything.

Letting her guard down, even for a moment, was a luxury she couldn't afford. Not now. Not ever.

CHAPTER 14

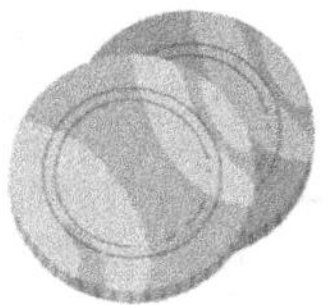

THE STORM HAD FINALLY PASSED, leaving behind a world refreshed and renewed, the sharpness of the air a reminder of the chaos they had endured. Yasher stretched his arms over his head as the caravan prepared to move, his muscles stiff from a restless night. The scent of damp earth and grass filled his lungs, invigorating despite the early hour. He turned to the tent where Farah stood, adjusting her rucksack. The way the morning light caught the edges of her figure, softening her sharp demeanor for just a moment, made him hesitate before speaking.

"Beautiful morning, isn't it?" he said, sauntering closer, his tone light and teasing. "Though not nearly as radiant as you, Phoenix."

Farah shot him a look that teetered between annoyance and disbelief. "Save your charm for the caravan leader's wife. She seemed more susceptible to it."

He smirked, placing a hand over his heart in mock injury. "I'm wounded. Truly. Here I am, offering you a compliment, and you dismiss me so easily."

Farah shook her head, clearly unimpressed. Whatever

had soured her mood during the storm was still there, but had lightened enough to have a small curve of a smile before she turned away from him.

"We're leaving soon. Try not to hold up the caravan, gharib."

As they packed the cart, his gaze wandered to the landscape unfolding around them. The once-flat plains had given way to rolling hills, their slopes covered in a patchwork of barley and sorghum. The fields rippled like a golden sea in the gentle breeze, the vibrant crops a stark contrast to the storm-darkened horizon of the day before. Farmers moved through the rows, their silhouettes bent in labor, a quiet rhythm of life that Yasher found soothing.

He leaned closer to Farah as she secured a bundle to the cart.

"You know," he began, his voice dropping slightly, "I've never been to Banima. Pouri spoke of the beautiful murals they decorate the entire city with. Do you think they'll be that bold as those stories you tell yourself to avoid admitting I'm not all bad?"

Farah paused, narrowing her eyes at him.

"You talk a lot for someone who nearly got himself swept away in a storm."

"Ah, but I didn't," Yasher replied smoothly, his grin widening. "Because I had you to keep me grounded."

Her sigh was exasperated, but the way her fingers lingered on the knot she tied suggested she wasn't entirely immune to his banter.

The caravan began its slow crawl forward, and he settled into his place beside Pari in the cart.

The little girl sat perched on a crate, her small hands busy with a piece of stitching Pouri had given her. He watched her for a moment, marveling at the ease with which she adapted to the rhythm of travel. It was a far cry from the whirlwind of chaos he often brought with him.

Pulling his cards out to give himself something to do, he watched the golden fields roll by like a sea of grain, the horizon punctuated by clusters of vibrant murals and the occasional conical tower rising like sentinels from the earth.

Banima must be close now, its bustling life spilling onto the road in the form of children's laughter, the clink of pots, and the soft murmur of voices.

He shifted his weight, glancing at Farah sitting at the front of the cart. Her gaze remained fixed on the road ahead, her posture straight but not tense. She seemed at ease in a way that Yasher hadn't yet seen, her expression softened by the golden light of the mid-morning sun. He leaned forward, resting his arms on his knees, and let his voice take on a teasing edge.

"You know, Farah," he began, his tone playful, "you have a way of making even the most beautiful landscapes seem dull by comparison."

She turned her head slightly, her dark eyes narrowing as she regarded him. "Do you practice these lines, or are you just naturally insufferable?"

Yasher's smirk turned into a full grin, his chest tightening with a strange, unexpected warmth.

Insufferable. It wasn't the word itself but the way she said it, her tone carrying just the faintest hint of something lighter, something almost fond. To anyone else, it might have sounded like an insult, but to him, it was progress.

"Insufferable," he repeated, letting the word roll off his tongue as if it were a badge of honor. "You know, I think that's the kindest thing you've ever said to me, Phoenix."

Farah rolled her eyes and turned back to the road, but

he caught the faintest twitch at the corner of her lips. Was that almost a smile? He liked to think it was.

His grin widened as he leaned back, the cards in his hands shuffling effortlessly. If Farah could call him insufferable, it meant she was at least engaging with him again. After the tension of the storm and the heavy silence that had followed, he'd take that as a victory.

For all her sharp words and colder edges, Yasher had started to see glimpses of something deeper—something more vulnerable and human. He wasn't foolish enough to think she'd forgive him outright for the relic swap, but maybe, just maybe, she was beginning to ease up. He liked to imagine that beneath her armor was someone who could one day trust him. Even if she didn't realize it yet.

"You are just a beacon for trouble," she mumbled, not looking at him.

"Trouble's where all the best stories come from," he added lightly, breaking the silence again. He flicked a card into the air, catching it with practiced ease.

"That, or trouble is where they end," Farah replied, her voice laced with exasperation. But this time, she didn't sound angry—just tired, maybe even amused. It was subtle, but he was learning to notice the small shifts in her tone, the little tells that spoke volumes.

"I like to think I have a knack for making my way out of trouble," he said, flashing her a roguish grin.

Farah didn't look at him this time, but her response was quieter, almost to herself. "You're lucky, that's for sure."

Yasher's grin softened, the teasing edge fading as he watched her.

"Maybe," he said, his voice low, "luck only takes you so far, Phoenix." He lifted his arm, showing off the bangle she'd placed on his wrist with a smirk.

Her eyes flicked toward him, a glare at the ready. Whatever fragile truce they had, he'd do his best to hold onto it. And that comment may have been a push in the wrong direction.

The cart crested the hill, and Yasher leaned forward, anticipation coursing through him as the faint outline of Banima began to emerge in the distance. The city was still a few miles off, nestled like a jewel at the foot of the rising hills and a confluence of rivers. The vibrant colors of its famed murals seemed to shimmer even from afar, though they remained indistinct, a tease of what lay ahead.

The air here carried a hint of change, the dry warmth of the plains giving way to something fresher, touched by the faint scent of fruit blossoms and distant water. The road beneath the caravan's wheels had grown smoother, more deliberate, as if the path itself were eager to lead them to their destination. To the left, the fields of barley and sorghum were replaced by orchards, the trees heavy with early-season fruits. To the right, the land stretched out in a patchwork of wildflowers, their hues vibrant against the backdrop of rolling hills.

Pari stirred, lifting her head from where she had been dozing off against a crate. Her dark eyes blinked sleepily as she took in the scenery.

"It's beautiful," she murmured, her voice soft with awe.

Farah, seated at the front of the cart, turned slightly, her gaze flicking over the horizon.

"Banima is one of the few places left that celebrates the old ways," she said, her tone carrying a weight that hinted at both relief and sorrow. "Its people are proud of their heritage and push to keep their traditions untouched."

Yasher watched her as she spoke, noting the way her shoulders seemed to relax just a fraction. It was rare to see her like this—unguarded, even if only for a moment. He filed the sight away, like a gambler holding onto a winning card.

"Untouched, huh?" he said, leaning back with a wry grin. "Sounds like the perfect place to start trouble."

Farah shot him a sharp look, her lips pressing into a thin line. "Not everything is a joke, gharib."

He held up his hands in mock surrender, though her rebuke didn't sting as much as it might have. The tension in her voice was familiar now, almost comforting.

The caravan halted briefly near a small rise where a cluster of shade trees grew. The caravan leader, seated atop his own cart, gestured for the group to rest and prepare for the final stretch before Banima. Merchants and travelers alike began to unload supplies for a short break, their chatter blending into the rustle of leaves and the occasional lowing of oxen.

He hopped down from the cart, his boots crunching against the gravelly road. Pari scrambled after him, her small hands reaching for his as she steadied herself on the uneven ground. Farah followed a moment later, her movements fluid and efficient as she surveyed their surroundings.

"What now?" Yasher asked, stretching his arms overhead. The long hours of travel had left his muscles stiff, and he welcomed the chance to move.

"We wait," Farah said simply, her attention already shifting to the caravan leader, who was speaking with one of his aides. "The leader wants to assess the path ahead before we move closer to Banima. Likely a precaution."

Pari tugged on his sleeve, her expression curious. "Why would they need to be cautious? Banima seems so peaceful."

Farah's jaw tightened, though she didn't immediately answer. Yasher caught the shadow that passed over her features and felt a flicker of unease.

"It's not Banima we're cautious of," Farah said finally, her voice low. "The roads can be dangerous, even this close to town. Bandits, deserters, or worse."

"Worse?" Yasher arched a brow, his grin returning. "Don't tell me the Unnamed Gods themselves walk these roads."

Farah didn't rise to the bait. Instead, she stepped closer, her tone quiet but firm. "There are those who prey on travelers, especially caravans like this one. Some for survival, others for cruelty. If you're smart, gharib, you'll keep your jokes to yourself until we're safely within Banima's walls."

Yasher's grin faded, but only slightly.

"Noted," he said, tipping an imaginary hat. "I'll try to stay out of trouble. No promises, though."

Farah huffed, shaking her head as she turned away. Pari giggled, the tension dissipating as the little girl tugged him toward the shade of the trees. Yasher let her lead him, though his thoughts lingered on Farah's warning. The roads here might look idyllic, but danger often lurked where least expected.

Under the shade, he dropped to a seated position, pulling out his deck of cards. Pari settled beside him, her curious eyes watching as he shuffled the cards with practiced ease. He glanced toward Farah, who had taken up a position near the cart, her gaze scanning the horizon.

"You know," he said, his voice carrying just enough to reach her, "you don't always have to be on guard. We're allowed to enjoy the view."

He caught the way her shoulders stiffened at his words. She turned to face him, her expression inscrutable.

"Enjoy it while you can," she said, her tone clipped. "It doesn't last."

Yasher tilted his head, studying her. There was a weight to her words, a sadness she couldn't quite hide. He wondered what she saw when she looked at the horizon—what memories or fears kept her from relaxing, even for a moment.

"Maybe that's why we should enjoy it," he said quietly, almost to himself.

Farah didn't reply, but for a fleeting moment, her gaze softened, her eyes meeting his before she turned away. He leaned back, shuffling the cards again as Pari leaned her head against his arm. The wind rustled through the trees, carrying with it the promise of Banima and whatever waited beyond.

CHAPTER 15

THE ROAD CURVED GENTLY, and Banima unfolded before Farah like an artist's masterpiece, its vibrant hues set against the vast expanse of the Emari plains on one side, the mountains and rivers on the other. She had almost forgotten how alive this city was.

The murals were a riot of color, each building a canvas for the tales of Banima's people—of triumph, sorrow, and the gods they revered. Vibrant blues intertwined with deep golds and fiery reds, their interplay telling stories that felt as old as the Azhdahak mountains that loomed over the city. Those peaks, their jagged forms etched into the horizon, seemed to stand watch over the town, a silent reminder of Emari's enduring strength.

The air was different here, infused with the mingling scents of jasmine with other wildflowers, fresh bread, and sun-warmed stone. Even the light seemed softer, refracted through the petals of blooming flowers that spilled out from every corner—windowsills, market stalls, and small gardens bursting with reds, purples, and yellows. It was a city that demanded to be seen, to be experienced, as if

Banima itself were alive and eager to tell its story to any who entered.

The caravan halted just outside the grand walls, their surface alive with sprawling murals. Unlike the smaller, personal paintings they had seen along the road, these were immense and intricate, depicting entire legends. Scenes of gods and mortals intertwined, the Yazatas bestowing blessings upon the people, and the Amesha Spentas guiding them through trials.

Her gaze lingered on one mural that dominated the center of the wall. It depicted Rashnu, the divine judge, his form towering and majestic, holding the scales that determined the fates of men. The colors seemed to shift under the sunlight, as though the painted god himself were watching them approach.

Yasher's voice broke through her thoughts.

"Quite the welcome, isn't it?" he said, leaning casually against the cart as if he were indifferent, but she caught the way his eyes flitted from mural to mural, taking it all in.

"Banima doesn't do subtlety," she replied, her tone softer than she intended. The city always had a way of softening her edges, even if she fought it.

Pari's small voice chimed in, filled with awe. "It's so colorful. I didn't know cities could look like this."

She crouched to Pari's level, brushing a stray lock of hair from the girl's face. "Banima is special. It's one of the few places where the people hold onto their traditions tightly. Everything you see here is a piece of our story as Emarians."

Pari nodded solemnly, her eyes wide as they took in the splendor around them. Farah stood, glancing at Yasher, who was grinning at her as if she'd just shared some great secret.

"What?" she asked, raising an eyebrow.

"Nothing," he said, the grin still firmly in place. "Just not used to seeing you as a keeper of tales. It's... refreshing."

She rolled her eyes, but the faintest hint of a smile tugged at her lips. "Don't get used to it, gharib."

The caravan began to disperse, the merchants and travelers making their way into the city or setting up their wares just outside the gates. Farah shouldered her rucksack, her gaze lingering on the gates for a moment before she turned to Pari.

"Are you planning to stay with us this time?" she asked, keeping her tone light despite the undercurrent of concern.

Pari fidgeted with the hem of her tunic, her usual boundless energy tempered by something quieter. "Rashnu said I should stay. For now."

Farah's chest tightened at the weight in the little girl's words. "Good. I'd rather have you where I can see you."

Yasher moved to stand beside her. "So, what's the plan? Do we storm the gates and declare ourselves as treasure hunters?"

She shot him a pointed look, but there was no real venom behind it. "First, we find a place to stay. Then, I have business to attend to."

"Business," Yasher echoed, his tone laden with curiosity. "Mysterious as ever, I see. Should I be worried?"

"Worry about yourself," she said, pulling her pack tighter against her shoulder. "You've managed to get by this far without me babysitting you."

"Hardly getting by," he quipped, but the teasing edge in his voice was gentler than usual. "I'm thriving. Just ask Pari."

Pari giggled, and she shook her head, leading the way

toward the gates. The cobblestone streets stretched out before them, alive with the buzz of activity.

Merchants called out their wares, their voices weaving through the laughter of children darting between stalls. Every corner seemed to hold a burst of color, from the woven tapestries hanging in shop windows to the overflowing bouquets carried by street vendors.

He fell into step beside her, his usual swagger tempered by the quiet wonder the city inspired. He glanced at the murals as they passed, his expression thoughtful.

"Do all of the mainland Emari cities look like this?" he asked, his voice low as if he didn't want to disturb the moment.

Farah shook her head. "No. Banima is... unique. Most cities have their beauty, but this? This is a testament to the people. They've fought to keep their traditions alive, even when others tried to take them away."

"You admire them," he said, his gaze flicking to her. "The people here."

"I admire their resilience," she admitted. "They've held onto something pure, something that has been chipped away at over time. That's rare."

The weight of the relic she sought in this city pressed on her mind, a way to recover from the damage her first task was sure to cause, mingling with the unease of trusting this man. Could she really rely on him for something so important?

They approached the bustling market square just outside the gates, the scent of spices and fresh bread mingling with the hum of conversation.

Stalls lined the streets, their vibrant fabrics and shining trinkets catching the light. Farah's gaze drifted to one stall selling intricate jewelry, the delicate pieces reminding her of the craftsmanship she'd seen in the Saffron Oasis, which was the last place on the island with the Citadel to still hold to the old ways.

"Careful, Farah," he said, his tone teasing. "You're starting to look like you might actually enjoy yourself."

"Don't be ridiculous," she replied, but her lips twitched in what might have been the beginnings of a smile.

Before she could say more, Pari tugged on her sleeve, pointing to a stall laden with colorful pastries. "Can we get some? Please?"

She hesitated, the weight of her responsibilities pressing against the simple request. But when she saw Pari's hopeful expression, she relented. "Fine. But only one."

As Pari darted toward the stall, Yasher leaned closer, his voice low. "You know, you're not as intimidating as you think."

Farah glanced at him, her expression cool. "Don't push your luck, gharib. You chose to leave me a leash if you get out of line." She pointed to his wrist.

He laughed, the sound warm and genuine. "Noted."

The moment hung between them, light and fleeting, before Farah turned her attention back to the bustling streets. The relic awaited, and with it, the weight of the Mashyana's expectations.

The vibrant city offered moments of distraction from her own thoughts as she led them through the streets. Every turn revealed more of the city's kaleidoscope of life. Banima was alive in a way the Citadel never could be— here, every wall, every stall, every laugh seemed to breathe with purpose.

Pari skipped ahead, her laughter blending with the music of the city. She darted between merchant stalls, her small form weaving effortlessly through the crowd. Farah kept her gaze on the girl, her steps purposeful as she navigated the streets. Yasher, as always, was at her side, his presence a mixture of amusement and curiosity.

"This place has a certain charm," Yasher said, his voice cutting through the din of the market. "Though I'm not sure if it's the murals or the pastries."

Farah shot him a sidelong glance. "You'd find charm in a mud pit if it meant a good grift."

"True," he replied with a grin. "But I prefer my charm with a side of adventure. It keeps the heart and mind strong."

She didn't reply, her attention drawn to a mural that stretched across the side of a building. It depicted the Yazatas standing in a circle, their forms illuminated by radiant colors. In the center stood Rashnu, his scales balanced, his gaze solemn. The artistry was breathtaking, each brushstroke telling a story of justice, faith, and balance.

Yasher followed her gaze, his tone softer. "Do you ever wonder if they're still watching?"

Farah paused, caught off guard by the sincerity in his question. "The Yazatas?"

He nodded, his eyes lingering on the mural.

"Whoever they are. Do you think they care about all of this?" He gestured to the city around them, his voice quieter than usual.

Farah's grip on her rucksack tightened. The relics she sought was tied to that very question, wasn't it? The Mashyana believed the gods protection was waning Emari, and the relics were their only hope of stability. But did Farah believe that? The weight of her doubt pressed against her chest, and she forced herself to shrug.

"Whether they care or not doesn't change what I have to do."

Yasher tilted his head, studying her. "Practical as always."

"Someone has to be," she replied, turning away from the mural and focusing on Pari, who was examining a stall filled with brightly colored fabrics. The little girl's enthusiasm was a small comfort.

Yasher fell into step beside her, his voice light again. "So, what's the plan? Or are you going to keep me guessing?"

Farah sighed, the tension in her shoulders easing slightly as they moved further into the city. "First, we settle in at the inn. Then we find the merchant. After that... we'll see."

"That's a lot of unknowns for someone who likes to have everything under control," he teased, but there was a note of encouragement in his tone.

She didn't respond immediately, her thoughts lingering on the merchant and the relic.

"I know when to adapt," she said, finally. "Sometimes plans show themselves."

He smirked. "Sounds like someone's been spending too much time with me."

She rolled her eyes, but the corner of her mouth quirked up despite herself. "Don't flatter yourself."

They continued through the streets, the sounds of the market fading slightly as they neared their destination.

The Golden Leaf Inn stood at the end of a narrow lane, its sign swinging gently in the breeze. The building was modest but well-kept, its walls painted with scenes of lush gardens and flowering trees. It exuded a quiet warmth, a welcome respite from the bustle of the market.

Pari ran ahead, her excitement bubbling over.

"This is it! I've seen this place," she exclaimed, pointing to the sign. "Can we go in?"

"We'll get rooms," Farah said. "Then we can figure out our next steps."

Yasher gave her a mock salute. "As you wish, Phoenix."

She shook her head, leading the way toward the inn's entrance. The door creaked slightly as it opened, the scent of warm bread and woodsmoke wafting out to greet them.

The interior of the Golden Leaf Inn was as inviting as its exterior, with polished wooden beams supporting a ceiling adorned with dried herbs and flowers. A stone hearth burned gently in one corner, casting a soft, flickering glow across the room.

The innkeeper, a middle-aged woman with a cheerful smile and hair wrapped in a colorful scarf, glanced up from behind the counter.

"Welcome to the Golden Leaf," she greeted warmly. "What can I do for you, travelers?"

Farah stepped forward, adjusting her rucksack. "We'll need two rooms for the night. Preferably close to one another."

The innkeeper nodded, her smile widening. "We have just the thing. Two rooms on the upper floor, directly across from each other. Perfect for families or companions traveling together."

Farah didn't correct the implication, though she could feel Yasher's grin forming at her side.

"Sounds ideal," Yasher said, his tone light but edging toward teasing. "We'll take them."

Farah shot him a look, silencing whatever additional comment he had been about to make. She reached into her rucksack and retrieved the necessary coins, placing them on the counter. The innkeeper took them with a nod of thanks and reached under the counter to retrieve two brass keys.

"Here you are," the woman said, placing the keys on the counter. "Rooms three and four. Upstairs, second door on either side of the hallway. I'll have fresh water to take off the road brought up shortly."

"Thank you," Farah said with a small bow of her head, taking both keys. She handed one to Yasher without a word and turned toward the stairs, motioning for Pari to follow. The little girl bounced after her, and he trailed behind, his footsteps light but deliberate.

The upper hallway was narrow but well-lit, sunlight streaming through a window at the far end. Farah paused at the doors marked with brass numbers. She handed Pari the key to their room and pushed open the door.

The room was modest but clean, with one large bed and a window that looked out over the bustling street below. A simple washbasin stood in one corner, and a neatly folded, colorful quilt lay at the foot of the bed.

"This will do," Farah said, setting her rucksack down on the bed.

Pari climbed onto the bed, her small hands running over the quilt.

"It's cozy," she said with a satisfied nod.

Farah glanced over her shoulder to see Yasher leaning casually against the doorframe of his own room across the hall, the brass key twirling between his fingers.

"Let me guess," he said. "Your room is exactly the same, but somehow you'll complain about it."

Farah rolled her eyes. "Some of us don't spend our time critiquing inns."

"Critique?" Yasher raised an eyebrow. "I was going to

compliment the craftsmanship of the beams. Clearly, I'm underappreciated."

She snorted softly, shaking her head as she began to unpack her things. His teasing might have grated on her nerves at first, but she was beginning to see the humor in it —or, at the very least, tolerate it.

Pari hopped off the bed and skipped to the window, peeking outside.

"I can see the market from here!" she exclaimed. "It's so lively."

Farah joined her, looking out over the colorful streets below. Merchants called out their wares, and the scent of spices and fresh bread wafted through the open window. She allowed herself a moment to take it in, the energy of Banima tugging at something deep within her.

Behind her, Yasher cleared his throat. "I'll let you two settle in. Don't miss me too much."

"Hardly," she replied without turning, though a faint smile touched her lips.

A servant nodded to her as they placed jugs of water in each room, Farah exhaled softly. There was a lot to prepare for—the merchant, the next relic, and whatever complications might arise. But for now, she allowed herself a moment of quiet, the vibrant city below a reminder that not everything was shrouded in duty and shadows.

She set her rucksack down on the bed and turned to Pari, who was already sprawled across the bed, fingers tracing the intricate patterns of the quilt. The little girl's face lit up with curiosity as she explored the room, occasionally running her fingers along the edges of the furniture or peeking into corners like an inquisitive sparrow.

"We'll clean up first," Farah said, breaking the comfortable silence. She picked up the small pitcher of water and the washbasin from the corner table, testing their weight. "No sense walking around the city looking like we've been dragged across the plains."

Pari looked up, her face scrunching in playful protest. "I'm not dirty."

Farah raised an eyebrow, a wry smile tugging at her lips. "You've been traveling the same road we have, Little Divine. You'll wash too."

Yasher, still leaning against the doorframe of his room across the hall, chuckled. "A command from the Hand herself. You'd better listen, Pari."

Farah shot him a look, but it lacked the sharpness she might've intended.

"You could do with a wash yourself, gharib," she said, her tone lightly teasing. "I've seen less dust on ruins."

Yasher grinned, brushing his hands against his travel-worn trousers as if to demonstrate the point. "Fair enough. But don't forget, I clean up well."

"Then prove it," she said simply, before focusing her attention on filling the washbasin. The quiet confidence in her voice seemed to amuse him more than deter him, and she caught his smirk as he retreated into his own room.

"Do you think they have a proper bathhouse here?" Pari asked, sitting up and hugging her knees as she watched Farah.

"They should," Farah replied. "We'll ask downstairs after we've cleaned up a bit."

With the washbasin filled, she handed Pari a clean cloth.

"Start with your face and hands," Farah instructed gently, turning back to grab her own small towel. The ritual of washing off the road felt grounding, a way to shed the weariness of travel and prepare for what lay ahead.

Across the hall, the sound of Yasher humming a cheerful tune floated through the open door. Farah paused mid-swipe, her cloth against her arm, and rolled her eyes. "Does he ever stop?"

Pari giggled, scrubbing at her cheeks. "He's funny."

"Funny isn't the word I'd use," Farah muttered, though her lips quirked upward for a moment before she resumed cleaning herself.

A short while later, they stepped back into the hallway, feeling somewhat refreshed. Yasher joined them, his hair damp and face free of the road grime that had clung to him since the caravan.

He spread his arms theatrically. "Well? Do I pass inspection?"

Pari giggled again, giving him an exaggerated once-over. "You look less dusty now."

Farah shook her head, a small smile slipping through despite herself. "Let's go downstairs. The innkeeper mentioned a meal, and after that, we can start asking around for the merchant."

They descended the staircase, the warm light of the common room enveloping them once more. The scents of roasted meat, fresh bread, and spiced tea filled the air, and Farah's stomach growled softly in response. Yasher caught the sound and raised an eyebrow, but she ignored him, leading Pari to a table near the hearth.

The innkeeper bustled over, her scarf swaying as she moved.

"I hope the rooms are to your liking," she said with a smile, setting down three cups of tea.

"They're wonderful," Farah replied, nodding gratefully. "And the warmth of this place is even better."

"Good to hear," the woman said, placing a small tray of

flatbreads and spreads on the table. "This will tide you over while we finish preparing the main meal."

Yasher reached for a piece of bread, but Farah intercepted his hand with a sharp look. "Wait for Pari."

"Of course, Phoenix," Yasher said, withdrawing his hand with an exaggerated show of contrition. Pari giggled as she grabbed a piece herself, and Farah allowed herself a soft chuckle before taking her own.

The meal that followed was simple but hearty, a welcome change from the dried rations of the road. As they ate, she began to plan her next move.

Yasher leaned back in his chair, swirling the tea in his cup. "So, what's the approach? Are we asking directly about this merchant, or do we keep it vague?"

"Vague," Farah said immediately, meeting his gaze. "We don't know who might be listening."

He nodded thoughtfully, his demeanor serious for once. "Fair enough. What do we know about this merchant?"

"Not much," she admitted. "But merchants who deal in rare items tend to leave a trail. Someone in the city will know where to find him."

Pari looked up from her plate, her expression curious. "Is the relic really important?"

Farah hesitated, then nodded. "It could be. The Mashyana believes it might help with the unrest from Tamidh and... other issues we're facing."

Yasher raised an eyebrow, his voice low. "Other issues? Like the rebels?"

Farah stiffened but didn't look away. "Among other things." Mozhde's gaunt face with her blood-speckled lips flashed in her mind.

The weight of her words hung in the air for a moment before Yasher leaned forward, his tone lighter. "Well then, I suppose we should tread carefully. Don't worry. I'll be the picture of discretion."

"I'll believe that when I see it," she replied, though her tone was more teasing than harsh.

They finished their meal in relative silence. She stood first, brushing crumbs from her tunic.

"I'll speak to the innkeeper," she said. "Stay here."

As she walked toward the counter, her thoughts swirled. Finding the relics, the rebels, the wasting disease, the Mashyana's expectations—everything felt precariously balanced.

CHAPTER 16

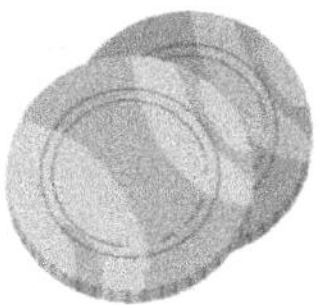

Yasher took a deep breath as he and Farah stood before the closed door of the antiquities shop, its heavy wooden sign creaking slightly in the breeze.

The street behind them bustled with life—merchants hawking wares, children darting between the brightly painted stalls—but the vibrant chaos seemed muted compared to the stillness of the shop. The frustration that radiated off of her wasn't helped by the fact that the shop was, apparently, shut tight.

They'd spoken with so many people, starting yesterday evening, picking back up this morning after a deep sleep on a real bed at the inn.

Farah glanced at the locked door, her arms crossed as she regarded it with a mixture of frustration and wariness.

"I guess the merchant isn't home," she said, her voice clipped. Disappointment flickered across her face but vanished as quickly as it came.

"Maybe he's just running late," Yasher offered, leaning back against the frame of the building and forcing a casual tone. "Or maybe he's having a meal. Everyone needs to eat."

Farah shot him a skeptical glance, her dark eyes sharp. "Midday, Yasher. This shop is supposed to be open."

"Well, I wouldn't expect punctuality to be a universal trait," he replied, a smirk tugging at his lips. "Especially not in a place like this, where everyone seems to run on their own schedule."

Her frown deepened, irritation visible in the taut line of her mouth. "This is the fifth shop we've visited, and we're no closer to finding the relic. We're wasting time."

He rubbed the back of his neck, his own unease surfacing. The long hours spent wandering the streets of Banima had left them with little more than vague rumors and frustrating dead ends. Pari, who had declared herself unnecessary for this leg of the journey, had wandered back to the inn hours ago, leaving the two of them to puzzle out their next steps alone.

"What do you suggest?" he asked, gesturing at the door. "Break it down? That would certainly get us noticed."

"I suggest we find someone who actually knows something," she replied, her tone laced with exasperation. She cast a glance down the street, her expression shifting to one of determination. "I'll check the traders near the square. They might have information we've missed."

"And leave me to... what? Knock on doors until someone answers?" Yasher arched a brow. "Not that I'm opposed to improvisation, but it would be nice to have a plan."

"Use your charm," she said, her voice dripping with sarcasm. "You're good at getting people to talk, aren't you?"

He grinned at that, leaning closer with a mock-serious expression. "Phoenix, was that a compliment?"

"It was an observation," she retorted, brushing past him and heading toward the square. "Don't waste it."

He watched her go, shaking his head in amusement. Despite her sharp edges, there was something new in her barbs, maybe even a little banter?

Turning back to the door, he knocked once for good measure. No answer. He sighed, stepping away and scanning the marketplace for a likely informant. The stalls sprawled out before him, their colorful canopies shielding an array of goods—jewelry, fabrics, spices, and more. The air was thick with the scent of roasted nuts and the faint tang of the river.

He wandered toward a stall draped with bolts of vividly dyed cloth, the colors shimmering in the sunlight. The merchant, a wiry man with a keen eye, looked up as Yasher approached.

"Looking for something special, gharib?" the merchant asked, his tone both curious and guarded.

"Depends on what you've got," Yasher replied with an easy smile, running a hand over the edge of a deep crimson bolt. "Beautiful work. But I'm actually looking for information."

The merchant's brow furrowed. "Information costs more than fabric, I'm afraid."

"Fair enough." Yasher pulled a few coins from his pocket, letting them glint in the sunlight. "I'm trying to find a particular merchant—someone who deals in... unusual items."

The man's eyes narrowed, but his interest was piqued. "Unusual, you say?"

"Antiquities, trinkets, that sort of thing." Yasher leaned in slightly, lowering his voice. "I've heard there's someone in town who specializes in rare finds."

The merchant stroked his chin, glancing around the market as if ensuring no one else was listening. "There's a man near the docks. Keeps to himself, but he's known for having oddities. If he likes you, he might show you something special."

"Sounds promising." Yasher slid the coins onto the counter, watching as the merchant's fingers deftly swept them away. "Anything I should know before I visit?"

The merchant hesitated, then shrugged. "He doesn't take kindly to time-wasters. Best go with purpose."

"Noted." He nodded, tossing a coin before turning toward the docks, the faint thrill of progress quickening his steps. At least it wasn't a shop they'd already scoured through, or been dismissed and delayed at.

The docks had their own rhythm, a pulse that thrummed beneath the city's surface like a hidden current.

The steady lap of the river against wooden pilings blended with the creak of mooring ropes and the low murmur of traders exchanging coin for cargo. Barges and flat-bottomed boats lined the waterfront, their hulls slick with river silt, their sails furled against the sluggish afternoon breeze.

The air was thick with the scent of damp wood, sun-warmed reeds, and the faint metallic tang of fish pulled fresh from the water. Here, the city's order frayed at the edges. Merchants haggled in clipped tones, dockhands called out as they hoisted crates of grain and dried fruit onto waiting carts, and the occasional ferryman maneuvered his narrow skiff through the tangle of vessels.

He spotted the shop nestled between two larger buildings, its weathered facade almost lost amidst the busyness of the docks. The wooden door was slightly ajar, and Yasher hesitated before stepping inside. The Eye thrummed faintly in his pocket, a quiet reminder of the luck that had brought him this far.

The shop's interior was dim, the only light coming from a few narrow windows high on the walls. Shelves lined the room, crammed with relics and curiosities—ornate jewelry, rusted tools, strange carvings. Each item seemed to whisper its own story, and Yasher couldn't help but feel a flicker of awe.

"Looking for something?" The voice was rough, gravelly, and it came from an elderly man emerging from behind a cluttered counter.

"I'm hoping you can help me," Yasher said, his tone carefully measured. "I've heard you deal in rare finds."

The man's eyes narrowed, his suspicion palpable. "Rare finds aren't for just anyone. What's your business?"

"I'm searching for something specific," Yasher replied, stepping closer. "A relic. I don't have much detail, but it's supposed to be important."

The merchant studied him for a long moment, his gaze sharp. "Relics are dangerous business, gharib. You sure you know what you're getting into?"

"I'm here, aren't I?" he countered, keeping his tone light despite the weight of the man's words. "Do you have anything that might fit the bill?"

The merchant's expression softened slightly, a hint of intrigue sparking in his eyes. "Perhaps. But information doesn't come free."

"Of course it doesn't," Yasher muttered under his breath, already reaching for his coin pouch. He handed over a few coins, watching as the merchant pocketed them with a satisfied grunt.

"There's a relic," the man said slowly. "But it's not here. If you're serious, I can point you in the right direction."

Yasher felt his heart quicken. "Where?"

The merchant gestured toward a shelf laden with maps. "There's a place outside the city, across the river in the ruins in the old city. If you're brave enough to go looking, you might find what you're after."

His luck swung back and forth in his mind, the pendulum moving as it did every time he was faced with a choice that it refused to help him with.

"Consider me brave," he said at last, and his luck warmed. "Where do I start?"

The merchant chuckled, a low, rasping sound that filled the dimly lit shop. He shuffled toward the shelf, his movements slow but deliberate, and plucked a rolled parchment from among the clutter. The map he unfurled was weathered, its edges frayed and stained with time. As he spread it out across the counter, Yasher leaned in, his curiosity outweighing the unease prickling at the back of his neck.

"This here," the merchant said, tapping a spot marked with faint lines and faded symbols, "is the place you'll want to look. The ruins sit just at the Azhdahak foothills, near a dry creek bed on the other side of the river."

Yasher studied the map closely, committing the landmarks to memory. The lines were crude, the details sparse, but he could make out the general direction.

"And what exactly should I be looking for?" Yasher asked, keeping his voice casual, though his pulse quickened.

The merchant straightened, his expression guarded. "You'll know it when you see it. These relics have a way of making themselves known to those who seek them."

"That's vague," Yasher muttered, his fingers tracing the map's faded lines. "Are you sure you can't be more specific?"

The merchant narrowed his eyes. "The less you know, the better. These relics aren't trinkets to be toyed with, gharib. They carry weight—power that most can't comprehend. The wrong hands can turn them into tools of destruction."

"Good thing I'm not the destructive type," Yasher replied, flashing a grin that he hoped masked the unease curling in his gut. "How far are we talking?"

"You'll need to hire a boat to get across the river, but it should be an easy trek to the ruins," the merchant said, rolling the map and handing it over. "But tread carefully. The area is treacherous, and you won't be the only one interested in what's hidden there."

Yasher accepted the map, his grip firm. "Thanks for the warning. Anything else I should know?"

The merchant's gaze lingered, sharp and searching. "Yes. Don't go alone."

Yasher frowned. "Why? Are there guards? Bandits?"

"There are things worse than bandits in those ruins," the merchant said cryptically. "And the relic doesn't give itself up without a price."

He bristled at the ominous tone but nodded. "I'll keep that in mind."

The merchant gave a curt nod, stepping back into the shadows of his cluttered domain. Yasher took a final glance around the shop, his eyes catching on a collection of tarnished artifacts displayed haphazardly on a nearby shelf. He had a fleeting thought to inquire further, but the merchant's retreat signaled the conversation was over.

Tucking the map into his coat, Yasher turned and pushed open the shop door. The vibrant energy of Banima's streets greeted him, a stark contrast to the oppressive air of the shop. The sun had shifted higher in the sky, casting warm light over the colorful stalls and bustling crowds. The scent of spices and fresh bread wafted toward him, grounding him momentarily in the lively chaos of the city.

Farah was waiting where they had parted, leaning against a stone pillar with her arms crossed. Her eyes locked onto him the moment he stepped out, narrowing slightly as if she could read the tension in his posture.

"Well?" she asked, pushing off the pillar and approaching him. "Did you learn anything, or should I start breaking into shops?"

Yasher smirked, her bluntness cutting through the haze of unease. "Relax, Phoenix. I've got a lead."

Her gaze flicked to the rolled map in his hand, suspicion etched into her features. "And?"

"And," he said, holding the map up like a trophy, "we've got a location. Ruins outside the city, on the other side of the river. Apparently, it's treacherous, so we'll need to be careful."

Farah's eyes narrowed further. "Treacherous how?"

"Didn't get specifics," Yasher admitted, shrugging. "The merchant was cryptic—something about the relic not giving itself up without a price."

Her lips pressed into a thin line. "Conveniently vague."

"Isn't it always?" he replied, offering a lopsided grin. "But I'm sure we can handle it. Between your... skills and my luck and charm, we make a decent team."

She rolled her eyes, though there was a hint of a smirk tugging at the corner of her mouth. "Let's hope your luck and charm is enough to keep us alive."

"Optimism suits you, Phoenix," he teased, falling into step beside her as they began making their way back toward the inn.

"Let's prepare for the journey," she said, ignoring his

jab. "We'll leave in the morning. If this lead turns out to be a dead end, I'm holding you responsible."

Yasher laughed, the sound light and carefree. "Fair enough. But you might want to save some of that frustration for whatever 'worse-than-bandits' surprises we're walking into."

Farah didn't respond, her expression turning serious as her gaze shifted toward the Azhdahak mountains in the distance. Yasher followed her line of sight, a thrill of anticipation sparking in his chest.

———

THE ROOM FELT COCOONED in warmth, the soft glow of the fireplace casting flickering shadows across the worn wooden walls of the inn. Yasher leaned back in his chair, a half-empty bottle of spiced wine on the table between him and Farah. They had spent most of the evening pulling a plan together, almost as equals, and now sat in companionable silence.

Pari was sound asleep in the adjacent room, her quiet snores faintly audible through the closed door. For once, he felt the weight of the day ease slightly. Here, in the quiet of the inn, with the firelight painting Farah's features in gold, it was almost possible to forget the looming danger of the ruins they'd face tomorrow.

She sat across from him, her posture relaxed but guarded. Her fingers curled around her cup, the rim just barely brushing her lips before she took a sip of the wine. She seemed thoughtful, her gaze flicking between the flames and the table, as though measuring the distance between two worlds.

"You know," Yasher began, breaking the silence, "you're

surprisingly good company when you're not trying to stab someone. That someone being me, of course."

Her brow arched, her lips twitching into what might have been the start of a smile. "That was a weak compliment from you, gharib."

"It's the best you'll get from me tonight," he replied with a grin, raising his own cup in a mock toast. "Don't let it go to your head."

She took another sip of her wine, her gaze steady on him now. "I should be insulted."

"Should you, though?" He leaned forward, resting his elbows on the table. "Because I think you're starting to like me."

Farah let out a quiet laugh, the sound low and almost unfamiliar. "You're delusional."

"Am I?" Yasher countered, his grin widening. "You've been less... sharp with me lately. Admit it. I've grown on you."

She shook her head, but the faintest trace of amusement softened her features. "You're insufferable."

"And yet," he said, lifting his cup again, feeling a strange rush every time she called him insufferable, "here we are. Sharing a drink. No daggers drawn, no sharp pain in my wrist."

She tilted her head, studying him for a moment. "Maybe I just haven't decided whether you're worth the effort."

"Oh, I'm definitely worth the effort," he replied, his tone playful. But then his smile dimmed slightly, sincerity creeping into his voice. "And I'm glad I'm here to help, Phoenix. Despite everything."

She looked away, her expression turning thoughtful.

The firelight caught the edges of her face, highlighting the quiet strength in her features.

"You don't have to be here," she said softly. "You could've left. Back when we got to Banima. Or even before that, moving on with the caravan."

"True," he admitted, leaning back in his chair. "But I didn't."

Her gaze shifted back to him, her eyes searching his face for something. "Why?"

"Because," he said, his tone turning serious, "you've got this way of making everything feel like it matters. Like these relics, this kingdom—it all means something to you. And maybe that's something worth sticking around for, just to see where it all leads."

For a moment, neither of them spoke. The crackle of the fire filled the silence, a comforting backdrop to the tension that hung between them. Farah's fingers tightened around her cup, and she looked down, as if the weight of his words was too much to meet head-on.

"You talk a lot," she said finally, her voice quieter now. "But sometimes, you say things that make me think you actually believe in something."

"Don't sound so surprised," he said with a soft chuckle. "I'm capable of more than just running my mouth."

Farah's lips curved into a small, genuine smile—brief but unmistakable. "I'll believe it when I see it."

They lapsed into a comfortable silence again, each lost in their thoughts. Yasher let his gaze wander, taking in the room's warm glow, the way the firelight painted everything in shades of gold and amber. For a moment, it felt like the weight of the world had lifted, like this quiet moment could stretch on forever.

He reached for the bottle, pouring another small splash of wine into his cup before gesturing toward hers. "More?"

Farah hesitated, then nodded, holding out her cup. "Why not? It's not like we'll get much sleep anyway."

As he poured, their hands brushed briefly, a fleeting contact that sent a spark up his arm. He glanced at her, wondering if she felt it too, but her expression was unreadable.

"To tomorrow," he said, raising his cup in a toast. "Hopefully with a relic at the end of the day."

Farah clinked her cup against his, her smile faint but present. "To surviving it."

They drank in unison, the warmth of the wine mingling with the heat of the fire. Yasher set his cup down, his fingers tapping idly against the wood.

"Farah," he said after a moment, his voice softer now. "I know I joke a lot, but... if there's anything you're worried about, you can tell me. I'm here. For whatever you need — to listen, to be a friend."

She didn't reply immediately, her gaze fixed on the fire. When she finally spoke, her voice was barely above a whisper. "I can't afford friends. Not even you."

"I get that," he said, his tone steady, "but maybe... you can do with some additional support."

Her eyes flicked to him, and for the briefest moment, he saw something raw and unguarded in her expression. Then she looked away, her walls sliding back into place.

"We'll see," she said simply, her voice carrying a note of finality.

He didn't press her. Instead, he let the silence settle between them. For now, it was enough to be here, drinking wine with someone he didn't think still wanted to kill him in his sleep.

CHAPTER 17

FARAH FELT the weight of the mountains pressing down on her shoulders as she, Yasher, and Pari stepped deeper into the ancient ruins. The air was crisp, carrying the scent of damp stone and moss. The remnants of what had once been a thriving city loomed around them, including structures built into the hills themselves. The ruins stood as silent sentinels, the cracked stone walls intertwined with vines and patches of wildflowers that had crept through the decay.

Pari walked just ahead of them, her small fingers grazing the faded murals that adorned one of the crumbling walls. The colors, though dulled by time, still spoke of a vibrant past, the images showing scenes of joyous festivals and offerings to gods long forgotten.

"Stay close, Pari," Farah called, her voice sharper than she intended. The unease gnawing at her made it hard to sound calm. "This place isn't safe. You pushed to us to come, but you have to listen, remember?"

The little girl turned, her eyes wide with curiosity.

"It's so beautiful," she whispered. "Do you think the gods still watch over places like this?"

Farah hesitated, then crouched down to Pari's level, brushing dirt from her small hands. "Maybe. But the gods would also want you to stay safe. So please, stay near the entrance while Yasher and I look around."

Pari nodded solemnly. "I'll keep watch. Rashnu says I'm good at watching."

Farah exchanged a glance with Yasher, and he gave a small shrug, as if to say, *What can you do?*

"Good," Farah said, placing a hand briefly on Pari's head before standing. "We won't be long."

As they entered the gaping archway indicated on the map, Yasher took a long look at the stone carvings above it.

"Looks welcoming," he said dryly, his hand resting on the hilt of his dagger.

Inside, the air was cooler, the dampness clinging to their skin. Shafts of light filtered through cracks in the ceiling, illuminating the floor in uneven patches. The stones were cracked and worn, a testament to centuries of abandonment. Farah's Talent hummed faintly in the back of her mind, an ever-present awareness of the scattered remnants of decorations and debris of metal embedded all around them.

"This is the place," she murmured, clutching the map tightly. Her heart raced as she studied the interior, searching for any signs of traps or hidden dangers.

Yasher crouched near a faded mosaic on the floor, his fingers brushing against its edges.

"Keep your focus," Farah said, scanning the corridor ahead. "This place wasn't meant to welcome visitors."

Her words were barely out when Yasher froze, his eyes

darting to a faint indentation in the floor a few steps ahead. "Farah, wait."

She followed his gaze, her chest tightening when she saw the faint outline of a pressure plate nestled among the worn stones. Her Talent flared, sensing the metallic mechanisms buried beneath the stone.

"Good catch," she said softly, kneeling beside it. She extended her Talent, guiding the unseen metal components to lock in place, rendering the trap harmless. The pressure plate clicked softly, and she exhaled in relief.

"One down," Yasher muttered. "How many more do you think there are?"

"More than I'd like," Farah replied grimly. "Stay alert."

They moved cautiously through the ruin, the walls closing in as the corridor narrowed. The silence was oppressive, broken only by the soft scuff of their boots against the stone. Farah's Talent continued to pulse faintly at the metal that surrounded them.

A sudden shift in the air made her pause. She held up a hand. "Wait."

"What is it?" he whispered, his voice low.

Farah pointed to the ceiling above them, where a network of wooden beams and stone fragments hung precariously, held in place by a system of ropes and pulleys. One wrong move would send the entire structure crashing down.

"It's another trap," she said, her voice tense. "Stay back."

She stepped forward, her Talent guiding her as she carefully manipulated the metal pulleys, easing the tension on the ropes until the trap was rendered inert above their heads.

"Clear," she said, stepping back. Her heart was pounding, but she couldn't afford to let the fear take hold.

"Efficient," Yasher said with a faint smirk. "I could have used you on a few... excursions in my past."

Farah gave him a withering look but didn't reply. The faint glow of a larger chamber up ahead caught her eye, drawing her forward.

They emerged into what had once been a grand hall, its walls adorned with murals depicting gods and mortals locked in a dance of devotion. Though faded, the images retained an ethereal beauty, the colors blending in a way that seemed almost alive.

Farah's breath caught in her throat. "There it is," she said, her voice hushed.

At the far end of the hall, bathed in a faint green glow, sat the relic in a semi-crushed ornate box. The Shard of Ameretat.

Its light pulsed faintly, a beacon amidst the gloom, a similar filigree to the relic that Yasher carried framing the green crystal. Dust covered the destroyed box and the large cedar beam that must have fallen on it years ago.

Yasher's gaze followed hers, his expression shifting to one of awe.

"It's real," he murmured. "The old man wasn't lying."

Farah moved cautiously toward the pedestal, her senses on high alert. The Shard's glow intensified as they approached, and her Talent hummed in response, the connection almost tangible.

"Careful," Yasher said, his tone serious. "If this place is as old as it looks, there's no telling what kind of protections it has."

Farah nodded, extending her Talent to scan the

pedestal for hidden mechanisms. Her fingers brushed against the stone as she searched for signs of danger.

"It seems—"

Before she could finish, a faint metallic click echoed through the chamber. Farah's eyes widened as she realized her mistake. Whatever trap she'd activated was with her Talent, not from mundane means.

"Back!" she hissed, grabbing Yasher's arm and pulling him away from the pedestal just as a section of the floor gave way, revealing a deep pit lined with sharpened stakes.

He let out a low whistle. "That was close."

Her heart roared as she steadied herself, her gaze fixed on the Shard.

She stepped forward again, this time more cautiously. A marble pedestal lay broken before the shard, its surface smooth despite the dust that had settled on the cracked division. The Shard of Ameretat sat in the center of it all, its glow a stark contrast to the dim chamber.

Reaching out, Farah cradled the relic in her palm. The warmth of it spread through her, a pulse of energy that seemed to echo the heartbeat of the ruins themselves.

"We have it," she said, her voice trembling with relief. But even as she spoke, a faint rustling sound reached her ears, sending a chill down her spine. "We have what we came for. Let's—"

Before she could finish, the door burst open, the hinges pulled loose but still attached, and a group of eight rugged figures stormed into the chamber, their expressions menacing. The sight of them made Farah's blood run cold.

"Look what we have here," one of them sneered, his gaze landing on the box. "Seems like we caught ourselves some treasure hunters."

"Back!" Farah shouted, instinctively stepping in front of

Yasher. She calmed her breathing as Rostam drilled into her before letting her emotions push her heartbeat into her ears. The bandits pushed Pari towards them, the little girl stumbling as she ran towards the two of them. She ran up and hugged Yasher's leg before cowering behind them.

Adrenaline pumped through her veins, sharpening her focus. She could hear Yasher moving beside her, ready to engage, but the bandits were overwhelming in numbers.

"Take Pari and get outside," she said, putting the relic in one of her interior pockets before grabbing her daggers from her belt.

"Twelve hells I will. There's too many of them for even you to take on your own." Yasher mumbled back before dropping down in front of the little girl.

"On my back, Little Divine." He said, helping her up. "We're going to need to move quickly. But if I tell you to drop, you drop and run for the boat as fast as you can. We'll be right behind, I promise."

She nodded solemnly, whispering something that Farah couldn't catch, but climbed up on his back, wrapping her legs around his waist and holding his shoulders.

With a swift motion, she pulled the metal from the walls as she hummed, turning nails and small metal pieces into projectiles, launching them towards the bandits. She took down three of them, their necks torn to shreds with the shrapnel she created, and injured three others, grabbing their legs and arms.

"Out, now!" Farah urged, her voice fierce with determination. She pulled two large plates from the walls, creating a barrier of sorts as they moved forward.

Yasher threw his boot dagger he'd grabbed as he stood up, Pari on his back, taking down another one of the bandits, his dagger stuck in his neck. They both moved

216

forward, Farah humming again and pulling the shrapnel she created that was not currently in one of the bodies towards her before launching it again.

They moved forward as one. The bandits in disarray, realizing half of their group was bleeding out on the floor.

One of the bandits charged toward Yasher, club raised high, aiming for Pari. Farah's heart skipped a beat, her muscles tensing, ready to move. But before she could react, Yasher was already in motion. He spun, pulling Pari off his back with one arm, yanking her out of harm's way as the bandit's strike sliced through empty air. In the same fluid motion, Yasher's other hand shot out, his dagger flashing like lightning before it sank into the bandit's side.

The man crumpled to the ground with a gasp, his body twitching once before stilling. Yasher stood over him, his breath steady, eyes cold and focused. Farah watched him, momentarily stunned. The way he moved was like he had done this a thousand times, each motion precise, effortless. There was no hesitation, no wasted movement. It was brutal, efficient, and she couldn't help but feel a flicker of admiration.

She pulled his boot dagger to her grasp with her Talent, tossing it back to him before pulling the shrapnel she'd created, spinning it around the remaining bandits to force them over to the side of the room.

He scooped up Pari, putting her on his back again before falling right behind her, running for the door. They each dragged one of the doors, pushing them back into place, Farah humming again to melt the hinges and remaining parts of the lock in place. They both leaned their heads against the door for a moment, and she couldn't control the grin that spread across her own face to match his own.

His eyes focused hard and quick, and before she could ask what was wrong he threw the dagger that was still in his hand directly over her shoulder. She spun, her own at the ready and watched another bandit who was standing in the shadows drop to his knees before completely collapsing at her feet.

"We need to get out of here." She took a deep breath in, putting her hand on the door as they banged and bashed on it from the other side. "This won't hold that long."

He walked over to the corpse, grabbing his dagger back and cleaning it off on the dead man's shirt.

"Let's go then." He picked up Pari, helping her onto his back. "Hold on tight, Little Divine."

They moved quickly, leaving behind the building they'd trapped the bandits in, and rushing out to the trees and scrub bushes, breaking into a run as soon as they could. Farah took one last glance at the ruins, the weight of the Shard pressing against her chest.

"Thank the gods we thought to hide the boat before," Yasher said, guiding Pari down from his back. He walked over to a layer of scrub and branches that hid their small dinghy they'd hired for the day. A knot released in her chest when she realized it was still there, intact.

They scrambled into the boat, Yasher taking the oars up, Farah pushing off from the shore, and Pari huddled in the middle of the boat.

***

FARAH FELT the need to hold her breath as they crossed the river, her gaze fixed on the distant shore as though the ruins themselves might reach out to pull them back. The knot of tension coiled in her stomach eased slightly as she looked down at Pari, who lay curled in her lap, her soft breathing as she calmed from the fight they'd just escaped. Yasher, seated at the stern, pulled the oars with steady determination, his expression tight with focus. Even when he glanced her way, offering a fleeting smile, the strain in his eyes betrayed his wariness.

The noise of the Banima docks hit her all at once as the small dinghy bumped against the pier. The shouts of dockworkers and the clatter of cranes lifting goods onto ships were jarring after the suffocating silence of the ruins.

The sun had begun its slow descent, bathing the waterfront in hues of orange and gold, but Farah felt no peace in the beauty of the moment. Her body ached, her Talent was depleted, and the relic pressed heavily against her chest, hidden within her vest.

Yasher helped Pari out of the boat, scooping her up in his arms when her legs wobbled. The little girl barely stirred, settling her head against his shoulder.

Farah lingered by the dock, her eyes flickering back toward the water's edge. The far shore was empty, but her unease remained. They had left the ruins, but the danger felt far from over.

"Well," he said softly as they moved away from the water, "that was invigorating." His voice carried its usual humor, but there was a weariness to it, a crack in his usual armor. "Please tell me we didn't risk our lives for nothing. Did we actually get the relic?"

She patted her vest, the weight of the Shard of Ameretat reassuring even as its presence seemed to draw a shadow across her thoughts.

"We have it," she said, her voice low. "But don't mistake this for a victory yet."

Yasher didn't reply, but his brow furrowed as he adjusted Pari in his arms.

They made their way through the bustling streets in silence, the sights and sounds of Banima muted to Farah's ears. The vibrant murals and fragrant market stalls, usually so lively, seemed distant and unreal after the cold, oppressive halls of the ruins.

By the time they reached the inn, Farah felt like her legs might give out. The warm, inviting air of the common room enveloped them as they stepped inside, the scent of spiced meats and fresh bread momentarily lifting her spirits. Yasher carried Pari upstairs, and Farah followed, the familiar creak of the wooden steps grounding her.

In their shared room, he carefully placed Pari on the bed, tucking her under the covers with a gentleness that caught her off guard after removing the little girl's shoes and her headscarf. She felt a pang of gratitude for the child's peaceful sleep, a stark contrast to the storm raging within her, the lack of her Talent reservoir in combination with the rest of the adrenaline she had yet to let go of. It could take hours if not days to restore her Talent, and the loss of it always left her feeling bare, vulnerable.

Her fingers twitched at her sides, as though expecting the familiar surge of power to return. But there was nothing. That hole inside her seemed to widen with every passing moment. Rostam had made sure that she had been trained to fight, to protect, without her Talent, but even his lessons had never been enough to quell the fear that crept in when it was gone. She had always been able to fall back on it, a shield, a force to control the chaos. Now, it felt like she was fighting without armor, exposed and vulnerable in a way that always left her unsettled.

Yasher leaned against the doorframe, his arms crossed.

"You look like you could use a drink," he said. "I've got another bottle in my room. Come on."

She hesitated, glancing at Pari's sleeping form. The pull of the relic weighed heavily on her, but the thought of sitting in her own thoughts, alone, was unbearable.

"Fine," she muttered, following him out of the room and leaving the door ajar.

His room was nearly identical to hers, but the warmth of the low fire and the faint scent of spices gave it a more lived-in feel. He moved to the fireplace, feeding it until the flames roared softly, casting golden light across the room. He poured two glasses from a dark bottle and handed one to her, his fingers brushing hers briefly.

"To surviving," he said with a crooked smile, raising his glass.

"To surviving," she echoed, taking a sip. The liquid was smooth and warm, spreading through her chest like a balm against the cold ache of her exhaustion.

She pulled the shard out of her vest pocket and placed it on the table, the cool surface of the relic grounding her as it sat there.

She stared at it for a moment, her eyes tracing the intricate details, the faint shimmer in the firelight. She felt the weight of her duty tied to this piece of the gods, pulling her back to the Citadel and the Mashyana.

Her gaze shifted, drawn to Yasher. He was sitting back now, his eyes focused on the flames, his usual playfulness absent. There was something different about him in the quiet of the room, the light catching his features in a way that made him seem more... present.

She blinked, feeling a slight tug of something unfamiliar in her chest. The relic, important as it was, felt like it had faded into the background, its weight momentarily lightened by the quiet presence of the man across from her.

"You know," he said, breaking the silence, "I didn't think we'd make it out of there."

She raised an eyebrow, taking another sip of her drink. "You're usually more optimistic."

"Not in ruins full of traps and people trying to kill us," he replied, his tone lighter now. "I mean, really. You could've warned me about the homicidal architecture. I guess that's what the old man meant by things worse than bandits."

She let out a quiet laugh, surprising herself. "And ruin the surprise? Where's the fun in that?"

He grinned, but then his expression turned serious. "We risked a lot back there. For something you're not even sure about."

She tensed, her fingers tightening around her glass. "I don't need certainty. I need results. This relic, it's part of something bigger. Something that could heal Emari."

"Or something that could destroy it," he said quietly, his eyes on the shard.

Her breath caught, the weight of his words sinking into her. She had thought the same thing, but hearing it out loud made it feel more real, more dangerous.

"I don't expect you to understand," she said finally, her voice steady. "This isn't your fight."

"Maybe not," he replied, his gaze shifting to meet hers, "but for now, I'm here, so it makes it, at least a little bit, my fight."

The sincerity in his voice made her chest ache, a feeling she quickly buried. "You don't owe me anything."

"No," he said with a faint smile. "But maybe I want to be here anyway."

Farah looked away, the firelight dancing in her peripheral vision. She didn't know what to say to that, so she said nothing, letting the silence stretch between them.

Yasher leaned back in his chair, swirling the liquid in his glass. "You know, at the end of the day, this is just a job. You pour your whole heart into this."

She shot him a look, but there was no malice in it. "I don't have a choice."

"There's always a choice," he said softly, his eyes searching hers. "You just have to decide what matters more. Your duty or yourself."

Her lips parted, but no words came. His question lingered in the air, unanswered, as the fire crackled on.

Her grip tightened on her glass as his words hung in the air. The firelight reflected in his eyes, making them appear deeper, more piercing than she cared to admit. She didn't like the way his words made her feel, like he'd peeled back a layer of her armor and left her exposed.

"I don't see the two as separate," she said finally, her voice quieter now. "My duty is who I am. Without it... there's nothing else."

He tilted his head, watching her carefully. "That sounds like something someone told you. Not something you decided for yourself."

She felt the sting of his words, but she refused to let him see how deeply they struck. "You don't understand. The Mashyana took me in when I had no one. She gave me a purpose, a family, a place in the world. My duty isn't just an obligation—it's everything."

"Everything?" He leaned forward, resting his elbows on his knees. "Even if it means giving up your own freedom? Your own happiness? I wasn't the one to bring your queen into this conversation."

She frowned, exhaustion warring with wanting to defend. "Freedom and happiness are luxuries for people who aren't one of the Beloveds, and especially not if you are the Hand."

"That's convenient," he said, his voice soft but edged with challenge. "If you tell yourself that enough times, you might even believe it."

Her jaw tightened, and she looked away, her gaze fixed on the flickering flames. She didn't have a response for him, not one she was ready to admit out loud. His words poked at something she had buried long ago—a longing for something more, something she had convinced herself wasn't for her.

"You're insufferable," she muttered, taking another sip of her drink.

"And yet, you're still sitting here with me," Yasher said with a faint smile, leaning back in his chair. "Makes you wonder, doesn't it?"

Farah shot him a look, her expression somewhere between irritation and amusement. "Don't flatter yourself."

He held up his hands in mock surrender. "Just calling it like I see it."

The tension between them maintained, the crackling fire filling the silence. She felt a strange sense of comfort sitting there with him, despite her instinct to keep her walls firmly in place. It was unsettling, how easily he could get under her skin and make her forget—if only for a moment —the weight of her responsibilities.

"Why are you here?" she asked suddenly, her voice cutting through the quiet. "Why do you care about this mission? About me?"

He blinked, caught off guard by her directness. For a

moment, he didn't answer, his gaze drifting to the fire. Then, he sighed, a soft, almost self-deprecating smile tugging at his lips.

"I don't know," he admitted. "At first, it was just... curiosity. You're intriguing, Phoenix. Different from anyone I've ever met. But now..." He paused, his fingers tapping lightly against his glass. "I guess I want to see where this all leads. To see if you're right about the Mashyana. And maybe... because I want to see you succeed."

Her heart stuttered at his words, and she quickly buried the flicker of warmth they sparked. She couldn't let herself get distracted—not now, not with everything at stake.

"Don't make this about me," she said, her tone sharper than she intended. "This is about the relics, the kingdom, the gods."

"Is it?" He leaned forward again, his gaze locking onto hers. "Or is it about you proving something to yourself? To the Mashyana?"

Her breath hitched, and she looked away, her chest tightening. His words hit too close to the truth, a truth she wasn't ready to face. She drained the rest of her glass and set it down with more force than necessary before scooping up the shard.

"I'm going to check on Pari," she said abruptly, standing and heading toward the door.

"Farah," He called after her, his voice soft but insistent. She paused, her hand on the doorknob, but she didn't turn around.

"Goodnight, gharib," she said, her voice steady but distant.

She stepped into the hallway, the warmth of the fire replaced by the cool air of the inn. Her footsteps were quiet as she made her way back to her room, her thoughts a swirling storm of frustration, doubt, and something she couldn't quite name.

Inside, Pari was still fast asleep, her small form tucked snugly under the covers. She leaned against the door, closing her eyes and letting out a long, unsteady breath. Yasher's words echoed in her mind, his gaze lingering in her thoughts.

She pushed it all aside, focusing on the steady rise and fall of Pari's breathing. Whatever his intentions, whatever feelings he stirred within her, they didn't matter. Not now. Her duty was clear, her path set. Everything else was a distraction.

And yet, as she lay down beside Pari, staring up at the ceiling, the flicker of doubt refused to fade.

CHAPTER 18

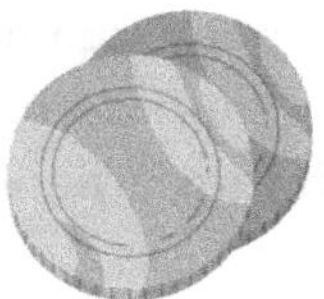

YASHER WOKE the next morning with a thudding head and a dry mouth, the sunlight piercing through the thin curtains of his room like daggers. He blinked a few times, trying to remember how he had ended up sprawled across the bed in last night's clothes. A groan escaped his lips as he sat up, the remnants of the previous night's bottle swirling in his mind like a relentless storm.

"Damn it," he muttered, rubbing his temples, wincing at the pounding in his skull. "What a brilliant way to handle an argument."

The bitter taste of regret for deciding to finish the bottle on his own settled in his stomach alongside the hangover, reminding him of the words they had exchanged, the doubts he had pushed to plant in her mind.

"Ugh," he groaned again, pushing himself to his feet. The wooden floor creaked beneath him as he stumbled toward the washbasin, splashing cold water on his face in an attempt to shake off the fog. It helped a little, but the reality of the situation still felt like a weight pressing down on his chest.

With a sigh, he opened the door and stepped into the hallway, checking her room first and finding it empty. He wandered downstairs to the common area.

The inn was quiet, the early morning sunlight spilling into the space where a few patrons quietly sipped their tea. He scanned the room for any sign of Farah but found only empty chairs and tables. She must have already left.

"Where are you, Phoenix?" he whispered to himself, a pang of unease twisting in his gut.

He needed to apologize, to mend the rift that had formed between them. It had been reckless of him to question her loyalty to the Mashyana, and he regretted letting his skepticism get the better of him.

Determined, he headed down the stairs and out into the bustling streets of Banima. The market was alive with activity, merchants setting up their stalls and calling out to potential customers. The vibrant colors of fruits and textiles filled his vision, a stark contrast to the dull ache still pounding in his head.

As he walked through the market, he kept his eyes peeled for Farah, but she was nowhere in sight. The crowd swirled around him, but he felt like an outsider looking in.

"Yasher!" a familiar voice called out, and he turned to see Pari running toward him, her small frame a whirlwind of energy.

"Hello, my Little Divine," he said, a smile breaking through his hangover haze as he released some of the tension he didn't realize was there.

"I'm hungry," she declared, her eyes shining with excitement. "I was waiting for Farah, but she's still looking for supplies to continue our journey. So, I came to find you!"

"Well, let's get you something to eat, shall we? We can wait for her together."

They found a small stall selling warm bread and pastries, the scent wafting through the air, making Yasher's stomach rumble despite his headache. They settled on a couple of freshly baked rolls, slathered with honey.

Pari dug in with enthusiasm, crumbs dotting her cheeks as she chatted away about the inn and how she wanted to help with the cooking again.

"You're quite the helper, aren't you?" he remarked, watching her with a mix of amusement and fondness.

"Of course! I help Shirin, I help you, I help Farah, I help Rashnu...," Pari replied with a proud grin.

"You are very special, Little Divine," he said, his heart warming at her innocent confidence. "But don't forget, the world can be unpredictable, especially to the special ones."

Pari paused mid-bite, tilting her head. "You're worried about Farah, aren't you?"

"Maybe a little," he admitted, his thoughts drifting back to their argument. "But she'll be back soon."

Pari nodded, but her expression shifted, and he could see a hint of concern in her eyes. "You really care about her, don't you?"

Yasher hesitated, caught off guard by her question.

"I care about both of you," he said, trying to keep his tone light. "We're in this together."

"But you and Farah... you argue a lot," she pointed out, her innocent curiosity digging deeper.

"Yeah, well, that does happen," he replied, brushing off her observation. "Sometimes people have different opinions."

After finishing her bread, Pari leaned closer, her voice

barely above a whisper. "You should tell her that you're sorry. I think she needs to know that you care."

"Good advice, Little Divine," Yasher said, his heart warming at her sincerity. "I will."

The little girl skipped beside him as they walked back to the inn, her energy infectious. Inside, it was still quiet, the rising sun casting a warm glow across the common room. They found a table by the window and settled in to wait.

But as the minutes turned to an hour, Yasher's worry grew.

"I'll go check outside again," he said, trying to reassure Pari. "Stay here, okay? I'll be right back."

"Okay," she chirped, her attention already focused back on the street. "Be careful."

Stepping outside, he gave himself a moment to feel the sun on his face and the cool breeze against his skin. Scanning the streets once more, he hoped to catch a glimpse of Farah among the bustling crowd. But she was still nowhere to be found.

As he wandered through the marketplace, a nagging doubt gnawed at him. What if she had left without him? What if she was angry enough to want to go on alone? He shook his head, trying to dispel the thoughts.

"She wouldn't do that," he muttered. "Not without taking Pari."

Just as he began to turn back, he spotted a flash of curly dark hair and embroidered vest across the square. His heart raced as he pushed through the throngs of people, weaving past merchants and customers, trying to catch up to her.

"Farah!" he called out, his voice barely carrying above the noise of the market.

But she didn't turn around. Instead, she slipped down a narrow alleyway, disappearing from sight. The urgency in his gut kicked in, and he followed her, dodging carts and people as he hurried toward the alley. The Eye shot through with a cold spike, anxiety running down his spine.

"Wait!" he shouted, but his voice was swallowed by the sounds of the people all around.

As he reached the mouth of the alley, he slowed down, the shadows from the buildings casting an eerie light on the cobblestones. He peered down the narrow passage, trying to spot her. "Farah?"

Silence met his call, and a knot of anxiety twisted in his stomach. Suddenly, he heard voices—low and menacing. Yasher's heart raced.

He crept forward, heart pounding in his ears as he maneuvered through the shadows. Peering around the corner, he froze at the sight before him.

Farah stood facing four figures, their postures tense and threatening. Arash, that little shit from the Citadel, and two others—other Beloveds of the Mashyana he assumed— stood menacingly close. They were dressed similarly, their eyes glinting with an intensity that made Yasher's blood run cold.

"What are you doing here, Farah?" Arash sneered, crossing his arms. "You think you can just run off, doing whatever you want to?"

"I thought you'd still be chasing birds in the Citadel," Farah shot back, her voice steady but laced with irritation.

He watched her chin raise up in defiance, his heart racing. The urge to rush in, to confront Arash, burned in his veins, but the cunning part of him cautioned against it. He was sorely outnumbered thanks to all of them having Talents, and a head-on confrontation would only put Farah in more danger.

"None of how I work or travel is your business," she replied defiantly, her eyes blazing.

"Everything about your situation is my business. The Mashyana is worried about you," Arash warned, his voice low. "We've been watching you to make sure that you did your duty."

Yasher's breath caught in his throat. *Watched?* The realization that they were being tracked sent a shiver down his spine.

"I will not let you jeopardize my own duty to Amma Behnaz," Arash threatened, stepping closer. "You're a liability, and I can't have you wandering around without oversight."

"Is that what you think?" Farah countered, her voice rising. "I can handle myself!"

Yasher felt a rush of anger rise within him, the desire to protect her overwhelming. He searched for something to create a distraction to get them away from her.

"Can you?" Arash laughed, the sound hollow and cruel. "Because it doesn't look like it. You're out here chasing relics haphazardly, no plan, hanging around caravans and foreigners that you can't even bring in properly. You think the Mashyana would send me if it wasn't serious?"

"I don't need your permission to do my duty," Farah insisted, her words fueled by determination.

"Right you are," he replied, a smugness creeping into his voice. "But you'd be wise to remember you're not the only one in this world who's been tasked with a mission. My purpose is to ensure you don't screw this up."

"Is that your only purpose?" Farah shot back, her anger evident. "Because it looks to me like you're just here to step in and distract me with your whining."

Yasher shifted in the shadows, his heart pounding

against his ribcage. The alley was narrow, the stone walls rising high on either side, creating a claustrophobic atmosphere that made him feel trapped. He needed to act, but how could he intervene without exposing himself?

Arash's voice grew low, dangerously sweet, "You're out here on your own, Farah. We can't have that. You need to understand your place."

"I am not your puppet," Farah shot back, her voice steady.

Yasher's anger simmered beneath the surface as he watched Arash's expression shift, filling him with dread. There was something ominous in the way his lips curled into a cruel smile.

"Of course you are, you mongrel. I deserve your role as Hand. You are just a mistake."

The words hung in the air like an omen. Yasher's blood ran cold as Arash lunged forward, a flash of steel caught the light.

Before she could react, Arash struck, the blade glinting menacingly before it sank into Farah's side.

The gasp that escaped her lips was a sound he would remember for the rest of his life as it echoed in the alleyway. She staggered back, her eyes wide with disbelief, hand instinctively clutching the wound in her side.

Drawing in a shaky breath, he quickly scanned the area, searching for anything he could use as a distraction.

The world around him felt alive, the market's sounds fading as his focus narrowed. A cart filled with barrels of apples caught his eye, sitting precariously close to the edge of the alley.

Yasher seized the moment as Arash turned, raising his dagger to make the killing blow. Reaching for the ground, he willed his senses to sharpen, for his luck to help him.

With a surge of resolve, he grabbed a few loose stones from the alley floor he hadn't seen before and hurled them toward the cart that had spilled apples, aiming for the barrels.

The stone struck true, sending a cascade of apples flying in every direction, creating chaos at the entrance of the alley. Market patrons reacted with alarm, rushing to avoid the rolling fruit, some moving towards the entrance of the alley.

With Arash momentarily preoccupied by the pandemonium, Yasher charged toward Farah, slipping out from his hiding place.

"Move!" He grasped her arm, helping to steady her, his heart pounding as he felt the warmth of her blood seeping through her clothes.

"We can't let him catch us," she whispered, eyes wide with fear. "My... my Talent is still recovering from yesterday."

"Let me help you," Yasher replied, steeling himself. "We have to get out of here before we worry about that."

He helped guide her down the alley, urging her to lean against him for support. Together, they moved through the shadows, their footsteps muffled by the noise of the market. The voices of the Beloveds grew distant as the chaos at the entrance drew them away.

"Yasher, I can't—" She gasped, the pain evident in her voice.

"Just a little farther," he urged, determination fueling his every word. "I won't let you go down like this."

He kept her close, weaving through the crowd, careful to avoid drawing attention. Every moment felt like an eternity, his mind racing with a mixture of dread and determination. What would happen if Arash caught up with them?

"Over there," he pointed to a stall selling colorful textiles. "We can hide for a moment."

They ducked behind a stall, Yasher's heart racing as he pulled Farah close. She leaned against the wall, breathing heavily, her face pale and clammy. The vibrant colors of the fabrics seemed to swirl around them, a stark contrast to the tension that gripped the air.

"I didn't..." Farah's voice was barely a whisper, her eyes glassy. "I didn't think he'd actually hurt me."

"Shh," he said, pressing a finger to his lips. "It's going to be alright. Just hold on."

The din of the market buzzed around them, and Yasher felt the weight of time pressing heavily on his shoulders. "You need a healer."

But before he could say anything more, he heard Arash's voice cutting through the chaos, sharper than glass. "Farah! Where are you?"

Yasher's breath hitched as panic flared in his chest.

"We need to move." He took her arm, urging her to follow him deeper into the market, away from Arash's looming presence.

With every step, he could feel the adrenaline coursing through his veins, the desire to protect her burning like fire. They pushed past the stalls, ducking behind crates and weaving through the throngs of people, blending into the chaos of the marketplace.

"Where are we going?" Farah gasped, her voice strained.

"Just keep moving," he replied, scanning their surroundings for a way out. "We'll find a place to hide."

As they rounded a corner, Yasher spotted a narrow alleyway that led behind a row of shops.

"In there," he said, guiding Farah toward the darkness.

They slipped into the alley, the shadows enveloping them as he pressed her against the wall. The distant sounds of the market faded into a muffled hum, and he took a moment to catch his breath.

"We need to bandage your wound until we can get you to a healer," he said, his voice steady despite the panic thrumming in his chest. He glanced at her side, where blood soaked through her clothing.

"I'll be fine," she protested, but he could see the pain etched on her features.

"No, you won't," he replied firmly. "We need to stop the bleeding, or you won't make it. Just let me help."

She hesitated. Finally, with a defeated sigh, she nodded. "Quickly."

Yasher reached into his pack, rummaging through the supplies. He pulled out a clean cloth and pressed it gently against the wound. Farah winced, but he kept his grip steady, applying pressure to stem the blood flow.

"Stay with me, Farah," he said softly, his eyes locked on hers. "You're going to be alright."

"I'm sorry," she murmured, her voice barely above a whisper. "He's always been hot-headed, but I never expected this..."

"Don't apologize," he replied, his heart heavy with concern. "Just focus on your breathing."

As he tended to her wound, his mind raced through all of the options they had to get out of this. He needed to find a way to get her back to the inn without getting caught.

He looked around as he took off his coat to hand to her. He knew they were at a disadvantage, but it was the only thing he could think of. She slowly put it on with his help, covering her distinctive vest and the wound.

The tension in the alley shifted. "We should go. We can't linger here."

With a final glance at her wound, he pressed the cloth into place, feeling the warmth of her blood seep through as he wrapped his arm around her waist to help her stand. "Can you walk?"

"I can manage," she replied, determination flickering in her eyes.

They moved cautiously through the alley, stepping carefully over the cobblestones as they emerged back into the bustling marketplace. The noise surrounded them once more, but Yasher kept his senses sharp, scanning the crowd for any sign of danger.

They finally reached the inn, he ushered her inside, relief flooding through him. He helped her get through the common area and up the stairs without gathering much attention from the few people in the area. He opened the door to her room, finding Pari standing with an unknown woman.

"Pari?" he said, pulling Farah behind him. "Who did you let in the room?"

The little girl's face was impassive. "Rashnu showed me that we needed a healer. She will fix Farah."

No time to deal with that, then. These gods gave them a healer, he'd use it.

He gently guided Farah over to one of the chairs, helping her get his coat and her vest off before the healer came over and got to work. Every time her eyelids dropped, his heart skipped a beat.

"We're safe for now," he murmured. "You are safe."

She nodded, the fight leaving her for the moment.

"It would be best if you take the strange girl out and

distract her, Aqa. This is a messy wound," The healer said, removing the cloth they'd used.

"We'll be right next door," he said, taking Pari's hand in his. He didn't move until he looked to Farah and she nodded at him, grimacing as the healer poked and prodded.

<hr>

THE ROOM FELT UNBEARABLY small as Yasher closed the door behind him, Pari's small hand gripping his tightly. His mind raced as he tried to process everything—the ambush, Farah's injury, and now this mysterious healer. He glanced down at Pari, whose face was a mask of calm, far too composed for a child her age.

"Rashnu sent her, did he?" Yasher asked quietly as they entered his room.

"Yes," Pari replied, her voice steady. "He said Farah needed help, and I had to find someone who wouldn't ask too many questions."

He arched an eyebrow at her, though his heart was pounding. Pari's cryptic relationship with Rashnu unnerved him.

"That's convenient," he muttered under his breath, but he didn't press further. There was no use questioning the divine, or whatever Rashnu claimed to be, when Farah was fighting to live next door.

Once inside his room, he sat Pari down on the edge of his bed and knelt to her eye level.

"Alright, Little Divine. I need you to listen to me. Farah's going to be fine, but the healer needs time to help her. So, you and I are going to stay here for a bit. Sound good?"

She nodded but looked at him with wide, curious eyes. "You're worried about her."

He let out a low sigh, running a hand through his hair.

"Of course I'm worried. She's…" He paused, searching for the right words. "She's strong, but even the strong need help sometimes."

She tilted her head, her expression thoughtful. "You like her."

He froze, her blunt statement catching him off guard.

"What makes you say that?" he asked, trying to sound casual.

"You look at her the same way Shirin says my baba must have looked at my maman to make such a pretty girl," Pari said with a shrug, as if it were the most obvious thing in the world.

He let out a dry laugh, shaking his head. "You're too clever for your own good, Little Divine."

"But do you?" she pressed, her gaze unrelenting.

He hesitated, the weight of her question settling over him. Did he? It wasn't something he'd dared to fully admit, even to himself. Yet the answer sat heavy in his chest, undeniable.

"I care about her," he said finally, his voice soft. "More than I probably should."

Pari smiled, as if she'd just uncovered a great secret. "Then you should tell her."

He chuckled, leaning back on his heels.

"It's not that simple, Pari. Farah's carrying more than anyone should, and I'm… not the man who can steady that weight."

"But you're here," she said matter-of-factly. "And that's what matters."

Her words hit harder than he expected, and for a

moment, he didn't know how to respond. Instead, he stood and ruffled her hair.

"Alright, enough matchmaking from you. Let's find something to keep us busy."

Pari nodded and hopped off the bed, wandering over to the small window. She gazed out at the bustling street below, her fingers tracing the edge of the glass. Yasher watched her for a moment before turning his thoughts back to the situation at hand.

Farah's safety came first, but Arash and the other Beloveds weren't going to stop hunting for the relics, or to finish the job with Farah. Remembering the look on Arash's face as he stabbed her, he wouldn't put it past him to prioritize killing her over anything else. They needed a plan, and fast. His mind turned over the possibilities until one solidified, a sly grin spreading across his face.

"Pari," he called, walking over to her. "How do you feel about helping me send those Beloveds on a bit of a chase to nowhere?"

Her eyes lit up with mischief. "What do we do?"

He crouched beside her, lowering his voice. "We're going to give them a trail to follow. One that leads them far away from us. I just need to think on it a little bit."

Pari's grin mirrored his, and for the first time that day, Yasher felt a spark of hope. Together, they would buy Farah the time she needed to recover and keep the relic out of the wrong hands. And maybe, just maybe, they'd come out of this in one piece.

YASHER SETTLED into his chair by the hearth, still searching for comfort after trying to sleep in it last night, the faint warmth of the fire a poor match for the storm brewing in his chest.

Pari sat on the bed near the window, idly twirling one of the ribbons from her braid between her fingers. Her quiet tension mirrored his own. Between putting together their plans to send the Beloveds on a useless chase and worry for Farah, neither of them got much sleep last night. The healer only called for a servant to bring her water and cloth throughout the night, with no word on how Farah was doing.

The soft knock at the door startled them both. Yasher exchanged a glance with Pari before standing, crossing the room in a few quick strides. He opened the door to reveal the healer from earlier, her expression grave but steady.

"Your Khānum is resting, finally," she said, stepping inside without waiting for an invitation. Her sharp eyes scanned the room before settling on Yasher. "She'll recover, but it was close."

Yasher's chest tightened. "How close?"

The healer set her bag down on the table, pulling out a small vial and rolling it between her fingers as she spoke.

"The blade didn't puncture her intestines, but it came dangerously close. Another inch or a less steady hand in stitching, and it could have been fatal."

Yasher clenched his jaw, his hands curling into fists at his sides. "But she'll recover?"

"She's young, strong, and stubborn," the healer nodded. "With rest, she should make a full recovery. But she shouldn't move too much for a few days, and I'd say a fortnight for a full recovery."

"The wound will need careful tending, and she can't afford to overexert herself." She paused, considering her words before continuing. "My Talent is... not the strongest, so there was only so much I could do to heal her. She will need to do the rest on her own and with time."

"Thank you. For everything." He ran a hand through his hair, the weight of the healer's words settling heavily on his shoulders. Grabbing his coin pouch, he poured out more than he should.

The healer inclined her head. "She's lucky, you know. Whoever did this clearly knew what they were doing. Precision like that isn't common in street fights. She's fortunate to have you and the little one here."

Pari stood and approached the healer, her small voice breaking the silence. "She's going to get better, right? The choices are muddy."

"Yes, little one," the healer replied gently. "But she needs rest. No running around or getting into trouble, understand?"

Pari nodded solemnly, her hands clasped tightly in front of her. "I'll make sure she's okay."

The healer glanced back at Yasher, her eyes narrowing slightly. "Keep her safe. Whoever attacked her isn't likely to give up easily. You've got a target on your backs now."

He nodded, his jaw tightening. "We'll handle it."

The healer packed up her things and left, leaving behind a heavy silence. Yasher sank back into his chair, his thoughts racing. The image of Farah, pale and bloodied, flickered in his mind like a haunting echo.

Arash had done this. That arrogant, smug bastard. And he wouldn't stop until he'd finished whatever twisted mission the Mashyana had sent him on.

"I won't let this happen again," he muttered, his voice low but filled with resolve.

Pari looked at him, her eyes filled with both fear and determination. "What are we going to do?"

"We're going to make sure Arash and his puppets never come near us again," Yasher said, standing abruptly. "I'll send them chasing their own tails across this damned country, and by the time they realize they've been duped, we'll be long gone."

Pari nodded, her expression fierce despite her small frame. "What we planned last night is a clear choice from Rashnu. I can help."

"You're helping by staying here with Farah," he replied, his voice softening. He crouched down to her level, placing a hand on her shoulder. "She needs you to keep watch and make sure she doesn't push herself too hard. I'll start working on the plan we came up with last night. Can you do that for me, Little Divine?"

Pari straightened, her chin lifting with pride. "I can do that."

"Good." He stood, determination hardening his features. "I've got some work to do."

As he gathered his supplies and prepared to head back into the bustling streets, the healer's words echoed in his mind. The wound had been close. Too close. He couldn't afford to let Arash get near Farah, or gods forbid Pari, again. Whatever it took, however far he had to go to lead them astray, he would make sure they were safe.

With one last glance at the little girl, who had returned to her spot by the window, he squared his shoulders and stepped out into the hall. The morning light spilled through the inn's windows, illuminating his path as he made his way down the stairs and out into the marketplace.

Arash wanted a relic or two? Yasher thought grimly as he merged into the bustling crowd. Fine. Let him waste his time digging through rubble and chasing phantoms.

CHAPTER 19

Six days. She'd been stuck in this small room for six days to heal. Thank the Unnamed Gods that Pari had brought in a healer with a small amount of Talent. The wound started to get infected after the first day, causing the healer to come back multiple times for more healing, tapping the poor woman's Talent to the edge.

Pari and Yasher seemed to take far too much joy in waiting on her, bringing her food from the market and helping her as much as she would allow them to. The only thing they fought her on consistently was leaving the bed. Any and all conversations about leaving Banima and Arash were cut off quickly. Yasher said that he had handled the problem of Arash and would not elaborate further.

The morning light filtered through the thin curtains, illuminating the dust motes that danced lazily in the air. They had left her alone so far today, giving her the chance to contemplate her next steps.

With a surge of energy after laying in bed for so long, Farah slowly stood and dressed herself, carefully avoiding any sudden movements that might aggravate her injury.

The wound was still tender, but she could feel her strength returning.

The healer had said that her Talent wasn't the strongest, but she gave Farah a better chance than if she'd only stitched up the wound. If she took it slow, she could be ready to travel again, perhaps in time to finish the task that had brought them here.

As she dressed, she noticed her vest draped across the back of a chair. The fabric felt familiar and comforting as she ran her hand over it. She marveled at the repair Pari had been working on—an imperfect yet heartfelt embroidery of a hawk mending the hole Arash had created, the vibrant threads of a patchwork of colors that reflected the little girl's creativity and care. A smile crept onto her face, a fleeting moment of warmth that felt like a balm against the weight pressing down on her.

"Farah—what are you doing up?" Yasher's voice sliced through her moment of reverie as he entered the room, a steaming cup of tea in hand. The surprise in his eyes quickly shifted to concern.

She shrugged, pulling the vest on and smoothing it down.

"It's time to leave," she declared, taking the cup from him and savoring the heat radiating through the ceramic. "Enough time has been wasted. I have to finish my work."

His frown deepened, the familiar expression that had become all too common over the last few days as they butted heads about her staying put and healing. Setting the cup of tea down, he approached her, hands on his hips, and let out a heavy sigh.

"Fine, fine." He stepped closer, his eyes narrowing with an intensity that made her heart flutter, albeit in frustration rather than attraction. "I'll go and negotiate with any caravans going south for passage. You are to stay here—no arguments."

"Yasher—" she began, ready to protest, but he placed a finger gently but firmly against her lips, silencing her.

"No. Arguments." The glint in his eye paused most if any thought at all, let alone to argue with him. "Otherwise, I will physically restrain you in that bed until you're healed fully."

She willed herself to move, to push him away, but her body betrayed her. Her heart hammered in her chest, so loudly she feared he could hear it too, expecting him to make some joke about the way it pounded against her ribs.

Her hand moved slowly, as if fighting against her own instincts, attempting to push his finger away from her face. But he didn't resist. He simply opened his hand and took hers gently in his, and in that moment, the world seemed to narrow. She forgot how to breathe as he leaned in, his face inches from hers.

The sound of Pari running up the stairs brought her back into herself and she stepped back a half-step, but kept her hand in his for just a moment longer as the little girl ran into the room.

"Farah!" Pari exclaimed, bursting into the room with uncontainable energy, her hands held high as if presenting a treasure. "I found a flower for you!"

She rushed forward, her small frame darting between them, and he took a step back, releasing his hold on her.

"Little Divine," he said, grinning down at Pari, "that's a beautiful flower."

"I want to give it to you so you'll feel better!" Pari said, holding out the sprig of jasmine.

Farah accepted the flower, her heart swelling at the

gesture, helping to calm the tightness she still felt from a few moments ago. "Thank you, Pari. It's lovely."

Yasher chuckled, stepping away from her to take a sip of the tea.

"Little Divine, you need to help Farah pack while I find us a way out of town." He knelt to Pari's level, placing a hand on her head affectionately. "Can you make sure that she doesn't hurt herself while I'm gone?"

"I will," Pari said solemnly, her tiny face set in determination. "Farah needs to heal for what's to come."

He straightened and glanced at Farah, concern still etched on his features.

"Well, that's not ominous at all," he muttered before turning to the door.

"I'll be back after I've secured our transportation to Tamidh. Remember what I said about arguing. Though, that could be fun too." He winked at her, closing the door behind him.

As the sound of his footsteps faded down the hallway, Farah sighed, the weight of uncertainty settling back onto her shoulders. She moved to the window, looking out over the bustling streets of Banima. The vibrant life below contrasted sharply with the turmoil inside her.

Her mind drifted to Yasher and the feel of his hand on hers, his breath so close. The tension between them had shifted, something unspoken crackling in the air.

The truth was, she found herself drawn to him in ways that confused her. The more time they spent together, the more she felt the weight of her responsibilities pull against the desire for something deeper with this insufferable gharib.

Every time she woke, he was there, sitting in a chair next to her bed. Every time she needed anything, he would jump up and retrieve it for her. Once she woke to him asleep, holding her hand. The things that he did were more than what she would have expected, given he was clear that he was only there to support her, not her tasks. Why did he care so much?

The sting of Arash's dagger piercing her side was a sharp memory, the pain a constant reminder of her vulnerability. It infuriated her that he had the audacity to threaten her, to stab her, to question her worthiness as the Hand. She had survived countless trials, yet here she was, feeling weak and powerless thanks to his hatred of her and her position.

There were very few rules between the Beloveds handed down from the Mashyana outside of a Beloved never killing another Beloved without her approval. And yet Arash didn't hesitate to plunge the dagger into her.

Was there a grain of truth in Yasher's earlier suspicions? Had the Mashyana sent her to collect relics for herself, not the kingdom, sending Arash and the Beloveds as he said to correct her path, her mistakes? The thought twisted her stomach. If she truly was just a pawn in the Mashyana's game, what would happen to her? To Yasher? To Pari?

The weight of Arash's threats lingered, and her resolve wavered. He had warned her about the dangers of straying too far from the path set by the Mashyana. Was he right? Did Yasher have a point when he expressed concern over her loyalty to the queen?

"Focus, Farah," she muttered to herself, hearing Rostam in her mind.

Steeling herself, Farah began to gather her belongings, moving with a purpose. She packed the scant supplies they had, her movements steady despite the lingering pain. Her injuries didn't matter. What mattered was the mission ahead and the relic they needed to retrieve. She had to be ready.

As she finished packing, she took a moment to breathe deeply, centering herself.

"I will finish what I started," she whispered, determination igniting within her.

Pari was still bustling about, excitedly chatting about the flower and what they could do once they left Banima. Farah smiled, the little girl's spirit infectious.

"Let's make a plan, Little Divine. We'll need all our wits about us if we're going into the deserts to reach Tamidh for the last relic."

"Yes! I have seen many things that will help us, whichever path we take." Pari exclaimed, bouncing on her toes.

"Exactly," Farah agreed, kneeling down to the girl's level. "You'll be our secret weapon."

As if sensing her inner turmoil, Pari spoke up. "You have chosen the better paths I was shown by Rashnu so far. We will struggle with more choices, but know that."

"You are a wonder, Pari," she replied, her voice steady despite the uncertainty clawing at her insides. "But it won't be easy. News coming from Tamidh was not positive, let alone just getting through the desert between us."

"We'll need to be careful," Pari said, her brow furrowing. "There are people who want to stop us, but there are people who want to help us too."

"We'll find a way," Farah reassured her, though uncertainty lingered in her heart.

Farah's thoughts drifted off again as Pari went to get them tea, intermingling her worries about Yasher and the Mashyana's plans. Arash said that he was sent to keep her in line, as if the queen didn't trust her to do her duty. What if the Mashyana's motives were not as pure as she believed?

She shook her head, trying to clear the thoughts. The Mashyana had always been there for her, guiding her on this path. But the flicker of uncertainty lingered, making her question all of the things that made up her life.

Voices outside of the door pulled her out of the swirl of her thoughts just before the door opened on Pari and Yasher, him taking the cups out of the little girl's hands before they spilled.

He handed her one of the cups before collapsing into the chair next to hers. "I have good news, and not good news."

She took a long sip before glaring at him. "Out with it."

"I did find transport for us, but no caravans are going south thanks to the rebels pushing out of Tamidh." He took a long draw of his own tea and put his boots up on the table, stretching his legs. "But I got a deal from one of the merchants and we have horses."

She sighed. "We'll need to stay to the southern side of the river then, to keep the horses usable until Tamidh, keeping to the foothills and stay out of the desert. It will take longer, but it may keep us out of the troubles the rebels will bring with them."

She stood slowly, rubbing her hand gently over the embroidery covering her healing wound.

"We'll need to get a few additional supplies for the horses, and we may as well grab an evening meal."

He focused on her hand, then lowered his feet back to the ground.

"I'll take care of that. You should rest." His hand came up and brushed her cheek. "Please."

Stopping herself from leaning into his hand was harder than she expected.

"Fine. But bring back something stronger than tea."

She tried to shake off the sensation of the warmth of his hand against her cheek, focusing instead on the tasks ahead, but the moment lingered in her mind like a sweet, stubborn melody. She felt his eyes on her, studying her as she turned away to hide the flush creeping into her cheeks.

"I'll see what I can do," he said, a teasing smile playing on his lips as he moved toward the door. "You know how the markets are at this time of day. Crowded and full of distractions."

"Food," she called after him, forcing the lightness in her tone. "If you take too long, I might just come looking for you."

"Wouldn't dream of it," he replied over his shoulder, the door swinging shut behind him.

As the sound of his footsteps faded down the hallway, she released a breath she hadn't realized she was holding. The tension in her shoulders eased slightly, though her heart still raced from the interaction.

She glanced at Pari, who was busy arranging the few belongings they had on the small table. The little girl hummed a tune under her breath, lost in her own world of imagination. Farah sat down and pulled out a novel about the Yazatas which they'd brought her while she was laid up in bed.

The door creaked open again just as the sun started to set, and Yasher reentered, balancing a small bottle and a bag of food in his hands.

"I present to you," he announced, his voice grand and theatrical, "gifts from the great people of Banima."

He set the items down on the table, the bottle glinting

in the dim light. "A lovely bottle of something far stronger than tea, as requested."

Farah's curiosity piqued as she leaned forward. "What is it?"

"Just a little something I found from a merchant who swore it would cure all ills," he said, winking at her. "At least, that's what he told me after I haggled him down to a reasonable price."

She laughed lightly. "When did you learn enough Emarian to haggle?"

"I am a wonder, didn't you know?" He poured two glasses, filling the air with a sweet, inviting aroma. "I figured we could both use a bit of fortification after these last few days."

He leaned back in his chair, the playful atmosphere around them weaving a cocoon of warmth that felt comforting after the heavy doubts that had plagued her. The evening meal was a simple affair, with freshly baked bread, fruits, and a small portion of roasted meat that Yasher had managed to barter for at the market.

As they shared the meal, Yasher and Farah fell into a rhythm of easy conversation, a banter that felt both familiar and new. Farah found herself drawn to the way he spoke, the way his eyes sparkled with mischief and confidence as he regaled them with tales of his adventures prior to meeting her.

"Did I ever tell you about the time I managed to outsmart a band of thieves?" Yasher said, his expression becoming animated. "I had a good run for my money, but let me tell you, it was all about the right distraction."

Farah leaned in, intrigued. "What did you do?"

He grinned, glancing at Pari, who was enraptured by his every word.

"Well, you see, I noticed that their leader had an affinity for shiny things, like a raven. So, naturally, I devised a plan to make my escape. I tossed a handful of coins into the air while I slipped behind a crate. They were too busy scrambling for the treasure to notice me sneaking out the back."

Pari gasped, eyes wide with awe. "You are very clever!"

He laughed, leaning back with a smug grin. "I prefer to think of myself as resourceful in the moment."

"Hero or rogue, you're still dangerous," she chimed in, raising an eyebrow playfully. "But I think we're lucky to have you around."

His expression softened, and he met her gaze with a sincerity that sent a ripple of warmth through her.

"And I'm grateful to have you two with me."

Farah felt a sense of peace settle over her as they ate. The tension from earlier was forgotten, replaced by the warmth of companionship.

Eventually, the meal concluded, and Pari yawned widely, her eyelids fluttering.

"I think I'm tired," she said, her voice a sleepy whisper.

"Good idea, Little Divine. You've had a busy day," Yasher said gently, leaning down to tuck her in. "Get some rest. We'll need your energy for tomorrow."

The way he cared for the little girl filled her with warmth, and in that moment, the attraction she felt toward him intensified, woven with the thread of admiration.

Once Pari was settled, he turned to her, a playful glint in his eye.

"Now, about that stronger drink..." He raised the bottle with a mock seriousness.

She laughed lightly, shaking her head. "You're going to get us in trouble, you know."

"Ah, but trouble is what makes life interesting," he replied, the lightness in his tone making her smile.

"Maybe for you, but I have responsibilities."

"Those responsibilities can wait a little longer," he countered, stepping closer, the teasing note in his voice laced with sincerity. "Besides, we've faced enough danger and stress in the past few days. A little celebration is in order."

"Celebration? Is that what you call it?" she teased back, though she couldn't help the flutter of excitement in her stomach at the prospect.

"Let's call it a toast to our adventures," he said, raising the bottle. "To friendship, and to the journey ahead."

"To friendship," she echoed, as she clinked her glass against his. Their eyes locked for a moment, and the world around them faded, leaving just the two of them suspended in that bubble of connection.

"Are you feeling better?" he asked, his voice dropping to a more serious tone.

"Yes," she replied, her breath catching slightly. "Stronger every day."

"Good." He leaned closer, a teasing smile on his lips.

With the last of the evening fading into a comfortable silence, she found herself inching closer to him, as if pulled by an invisible force. The intimacy of the moment enveloped them, and she could feel her heart pounding against her ribs, urging her to take a leap of faith.

Just then, Pari stirred in her sleep, breaking the spell.

"Farah?" she murmured, her voice small and drowsy.

"Shh, sleep, Little Divine," She whispered, glancing over at the girl. "Everything is alright."

He chuckled softly, the lightness of his tone returning.

"See? Even she knows when to speak up. Maybe we

should save the deep conversations, and other things, for another time."

"Yes, perhaps." She felt the warmth of his presence still lingering beside her, the air thick with unspoken words.

With a contented sigh, Farah settled into the moment, letting the exhaustion of the day catch up with her.

"Well, my lovely Phoenix," he said, standing. "I shall leave you to sleep. Dawn comes early." He pulled away reluctantly, pausing in the doorway. "Goodnight, dear Farah."

"Goodnight," She said, waiting until he'd closed the door to move. She placed her vest lovingly on the chair, and then laid down next to Pari.

CHAPTER 20

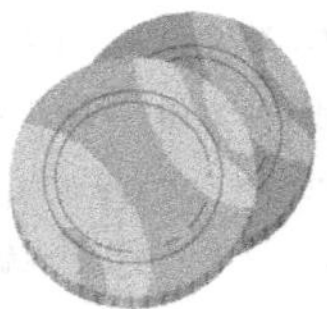

THE LONGER THEY TRAVELED, the more Yasher could see that Farah was flagging. Her side still bothered her, but she stayed silent as they made their way around the southern tip of the Azhdahak Mountains.

If he had any other option, they would have waited until she was fully healed, or they could have taken their time with a caravan had any been going along the more direct route they needed. He cursed under his breath, wishing that his luck could somehow steer him toward better choices for her, but it had gone silent again.

The sun hung low in the sky, casting long shadows across the dusty path that snaked through the foothills. The scent of earth and the whisper of the wind provided a momentary distraction, but his mind remained fixated on Farah. Each time she had to adjust her seat on her horse seemed to require an effort far greater than it should have.

The determination etched on her face was commendable, yet it did little to quell the anxiety gnawing at his insides. She was strong, but he couldn't shake the feeling that pushing herself could lead to further complications.

"Let's stop here," he suggested, gesturing toward a small mining village that appeared on the horizon.

The settlement was modest, with wooden structures jutting from the rocky terrain, their exteriors weathered by years of labor and hardship. He could make out the silhouettes of villagers going about their day, their movements quick and purposeful.

"Are you sure?" Farah asked, her brow furrowing as she glanced at the village. "We can't afford to lose any more time."

"We'll rest the horses and see if we can gather more supplies," Yasher replied, keeping his tone light, though he felt the weight of urgency pressing down on him. "Besides, you need to recuperate. It won't do anyone any good if you push yourself too hard."

She hesitated, but he saw the slight nod of agreement as she turned her attention to Pari, who bounced ahead, excitement radiating from her small frame.

As they approached the village, Yasher noticed the cautious glances of the villagers. Their eyes flickered to him, lingering a moment longer than they did on Farah. He couldn't blame them. He was a foreigner in a land rife with uncertainty, and foreign faces weren't always welcome.

"Stay close to me," he murmured to Farah as they stepped into the village, the dusty ground crunching beneath their boots. He lowered his voice, leaning closer. "I'll handle this."

She shot him a sidelong glance, an eyebrow raised. "You stand out much more than I do."

He shrugged, feigning nonchalance.

"All the better, right? Just play along." He scanned the area, taking in the layout of the village. The small market was bustling with activity. Vendors shouted out prices, children darted between stalls, and the air was thick with the scents of spices and baked goods. It felt alive, a stark contrast to the burdens they carried.

"Look!" Pari exclaimed, tugging on Farah's arm as she darted toward a stall selling fabric flowers. "Can we get some of those? They're so pretty!"

"Maybe later," She replied, her voice softer as she watched the little girl. The corners of his mouth lifted at the sight, but his amusement was short-lived as he turned his attention back to the villagers. He couldn't shake the tension that wrapped around him like a cloak.

"Let's see if we can find someone to talk to," he said, guiding them toward a merchant who appeared to be more approachable than the others. The man was older, his face weathered by years of labor, but his eyes sparkled with a hint of mischief.

"Ah, travelers! What brings you to our humble village?" the merchant called out, his voice warm despite the evident skepticism in his gaze.

Yasher stepped forward, putting on a charm that he had honed over years of navigating markets. "We're looking for supplies and information about the road ahead. We've heard that things are... complicated."

The merchant's expression shifted slightly, the mirth fading.

"Complicated is one way to put it. We've had our fair share of trouble with the rebels," he replied, his voice dropping to a conspiratorial tone. "You're lucky you're not associated with The Citadel."

"Why's that?" Farah asked, her curiosity evident. She seemed to forget her fatigue, her posture straightening.

"The Mashya was taken hostage," the merchant said, glancing around as if ensuring they weren't overheard.

"Word is that the rebels are moving toward the mountains, and many are saying it's all the fault of the Mashyana. They say she's been hoarding power and treasures while the people suffer. There's a plague burning down anyone with a lick of Talent that no one can explain."

His heart sank at the mention of the Mashya. He'd heard the rumors even when they were in Banima, but chose to keep that to himself while she recovered. The weight of the news settled heavily in the pit of his stomach as he watched Farah's reaction. He had tried to keep it all from her.

"Is that what people believe?" he asked, trying to keep his voice steady.

"Believe?" the merchant scoffed, folding his arms. "People believe what they want to believe, especially when times are tough. They see the Mashyana as someone who doesn't care about their struggles. Some folks are angry enough to consider rebellion themselves."

Her expression darkened at the merchant's words, her brow furrowing as she absorbed the implications. Yasher felt the tension rising again, the uncertainty swirling around them like a storm.

"I see," he said, forcing a calmness he didn't feel. "And what of the Mashya's situation? Is there anything we can do to help?"

"Help?" the merchant chuckled dryly. "Unless you're planning to march into the mountains and confront the rebels, there's not much anyone can do. Besides, you should be more worried about yourself. Tensions are high, and it's best to keep your heads down. That's how you stay safe in these parts."

Farah remained silent, her eyes narrowed as she contemplated the merchant's words.

"Then let's focus on the immediate needs," Yasher said, forcing a smile. "We'll need provisions for our journey. Can you point us in the direction of someone who sells food for ourselves and our mounts?"

The merchant waved a hand toward a stall nearby. "You'll find plenty there. But if I were you, I'd keep moving as soon as you can. The longer you linger, the more you risk being noticed. People are on edge, gharib. No offense, but you are not a common sight around these parts, no matter how well you speak Emari."

"Thank you for your help," Farah said, her voice barely above a whisper as she turned away from the merchant.

Yasher took a moment to study her, the worry etched into her brow. He could see that the merchant's words had struck a nerve, that doubt was creeping into her mind.

"Hey," he said, placing a hand gently on her shoulder. "Is your wound bothering?"

"I..." She hesitated, her gaze distant as she processed everything. "It's just... this was supposed to be about retrieving the relics to save the kingdom, not... not causing me to question my loyalties."

He felt a surge of frustration at the doubts swirling in her mind. "It doesn't matter what the villagers think."

"But what if there's truth to what they're saying?" she pressed, her eyes searching his for reassurance. "What if I am just a pawn in a game I don't fully understand?"

"You're not a pawn, Farah. You have your own agency," he said firmly, trying to anchor her back to the truth. "Don't let a few angry villagers shake your confidence."

"Easier said than done," she muttered, her gaze shifting back to the bustling village square. "It's just... I owe my life to the Mashyana. To hear that people believe that she is to blame for all of this is too much."

"We'll figure this out," he said, stepping closer, his voice low and earnest. "But you can't let the fear of what might be cloud your judgment. You have to trust in yourself first."

"Trust. Such a fragile thing," she said, her voice laced with doubt.

"Always," he spared a glance to her. "Now let's grab those provisions and keep moving."

While Farah haggled with the vendor as he couldn't keep up with the accent well enough, he stepped back, observing her. Her spark of fire was still there, but dulled between her injury and the rumors swirling around them.

Once they secured the provisions, they made their way back toward the horses, the tension in the air palpable. Yasher couldn't shake the feeling that the villagers were watching them, eyes lingering too long. He refused to let it faze him. He'd been in tighter situations and gotten out just fine.

"Let's get out of here. We seem to be on display," he urged.

He offered a hand to Farah, who swung herself up gracefully, the slight wince she tried to hide not escaping his notice.

"Thank you," she said, her voice steady once she settled in the saddle.

"Of course. I wouldn't let you take a tumble after all the trouble we've gone through," he replied, shooting her a playful grin.

With Pari perched between them on her smaller horse, they set off down the trail, leaving the village behind.

As the sun began to dip behind the mountains, casting a warm golden hue across the landscape, he took a deep breath, feeling the crisp air fill his lungs. They still had a few hours of daylight before they'd stop to make camp, and she would want to make the most of them.

And he would do everything in his power to help Farah find her way, even if that meant challenging her beliefs about the Mashyana and her place in it all.

They rode in companionable silence, the rhythm of the horses' hooves a steady reminder of their resolve. The world around them faded into a blur, a tapestry of greens and browns painted by the sun.

THE FIRE they'd started at dinner had cooled down to just embers by the time Yasher noticed that Farah and Pari had fallen asleep. The night was quiet, save for the occasional rustle of the scrub brush and the distant calls of nocturnal creatures. He sat a few feet away, the warmth of the fire still lingering in the air, a stark contrast to the storm of thoughts swirling in his mind.

Here he was, far from home, caught up in a quest that felt increasingly beyond his control. He glanced over at Farah, the flickering light illuminating her features, casting shadows that danced across her peaceful expression. There was strength in her even in sleep, a quiet resilience that pulled at something deep inside him.

He reached towards the pocket in his vest where the Eye of Rashnu stubbornly stayed, patting it.

"What's happened to you?" he whispered, his voice barely above the hush of the night. It had once felt like a beacon of luck, guiding him through challenges and uncertainties. Yet, lately, it seemed to have lost its power. The charm that had once protected him now felt like a heavy reminder of his failures as it sat silent.

The last few days had been riddled with near misses, decisions that had felt wrong even as he made them. Arash's ambush had put them in jeopardy, and now they were in the midst of a brewing storm—rebels on the move, uncertain allegiances, and Farah's internal struggles, let alone the fact that she was still healing from the attack. His relic was supposed to bring him luck, but lately, it felt more like a shackle than a safeguard.

It was absurd when he thought about how he'd ended up sitting around a fire, in the middle of a country on the brink of war, traveling with a woman he barely knew yet wanted to be around all of his time and a little girl who somehow believed he could be a hero.

The life he had led, the choices he had made, had all been in service to himself, to his own survival for so many years. Yet, here he was, entangled in their fates, questioning his own motivations.

It had started as a simple quest for relics, a chance to earn a little gold and perhaps even a bit of fun. But as he looked at Farah, the light from the embers flickering across her face, he realized there was more to it than that. The way she moved, the fire in her spirit, it ignited something within him. Something he hadn't expected to feel again, something he had buried away.

With a sigh, he leaned back against the rough boulder behind him, eyes trained on the stars twinkling overhead. He was entangled with Farah deeper than he wanted to be, more than just being a shoulder for her to lean on regardless of her acceptance.

And what of Pari? The girl had a light that seemed to shine through the darkness, and he couldn't help but admire her spirit. She was a part of this strange family they had formed on the road.

As if sensing his thoughts, Pari stirred awake, rubbing her eyes as she blinked against the dim light.

"Yasher?" she mumbled, her voice still thick with sleep.

"Right here, Little Divine," he replied, a smile tugging at his lips.

"What time is it?" she asked, yawning as she stretched.

"Late. But you're just in time for the night's stories." He gestured to the embers, trying to lighten the mood. "I was just telling myself how fortunate I am to have you and Farah with me on this journey."

She sat up, her little face brightening. "You were? I like stories! Tell me more!"

Yasher chuckled softly, grateful for the distraction.

"Well, there's not much to tell, really. Just me wondering why my lucky charm seems to have abandoned me." He gestured to the Eye of Rashnu, feeling a mix of humor and frustration. "I guess it can't always be good fortune, can it?"

Pari tilted her head, a thoughtful expression on her face. "Maybe it's not about luck. Maybe it's about trusting yourself."

His heart skipped a beat, the simplicity of her words striking him with unexpected clarity.

"Trusting myself?" he questioned, trying to mask the way her insight rattled him.

"Rashnu says that we have to believe in ourselves, even when it's hard," she continued, her eyes shining with conviction. "You can do great things, Yasher. You just have to trust. Without it, all I can see is failure."

"I'll remember that," he said, his voice laced with sincerity. "But you know, it's easier said than done."

"I know," she said, nodding. "But you've already done

so much. You've helped us escape the bad men so many times, and you're always there when I need you."

The warmth of her faith in him sent a surge of determination through his veins. "I'll do my best. I promise."

Her eyes sparkled with approval.

Just then, he heard the faintest rustle in the underbrush by the horses, a sound that made his heart race.

"Stay close," he whispered, his instincts kicking in as he scanned the shadows. He felt the tension in the air shift, a sense of foreboding creeping into the night.

"Is something wrong?" Pari asked, her voice barely above a whisper.

"Not yet," he said, keeping his tone calm. "But I need you to stay quiet. Just for a moment."

He sat up and went to his knees, not wanting to give anyone a potential target. He moved in front of the little girl and placed his hand to cover the small light from the dying fire to adjust his vision.

Then he saw it—multiple figures emerging from the darkness, their movements stealthy and deliberate by the horses, just out of sight from the firelight. He pulled one of his daggers out, holding it loosely.

"Phoenix!" he hissed, urgency lacing his voice. "We've got company."

She sat up but stayed low, a dagger already in her hand.

"Where?" She matched his whisper, looking around.

He put a finger to his lips, then pointed over to the horses, his open hand low. The three of them were slightly sheltered by the outcroppings of boulders from the strangers, but they had to have heard his voice as he and Pari spoke.

"We know you see us, gharib." A gruff male voice spoke from the dark. "Drop the knife, and put your hands up."

Yasher was a little thrown at how clear the Common the figure spoke was, with no hint of the normal Emarian accent.

He stood slowly, making a production of leaving his dagger on the ground close to Pari and stepped around Farah, holding his arms out wide while he caught her from the corner of his eye slipping around, low to the ground behind him. He walked towards the shadows, wishing he still had his coat on to make him look a little larger to help cover her movement.

"Hail, gents," he said, making his voice loud and leaning into his Northern accent. "The dagger is down. While I'd ask that you leave the horses, I understand if that's not an option. If you could leave the food for the little girl, it would be a kindness."

A harsh bark of a laugh came from one of the shadows. "Kindness is in short supply in Emari, gharib."

The shadows separated into four distinct shapes, and Yasher took advantage of checking on Pari to turn slightly, making sure that Farah was out of sight.

One of the men stepped into the dying light of the fire that Yasher could finally see his homespun tunic and pants, and boots that looked to have been military conscription once upon a time. His face was lined with a long scar running down it and streaks of gray in his dark hair, but his large build made Yasher very glad that he didn't attempt to fight them.

No, he left that to Farah.

He blinked and all of a sudden, she'd dropped two of the other shadows and had her dagger against the throat of the older man in front of him. The last man rushed from the dark but stopped as she nicked the man's throat, a drop falling on his bright blue scarf around his shoulders. She threw another dagger at the second man, knocking his cudgel out of his hand and into the night.

This woman made his mind a mess when she looked like that.

She glanced back at Yasher, as if she could hear his thoughts, a small smile appearing for a moment before she looked up at the older male's face. The smile disappeared and she stumbled back, lowering her dagger.

"Rostam? What in the Shining Halls! You're... you're alive!" She said, stepping far enough back from the older man that she almost fell into Yasher's arms, shock written all over her face.

"I am. And here I was just about to ask why you were in the mountains with a gharib, Farahnaz." The older man, Rostam, touched his neck where she'd cut him. "We have much to talk about, it seems."

Yasher wrapped his arm around Farah, helping to hold her up.

What in the twelve hells was happening?

CHAPTER 21

Farah shifted uncomfortably as the cart jolted down the rocky path, her wrists chafing against the coarse ropes binding her hands. The healing wound on her side throbbed with each jolt, but she was too numb to feel the full extent of it. Every ache, every bruise felt distant, like they belonged to someone else entirely.

She kept her gaze fixed on Rostam's back as the sun rose, just ahead on horseback, willing him to glance back, to give her some hint that this wasn't real—that the man who had once been her mentor, her friend, hadn't truly turned against her, against Emari.

Yasher leaned against her shoulder, his warmth a quiet reminder that she wasn't completely alone.

"You're looking at him as though you could set him on fire by glare alone," he whispered, his voice barely louder than the rattling cart.

She didn't reply. Instead, she focused on steadying her breath, anchoring herself against the ever-rising tide of anger and betrayal.

Rostam, the man who had taught her how to fight, how

to care for others, how to love her duty and country. He had stripped them of all their weapons, their armor, everything metal. Even now, he kept his distance, knowing exactly the limits of her Talent.

Rostam was supposed to be dead. They had mourned him in the Citadel, honored him with stories of his valor and sacrifice. And now here he was, not just alive but working with the rebels he had supposedly fought and died against.

A familiar, biting anger simmered just beneath her skin, even as she tried to douse it. She'd mourned him—Damned Divine, she still mourned him. Trusted him. And now he was here, speaking as though he hadn't abandoned everything she believed in. As if his betrayal didn't matter.

As dawn crept over the horizon, bathing the landscape in a muted glow, Pari stirred, nestled in Farah's lap.

She turned her bright eyes up to Farah and whispered, "Things are not as they seem."

Farah looked down, surprised by the child's calmness, but a part of her bristled.

"He is a traitor," she hissed back, voice tight. "That much is plain."

"Well," Yasher interjected quietly, glancing over his shoulder at the surrounding rebels, "he didn't kill us. That's something."

"Yet," she muttered, unable to tear her eyes from Rostam's back. "Not yet."

Silence fell over them as the cart rolled on, and Farah leaned her head down, her chin resting on the top of Pari's head. She let her thoughts slip into a meditative state, keeping her focus on the feel of Pari's steady breathing, grounding herself in that simple rhythm. She would need all her strength and clarity for whatever that man had planned.

By midday, the distant sound of clanging metal, voices, and the muted din of a camp drifted toward them. They'd reached the rebel encampment, tucked away in the foothills on the southern side of the mountain range. Her mind took note of every detail, every potential exit and blind spot.

When they finally came to a stop, Rostam swung off his horse and strode over. His gaze met hers briefly, an unreadable glint in his eyes, before he ordered the rebels to pull her, Yasher, and Pari from the cart. His face, once so familiar and steady, now held a sternness that felt foreign. For a moment, he looked every bit the stranger she feared he'd become.

"You'll remain bound until you can prove you're no threat to anyone here, Farahnaz," Rostam said, his tone measured but edged. Farah flinched, hearing her full name fall from his lips—a name he used to say with pride, now said with a coldness that hurt her just as much as his betrayal.

She raised her chin, staring him down. "Is that how you greet those you betrayed? With bonds?"

Rostam's face flickered with something like regret, but it vanished as quickly as it came.

"If betrayal means standing against someone who would poison our people for their own rise in power," he said, voice low, "then, yes, I'll own that."

She stared at him, barely hearing the rest of his words as the shock of what he'd just said settled over her. Poison. Was he speaking of the Mashyana, the woman he once protected?

"You're a fool if you think she'd do that," she shot back,

her voice laced with disdain. "The Mashyana wants only to protect Emari."

"Is that what you believe?" he asked, his tone gentle, as if he were speaking to a child. "Or is that what you were told to believe?"

With a rebel's grip on her arm, Farah was led forward, separating her from the others. She glanced back, seeing Yasher and Pari being taken toward the camp's center, and something clenched in her chest.

She wanted to run to them, to take their hands and turn back, to flee this nightmare. The rebels pulled her towards the largest tent, away from the two of them, she straightened to accept her fate.

Inside, the dim lighting cast the figure before her in half-shadow, his face thinner, a scar slicing across his cheek, rough stitches closing the wound. The man's left arm was bound in a sling, and he sat at a camp desk, reviewing maps. It took her a moment to fully recognize him, but when she did, her breath stopped.

The Mashya. Alive. Not bound as she was, but free.

The world seemed to tilt, and Farah's pulse pounded in her ears. She'd heard at every town and way station since they'd left Banima that the rebels had captured him. That he was missing, likely dead. But here he was, alive, and beside him was Rostam.

"Your Grace," she managed, her voice wavering. Her hands ached from the restraints, her skin raw, yet all she could do was stare.

He looked at her with an expression she couldn't decipher—part sympathy, part sorrow, a strange warmth flickering behind the exhaustion in his eyes.

"So she sent you, did she?" he asked quietly, his voice rough, weakened. "To finish things off?"

Farah swallowed, struggling to keep her composure, though her world felt as though it were slipping out from under her feet. "The Mashyana… it was said the rebels had taken you. She feared for your life."

A bitter smile twisted his lips, and he exchanged a glance with Rostam, one that spoke of understanding, of shared suffering.

"Feared for my life? She sent me here under the guise of negotiation, begging me for the good of the country. But it was a trap, her assassins were waiting for me. When they failed, she planned to lay the blame on the rebels. An easy way to unite Emari under her rule through manufactured outrage and grief." A bitter smile crossed his face. "I'm sure that my state funeral has already happened at the Citadel."

The Mashya's words settled over her like a dark shroud, stifling, heavy. Her queen—the woman she had trusted with her life, the woman she had fought for—had betrayed not only Emari but her own king, her husband?

"No…" she whispered, her voice trembling with a desperation she couldn't contain. "No, she wouldn't. The Mashyana… she wants peace for Emari."

"She wants power," Rostam interjected, his voice colder now. "And she'll sacrifice anyone, even her own people, to get it. Farah, the disease that's been ravaging the people, it isn't natural. It's something she unleashed to weaken the people and take their Talent."

Farah's mind reeled. Her thoughts spun, trying to make sense of what they were saying. The Mashyana with the Mashya had spent years strengthening Emari, bringing stability, unity. How could it all be a lie?

"Why?" she demanded, her voice choked. "Why would she do this?"

"Because power is never enough," the Mashya

answered, his voice sad but steady. "For some, the need to control becomes insatiable. I saw it in her years ago, but I ignored it, believing she would grow wiser, see reason, see that we can achieve peace and prosperity without looking to darker motives. But I was wrong."

She felt as though she were being ripped in two. She wanted to shout at him, to deny every word, to hold onto the loyalty she'd devoted her life to. But the images of the sick, the memories of her queen's strange, calculating gaze, the unease she'd ignored for so long—they clawed at her, demanding to be acknowledged.

A wave of nausea hit her, and she fought to keep her balance, the weight of betrayal nearly buckling her knees.

"Farah," Rostam said softly, and she felt his hand settle on her shoulder, warm, steadying. "I know this is a lot to bear. But this is the truth. You've been trained to follow orders, to believe without question. But now... you have a choice."

She jerked her shoulder away from him, the anger returning, fierce and blinding.

"A choice? What choice, Rostam? You stand here, telling me that everything I've fought for is a lie. That the Mashyana, the woman who saved me, who gave me a purpose, is a monster. And you expect me to just... abandon her?"

"No," the Mashya said, his voice soft but resolute. "But I expect you to see her for who she is. And when the time comes, to decide what you're truly fighting for."

Farah's fists clenched, the skin around her wrists raw from the rope. Her mind spun with doubts, questions, loyalties torn to shreds. She wanted to scream, to tear herself free of this place, this twisted reality.

She looked to the Mashya. "I give you my oath I will not kill your people Release these bonds."

He nodded, and Rostam untied her wrists. She rubbed them lightly, then spun around and stalked out of the tent, looking for anywhere to run. Away from her king and her commander, away from the things that they said. Her anger burned brightly, fighting against the pit of fear that her queen caused all of this. Killed so many people for their Talent, all for power.

She avoided the people milling around, going about their business in the camp as if the world still stood unharmed. Making her way to the ruins of the ancients that were built into the foothills, she scrambled, half-climbing up to one of the lower buildings before she stopped, her side screaming at her and her breath shallow and fast. She sat, her legs hanging down into the air and just stared at the horizon while her thoughts ran rampant. Her world had shattered, leaving her with nothing but pieces, fragments of loyalty and purpose she could barely recognize.

PEOPLE MOVED IN EVERY DIRECTION, cooking, cleaning, tending to horses, and preparing weapons, their energy infectious. Yasher and Pari, led by two rebels who communicated in a mix of broken Common and hand gestures, wandered through the maze of tents. The air was thick with the scent of woodsmoke and the earthy tang of sweat, the sounds of daily life all around them.

Yasher tried to keep his bearings, but the camp was vast, and everything was new. The rebels pointed out different areas, explaining in simple words where the food was prepared, where people slept, where the horses were kept, including the three that were originally theirs. His Emarian was getting better, but it was still hard to follow the fast flow of speech. His eyes darted around constantly, staying aware of their surroundings, but he felt like a stranger here, unsure of who to trust or what to make of this world that felt so foreign.

Pari, on the other hand, had already made herself at home. She was like a spark in the midst of the busy camp, her energy catching the attention of everyone around her. A few children, drawn to her curiosity, quickly surrounded her, and she was lost to them, laughing and chatting in her usual exuberant way.

He watched her, a small smile tugging at his lips despite the tension in his chest. She was so natural in this place, her innocence making the camp feel less threatening. It was almost as though she belonged here, effortlessly adapting to the movement and rhythm of the camp.

By midday, they had been shown around the camp, stopping for a meal near a cooking fire. A group of women had prepared a hearty stew served in large bowls, and they were kind enough to offer it to the two of them. The warmth of the food soothed his hunger, the simple act of eating grounding him for a moment in the chaos of his thoughts.

Pari dove into her meal with enthusiasm, her chatter filling the space between them as the women around her listened, delighted by her. Yasher was more reserved, his thoughts still consumed by the uncertainty of their situation.

Where was she? What had they done with her? He looked at Pari, watching her without her usual sense of worry or fear, and he couldn't help but feel the weight of his responsibility. He'd promised to protect her, but he was also worried about Farah.

As the afternoon wore on, the sun climbing higher, the camp settled into a familiar rhythm. Children played near the fire, soldiers sharpened their weapons, and others moved between tents, carrying out tasks. Yasher, despite his unease, couldn't help but notice how the rebels worked together. There was a unity here, a shared understanding among them, and he found himself watching them with a sense of curiosity.

But despite the warmth of the camp, his thoughts kept drifting back to Farah. The longer she was absent, the more his anxiety grew. He had no idea where she was, what the rebels had planned for her, and with each passing hour, the knot in his stomach only tightened.

Pari, oblivious to his spiraling thoughts, had begun helping the women with a task, her small hands quick and nimble as she assisted in preparing the next meal. The women spoke to her kindly, smiling at her as she worked.

The shadows of the camp stretched longer, and the activity began to slow. Yasher could feel the weight of the day pressing on him, his frustration at not finding Farah mounting. He couldn't keep putting off the inevitable, and he knew it was time to leave Pari and go search for her.

Pari, sensing his change in mood, stopped what she was doing and walked over to him. Her expression was calm, knowing, and she spoke with the same quiet certainty she always had.

"It's okay," she said, her voice soft but firm. "You need to go find her now. I'll be fine here."

He hesitated, his protective instincts flaring as he looked at her, but her gaze softened, reassuring him. "Go. She's going to need you. And I'm not alone."

He looked at her for a long moment, searching her face for any sign of hesitation, but found none. She was more than capable of handling herself, and despite the discomfort he felt leaving her behind, he knew she was right. He had to find Farah.

With a reluctant nod, he patted Pari's head and gave her a small smile. "Stay safe. I'll be back as soon as I can."

Pari smiled back, giving him a wave as she returned to the group of women, already lost in their chatter. Yasher stood for a moment, watching her, then turned, his resolve solidifying as he started moving through the camp again, his eyes scanning the people around him.

He had no time to waste. He needed to find her. But he had no idea where to start. The paths of the camp seemed to stretch on forever, and with each step, he felt the weight of his uncertainty grow. The more he walked, the more he became disoriented, the maze of tents blending into one endless stretch of uncertainty.

His steps slowed, frustration creeping in as he realized he had no clear direction. He had no idea where to go or how to find her in this sprawling camp. The faces of the rebels, who had once seemed so familiar, now blurred around him.

He started watching anyone who wore the bright blue headscarf and their movements to a certain area of tents. That had to be where they'd taken her.

He knew that not even his lucky charm would help them escape as they were literally in the middle of nowhere, but the longer that the three of them weren't together, the more he worried that Farah had been moved to whatever they had as a jail in this temporary village at best, or just took her out into the foothills and killed her at worst. He wouldn't put it past her that she'd taken someone's dagger who'd gotten too close and stabbed Rostam as they walked, honestly.

He found Rostam coming out of a tent, speaking to a few of his men. He slipped into the shadows and waited for him to pass.

"Where is Farah?" he said, sliding next to the man and matching his stride. He kept his hands behind his back, trying to not present as a threat.

"Aqa... Yasher," Rostam replied as if they were greeting one another at a formal event. "Correct?"

"Yasher of Gavrilov," he bowed slightly, still matching the larger man's stride. "At your service. And where is Farah?"

He sighed deeply, looking up to the foothills. "My men say that she is burning off some of her anger up in the hills. I fear that she has many things to work out. Painful things. She has always struggled with change that was not of her making."

"I'd say that she is more competent at that than you give her credit for, Commander." He straightened his back, feeling just a bit of that same anger for her as he was sure she was 'working out'. "In fact, I think that she is more than capable of handling whatever is thrown her way."

"Her queen, the only woman who Farah ever really trusted," the older man said, stopping and turning to Yasher, "is causing a plague in this country in more ways than one. Give her space."

Twelve hells. He didn't really like being right that there was something wrong with the Mashyana and Farah's blind trust in her, but he wasn't expecting it to be so plainly spoken by this man. His Phoenix needed support, not space.

"You may have known Farah once, Commander." he

bites. Without thought he raised his hand, pointing right at the older man's face. "But you don't seem to know the woman that I do."

Rostam straightened up, raising his own hand to snatch Yasher's away and then his shoulders fell as he ran his hand across his own short beard.

"Go to her then," he said softly. "This is not something that she should be going through alone, though she was trained her whole life to do so."

Yasher didn't need to hear any more. He turned back to the hills surrounding, moving around the tents to find the rough pathway up to the ancient buildings. In the dimming light, he saw her, sitting on a ledge of one, staring at the sun behind him. He scrambled up the walkway, at one point climbing over what was once a roof until he figured out how to get to her.

Finally navigating the pathways, he walked up to where she sat, moving next to her. He let his legs hang off the ledge, clasping his hands together in his lap in silence, looking out to the horizon.

"I'm sorry," he whispered, putting his hand out. She ignored it for a moment and then clasped it tightly, still staring at the horizon. He turned to her just as fresh tears fell, retracing tracks that ran down her cheeks.

"I don't know who I am," she whispered back. He squeezed her hand, releasing it, and wrapping his arm around her shoulders, letting her cry into his chest.

He watched the stars pierce the darkening sky, letting the silence settle between them as she leaned against him. Her tears were warm on his chest, a quiet testament to the turmoil she kept locked away behind her hardened exterior. Farah was a fortress, built of iron will and loyalty that most couldn't fathom. But tonight, those strong walls had been destroyed, and he felt the weight of that collapse. He tightened his arm around her, wishing he could shoulder the storm of emotions tearing through her.

He let the moments drift by in silence, his fingers lightly tracing patterns on her shoulder, waiting for her to speak. She needed space to let her thoughts settle, and he was willing to give it, even if the quiet gnawed at him.

Finally, her voice broke through the night, a soft murmur that he had to lean closer to hear. "Everything I believed... it feels like a lie. The Mashyana saved me from dying a pauper in a ditch, gave me a purpose. I dedicated my life to her. And now..."

She trailed off, her voice catching, and Yasher felt her trembling slightly, as if the words themselves were too painful to bear. He brushed a loose strand of her hair behind her ear, his fingers lingering.

"Sometimes... sometimes the people we trust, the ones we're meant to look up to, they can fail us," he said gently, his voice barely above a whisper. "That doesn't mean you're wrong, Farah. You are still the person you've always been. You haven't failed. She has failed you."

She shook her head, pulling back slightly to meet his gaze, her eyes searching his face for something—reassurance, understanding, maybe even absolution.

"How can you say that? Everything I did was for her, for Emari's unity. And now I find out she's... she's causing the very suffering I was raised to protect the people from. To know that by following her I may have caused any of this. It's too much to bear."

Yasher's heart ached as he saw the confusion and betrayal etched across her face. He could see the fracture lines of her faith splintering beneath the surface. He didn't need to know the details of the betrayal that she'd been shown by the Commander and the rebels, he could see it etched on her face.

"I can't imagine what it feels like to be betrayed at this level," he said, choosing his words carefully. "You don't have to believe in her. Not anymore. The loyalty, the strength you gave her, it was real. And it's still a part of you. It's yours to choose where it goes now."

She let out a shaky breath, her shoulders relaxing slightly as his words sank in. She looked down, her fingers tracing absent circles on the stone ledge, her eyes distant.

"I don't know who to trust," she said softly. "I trusted Rostam, the Mashya... and yet, they're asking me to turn against everything I've been taught."

He bit back his own certainty, knowing it wouldn't help. Instead, he spoke the one truth he was sure of.

"Trust yourself, Farah. Your instincts, your judgment. They've brought you this far, and they're worth more than anyone else's words."

She looked up, a flicker of something familiar returning to her eyes. "You always know the right thing to say, don't you?"

He chuckled softly, giving her shoulder a gentle squeeze. "Only with you. The rest of the time, I'm as lost as a desert wanderer without a compass."

A faint smile tugged at her lips, and Yasher felt a warmth spread through him at the sight, relief seeping into his bones. He shifted his hand, sliding it down her arm, letting his fingers intertwine with hers. He could feel the tension still thrumming through her, but her hand tightened around his, grounding them both.

They sat in silence, watching as the last sliver of sun disappeared, the sky deepening into indigo. The stars were clear and bright, their light sharp against the darkness.

After a while, she leaned her head on his shoulder, and he could feel the soft exhale of her breath.

"Thank you," she whispered. "For being here. For... listening."

He tilted his head down, letting his cheek brush against her hair. "As long as you allow me to be, I'll be right here, next to you."

Her hand tightened in his, and the air between them grew heavier. His pulse quickened as he felt her shift, tilting her face up toward his. Her eyes caught his, and for a moment, they were both frozen, held in a cocoon of quiet intimacy.

She closed the space between them, her lips soft and tentative against his, as though testing the edges of the feelings that had pushed and pulled against them. His heart raced, and he returned the kiss, his hand finding the small of her back, pulling her closer.

Her hands moved to his chest, her touch hesitant but growing bolder, and he felt his own restraint slip away. He poured all the unspoken promises she created in him, the comfort he couldn't put into words, into the press of his lips against hers.

Their lips parted briefly, and he met her gaze, searching her face, making sure this was what she wanted. Her eyes, still glassy with tears, held a fire he wanted to dance in. She gave a small nod, almost imperceptible, but it was enough to banish any lingering hesitation.

She reached up, her hands cupping his face, fingers grazing along his jaw. She pulled him down into another kiss, her movements bolder, almost desperate, as if trying to erase the weight of the night.

He responded in kind, letting his hands trace a path down her shoulders, over the curve of her arms, pulling her closer until there was no space between them. The distant sounds of the camp, the murmur of rebels' voices, the crackling of fires—all faded into nothing. There was only her, warm against him, the steady, grounding rhythm of her breathing, the feel of her heartbeat as it quickened in time with his own.

Slowly, she tugged him gently, guiding him down onto the stone ledge beside her. His breath hitched as he moved to rest beside her, the coolness of the stone beneath him a sharp contrast to the heat between them. She shifted, turning toward him, her eyes dark and intent, a vulnerability mingling with the steel resolve he knew so well.

"Yasher..." she whispered, her voice barely audible, as if testing the sound of his name in this new, tender space. He smiled softly, pressing his forehead to hers, breathing in the moment, savoring it.

"I'm here," he murmured, his voice low, comforting, a promise etched into his words.

They lay next to one another, their breaths mingling, the touch of her fingers gliding along his arm, tracing paths that left trails of warmth. He moved his hand, tentative at first, brushing his fingers lightly along the line of her jaw, down her neck, feeling her pulse beneath his touch.

She reached up, her hands threading through his hair, drawing him closer as their lips met again, this time slower, deeper, each kiss a promise, an anchor. He let himself get lost in her, his hand moving to her waist, pulling her even closer as if he could protect her from all the hurt and doubt that had haunted her.

When their lips parted, he pressed his forehead to hers, their breath mingling in the quiet.

"Are you alright?" he asked softly, brushing a stray tear from her cheek.

She hesitated, her fingers tracing his jawline as she searched for the words.

"I don't know," she admitted. "But this... being here with you—it's the only thing that feels real right now."

"You're real," Yasher said firmly, cupping her face in his hands. "Everything you've done, everything you've endured—it's all you. And you're more than enough."

"You deserve everything," he said, his tone serious as he tilted her chin to meet his gaze. "You've given so much of yourself to others—your queen, your country, your people. Let someone give something back to you for once."

She let out a shaky breath, leaning into his touch, her forehead resting against his.

"And what is it you're giving me?" she asked, her tone both teasing and vulnerable.

"Everything," he said simply, his voice steady and full of conviction. "Whatever I have to give, it's yours."

Her response wasn't verbal, but in the way she kissed him again, her lips finding his with more urgency this time. Her hands slid to his shoulders, and he responded, pulling her closer, his movements growing bolder as the barriers between them crumbled.

He pulled back for a moment, his breath uneven as he searched her face. "Farah... are you sure? I don't want to—"

She silenced him with a kiss, her fingers curling into the fabric of his tunic as she pressed closer.

"I'm sure," she murmured against his lips, her voice filled with a quiet determination. "I need this. I need *you*."

His heart pounded as her words sank in, and he felt his own resolve solidify.

"Then you have me," he whispered, brushing his lips across her temple.

Her hands found their way beneath his tunic, her

fingers grazing his skin, and he shivered at her touch. She guided him gently, her movements confident despite the vulnerability between them, and he let himself be led, his own hands exploring the contours of her body as he pulled her tunic away.

He savored every moment, every touch, every soft sound she made, committing it all to memory in case it was all ripped away later on in the light of day.

He shifted slightly, his hands sliding down her back to grip her hips, guiding her movements as they explored the edges of the feelings they had long kept hidden. Her breath hitched against his lips, a sound that sent a thrill through him, and he let himself lean into the moment fully, letting her set the pace as her hands moved to his back, pulling him closer.

As the stars shone brightly above and the night wrapped around them, they stayed in that space together, letting the intimacy between them deepen, both in body and in spirit.

CHAPTER 22

THE MORNING LIGHT seeped through the cracks in the crumbling walls of the ruins, casting a soft, muted glow across Farah's face. She blinked against the brightness, her eyes adjusting as memories of the night before filtered in.

The steady warmth of Yasher's arm draped over her waist, his slow, deep breaths against her shoulder were a strangely welcome way to wake. They'd sheltered under his coat after they'd shared themselves with one another, a weak blanket against the chill to their bare skin.

Farah's pulse quickened, and she lay still, caught between the comfort of his presence and the awkwardness of what it meant. This was Yasher—unpredictable, frustrating, the last person she would have expected to be here with like this. And yet, she couldn't deny the warmth that spread through her, even as she felt a flicker of uncertainty, wondering what he was thinking.

Yasher stirred beside her, his arm shifting slightly as he blinked, his eyes slowly opening. She felt him freeze for a second, as if he too was trying to process where he was, the weight of her body beside his. His gaze met hers, his expression softening in a way that made her heart skip.

"Morning," he murmured, his voice rough with sleep, a hint of his usual smile tugging at the corner of his mouth.

"Morning," she replied, her voice a little stiffer than she'd intended, a strange heat creeping into her cheeks. She shifted slightly, trying to create a bit of space between them without being too obvious, but the movement only drew his attention.

"Didn't think I'd wake up with you still here," he said, his tone light but his gaze searching, as if he were trying to read her reaction.

She cleared her throat, her gaze dropping as a wave of self-consciousness washed over her.

"I didn't think I would either." She kept her tone neutral, though her pulse quickened under his steady gaze.

A silence settled between them, not tense exactly, but charged, filled with unspoken words. She fumbled for something casual as she pulled her tunic on, something to defuse the feeling that lingered, even as she felt Yasher's eyes on her, his hand resting near her, as if he too was unsure of how to bridge the gap left by last night.

"You sleep like a rock," she commented, finally managing to find a lightness in her voice. "I almost thought you'd forgotten where we were."

He chuckled, rubbing the back of his neck, his own awkwardness apparent.

"Well, it's not every night I... end up like this," he admitted, a small grin surfacing before he cleared his throat, looking away briefly. "Guess you make good company."

She raised an eyebrow, feeling a reluctant smile tug at her lips. "Good company? I seem to remember you getting an elbow to the ribs at one point."

"That was just instinct," he said with a grin, his eyes twinkling. "Didn't know you were so ticklish."

The playful exchange settled some of the awkwardness, allowing a comfortable silence to take its place. But as they sat up, gathering their things and dressing, their hands brushed, and Farah felt a spark of awareness shoot through her, reminding her that, beneath the banter, something deeper lingered.

They both straightened, each giving the other a side-long glance, unspoken questions hanging in the air. For Farah, the night had been a rare vulnerability, a quiet comfort amid the chaos of recent events, yet she was hesitant to name it, to let it change things between them. She didn't know how to voice that, and perhaps, neither did he.

He looked down, absently adjusting his belt, and she couldn't help but notice his slightly flustered expression.

"So... back to reality?" he asked, a touch of humor masking his uncertainty.

She nodded, her hand briefly resting on his arm, a gesture that felt natural yet strange at the same time.

"Back to reality," she echoed, her voice softer.

He pulled her towards him, his head bent down, a breath away from her.

"Wait." He kissed her roughly, pulling the rest of her body up against him. She felt herself melt into his embrace, wanting nothing more than to slip back down and tangle herself with him again.

He pulled away after both forever and not enough time, his irritating grin already on his face that made her want to slap him.

"That's better. Let's go, Phoenix."

The strange warmth of their shared night coursed

through her as they made their way back to the camp, hand in hand.

The awkwardness of the morning after had faded into something subtler that neither of them seemed eager to disrupt. They walked in comfortable silence, exchanging glances but saying little, afraid to break the moment. She pulled away from him, releasing his hand only as the camp came into view begrudgingly, rebels bustling around as the sun rose higher.

As they entered the heart of the temporary village, a voice called out to her.

"Farahnaz."

She turned to see the Mashya, standing outside his tent. His gaze was intense, his posture a bit more formal than she'd seen yesterday. He gave a small nod to Yasher but held Farah's gaze with a silent insistence.

"Farah," he repeated, his tone softer, almost private. "Might I speak with you?"

"Of course, your Grace." She glanced at Yasher, who met her gaze with a look that seemed to say, I'll be close. She nodded back at him, then followed Enayat into his tent, where the muted light and quiet atmosphere offered a stark contrast to the camp outside.

The tent was sparsely decorated, with only a few chairs and a table covered in maps, scrolls, and weathered papers. A simple camp cot that seemed out of place for someone like the Mashya set in the corner.

She took a seat across from him, studying her with a gaze that felt both familiar and weighted.

"We left much unspoken yesterday. There's much you still don't know," he began, his voice low and somber. "I realize I've given you pieces, fragments of the truth, but not the full picture. I owe you more than that. You deserve to know what you're up against. And why I've come to this point against the woman I gave my heart to."

Farah held his gaze, her heartbeat quickening. This was the moment she'd both dreaded and anticipated, the confirmation of everything she'd been afraid to believe.

She gave him a slight nod, her voice steady. "I am ready to hear it, your Grace."

Enayat let out a heavy sigh, his face lined with the weight of memories. "Behnaz and I once shared a vision of Emari united. We were not just rulers. We were partners in creating something better than ourselves. When I say I loved her, it is not a small thing. I fought my advisors to marry for love or at least companionship, not just for political gain when my father forced me to find a bride. Behnaz and I seemed to not only be compatible, but there was a genuine connection from the moment we met."

He paused, gathering his thoughts, and she noticed the tension in his face.

"When we first came to power," he continued, his voice soft but unwavering, "she was as compassionate, loyal to Emari's well-being as I was. But over time, she began to seek out... darker influences. She had always been ambitious, always looking at ways to expand a Talent, collecting you and your other Beloveds, some from poverty like yourself, thinking that there were ways to collect the Talents to share them to those not blessed, but this was different. She wanted power not just for Emari's unity, but for herself. And in time, she found something—or rather, something found her that she could use, which twisted all of her grace and compassion into something hard and unforgiving."

Farah felt a chill creep down her spine, the words resonating with the whispers she'd heard in the past, the rumors she'd always dismissed as court gossip.

"What kind of power?" she asked, her voice barely above a whisper, afraid of the answer.

"Something older than Emari as we know it," he replied, his voice hardening. "A darkness that existed before our kingdom, a force that feeds on life, on strength. Something that should have abandoned our plane as the gods did, but stayed in the darkest corners, hiding. She struck a bargain with it, allowing her to tap into a power that could keep her in control for lifetimes, for generations. But there was a cost—a cost she was willing to pay at the expense of Emari's people."

Farah's stomach churned, the pieces falling into place with a sickening clarity. The sickness spreading through the Talented in the country — this was no accident. It was all by design, an elaborate, cruel scheme to feed her power.

"The wasting sickness," she murmured, almost to herself. "She's using it to weaken the people, to draw their Talents to herself..."

Enayat nodded, his expression grim. "Yes, that is the only thing that it can be. Each Talent she drains is another layer of power she adds to herself. Part of the appeal of her House to my father was the strength of the Talented in her line, but she has outpaced and outstripped anyone in their history. The people suffer while she grows stronger, and with each passing day, her hold on Emari tightens, distorts and grows resentments and disorder as if this Darkness can feed off of that as well. I discovered this too late. When I confronted her, she attempted to silence me, first with persuasion, then with threats, and finally with an assassination attempt."

Farah's fists clenched, anger flaring hotly within her. "And when that failed..."

"Yes, when that failed." The Mashya's voice held a note

of bitterness, looking down at his arm, and then touching his face and the scar tenderly. "The rebels have been her scapegoats, her excuse for control. By painting them as violent insurgents, she can justify any level of oppression, all under the guise of maintaining order. Rostam joined them after he found out she was the reason his younger brother, Darius, died. He was one of her first Beloveds... and one of the first experiments with the sickness after she made him Hand."

She stared down at her hands, the realization settling over her like a heavy fog. Her memories of Darius were colored by the rumors that swirled through the Beloveds after he died.. She did remember the pain that it had caused Rostam, and how he'd trained her harder after his death to be able to protect herself with or without her Talent.

She had spent her entire life serving a woman she had believed in, a queen she had thought giving and just, only to discover that her loyalty had been built on lies. She felt as though the ground had opened beneath her, as though her very purpose had been ripped from her.

"Why didn't you stop her? Before she'd taken in that much power?" she asked, a sharp edge to her voice warring with the idea that she spoke so plainly to her king. She hated the desperation in her own tone, the need to make sense of the senseless. "You are the Mashya, anointed by your ties directly to the Unnamed Gods. Couldn't you have done something?"

His face softened, a look of regret darkening his features. "I tried. I tried in every way I knew. But her power grew beyond my reach, her influence poisoning the court, turning allies into enemies. By the time I realized the extent of her corruption, it was too late. She had already sealed her bond with the Darkness, and my influence was limited even within my own court. I became a threat to her, a loose end to be eliminated and discarded."

She clenched her jaw, grappling with the anger and grief roiling inside her. All this time, she'd been serving the Mashyana, convinced she was protecting Emari. But now, every order she'd carried out, every act of loyalty, felt hollow, tainted.

"Is there no way to break her hold?" she asked, though her voice wavered with doubt. "If her power comes from this Darkness, can't it be undone?"

"There is one hope." His expression grew solemn, his gaze steady as he met her eyes. "The relic we spoke of, the one she sent you here for, hidden in the Forgotten Temple. Ancient writings describe it as a weapon forged to combat Darkness, a force that could balance the scales and strip power from those who would abuse it. We believe it lies somewhere in the caves near here. That is why we have camped here, to try and find it."

Farah's heart raced, the familiar pang of her mission surfacing. The third relic the Mashyana had tasked her with retrieving. If this relic was the same one, then she had been manipulated into a quest that could lead to Emari's destruction. Her stomach twisted at the thought, the realization cutting deeper than any wound she'd ever received in battle.

"So she sent me to retrieve this relic for her," she said bitterly, the betrayal sinking in. "She must have known it could either strip her of power or seal her control over everything. She used me."

His eyes softened with sympathy, though his expression held a grim resolve. "She chose you not just because of your drive and Talent, but because she knew you were loyal, because she knew you wouldn't question her. But now that you know the truth, you have the power to stop this. To stop her. I... don't have that power."

She took a shaky breath, feeling the enormity of her decision settle over her. She had always been the most loyal of Mashyana's Beloveds, following her will without question. But now, that loyalty felt hollow, a broken promise bound to a queen who had betrayed her people.

She closed her eyes. The knowledge, the murky path stretching before her. She had never questioned her loyalty, had never felt the need to. But now, as she stood on the edge of a new truth, the doubt clawed at her, leaving her feeling as though she were walking blindly into darkness.

"I don't know if I am that person," she whispered, the vulnerability in her voice unfamiliar and raw. "I've spent so long believing in her, in her vision. I don't know if I can see clearly anymore."

His hand found hers, the warmth of his touch grounding her. "Farah, trust isn't a thing easily regained, especially when it's been broken by those we hold dear. But questioning yourself, doubting—that's part of the journey. It means you're willing to see beyond what's been shown to you."

She looked up, meeting his gaze. In his eyes, she saw the weight of his own regrets, his own pain. He wasn't just a king without a throne; he was a man who had lost everything he had once protected and fought for, including the woman who held his heart. And yet, he remained here, willing to confront the darkness that had overtaken his kingdom.

With a deep breath, she nodded. "I'll stop her."

The Mashya's face softened, and he nodded, a faint smile breaking through his stern expression. "Thank you, Farah. Emari needs more people like you—those who are willing to fight for more than power, for more than themselves."

The words sank into her, filling the hollow places left by her broken loyalty. She had fought for the Mashyana, thinking that she was fighting for the people, but now she would fight for Emari, for the people whose suffering she had been blind to.

"Be patient and recover from your travels here with my blessing. We are sending out scouts to cover the foothills surrounding the area. If the Forgotten Temple is here, we will find it."

As she rose to leave, the Mashya's voice called her back one last time.

"I asked Rostam to make sure that you are welcomed into the camp by the people here. You and your companions," he said, leaning back in his chair and running his free hand against his injured arm, the exhaustion visible.

Stepping out of the tent, she felt the cool morning air brush against her face. She spotted Yasher waiting nearby, speaking with Rostam, his eyes lighting up as she approached. She felt a surge of warmth and felt a small smile cross her face.

Rostam smirked at her, leaning against a staff. He stood up straight and tossed the staff to her.

"It's been too long since we've sparred," he said, taking another staff from one of his men nearby. "Let us see how rusty you are, if you are not too stiff from sleeping... in the elements." He glanced at Yasher before walking away, and she could feel the heat crossing her face.

She caught Rostam's smirk and narrowed her eyes, she could almost hear the unspoken judgment in it. Though she had not been a student of his since he'd left on his mission to Tamidh before the Trials, if there was anything — or anyone — that took her away from her training, he took personal affront to them.

She took a steadying breath. If he wanted a sparring match, she'd give him one. He owed her in his skin for the grief she'd suffered, first for his departure, then for his supposed death.

Yasher moved back, giving them space, though she could feel his gaze lingering on her, a quiet support that steadied her in ways she didn't want to admit to herself quite yet. The warmth from their shared night still lingered, though it felt fragile under the scrutiny of Rostam's watchful eyes. He might be a friend, a mentor, but she knew this spar was more than just exercise. It was a test.

"Are you healed enough to spar?" Yasher asked, tension in his shoulders as he took a step back towards her.

"I'm fine. I promise," she said softly, brushing her hand on his arm before moving to face Rostam. She could keep up with her old mentor, even if she was still a little stiff from their encounter and sleeping rough last night.

The old man swung his staff in a smooth arc, testing its weight, his gaze steady on her, evaluating.

"I taught you better than that stance," he remarked, arching an eyebrow.

She set her feet, her grip firm, her muscles tense as she raised her staff.

"Is this better, Commander?" she shot back, the title slipping out with a hint of edge. "Or are you just rusty on remembering my style?"

His eyes narrowed, but there was a hint of amusement in them.

"You haven't lost that bite, then. Good." Without another word, he lunged, his staff sweeping low toward her ankles. "Let's see if you remember anything I taught you."

She dodged swiftly, spinning the staff to deflect his attack and using the momentum to strike toward his shoulder. He blocked her move, his strength almost dislodging the staff from her hands. The force behind it reminded her that he wasn't holding back, that this was no spar to go easy on.

"Good. You've kept your speed," he muttered, his gaze sharp as they circled each other. "But have you kept your focus? Sleeping rough does wreak havoc with staying on task."

Her lips pressed into a line, the jab hitting closer than she'd like. She met his next move, twisting her body as their staffs collided with a resounding crack.

"My focus is strong, old man," she replied, her voice taut.

He stepped back, giving a slight nod, his face unreadable. "Don't let distractions lead you astray." His gaze flicked briefly to Yasher, his eyes narrowing before he looked back at her.

Farah tensed, but she refused to let it affect her stance, pushing him back with a series of rapid strikes.

"Distractions such as faking my own death?"

His expression hardened, his stance shifting as he braced for her blows, parrying each one with practiced precision.

"Loyalty to the wrong person... is worse than no loyalty at all." His voice was clipped, each word landing like a blow of its own.

Her jaw tightened, her muscles straining as she met his strength, her frustration building with each block and strike. He didn't trust her judgment—no, it was worse than that. He didn't trust her.

"Is that what you think?" she spat, her voice sharper

than intended. She swung low, and he dodged, his footwork light despite his age. "That I'm unable to see clearly?"

His eyes flashed with something unreadable, his tone rough. "I think that you've faced choices you shouldn't have had to face. And that can distort your vision."

He blocked her next strike, his staff twisting to hook under hers, using the leverage to pull her closer, almost forcing her off balance. She didn't flinch, meeting his gaze with defiance.

"You don't get to decide who I trust," she said, breathing hard, her voice steady despite her frustration. "You taught me to be strong. Let me."

For a moment, there was silence, broken only by their labored breathing. Rostam's eyes softened, and Farah saw a flicker of something—a hint of regret?—pass through his features, but it was gone almost immediately. He stepped back, releasing her staff with a swift movement, giving her space.

She wasn't done, though. There was one thing he needed to hear, one thing that would shake him more than any of their sparring could.

"The Mashyana sent Arash to Banima to follow me," Farah said, her voice cutting through the silence. "She didn't trust me either."

Rostam froze, his expression shifting, his usual calm now cracked. His eyes widened ever so slightly, his brow furrowing in a rare show of disturbance. The shock hit him harder than any of her strikes had. He hadn't expected that —none of them had.

His breath faltered as he processed the information.

"Arash followed you?" His voice was tight, a surge of disbelief and anger clouding his features. "To Banima?"

Farah nodded, meeting his gaze with a steady look, her chest tight with the weight of it all.

"Yes. But Yasher... Yasher sent him away." Her words were like a weight lifted from her shoulders, letting them hang between them as the tension crackled. She nodded her head over to Yasher standing to the side. "He made sure Arash didn't follow us into the mountains."

Rostam's face darkened, his grip tightening on his staff as if the news had physically unsettled him.

The world seemed to hold its breath as she stood, watching him. He opened his mouth to speak but seemed at a loss for words. His gaze softened, but the sharp edge of his thoughts was evident.

"Well," he finally murmured, his voice low and measured, "perhaps this isn't about trust at all." He paused, looking at her with a mix of frustration and something else she couldn't quite place. "But if she's sending him after you, then I've underestimated what she's willing to do."

The words hung heavy in the air, and Farah felt a strange shift between them.

She raised her chin, her stance firm. "I'll manage, Rostam. You taught me how to fight. Now let me protect what's mine."

For a brief moment, he looked at her with something unreadable in his gaze, but he nodded slowly. "Very well. Then show me."

She attacked with renewed focus, her frustration boiling over into each strike, each precise swing of her staff. She could feel her strength returning, the doubts that had haunted her dissipating as her body moved with the familiar rhythm of combat. This was where she felt sure, where she felt grounded—where no one could question her loyalty but herself.

He met her attack with equal ferocity, and for a while, they danced around each other, locked in a fierce exchange of blows. She noticed his shortness of breath, the slight tremor in his stance, and though he was still formidable, she sensed he was holding back—just slightly, but enough for her to know he was testing her.

"Good," he muttered, nodding approvingly as he stepped back, allowing a moment's pause.

Farah lowered her staff, her breathing heavy, her heart pounding as she held his gaze.

"I am no wilting flower," she said, though the words came out softer than she intended, a hint of vulnerability creeping in.

He nodded, the harshness in his expression softening.

"I don't doubt your strength, Farah. I doubt the intentions of those around you." His gaze flicked to Yasher, who had been watching from a short distance, his expression unreadable, his posture tense.

Her fists clenched around her staff. "He's proven himself," she said, her voice firm.

His eyes narrowed, a brief flash of annoyance crossing his face. "And why should I believe that? A foreigner wandering into Emari, aligning himself with our cause because he wants to bed you?"

She stepped between them, her gaze sharp, daring him to question her judgment further.

"Enough, old man," she said, her tone cold. "He has been honest with me, even when I didn't want to hear the truth. Unlike you."

Rostam looked at her, his expression a mix of frustration and something else—something she hadn't seen in him before. Grief that cut through the usual mask of command. Her hands tightening around her staff, knowing that her words had cut him worse than she could have with the fight.

"Very well," he said at last, though his tone held a trace of reluctance. "But be cautious. Those we bring into our circle can fall short at the wrong moment."

She lowered her gaze briefly, the weight of his warning settling over her. But she nodded, acknowledging the truth in his words, even as she held firm in her trust of Yasher.

"Thank you," she murmured, her voice softer, laced with both gratitude and finality. She would listen to his advice as she'd done most of her life, but she wouldn't let it dictate her choices. Not anymore.

His gaze lingered on her for a moment, and then he nodded, his expression a mixture of pride and resignation.

"You've grown strong, stronger than I had anything to do with," he said, his tone carrying a hint of respect. "Hold that strength close. You'll need it."

He stepped back, nodding to her before turning to walk away. His posture was as stiff and proud as ever. She watched him go, feeling the ache of their sparring settle into her muscles, but she welcomed it. The fight had left her feeling clearer, more grounded.

Yasher approached her, his gaze warm but concern etched across her face.

"All is well?" he asked, his voice gentle as he reached out, his hand brushing hers.

She nodded, giving him a faint smile. "Yes. Rostam and I... we needed that."

He chuckled softly, his fingers lingering against hers. "I gathered as much. Though I can't say he's entirely thrilled about me."

Farah laughed, a quiet, tired sound, and squeezed his hand gently. "Give him time."

His gaze softened, a look of gratitude and a tenderness that made her heart ache, in a way that was both comforting and terrifying. "For you, I'll give him all the time in the world," he murmured, his voice barely audible.

She felt her breath catch, and she held his gaze, the warmth of his words settling over her like a balm.

———

THE SPARRING MATCH had left Farah's body strained with exhaustion, her muscles sore from the brutal pace Rostam had set. The sharp ache of each movement reminded her of how he fought—precise, relentless, and unyielding. But it wasn't just the physical strain that lingered. His words clung to her like a second skin, needling at her thoughts.

He had always been a complicated figure in her life. Protector, mentor, deserter. His reappearance had shattered more than her trust. It had broken pieces of herself she wasn't sure how to put back together, separate but no less painful than the Mashyana's betrayal.

After a quiet meal and invocation, finding Pari fully ensconced with the camp cooks, Yasher was a quiet presence at her side as they found their way to their tent. He didn't fill the space with his usual banter for once.

The camp was alive with activity. Fires crackled, voices rose in animated discussion, the clang of weapons being cleaned and repaired echoed through the air, but it all felt distant, as if they were moving through a different world entirely. His hand brushed against hers, sending an electric jolt through her, grounding her in the present.

When they stepped inside their tent, the warm air wrapped around her, carrying the faint scent of canvas and herbs. She paused, her eyes adjusting to the dim light filtering through the fabric walls. The space was small but familiar, the bedding neatly arranged, their packs stacked in one corner. The noise of the camp outside dulled to a low hum, leaving them alone in the soft stillness.

She rolled her shoulders, wincing as the tension from Rostam's strikes flared up again. Yasher's sharp eyes caught the movement, and he was at her side in an instant, his hand brushing over her arm. His touch was light, hesitant, but it sent a warmth through her that she hadn't expected.

"You're hurt," he said, his voice low and tinged with concern. His gaze lingered on the bruise forming along her forearm, and she could see the subtle tightening of his jaw.

"I've had worse," she replied, shrugging it off. But she didn't move away, letting his fingers linger against her skin. The truth was, she didn't want to push him away.

He tilted his head, his lips curving into a teasing smile that didn't quite reach his eyes. "Rostam doesn't pull his punches, does he? It's like he's still trying to prove something."

She huffed a quiet laugh, the sound dry but not unkind.

"He doesn't have to prove anything to me," she said, her tone softening. "I think he's just trying to make up for lost time."

He studied her for a moment, his smile fading into something quieter, more contemplative.

"And what about you?" he asked, his voice gentle. "How are you holding up?"

The question caught her off guard, its simplicity

masking the depth of what he was really asking. She looked away, her gaze falling to the floor as she struggled to find the right words.

"I don't know," she admitted finally. "I feel... unmoored still. Like everything I thought I knew is slipping through my fingers."

He reached for her hand, his touch steady and grounding.

"Don't carry it alone, Phoenix," he said softly.

His words, so simple yet so earnest, broke something loose inside her. She turned to him, her eyes meeting his, and for the first time in what felt like an eternity, she let herself lean into his presence without any of her pride blocking it.

"Thank you," she whispered, her voice trembling.

His hand slid to her cheek, his thumb brushing lightly against her skin.

"You don't have to thank me," he murmured, his voice low and steady. "Just let me be here for you."

Her heart clenched at the tenderness in his gaze, the way he looked at her like she was something precious. She leaned into his touch, her eyes slipping shut as she let the warmth of his presence wash over her. And then, as if drawn by an invisible force, she tilted her head, her lips brushing against his in a tentative kiss.

The contact was soft, hesitant, but it sparked a fire that had been smoldering between them since they woke in each other's arms this morning. He responded immediately, his lips moving against hers with a gentle urgency, his hand sliding to the back of her neck to pull her closer.

She melted into him, her hands finding their way to his chest, her fingers curling into the fabric of his tunic, pulling it up and off him. He returned the movement in kind, their skin needing to not have a barrier between them.

Their movements grew bolder as she pulled his face back to hers. His hands roamed her back, his touch firm and reassuring, grounding her in a way that nothing else could. She let herself be swept away, focused on the warmth of his embrace, the steadiness of his touch.

They broke apart briefly, their foreheads resting together as they caught their breath. His eyes searched hers, his expression a mix of awe and vulnerability.

"Tell me this is what you want, Phoenix. Farah," he whispered, her name like a prayer on his lips.

She pulled him back into another kiss, her hands slipping to his loose trousers and their ties. He groaned softly, the sound vibrating through her as his hands found her waist, guiding her closer until there was no space left between them.

They moved together, shedding any clothing remaining with a mix of urgency and reverence, their touches growing more deliberate, more intimate. Her fingers traced the scars that marked his body, her touch soft but insistent, as if committing every inch of him to memory. His hands explored her body in kind, glancing over the scars she carried, his touch leaving a trail of warmth in its wake.

The world outside their tent ceased to exist, the noise of the camp fading into nothingness as they lost themselves in each other. Farah let herself surrender, let herself be held, let herself feel.

As the night stretched on, their movements slowed, the urgency giving way to something softer, more profound. They lay tangled together, their breaths mingling, their hearts beating in sync. She rested her head against his chest, her fingers tracing lazy patterns along his skin as a sense of quiet contentment settled over her.

In that moment, wrapped in his arms, she felt something she hadn't felt in a long time—peace. It wasn't the kind of peace that came from certainty or resolution, but the kind that came from knowing she wasn't alone. And for now, that was enough.

CHAPTER 23

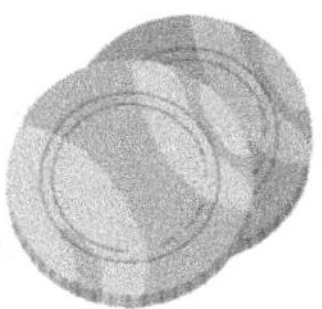

YASHER LEANED against the post of the supply tent, staring absently at the bustling camp, his thoughts drifting back to the evenings he and Farah spent together to calm the temper that another argument with Rostam had raised in him.

It never mattered what he said or did, the Commander had decided that he was wrong and did everything in his power to share his opinion to the small camp. The days had turned to weeks as they waited for word from the scouts, and Rostam's sheer presence made them drag along even longer.

The nights, though, wrapped in the dim light of a camp lantern they unraveled pieces of each other. She told him about her childhood at court, training with Rostam, even Shirin's care and attention.

In turn, he had shared fragments of his own past—stories of the North and the snow that stayed on the ground not just high up in the mountains, traveling across vast forests, and the life of a drifter with no ties. He held back some of the darker parts of his own story, glossing over the reason he wandered through life, leaning into learning as much as he could about her story, and then her body as their relationship grew.

Those nights had been transformative, pointing out to him that he was always outside looking in, and until recently, that was enough.

For years, he had thrived on impermanence, leaving before things became too complicated or expectations grew too heavy. But with Farah, the thought of leaving didn't feel like a relief—it felt like a betrayal. Her trust, her quiet strength, and the way she looked at him with equal measures of exasperation and affection made him feel seen in a way that unsettled him, making him crave more.

He wanted to be a part of her life, to not be the man that Rostam thought he was. And that terrified him. Because if he let himself believe he could be that man, the fear of falling short loomed even larger.

"Yasher!" Pari's bright voice cut through his spiraling thoughts, and he straightened as she bounded toward him, her braids bouncing and her small face glowing with excitement.

"Little Divine," he greeted with a grin, crouching to meet her as she came to a halt in front of him. "What mischief are you up to now?"

"I'm helping cook again!" she announced proudly, holding up a basket filled with herbs. "They said I'm the best at picking the fresh ones."

"Of course, they'd be lost without you," Yasher said, tapping her nose lightly with a finger. "What else have you been up to? Made any deals I should know about? Running a card game in the children's tent? Wrangling horses in the plains?"

Pari giggled, her eyes sparkling. "You are so silly.

Everyone here is so nice. I have so many friends already. They let me help with everything!"

His smile softened as he watched her. Pari had an uncanny ability to weave herself into any community as if she'd always belonged. The rebels adored her, welcoming her into their routines without hesitation. She flitted from one group to another, always eager to assist, her bright energy lifting even the most somber faces. Genuinely. Honestly.

He envied her for that. His community was always transactional.

For him, the camp was a space he navigated carefully, mindful of the wary glances and whispered skepticism. He didn't blame them. After all, he was the hanger-on to the Hand with no clear stake in their cause, as certain folk declared at every opportunity.

What if he couldn't change? What if his nature won out and he spoiled this fragile thing that they had? What if she looked at him the way that she did not so long ago in an alley at the Citadel, ready to gut him like a fish, because he did something that was unforgivable?

"Yasher?" Pari's voice broke through his internal turmoil, and he blinked, realizing she was watching him closely, her head tilted. "Are you okay?"

"Of course," he said, ruffling her hair with a grin that he didn't quite feel. "Just thinking about what kind of trouble you're going to drag me into next."

She giggled, her earlier concern forgotten. "I know, I'll teach you how to cook! You're really bad at it."

"Hey now," he said, mock-offended. "I'll have you know I make an excellent... no... uh... you know, never you mind. Teach me, Little Divine. I am a lost soul in need of instruction."

She dissolved into laughter, clutching her basket of herbs as if it were the most hilarious thing she'd ever heard. He couldn't help but chuckle along, the sound of her laughter a balm to his troubled thoughts.

"Let's get those herbs to the cooks before they start sending out search parties for their star helper," he said, standing and offering her his hand.

She slipped her small hand into his, her trust in him unwavering despite the doubts he carried within himself. As they walked toward the cook fire, the warmth of the campfire and the chatter of the rebels around them filled the air.

He lingered by the fire, hands resting lightly on his hips as he watched Pari animatedly explain something to the cooks. Her small hands gestured wildly, her braids bouncing with each word, and the people around her laughed, clearly charmed by her infectious enthusiasm.

He stepped back slightly, letting her work her magic, his gaze drifting toward the surrounding tents. Smoke curled lazily upward from scattered fires, and the late afternoon sun cast golden hues over the camp, softening its rough edges. The rebels moved with purpose, preparing supplies, sharpening weapons, and exchanging quick words.

He reached into his pocket and felt the smooth surface of the Eye of Rashnu, its cool weight grounding him. It still wouldn't let him take it out of the pocket, but it would let him at least touch the relic again, as if he'd proven himself to it. It reassured him, a gentle pulse against his fingers, as if saying, 'Stay. You can do this.'

A ripple of warmth spread through him, though it did little to silence the darker thoughts that lurked beneath. *I'm no hero.* And he couldn't help but think that Farah needed one of those.

"Yasher!" Pari's voice cut through his thoughts again, and he turned to see her running toward him, her basket now empty. "They said thank you for helping me bring the herbs. And the stew will be ready soon!"

He knelt slightly, meeting her eager gaze. "Stew, huh? Did you save me the best bowl?"

She tilted her head, pretending to consider. "Mmm... maybe. But only if you promise not to make the face you made last time this time."

"I make no promises," he replied with a dramatic sigh. "I'm a man of danger, Pari. I live life on the edge."

She giggled, grabbing his hand and tugging him toward the fire. "Come on, let's sit down. You can tell me more stories about all your dangerous adventures."

"Oh, you want stories, do you?" he said, following her with a grin. "Let me see... Did I ever tell you about the time I outwitted three merchants and a guard captain in one afternoon?"

Her eyes widened with curiosity. "No! What happened?"

He settled onto a log near the fire, pulling Pari into the seat next to him. People passed by with bowls of steaming soup, nodding to him or offering faint smiles, and he returned the gestures, his charm as much a shield as a tool.

"Well," he began, leaning in conspiratorially, "it all started with a set of dice, a lousy hand of cards, and a very, very angry captain..."

As he spun the tale, embellishing details and drawing laughter from her, he felt some of his tension ease. For a moment, the doubts and fears melted away, replaced by the simple joy of making her smile. He caught glimpses of others listening in, some chuckling softly at his antics. It wasn't much, but it felt like a small step toward something he hadn't dared to hope for: belonging.

The story wrapped up with a flourish, Pari clapping her hands and laughing as he made an exaggerated bow from his seat. He looked up to see Farah approaching from the direction of the main tents, her expression softening as she caught sight of them by the fire.

He rose as she drew near, his grin faltering slightly as he read the weariness in her face.

"How'd the meeting go today?" he asked, his tone light but his concern genuine.

She sighed, running a hand through her hair. Her hair was loose today, and all he wanted to do was bury himself in it.

"The scouts are still searching the foothills, but there's tension in the ranks to move on Banima. The Mashya is pushing for faster progress from the scouts and to hold on moving on, but Rostam thinks we're risking too much with these searches. It's... complicated."

He offered a crooked smile, hoping to lift her spirits. "You are wonderful at navigating complicated men, Phoenix."

Her lips twitched at the nickname, and she shook her head. "You're so insufferable."

"And yet, you keep me around," he quipped, his gaze softening as he stepped closer. "Come on, sit with us. Pari's been schooling me in the finer points of stew etiquette."

She arched an eyebrow but allowed herself to be guided to the log. Pari immediately leaned against her side, chattering about the herbs and her role in the kitchen. He watched them, his chest tightening with an emotion he couldn't quite name.

This was what he wanted. This fragile, imperfect

harmony. And for the first time in a long while, he let himself hope that he could be the man they needed him to be.

———

THE FIRST LIGHT of dawn filtered through the thin fabric of their tent, painting everything in soft, golden hues. Yasher blinked awake, the world around him quiet except for the sounds of the rebel camp beginning to stir around them. For a moment, he lay still, the warmth of the blankets and Farah's presence beside him a cocoon he didn't want to break.

Her hair spilled across her face in dark waves, her breathing steady and deep. He watched her, his heart a steady drumbeat in his chest, a sound he was suddenly keenly aware of.

She looked so peaceful like this, her usually sharp and guarded features softened by sleep. It was a side of her he rarely saw, a vulnerability she didn't let the world witness, and he felt an ache in his chest that he couldn't quite name. Or rather, he could, but he wasn't sure he was ready to admit it fully.

I'm in so much trouble, he thought, a wry smile tugging at his lips.

Farah shifted slightly, her hand curling tighter against his ribs as if she could sense his thoughts even now. His grin faded, replaced by something deeper, more vulnerable.

It wasn't just her beauty, though that was undeniable. It was her strength, her fire, her unyielding determination to do what she believed was right—even when it tore at her. It was the way she let him see glimpses of the woman beneath the Hand, the warrior. The way she trusted him, even when he didn't trust himself.

That trust scared him because he wasn't sure he deserved it. Because she deserved someone better—someone who wasn't used to running when things got hard.

But he wanted to stay. For her, for Pari, for this fragile connection they were building. And maybe, just maybe, for himself.

A soft knock at the tent's entrance broke the silence, and he tensed. She stirred, her brows furrowing as she groaned softly, burying her face against his shoulder. The knock came again, more insistent this time.

"Kānhum Farah," came a low voice from outside. "The Mashya needs to see you. It's urgent."

Her eyes fluttered open, sleep still heavy in her gaze. She blinked up at him, her expression shifting from confusion to awareness in a heartbeat.

"What time is it?" she murmured, her voice husky with sleep.

"Too early," He replied, his hand brushing a strand of hair from her face. "But apparently, the Mashya doesn't sleep in."

She sighed, pushing herself upright, the blankets falling away to reveal the sharp angles of her shoulders and collarbone.

"Come with me," she said, already reaching for her tunic. "If it's urgent, I want you to hear it too."

He hesitated for a moment, then nodded, following her lead as they quickly dressed. The early morning air was crisp as they stepped outside, a faint mist clinging to the ground. The rebel who had knocked, a young man with dark circles under his eyes and his blue headscarf dusty and stained, nodded toward the central tent.

"They've found something," he said simply, falling into step beside them.

Farah's pace quickened, her expression sharpening. He stayed close, his eyes scanning the camp as they moved. The usual hum of morning activity seemed subdued, the rebels speaking in hushed tones as they exchanged glances.

The Mashya's tent exuded a quiet authority, the soft glow of lanterns casting flickering light across the weathered canvas walls. The air was thick with the mingling scents of parchment, leather, and the faint tang of oil. A map lay spread across the center table, its edges weighted down with stones. Around the table stood the Mashya, Rostam, and a handful of scouts, their expressions a mixture of anticipation and unease as they entered.

The Mashya's presence dominated the room. Not with force, but with a quiet gravitas that drew all eyes to him. This man was the true power, the king of Emari, even if his throne was leagues away and held by his estranged wife who had convinced the entire country that this man was too ineffectual to lead them.

For every bit of resentment Rostam had built up for Yasher, the Mashya's clear voice calmed his fears of being led out of camp, away from Farah. His gaze held a spark of urgency as he gestured toward the map.

"The scouts have found it," he said, his voice deep and steady. "The cavern entrance lies within the foothills, hidden behind brambles and stone. It matches the ancient descriptions, untouched by scavengers or time."

Farah leaned forward, studying the map with intense focus. Her fingers brushed the edges of the parchment as her eyes traced the scouts' markings. He stood just behind her, watching her slip into her more rigid personality of Hand. Sharp, determined, a force of nature. The Hand, not the woman who just slept curled up next to him a few minutes before.

The lead scout, a wiry man with dirt smudging his face and an air of weary pride, stepped forward.

"We scouted the perimeter but didn't enter," he reported. "The air near the entrance feels... heavy. There's something about the place that doesn't sit right. We saw no signs of others, but that could change quickly."

She nodded, her expression thoughtful.

"You've done well," she said, her voice steady. "We'll need to move quickly. I've been away from the Citadel long enough that the Mashyana will have the Beloveds well on their way to take up my tasks. They could find their own path here at any point."

Rostam crossed his arms, his stance rigid.

"Quickly, yes." His deep voice cut through the quiet. "But we cannot be reckless. The Forgotten Temple is no ordinary ruin. If the stories are true, we're walking into a place that was never meant to be disturbed. We need caution."

"Reckless? Us?" Yasher grinned, the corners of his mouth tugging upward in a playful smirk. He was ever the opportunist to poke at the bear that was the old Commander, couldn't resist breaking the tension. "I thought that was the plan. Dive headfirst into danger, hope for the best?"

Rostam's eyes narrowed, his sharp gaze cutting through his lighthearted tone. "This isn't a game, gharib."

"Rostam," the Mashya interjected gently, his tone softening as he turned to the older man. He placed a hand on the Commander's arm, his fingers brushing with a quiet intimacy. "He's only trying to ease the weight of the moment. Let him."

Rostam's stern expression faltered, his shoulders relaxing ever so slightly under the Mashya's touch. Yasher didn't miss the subtle exchange between them—the way Rostam leaned almost imperceptibly into the gesture, the faint warmth that softened the lines of his face. He recognized the same every time Farah touched him.

The Mashya's gaze lingered on Rostam for a heartbeat longer before he turned back to the group, his calm authority returning.

"Farah has chosen her team. Herself, Yasher, you, and the team of scouts that found the location. A small group will move quickly and draw less attention. You'll leave at dawn."

The Commander nodded, though a flicker of hesitation crossed his face.

"I'll ensure we're ready," he said, his tone gruff but lacking its usual edge. He turned to the scouts. "Gather supplies. Four days' worth. Weapons, climbing gear, and light rations. I want everything ready by first light."

The scouts moved to carry out their orders, their footsteps fading as they left the tent. Only then did the Mashya turn his attention to Yasher, studying him.

"Aqa Yasher," he began, his voice measured. "You've found a place here, though it isn't an easy road. Rostam's... harsher criticisms are born of love, not malice. I hope you understand that." The Mashya glanced over at Rostam for just a moment, then back to Yasher.

He shifted under the Mashya's gaze, his usual charm slipping into something more subdued.

"I'll do my part, your Grace," he said, his voice quieter than usual.

Enayat inclined his head, a faint smile tugging at his lips. "I believe you will."

Farah, standing close enough that he could feel her presence like a steady flame, broke the silence.

"The relic isn't just another artifact," she said, her voice resolute. "If it's truly there, it could change everything, for better or worse. We'll retrieve it, but we won't take unnecessary risks."

The Mashya nodded, his expression grave. "Good."

Farah's gaze flicked to Yasher, and he saw something in her eyes that made his chest tighten. An unspoken trust, a quiet acknowledgment that she valued him. He straightened, the weight of her faith in him settling over his shoulders like an invisible mantle.

Rostam, watching the exchange, sighed and placed a hand on the Mashya's shoulder. "We'll see this through," he said, his voice low but steady. "All of us."

Enayat turned toward him, his expression softening once more. "We always do."

As they stepped out into the crisp morning air, the camp bustled with activity. Supplies were being packed, weapons sharpened, and quiet conversations carried on the cool breeze. Yasher fell into step beside Farah, their strides matching as they made their way toward their tent.

"We'll leave the Shard with Pari," she said as they walked. "It's the only way we can keep it safe."

He nodded, pulling her swinging hand to his, placing a chaste kiss to it.

"Are you ready for this?" he asked, his voice light but edged with genuine concern.

Farah glanced at him, her lips quirking into a faint smile. "I have to be."

CHAPTER 24

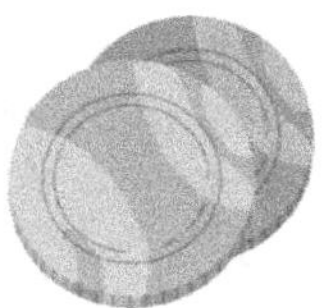

THE LANDSCAPE that stretched before them was stark, an expanse of rugged foothills and high plains. The ground was dry and cracked in places, dotted with scrubby brush and hardy plants that clung to life despite the harsh environment.

The southern foothills of the mountains loomed in the distance, a jagged line of stone and shadow under the morning sun. The air was hot and dry, and the distant cry of a hawk echoed across the open plains.

Yasher adjusted his pack, feeling the weight of his supplies settle against his back as he followed Farah and the scouts along the winding path that cut through the plains. The light was blinding, reflecting off the pale rocks and sparse patches of sand. It felt strange to be so exposed, the vastness of the landscape around them offering no shelter, no cover. The mountains beckoned ahead, silent witnesses to centuries of history—and, if the rumors were true, to secrets hidden deep within their caverns.

Farah walked a few paces ahead, her posture straight, her gaze fixed on the path. Her determination was palpable, even from a distance, and he found himself drawn to it, caught between admiration and a creeping sense of dread as they marched closer to this Forgotten Temple.

He kept his hand near his pocket as they walked, feeling for the reassuring weight of his lucky charm, though it felt strangely cold, almost dormant. Again. Twelve hells, knowing he was on the right path would have been helpful.

Rostam trailed behind, his sharp gaze scanning the path, ever-watchful. He could feel the Commander's eyes on him now and then, and he fought the urge to turn back and meet that wary glare head-on. He was here for Farah, and whatever doubts the Commander held would have to wait.

As they continued through the high plains, the chatter of the camp faded long ago, replaced by a quiet that felt thick and heavy. The only sounds were the crunch of gravel beneath their feet and the faint breeze that stirred the dust along the path.

The heat was relentless, but he forced himself to keep pace, matching her stride as the sun climbed higher.

After some time, she slowed, glancing back at him. Her expression softened, a hint of a smile playing at her lips.

"You're keeping up well," she said, her voice light but with a note of encouragement that made his pulse quicken. "The blue shemagh goes well with your eyes."

He shrugged, feigning nonchalance as he tugged at the headscarf that covered his fair skin. "I'm tougher than I look. Though I'd take the shade of a forest over this any day."

She chuckled, the sound a brief relief against the oppressive silence. "Not much shade out here, I'm afraid. Just more of the same—rocks, sand, and sun. We'll find a nice oasis for you when this is all done and laze around for days."

He stumbled and looked ahead at her, his chest tightening at the image she painted. He didn't think that far ahead, purposefully. His life was about surviving, never about what came after.

Long ago he learned that the future was a fragile thing, so easily broken, so easily lost. His vision blurred for a moment, overlaying an image of a time long-gone.

He rubbed his neck to pull away the image and lock it back into his memories and forced a casual smile that didn't quite reach his eyes as she looked to his silence. "If it's an oasis you want, maybe we'll have to take a detour before we head back. Can't let you down, can I?"

He laughed lightly, but the sound was strained, tinged with something he wasn't ready to face. The silence stretched, thick with the things left unsaid.

The scouts led them around a sharp bend, and he felt a thrill of unease as the foothills rose around them, the jagged stone formations casting twisted shadows across the ground. These hills had a strange energy about them, a quiet warning that prickled at the back of his mind. The Eye warmed slightly in his pocket, and he frowned, feeling its unpredictable weight settle uneasily against him.

She noticed his expression, her brow furrowing as she glanced at him. "Are you alright?"

He hesitated, choosing his words carefully. "It's... just a feeling. This place feels wrong somehow. But that might just be nerves talking."

She studied him for a moment, then nodded.

"I feel it too." Her gaze lingered on him, and he thought he saw a flicker of something more. Concern, perhaps, or worry.

Rostam's voice broke the moment, his tone clipped and impatient. "If we're all done with the small talk, I'd suggest we focus on the task ahead. We're close, and we don't need distractions."

He bit back a retort, clenching his jaw as he shifted his gaze back to the path. He knew better than to engage with Rostam logically, but old habits to poke and prod were harder to break. As much as he wanted to prove himself to him, he knew it would take more than words to change the Commander's mind.

They continued onward, the ground sloping upward as they approached the base of the mountains. The high plains began to give way to rocky outcroppings and narrow ridges, the landscape growing more treacherous with each step. The scouts paused occasionally to check their bearings, exchanging low words in Emarian he couldn't quite capture as they navigated the rocky terrain.

Finally, one of the scouts raised a hand, signaling for them to stop. He pointed toward a shadowed crevice in the side of a ridge, half-hidden by an outcrop of rock. The entrance was barely visible, a dark slash against the pale stone, but he could feel the air shift, a strange chill cutting through the heat as they approached.

"This is it," the scout said, his voice a low murmur. "The entrance to the cave network. It's said that one of the deeper tunnels lead to the temple."

Farah stepped forward, her gaze fixed on the entrance, her expression unreadable. He watched her, feeling a pang of worry. This journey wore on her, he could see it in the tension of her shoulders, the faint lines around her eyes. But she held herself steady, her shoulders straightened and head held high.

"Let's go," she said quietly, her voice steady.

Rostam gave her a firm nod, though his eyes betrayed a glint of his own apprehension as they moved toward the entrance.

He felt the weight of the darkness pressing against him as he stepped closer, his grip tightening instinctively on the hilt of his blade. The Eye warmed again, a flicker of warning that sent a chill down his spine. He glanced at Farah, who met his gaze with a look of quiet understanding.

As they crossed the threshold into the cave, the light from outside faded, replaced by a dense, almost suffocating darkness that clung to the air. His heart pounded in his chest as they descended, each step echoing in the silence, the weight of the unknown pressing down on him like the cavern walls with every breath.

***

THE AIR GREW heavy the moment they stepped into the mouth of the cave, like stepping into the belly of some ancient creature that had waited eons to devour them. Farah felt it press around her shoulders, thick and dense, whispering of secrets too dark for light to touch.

The faint scent of dust and damp stone lingered in the stale air, mixed with something sharper, metallic, and far too old. Her grip on her staff tightened as she took a cautious step forward, her eyes adjusting to the dimness, tracing the contours of the narrow path ahead.

The cave walls were rough, jagged edges catching the sparse light of their torches, creating dancing shadows that shifted with every movement. Each shadow seemed to promise a threat, some lurking force ready to reach out from the darkness. She kept her gaze steady, her breathing measured, trying to push down the instinctive dread crawling up her spine. She was no stranger to caves, to darkness, but something about this place felt deeply wrong, as though it resented their intrusion.

Yasher walked beside her, his presence a quiet reassurance. She could sense his unease, though he held it in check, his jaw tight, hand resting near his weapon. She wanted nothing more than to take his hand in hers, but stopped herself short, occasionally brushing the back of her hand against his instead.

Behind them, Rostam's steps were steady, cautious, his gaze darting over every nook and cranny as though expecting something to leap out at any moment. The scouts moved in silence, their expressions grim but determined.

The cave stretched on, narrow and winding, the walls occasionally widening into small alcoves where water dripped from above, carving pathways in the rock over the centuries. Each drop echoed, the sound sharp in the thick silence.

The ground was uneven, sloping downward, the path twisting in unexpected directions. She placed her feet carefully, testing each step, mindful of loose stones that could betray them. There was a sense of age here, as though the earth itself had folded around some ancient wound and hidden it away.

After what felt like hours of tense silence, with each step taken in measured, careful movements, they finally emerged into a wide, round cavern. She stopped abruptly, her breath catching as she took in the sight before them, her torch casting a warm but faint glow over the space.

The cavern was vast, stretching out in every direction. The walls arched high above them, curving like the dome of some ancient cathedral, disappearing into shadow beyond the reach of their lights. The air was thick and still, untouched by time and people, as though this place had been waiting for centuries. Along the curved stone walls, faded murals ran in intricate bands, telling a story she could barely comprehend but felt in the marrow of her bones. The figures were elongated, their faces indistinct, shrouded in flowing robes that seemed to ripple even in stone. She traced one figure with her eyes—a woman, tall and imposing, her arms raised as though summoning light or power from unseen forces around her, placing it into what looked like a gemstone.

"Are those..." Yasher's voice was hushed, filled with awe as he stepped up beside her. "The creation of the relics?" His torch held higher, casting a broader light over the walls.

She nodded, swallowing the dryness in her throat.

"It looks like it. Or something ancient enough to be mistaken for them." Her voice was low, the reverence in her tone matching the stillness around them. "I wonder who carved these murals... or why."

He took a step closer to the wall, studying a scene in which two figures appeared to be holding up a circular shape, not unlike the Crown of Emari between them, almost as if sharing the burden.

"It's like they're telling a story. Look at the way their faces are angled, like they're... struggling with it." He looked over his shoulder at her, his eyes dark with wonder. "Do you think this is where it began? All the stories of Emari's relics?"

She shook her head slowly, her fingers tracing a faded line in the mural. "Maybe. But it feels older than that, doesn't it? Like this isn't just history. It's something... sacred. Forgotten, even by those who built it."

They continued to move around the cavern, their footsteps soft, their voices barely more than whispers. Strewn across the floor were ornate stone boxes, some shattered, spilling their contents across the dust-covered ground, others still intact, though aged and brittle-looking. Each box was adorned with intricate carvings, symbols etched in geometric patterns, and inlaid with gemstones that had long since lost their luster. Some of the boxes had been damaged, others fully destroyed, whatever they held lost to tomb raiders and time.

"These look just like the box we found in Banima," she murmured, crouching by one of the few intact boxes, her fingers brushing the carvings lightly. She could feel a faint hum beneath her fingertips, a whisper of energy hidden in the stone. "The one that held the Shard of Ameretat…"

He knelt beside her, his gaze fixed on the box, his brow furrowing as he reached out a hand, his fingers hovering just above its surface.

"Do you think… another relic could be still be here? Just out here, in the open?" His voice held a quiet, cautious hope, tinged with a touch of fear as he looked at the broken and destroyed boxes.

"It's possible." Her voice dropped, her eyes scanning the various boxes in their states of varying disrepair. "But we'll have to be careful. Whatever is in these boxes was meant to stay hidden. Guarded."

She glanced at him, their eyes meeting in the dim light. She could see his own wariness mirrored back at her.

"Do you ever think about what these relics could do in the wrong hands?" he asked, his voice barely above a murmur. His hand dropped to his side, fingers brushing the pocket where he kept the Eye of Rashnu, a nervous gesture that didn't go unnoticed by her. "How many of these are already out there in the world?"

She exhaled slowly, her own mind echoing his fear.

"All the time." She let her gaze drift to the rows of murals, the ancient figures watching them from the walls, their silent faces filled with secrets. "These relics are tools. In the right hands, they can help, but in the wrong hands…"

He nodded, his eyes darkening with thought. "Should we be trying to find it at all then? I mean, if it could tip the balance one way or another…"

Farah's heart skipped, and the weight of his words sank deep into her gut. *Throw everything away.* Everything they had done, everything they had risked to come this far, to learn, to piece together the puzzle. And now, he was suggesting they walk away, abandon it all. The thought was like a shard of ice in her veins. She knew he wasn't dismissing all this work, not really, but it was too much.

Her fingers hovered over the carvings on one of the boxes, her mind reeling, a storm of frustration and doubt swirling inside her. The anger flared, sharp and biting, but she held it back, barely.

"We cannot allow the Mashyana to find it," she said, her voice tight, controlled. Her hand clenched into a fist. "If that means we must hold it to keep it from her, I will do it."

The words slipped out before she could stop them, heavier than she expected, more final than she wanted. She could feel the weight of them, the irrevocability of her commitment settling in. She wasn't just defending the relic. She was choosing a side.

But as she said it, she felt the tension between them crackle, that what she had just promised might be more than she was prepared for. His gaze didn't waver, but his silence now hung between them, heavy, full of a thousand unspoken questions. She met his eyes, steeling herself against whatever he might say next.

One of the scouts moved toward a passageway, his torch held high as he peered into the darkness beyond.

"There's a tunnel here, unblocked," he called back to them, his voice low but urgent.

They exchanged a glance, both sensing the same unease creeping over them. She rose, moving toward the scout. The ancient murals seemed to press down on her, as though they were watching, judging.

"This feels too easy," Yasher muttered behind her.

They approached the tunnel entrance, the light of their torches barely cutting through the heavy shadows within. The air was thick with the musty scent of damp stone, and every step seemed to echo through the stillness. The scout stepped forward, his boot heel scraping softly against the stone floor. He shifted his weight, peering deeper into the passage, his breath quiet.

Farah's senses were on high alert, the subtle pull of metal against her mind. She could feel it before she saw it, a shift in the air, the hum of something hidden beneath the stone. Her Talent prickled at the edges of her awareness. She narrowed her eyes, instinctively following the sensation. A faint, glinting metal mechanism embedded in the stone—a trap.

Her pulse quickened, and the moment her Talent flared with that familiar pull of danger, the faint click of the mechanism seemed to vibrate through her body, echoing deep within her chest.

"Get back!" Farah shouted, both she and Yasher lunging toward him, but it was too late.

With a sickening crunch, the ground gave way beneath the scout, and he vanished, his scream cut short as a hidden pit opened beneath him. The pulley system, covered in cobwebs and a large weight followed quickly behind the poor scout. She staggered back, pulling Yasher with her. She stared at the spot where he had been standing, now little more than a dark, gaping hole.

Yasher clutched his hand, blood trickling from two fingers that were obviously broken as he'd tried to reach for the scout and was caught in the mechanisms for the trap that had broken.

She held his shoulder, steadying him.

"Let me see," she murmured, her voice tight with worry, though her gaze flicked back to the trap, a horror settling in her gut.

He shook his head, gritting his teeth.

"I'm fine. Just... just a scratch." But she could see the pain in his eyes, the tension in his jaw as he fought to keep his composure.

Rostam's expression was grim, his gaze fixed on the gaping hole. "The relic won't matter if we're dead. May the Unnamed Gods protect your soul, Meysam."

She lowered her head in response to the prayer, still feeling the faint hum beneath her fingers, the pull of something powerful within these walls, but she knew Rostam was right. They had to be cautious, or they wouldn't leave this place alive.

Taking a steadying breath, she turned to Yasher, her voice softer. "Let me wrap your hand. We can't risk an infection down here."

He gave her a faint nod, allowing her to bandage his hand with a strip of cloth from her bag. Though his gaze remained fixed on the shadows around them, a deep wariness etched into his features. She could sense his frustration at the injury, his desire to push forward despite the danger, and she felt it, too. They were so close to tipping the scales in their favor, yet each step seemed to draw them further into the jaws of potential defeat.

Just as she finished tying the bandage, a sound echoed through the cavern, a low, mocking laugh that sent a chill down her spine.

"Foundling Farah... So, the Mashyana's loyal pet survived after all."

Her breath froze as she turned, her eyes landing on a figure emerging from the shadows near the entrance. Arash. He stood with a cold, calculating smile, his eyes glinting with malice. He had not fared well on the road since she'd last seen him, his face drawn and a scruff of a beard starting on his usually pristine face. Behind him, a contingent of the Mashyana's Beloveds filed in, their faces pale and gaunt, their eyes hollow, ravaged by the unmistakable signs of the wasting sickness.

Arash's gaze settled on her, his smirk widening. "I am disappointed in myself, honestly. I thought I'd left you to die in that alley."

Her grip on her staff tightened, her breath steadying as she forced herself to meet his gaze.

"You'll have to try harder than that," she said, her voice cold.

He chuckled, stepping further into the cavern, his Beloveds spreading out behind him like a dark tide.

"Oh, I intend to."

The Beloveds moved with a strange, unnatural grace, their movements slow but precise, as though something unseen guided them, compelling them forward with an eerie sense of purpose. Farah's heart twisted as she recognized a few of their faces, once vibrant and strong, now pale and twisted by the sickness, yet they still stood in a parody of all those that died to it. Yet despite their frailty, they moved with an iron will, their steps unnaturally coordinated, each Beloved like a puppet on invisible strings.

The hollowed shells of the Beloveds stared back at her, their eyes empty, robbed of the fire and personality that had once made them who they were. If not for a few different choices given to her on her path, Farah would be standing with them, or leading them in place of Arash.

She could feel the current of Talents pulsing around her, each one distinct yet subdued, as though the disease had taken their natural power and bent it to the Mashyana's will. One Beloved, whom she recognized as Youseff, a master of stone, moved with slow deliberation, his hands trailing over the rock walls, his Talent shimmering faintly in the air, reinforcing the cavern walls as they moved to prevent their escape. Another Beloved, Leyla, a Healer, stood at the back, her once-warm hands now trembling as her Talent warped, the life-draining energy of the disease feeding off her strength rather than using it to restore. She must be the one holding the disease in stasis for the others.

And at the front of them all stood Arash, his smirk twisting as he met her gaze. She could feel his power crackling around him, the air itself bending to his will. His Talent moved with him like an invisible cloak, the faint hiss and murmur of swirling air surrounding him, bending the dust and light around his form in a barely visible haze. She could feel the wind shift at his command, subtle currents swirling through the cavern, tugging at the edges of her clothes, whispering of danger.

His eyes glinted, a sick satisfaction in his gaze as he lifted a hand, a gentle flick of his fingers sending a sharp gust of wind cutting through the cavern toward them. Farah ducked instinctively, the wind grazing her cheek, sharp and biting like the edge of a blade. Behind her, Yasher cursed, raising his hand to shield his face as the gust swept past, rattling the broken boxes and stirring up clouds of dust that filled the air with an acrid, ancient scent.

"I wonder how she'll feel when she learns you've truly turned against her instead of just being absolute shit at your job," Arash sneered, his voice dripping with disdain.

Farah clenched her jaw, forcing herself to meet his gaze.

"The Mashyana doesn't care about loyalty," she shot back, her voice steady despite the roiling anger in her chest. "She only cares about power—and she's using you all to get it."

Arash laughed, the sound hollow, empty.

"You think I don't know that? You think any of us don't? But we have purpose under her. We are Chosen, not left to rot in obscurity like the rest of Emari." His voice hardened, his gaze narrowing. "She values strength. And we... we are strong."

Farah's heart twisted with grief and fury. "Is this what strength looks like to you? A life spent as a pawn, a shell of who you once were?"

But Arash only sneered, his fingers curling as he gathered the wind around him, the air rippling with his power.

"Spare me your pity, Mongrel. I am the wind itself. I can tear down mountains, raze cities. Amma Behnaz has shared her bounty with me to crush you. I am stronger than you ever were, and you'll ever be."

He raised his hand, and the wind surged forward, a powerful gust spiraling toward her with deadly precision. Farah braced herself, using her staff to anchor her stance, the force of the wind pressing against her, threatening to knock her back. Yasher stepped closer, his injured hand clutched to his chest.

Beside Arash, the other Beloveds stirred, their Talents flaring faintly as they took their places, forming a wall between Farah's group and the exit. Youseff lifted his hands, and the earth beneath them rumbled, subtle shifts in the stone as he prepared to trap them in. A woman with faintly glowing eyes stepped forward, who she recognized but could not name, her Talent emitting a low hum that made Farah's skin crawl, a manipulation of sound that could disrupt focus, disorienting them if they tried to move.

Rostam positioned himself at Farah's side, his stance solid, his gaze fierce as he raised his blade.

"We can't let them get to the relic," he murmured, his voice tight with determination.

She nodded, her grip tightening on her staff as she focused, letting her own Talent pulse to life. The familiar hum of metal in the earth around her called to her, in the weapons they held, and she reached for it, pulling the energy close, feeling it settle in her bones like a familiar friend. She could sense the faint traces of metal hidden in the Beloveds' armor, their weapons, small fragments that she could use if the need arose.

She didn't wait for Arash's next move. With a swift motion, she swung her staff, sending a wave of shrapnel toward him, the fragments of metal in the cavern resonating with her call. He dodged, the wind wrapping around him like a shield, deflecting her strike, but she pressed forward, refusing to give him the upper hand.

The cavern filled with the sounds of battle, the clash of metal and the hiss of Talents colliding. The scouts fought beside Rostam, their expressions grim, their movements swift as they dodged the Beloveds' attacks, each one trying to hold their ground. Yasher moved with them, his own movements careful but precise, his injured hand hampering him slightly but not enough to keep him from fighting.

She focused on Arash, her gaze locked on his, her Talent pulsing through her veins. She could feel the raw power in him, the strength of his Talent barely contained, like a storm waiting to be unleashed. He moved with a deadly grace, the wind whipping around him, slicing through the air with a force that made her heart pound.

"You can't stop us," he taunted, his voice carried on the wind, filling the cavern with a chilling echo. "The Mashyana's power is endless. And with the relics, she'll be unstoppable."

Farah's eyes narrowed, a surge of determination flooding her.

"These relics don't belong to her," she spat, her voice filled with defiance. "It was never meant to be a weapon for the Mashyana's greed."

Arash's expression twisted, anger flashing in his eyes. He raised his hands, the wind swirling around him, gathering strength, and Farah braced herself, knowing the force he was about to unleash.

But before he could strike, Yasher lunged forward, his uninjured hand gripping one of his many daggers, hurling it at Arash with all his strength. It wasn't a powerful strike, but it was enough to throw him off balance, his concentration faltering as he deflected the projectile with a sharp gust of wind.

"We need to move!" Yasher shouted, his voice carrying over the chaos.

Arash's smirk widened as he stepped closer, his steps

deliberate and his expression brimming with cruel amusement.

"Rostam," he drawled, his voice cutting through the cavern like the gust of a blade. "I must admit, I didn't expect to see you alive. You were always too loyal for your own good."

She felt Rostam shift beside her, his stance bracing as if Arash's words themselves were a physical attack. She glanced at him, seeing the flicker of something in his eyes—a sharp mix of regret and anger—but he said nothing. His silence was a shield, but Farah could feel the weight of the unspoken between them.

"Surprised?" Farah snapped, stepping forward to draw Arash's attention away from the Commander. "You shouldn't be. Loyalty to Emari over the Crown isn't as easily snuffed out as you think."

Arash chuckled, a low, mocking sound that sent a chill down her spine.

"Oh, I know that well. But him?" He shook his head, his expression twisting into something almost pitying. "I thought you'd have gone down fighting for her, singing the Mashyana's praises until your last breath. And yet, here you are. Just another traitor."

Rostam's jaw tightened, his grip on his blade steady. His voice, when it came, was quiet but firm. "I fight for Emari. Not for her. Never for her."

Arash's sneer deepened, his gaze flicking back to Farah.

"You see, that's the difference between us. You," he gestured toward her, his fingers curling as a faint breeze stirred the air around him, "and your merry band of rebels —you're all deluded, clinging to ideals long crushed beneath the Mashyana's heel. Meanwhile, we stand with the future. With strength."

Farah met his gaze, her chin lifting as she took a step closer.

"You're not strong. You're desperate. You're puppets on strings, parading your Talents as if they're still your own when we all know they belong to her now thanks to the wasting sickness."

His expression darkened, the smirk slipping from his face. His hand twitched, and the air around her grew colder, sharper, as though his anger was bleeding into the very atmosphere.

"Careful, Foundling," he said, his voice low, menacing. "I might take your words as a challenge."

"Maybe you should," she shot back, her tone steady even as her heart pounded against her ribs. She shifted her stance, the hum of her Talent stirring in her veins as she prepared for whatever he might throw at her. She couldn't afford to show fear, not to him.

His laugh came again, hollow and mocking, echoing off the cavern walls.

"You're bold, I'll give you that," he said, his voice dripping with condescension. "But boldness won't save you. Neither will Rostam or your ragtag band of misfits."

Behind her, she felt Yasher move closer. She didn't look back at him, but the faint brush of his arm against hers was enough to remind her she wasn't alone.

"You talk too much," she said, her voice sharp as she took another step forward, her staff angling slightly in preparation. "Let's see if you fight as well as you think you do."

Arash's smirk returned, though his eyes burned with a flicker of irritation. "Oh, I intend to."

The wind around him surged suddenly, but Farah was ready. She shifted her weight, her staff coming up in a swift arc to deflect the force, her Talent flaring to steady her footing against the gust. The wind howled around her, tugging at her clothes and hair, but she held her ground, meeting Arash's gaze with unwavering defiance.

Rostam stepped up beside her, his blade raised, his movements calculated.

"You're not taking her," he said, his voice cutting through the wind like steel.

Arash's gaze flicked to him, his smirk twisting into something darker.

"Taking her?" he echoed, mockery lacing his words. "No, Rostam. I'm here to destroy her, rip her apart limb from limb."

Her grip on her staff tightened, her jaw clenching as her Talent surged in her veins, ready to meet the storm.

"Big words for such a small man," she said, her voice steady, unyielding.

Arash's laughter filled the cavern, a harsh, grating sound that echoed like a taunt. "Then let's see what you're made of."

She didn't hesitate. They were outnumbered, outmatched, and every moment they lingered put them at greater risk. She caught Rostam's eye, a silent understanding passing between them, and he gave her a nod, his stance shifting to hold the line as she and Yasher began to back toward one of the unblocked tunnels, praying that they weren't trapped as well.

Rostam and the remaining scouts closed ranks, their faces set with grim resolve as they engaged the Beloveds, their weapons clashing in a brutal, desperate dance. Arash sneered, his gaze flicking between Farah and Rostam, his lips curling in satisfaction.

"You can't hide from the Mashyana," he called after them. "You can't hide from her power!"

But she ignored him, her focus on Yasher as he pulled her into the tunnel, away from the fight, into the shadows where they could regroup, where they could find a chance to breathe.

They slipped deeper into the darkness, the sounds of battle fading behind them, hoping they could find what they were after before Arash did.

CHAPTER 25

THE ECHOES of battle grew faint as they moved deeper into the tunnels, the twisting stone passageways swallowing the sound into an oppressive silence. The weight of the mountain seemed to press down on Farah's shoulders with every step, the cool, stale air thick with unease. The torchlight flickered in her hand, casting long, shifting shadows against walls that seemed to close in tighter as they advanced. Each step felt like a betrayal—leaving Rostam and the others behind gnawed at her conscience like a blade scraping bone.

She glanced at Yasher ahead of her, his form a silhouette against the dim glow of a torch he'd found. His gait was steady, his posture sure, but she knew him well enough now to catch the tension in the set of his shoulders. He seemed to trust some instinct—or his cursed "luck"—that carried him forward with a confidence she couldn't muster.

"Yasher," she whispered, her voice sharp but low, slicing through the thick silence. "We can't just leave them... they could be dying back there."

Farah froze mid-step, her breath catching as she watched him move ahead, his hand brushing against the pocket of his tunic. The gesture was so natural for him now, a quiet habit that she'd come to associate with his unwavering trust in the Eye. She couldn't stop the wave of frustration that surged within her towards the relic. That charm, that inexplicable thing, had brought them here, through every impossible escape and narrow path. But now? Now it felt like it was asking too much.

He stopped, turning back toward her, the torchlight catching on the sharp planes of his face. There was no grin this time, no deflection in his expression. His eyes, steady and darkened with the shadows, met hers, and for a moment, he looked almost vulnerable.

"It's not just luck," he said quietly. "You've seen it, haven't you? Every step it's guided us through, every time it's pulled me out of a grave. Rashnu told Pari I needed to keep it. Doesn't that mean something?"

Her chest tightened. Pari's words rang in her mind, the way the girl had spoken with such conviction, so certain of what Rashnu had said. It had felt like a command from the Yazata himself. She had questioned it then, even now, but she couldn't ignore the truth he was pointing toward. They had followed the Eye this far. And, somehow, it had brought them here.

Her voice trembled as she spoke, the weight of their situation pressing down on her. "And what if Rashnu was wrong? What if we've been wrong to trust it?"

He stepped closer, the flame of his torch flickering between them, illuminating the raw sincerity in his face.

"Farah, if we don't follow this, we're just... lost. If we turn back now, we'll die with the others. If you don't trust me enough, trust it."

She stared at him, her heart pounding. The words hit her harder than she wanted to admit. She thought of Pari's bright, determined eyes when she'd told them what Rashnu had said.

Yasher has to keep the Eye.

Pari had believed in it—believed in Yasher. Maybe Rashnu had seen this moment, seen how it would all unfold. Maybe they were here because of this very decision.

Her fingers flexed on her staff as the realization settled over her. It had always been about bringing them here, to this moment. The Eye wasn't just guiding Yasher. It was guiding them both.

She swallowed hard, glancing down the dark tunnel ahead before meeting his gaze again. "And if it falters? If this 'luck' of yours runs out, what then?"

His expression softened, and there was only the quiet weight of certainty. "Then I fall. But not before I've done everything I can to make sure you make it out."

Her breath caught at the rawness of his words, the depth of conviction in his voice. She hated how much she wanted to trust him, how much she wanted to believe that his faith in the Eye wasn't misplaced. But she also knew they couldn't afford hesitation—not now.

"Fine," she said, her voice low and firm. "Lead the way. But if this so-called luck gets us killed..." She let the warning linger, though she couldn't bring herself to finish it.

He gave her the faint, lop-sided smile, one that softened the sharpness in her chest just enough to let her breathe. "You'll get to say 'I told you so' in whatever afterlife awaits."

He turned back to the tunnel, his torch casting shadows along the ancient walls. She followed, her steps steady despite the storm of emotions within her. The whispers of the past, of Rashnu's words, and of the Eye's pull lingered in her mind, intertwining with the flickering light.

The tunnel twisted and turned, its walls narrowing and sloping, the air growing colder with each step. Ancient murals adorned the stone, illuminated in flickering fragments by their torches. Figures stretched long and thin danced across the walls, their faces indistinct, their postures speaking of triumphs and tragedies that predated Emari as she knew it. Faint symbols surrounded the figures, etched with delicate precision, their meaning lost to time.

The murals seemed to shift under her touch as her fingers trailed over the carvings, the figures' outlines catching the light in a way that made them feel alive. She stopped, studying a scene of two robed figures bowing before a radiant object that gleamed even in the stone.

"Do you think they knew what they were leaving behind?" she murmured, half to herself.

He paused beside her, his torch casting the mural in golden hues. "Maybe. Or maybe they didn't have a choice. They might have been like us—trying to figure it out as they went."

She looked at him, her thoughts a tangle of doubt and duty. "And if they buried this thing to keep it hidden? To protect us from what it can do?"

"Then we need to make sure it stays that way," he replied quietly, his fingers brushing against his pocket again. "Or keep it out of the wrong hands. Either way, your Mashyana can't have it."

They continued deeper, the path narrowing until the walls nearly brushed their shoulders. The air grew colder still, and the faint hum of ancient energy seemed to hum through the stone. She could feel it in her bones, a quiet vibration that resonated with the shards of metal buried within the rock surrounding them, like the cave itself was alive and watching.

A low rumble echoed from behind them, and she froze, her heart leaping into her throat. The ground trembled, dust falling from the ceiling as a sharp crack split the air. She spun, gripping her staff tightly as a section of the tunnel collapsed behind them, sealing their path with a wall of stone.

Her pulse thundered in her ears.

"We're trapped," she said, her voice tight, her knuckles white around her staff.

He turned, his face set with a determination that both reassured and infuriated her.

"Not trapped," he said, stepping forward. "Just redirected. Come on."

She stared at the blocked path, a sense of finality settling in her chest. There was no turning back now. Swallowing hard, she followed him, her footsteps hesitant but steady. The air grew denser, the silence broken only by the faint crunch of their boots on loose gravel.

Then, up ahead, the tunnel opened into a vast cavern, its ceiling disappearing into shadow. A soft, ethereal light illuminated the space, emanating from hundreds of glowing orbs embedded in the walls and ceiling.

She froze, her breath shallow as she took it in. A bridge stretched out before them, its broad expanse gleaming in the ghostly light reflected off of the vast, still lake. The stone was impossibly smooth, polished to a mirror-like sheen. Ornate carvings adorned its edges, running along the railings and arching pillars. Stars and swirling constellations intertwined with depictions of animals and abstract patterns, their lines intricate and deliberate, as though etched by hands that had known the weight of the cosmos.

The bridge's surface glowed faintly, not from the orbs above but from the stone itself, which seemed to pulse with life. It radiated an almost imperceptible warmth, a sense of presence that made Farah shiver. It was alive in its own way, and it was waiting.

The water beneath glowed faintly, a soft, bluish-white light that seemed to rise from its depths, creating an effect both calming and unnerving. The mist swirled in lazy spirals, its movements deliberate, as though it were alive, responding to their presence.

Farah stepped closer, the edges of her boots brushing the polished stone. The carvings along the bridge shifted subtly under the light, the stars seeming to shimmer, the animals almost moving in their poses. Her fingers brushed the railing, and the cold stone sent a jolt through her, a sensation not of ice but of clarity, as though the bridge itself had acknowledged her touch.

"This... this is the Chinvat Bridge," she whispered, her voice breaking the stillness like a pebble dropped into a calm pond.

Beside her, Yasher stepped forward, his torch casting warm highlights against the pale glow. His gaze flicked between the bridge and the lake, his lips parting in awe.

"The bridge souls cross to meet Rashnu," he murmured, repeating her earlier words as though trying to anchor them in reality. "I thought it was just a story."

Farah turned to him, her voice trembling. "It's not just a story. This is... this is where the dead are judged. This bridge... it's not meant for the living."

His brow furrowed, and he glanced back at the tunnel they'd emerged from, as though expecting to see shadows of their own death following them. But when his gaze returned to her, his lips quirked into a faint, almost irreverent smile.

"If this is where the dead are judged," he said, his voice soft but edged with humor, "then I've got questions. Like why I'm here and not some poor fool on a battlefield that's from this country."

Despite herself, Farah felt a laugh escape, shaky but real. "Maybe Rashnu does enjoy a challenge, bringing an insufferable gharib to judge his poor choices."

His smile widened, and for a moment, the overwhelming weight of the place seemed to lift. But as she looked back at the bridge, her unease returned, settling like a stone in her chest.

The carvings seemed to shift again, the figures on the pillars appearing to glance toward her, their expressions solemn. She traced the edges of a constellation etched into the railing, feeling the faint vibration of energy beneath her fingertips. It wasn't a welcoming sensation—it was watchful, judgmental.

"Do you feel it?" she asked, her voice low, her eyes fixed on the bridge. "It's not just stone. It's... alive, somehow."

He nodded, his gaze traveling over the glowing surface, his hand brushing one of the intricate arches.

"Yeah," he said, his voice quieter now. "Like it's waiting for us."

Her pulse quickened. The weight of the bridge's presence was suffocating, but the stillness of the lake beneath it felt even more ominous. As though it, too, was aware of their intrusion. The water's glow was brighter near the edges of the bridge, faint tendrils of light reaching upward, beckoning them to continue.

The carvings along the arch nearest them drew her

attention—a figure, shrouded and faceless, holding a scale in one hand and a blade in the other. She reached out, her fingers hesitating inches away. The air around the carving seemed to hum, a faint vibration that resonated in her chest, like the tolling of a distant bell.

"Farah." Yasher's voice drew her back, and she turned to see him watching her, his expression cautious. "What is it?"

She nodded, though her fingers still trembled.

"It's a test." Her voice wavered as she met his gaze. "If we cross it, there's no guarantee we'll come back."

He stepped closer, his presence steadying her in a way she didn't understand.

"We've come this far. If there's a relic at the other end, it might be our only shot at stopping the Mashyana." His tone was calm, but his eyes held the same mix of awe and fear she felt. "You said it yourself—this place isn't for the living. But maybe that's why we need to be here."

She wanted to argue, to tell him they had no right to be here, no right to disturb this sacred space. But the urgency in his voice matched the pull in her chest, the sense that they were being drawn forward not just by necessity but by design.

She glanced back at the carvings one last time, her fingers brushing the cold stone. Then, with a deep breath, she stepped onto the bridge.

The air shifted around her immediately, the faint hum growing louder, resonating in her bones. The carvings and constellations sparked to life, their patterns swirling and shifting as though aligning to something unseen. Each step felt heavier, the weight of the bridge's judgment pressing against her shoulders.

Yasher followed, his footsteps careful but deliberate, his

hand brushing the railing as though seeking reassurance from the stone itself.

"Do you think it's safe?" he asked, his voice barely above a whisper.

Her gaze swept over the bridge, the lake, the mist swirling below. "I think," she said carefully, "that safety isn't the point."

They walked in silence, their footsteps echoing faintly in the cavern. The bridge stretched endlessly before them, each step revealing new carvings, new constellations, new figures etched in stone. The glow of the lake intensified as they reached the center, the light rising in faint tendrils that seemed to beckon them closer.

But with every step, the pressure around them grew heavier, the hum vibrating in their bones like the toll of a distant bell. Farah's heart pounded as she looked ahead, the far end of the bridge disappearing into shadow.

And then the tremors began.

Farah braced herself against the sharp tremor that rocked the bridge beneath her feet. The stone beneath her boots groaned, and dust rained down from the ceiling, catching the soft light of the orbs above. Her hand gripped the railing, its carvings cool and steady beneath her palm, even as her heart thundered in her chest.

She glanced at Yasher. His face was tense, his usual easy demeanor replaced by grim focus. She could see his knuckles whiten as he tightened his grip on the bridge's edge.

"Did you feel that?" she asked, her voice tight, though she already knew the answer.

He nodded, his free hand brushing against his pocket. "We need to move. Now."

She nodded, trying to suppress the rising wave of

panic that threatened to engulf her. The carvings along the railing seemed to shimmer faintly in response to the tremor, their intricate patterns shifting like ripples in water. As they pressed forward, her steps quickened, each footfall echoing across the expanse of the bridge. The lake below was an endless mirror of blackness, its surface unnervingly still even as the bridge quaked above it.

They had only managed a few more strides when the second tremor hit, stronger this time. The bridge swayed precariously, cracks spidering along the stone beneath their feet. A deafening crack split the air, and she turned just in time to see a massive section of the bridge behind them collapse into the lake. The sound of shattering stone echoed through the cavern like a death knell.

"Run!" Yasher shouted, his voice sharp with urgency.

She bolted forward, her pulse pounding in her ears. The ground beneath her feet trembled with every step, and she forced herself not to look back, not to think about the pieces of the bridge falling away into the abyss behind them. Yasher was close by, his footsteps heavy and uneven against the stone.

Another tremor rippled through the bridge, this time accompanied by a cascade of debris from the cavern ceiling. She threw up an arm to shield her face as chunks of rock crashed down around them, one narrowly missing her shoulder. She heard Yasher curse, and she turned in time to see him stumble, his body jerking as a sharp shard of stone lodged deep into his calf.

"Yasher!" She screamed, skidding to a halt and running back toward him.

He had fallen to one knee, his face pale with pain. Blood seeped through his pants, staining the stone beneath him.

His teeth were clenched, but he waved her off with a shaky hand.

"Keep going," he managed, his voice strained. "You have to get to the other side."

Farah's chest tightened at the sight of him, his usual cocky exterior stripped away, leaving only raw determination and pain. She dropped to her knees beside him, her hand already moving to press against the wound.

"I'm not leaving you here," she said fiercely, her voice shaking. "Not like this."

"Phoenix." His voice was sharper now, cutting through her panic. "You don't have time. This bridge is falling apart, and you—"

"I said no," she snapped, her eyes blazing as she met his gaze. "We both get across, or neither of us does."

For a moment, he looked as though he might argue, but then his expression softened, his lips curving into a faint, rueful smile.

"Stubborn as ever," he murmured, his voice tinged with something that almost sounded like pride.

She tore a strip of fabric from her sleeve and wrapped it tightly around his leg, her hands moving with practiced efficiency despite the trembling in her fingers.

"We're getting up," she said, her tone leaving no room for argument. "Lean on me."

He nodded, gritting his teeth as he shifted his weight. She slipped her arm under his, bracing herself as she helped him to his feet. He let out a sharp hiss of pain but managed to stand, his arm slung heavily across her shoulders.

"Let's go," she said, her voice steady despite the fear clawing at her throat.

Together, they stumbled forward, the bridge groaning ominously beneath them. Farah's muscles burned with the effort of supporting his weight, but she refused to slow, her focus fixed on the far end of the bridge. The light at the other side seemed impossibly far away, a faint beacon in the endless expanse of stone and shadow.

Another tremor shook the bridge, and Farah felt her stomach lurch as a section ahead of them crumbled, leaving a jagged gap. She stopped short, her breath coming in ragged gasps.

"We have to jump," she said, her voice firm despite the fear twisting in her chest.

His eyes flicked to the gap, then back to her. "You first. I'll follow."

She hesitated, but the look in his eyes left her no choice. Nodding tightly, she let go of his arm and stepped back, her heart pounding as she gauged the distance. Taking a deep breath, she pushed off the ground and leapt, her body stretching across the void. Her hands caught the far edge, her arms straining as she hauled herself up onto solid ground.

"Your turn!" she called, scrambling to her feet.

He nodded, his face tight with pain as he limped forward. He paused at the edge, his gaze meeting hers.

"Catch me if I miss," he said, a flicker of his usual humor breaking through the tension.

Her chest tightened, but she nodded, her hands outstretched. He took a deep breath and jumped, his body arching over the gap. His injured leg faltered on landing, and he collapsed forward, his hand grasping desperately for the edge. Farah lunged, her fingers closing around his wrist.

"I've got you!" she said, her voice straining as she pulled him up with every ounce of strength she had left.

The bridge rumbled again, and her stomach lurched as

another section behind them crumbled into the abyss. Dust and shards of stone filled the air, stinging her eyes and throat. She could barely hear his strained breaths over the deafening cracks of the collapsing structure.

They had barely reached a patch of stable stone when another tremor rippled beneath their feet. The bridge's groans became deafening, and the fractures in the stone spread like spiderwebs. The entire structure was on the verge of collapse.

She glanced at his leg, where blood seeped through the makeshift bandage she had tied earlier. His face was paler than it should be, and his breaths came in labored gasps, but his eyes remained focused.

He tightened his grip on her arm and shook his head.

"You have to go."

"What?" she snapped, incredulous. "No! You're coming with me."

Another chunk of the bridge fell away, sending a shock-wave through the stone beneath their feet. He winced, his injured leg buckling beneath him.

"Phoenix," he said, his tone soft but unyielding. "You have to go ahead without me. You're not going to make it if you're dragging me along."

Her jaw clenched, her mind racing. "I'm not leaving you here alone. I can carry you—"

"No, you can't," he interrupted, his voice firm despite the pain lacing it. He reached into his pocket, pulling out the Eye of Rashnu. Its filigreed surface glinted faintly, its warmth visible even in the cavern's dim light. "Take this."

Her eyes widened, and she shook her head, backing away slightly. "No. That's yours—it's your luck. I'm not taking it from you. Pari said..."

"Farah." His tone was sharp, cutting through her

protest. He grabbed her hand, forcing the Eye into her palm. Its warmth hummed against her skin, and she felt a pulse of energy rush through her.

"You need this more than I do now. Rashnu wouldn't have put us on this bridge if you weren't meant to make it across. Go. Finish this."

She stared at him, the weight of his words crashing over her like a wave. "I can't just leave you here. If the bridge collapses..."

"I'll figure something out," he said, a faint smirk tugging at his lips, though his eyes were filled with something far more serious. "You've seen me squirm out of worse, haven't you?"

A bitter laugh escaped her lips, though it held no humor. She clenched the Eye tightly in her fist, the warmth of it grounding her. "I don't want to leave you."

He smiled faintly, his eyes meeting hers with an intensity that made her chest ache. "You have to, Farah, for all of this to mean something."

She shook her head, tears streaking her dusty cheeks. "Don't do this. I can—"

"Farah," he interrupted, his tone firm but gentle. "If I don't make it back..." He paused, his smirk softening into something more vulnerable, more real.

"Know that you were everything I never knew I needed. That I always—" His voice caught, and he glanced away briefly before meeting her gaze again. "That I cared for you more than I ever thought I could."

Her breath hitched, her heart shattering as the words hung in the air between them. Another rumble shook the bridge, and she staggered, forced to step back onto more stable ground.

"Run, Phoenix!" he shouted, his voice filled with an urgency that tore through her. "Run!"

With tears blinding her vision, she turned and sprinted toward the far side of the bridge, her heart pounding with every step. She didn't dare look back, even as the sound of stone shattering filled the cavern, echoing in her ears like a haunting refrain.

When she finally reached a stable section of the bridge, the tremors slowed, she collapsed onto her knees, clutching the Eye of Rashnu so tightly it cut into her palm. Its warmth pulsed against her skin, steady and insistent, as if trying to anchor her to the moment.

Farah's sobs wracked her chest, but she forced herself to stand, her fingers brushing the edges of the Eye as she whispered, "I'll come back for you. I promise."

CHAPTER 26

Farah's chest heaved as she raced across the shimmering surface of the bridge, the ethereal light rippling with every desperate step. Her knuckles whitened around the Eye of Rashnu, its warmth pulsating against her palm as if alive, as if it understood her terror. She had left Yasher behind. The thought crashed over her, suffocating her with guilt and fear.

He's going to die, and it's my fault.

The echo of her hurried steps filled the void around her, amplifying her anguish. The Chinvat Bridge stretched ahead, a translucent path of light suspended above an endless chasm that seemed to swallow sound and thought alike. Behind her, the edges of the mortal world faded into mist, separating her from everything familiar. The stillness of the place felt suffocating, as though even the air itself was holding its breath.

Farah slowed, stumbling to a halt, her breath ragged. She glanced down at the Eye, its glow soft and steady. She understood now. Every moment with the relic, every gamble, every miraculous escape—it had all been to guide them to this moment. Yet, she couldn't shake the image of Yasher, slumped and bleeding, forcing her to leave him behind.

She tightened her grip on the Eye, its heat grounding her as she fought to breathe through the panic.

You left him to die.

Her chest ached with the weight of it.

You left him.

A faint sound broke through the silence, like feathers rustling in an unseen breeze. Farah froze, her head snapping up. Ahead, the air shimmered, bending and twisting, as a figure emerged from the brilliance of the bridge.

Her breath caught.

He was more than she had imagined. More than any mural or effigy could ever capture. His form towered, nearly twelve feet tall, with the powerful body of a man, draped in robes of pristine white that shimmered as if woven from stardust. His face was that of a great white hawk, fierce yet wise, golden eyes gleaming with a depth that seemed to reach through time itself. Massive wings, blindingly white, folded behind him, their feathers rustling softly in the stillness of the bridge.

"Farah," the figure spoke, his voice soft yet resonant, like the hum of a distant drum. "You have crossed the threshold."

"Rashnu," she breathed. She felt a tug of reverence, awe. This was Rashnu, the divine being whose name was whispered in prayers of justice and truth to those that had crossed into the afterlife. Here he was, no longer an abstract figure but real, solid, watching her.

Rashnu tilted his head, his eyes gleaming with something that bordered on sorrow.

"You have brought me the Eye," he said, his hand

extending toward her. She hadn't even realized she still held it, but there it was, glowing softly in her grasp, as if responding to his presence.

Reluctantly, she offered the relic, and he took it from her, cradling it in his large, feathered hand as though it were the most precious of treasures.

"You have done well to bring it here," he murmured. "The Eye has missed its home."

A shiver ran down her spine. "Home?" she asked, her voice barely more than a whisper.

"Indeed," he replied, his gaze shifting beyond her, as though seeing far into realms she couldn't comprehend. "You, like the Eye, were destined to walk this path. And in doing so, you have uncovered much... too much, perhaps."

She swallowed, a knot of anxiety forming in her chest. "What do you mean?"

His golden eyes returned to her, filled with a deep, knowing sadness. Rashnu's wings rustled, and he shifted, his gaze moving past her, as if seeing into realms beyond her understanding.

"Behnaz à Radan," he began, his voice heavy with sorrow, "is not what she appears. The power she wields was never meant for her alone. She has become a vessel for something far darker. A Darkness that we, the gods, cannot perceive fully. It is insidious, ancient, and it hungers."

Her stomach tightened. She had always known the Mashyana was ambitious, but this... this was beyond anything she could have imagined.

"She's feeding it, isn't she?" she asked, her voice barely a whisper.

Rashnu's gaze returned to her, solemn. "Yes. Every Talent she siphons, every relic she gathers, strengthens the Darkness. It grows within her, consuming the essence of the gods, using her as a conduit. And should it succeed in devouring us fully, our world will be left defenseless."

Her heart clenched, her pulse thundering in her ears. The weight of his words settled over her, pressing down like an iron shackle.

"The prophecy…" she murmured, her voice hoarse. "If the gods die, so does the world."

Rashnu nodded slowly. "But the Darkness seeks to twist this prophecy, subvert it, to kill the gods without killing the world, to rule what remains as its own. Your people, Farah, would be left at its mercy. "

A tremor ran through her. She thought of her people, of Emari, of the lives caught in the Mashyana's ruthless grasp, each one unknowingly feeding the very Darkness that threatened to destroy them. It was too much, too vast and impossible to comprehend.

None of the relics that she'd touched could go against that kind of power. Except…

"What about the relic that we were here to gather against her?" She stood tall. "We were looking for the thing that they said would turn the tide for good or ill, restore the balance."

She was surprised at the deep sigh from the god as he dropped his head down.

"There is no such thing," he said, sorrow filling the space between. "We have nothing that can restore the balance that has been tipped. That is the role that you as a people play. We can only provide the places and the things, and the people to help you against the Darkness."

Every fiber of her being froze, then broke apart into a million shards. There was no way to break the control that the Mashyana and the Darkness possessed.

"I am sorry," he said. "For the soul of Emari, you must

fight back the Darkness in all things. That is how the restoration will happen."

Rashnu's gaze softened, and he took a step closer, his presence filling the bridge with an aura of quiet strength.

"You have done well, Farah. But now, I offer you a choice as you have walked the Bridge to be Judged. The path ahead of you is difficult, more so than any you have walked. But I will not ask you to bear it unless you choose it willingly."

Farah looked up at him, feeling the weight of his words settle into her bones. "What... what choice?"

He extended one hand, gesturing toward the far side of the bridge.

"Continue forward, and you will reach the House of Song. There, you would find peace—a release from the burdens you carry, an end to the suffering, the endless battles. Your soul would be free, your struggles left behind."

The promise of peace was both a balm and a torment, tempting her with its soft allure. To let go of all this—of duty, of pain, of fear. She could almost feel it, the warmth of rest, the final release.

Rashnu's voice broke through her thoughts, his tone softer now.

"Or, you may choose to return, to carry the weight of this knowledge. You would remember all that you have learned and be armed with the truth. But the fight you would face is not one of honor or certainty. It is a fight against the very essence of darkness. You must fight, Farah. Not just for yourself, but for the soul of Emari."

She looked down, her hands trembling. Peace, or the burden of truth. The choice felt both simple and impossible. She could be free, finally, from the endless cycle of struggle, or she could bear the truth, knowing the fight ahead would be harder than anything she had faced.

She thought of Rostam, of the scouts who had followed her into danger. She thought of Pari, waiting for her back at the camp, who spoke to the Yazata stood before her, but was still just a little girl, living her life. She thought of the Mashya, fighting against the woman he'd sworn his soul to and shared the country with. She thought of the people of Emari, each one living in a world they believed safe, unaware of the darkness that lingered so close.

The thought of Yasher, of his steadfast presence, his quiet strength, filled her mind. He had always been at her side, even when she had doubted him. With him, she felt... whole, as if he balanced the pieces of herself she had long struggled to keep aligned. She felt a strange, bittersweet longing twist within her, but it was laced with purpose, not despair.

Yet the question hung heavy in her heart, suffocating her with its weight.

Is he even alive?

The image of him slumped against the wall, bleeding, flashed before her eyes. The blood pooling beneath him, his pale face, the wounds that should have broken him—they all haunted her. She gripped her trembling hands into fists, her knuckles whitening as fear clawed at her chest.

Farah turned her gaze up to Rashnu, desperation burning in her eyes.

"Is he..." she whispered, her voice breaking, "is Yasher alive?" The words cracked like brittle glass as they left her throat.

Rashnu's golden eyes softened, his immense form radiating a quiet, almost sorrowful empathy.

"He lives yet," he said, his voice resonating like a low

hum through her bones. "Though his path is fraught with peril."

Her shoulders sagged with relief, though the knot in her chest remained.

"I left him," she admitted, guilt dripping from every syllable. "He was bleeding, hurt because of me. And I left him there to die."

Rashnu's feathers rustled as he stepped closer, his towering presence casting a soothing warmth over her.

"You did not abandon him, Farah. You were brought here to see, to understand. To carry the truth forward. Without it, neither of you could face what is to come."

Her decision crystallized within her, her choice as clear as the light of the bridge. She looked up, meeting Rashnu's gaze with a steady resolve.

"I can't abandon them," she said, her voice quiet but unwavering. "Not when I know the truth. I'll fight. I'll return."

A faint smile curved at the edges of Rashnu's beak, pride gleaming in his golden eyes.

"Then go, Farah. Bear the truth, and let it guide you. May it be the light that pushes back the Darkness."

"Farah," Rashnu said, his voice drawing her gaze back to him, "He will miss the Eye... yet his luck is his own, not a borrowed blessing."

Her chest tightened, a warmth flooding through her as she realized the weight of Rashnu's words. Yasher's luck was his own. He had believed it was the relic's doing, a gift that guided him, but it was him—his own Talent, woven into the fabric of his being. And she had seen it, hadn't she? The way he moved through danger, always just a step ahead, a force she hadn't fully understood until now.

In an instant, the light of the bridge began to fade, the ethereal realm dissolving into shadows as the weight of her own body settled upon her once more. Rashnu's form blurred, his presence fading into the mist, his voice an echo in her mind.

You were always meant to be more than a mere Hand. No relic will ever change that.

The words settled within her, resonant and true. The Mashyana had once held her close, like a prized possession, a crafted weapon. She had wielded her Talent, her loyalty, as easily as any blade.

Farah was no longer that obedient, unquestioning girl. She had seen the truth, felt the burdens, and made her choice. Her steps quickened.

Ahead, the mist grew denser, swirling as if in answer to her resolve. She could feel the pull of the mortal world strengthening, the weight of her body returning to her. Her memories flooded her mind—The Citadel's bustling markets, the vibrant murals that lined Banima's walls, the quiet wisdom of Shirin at the tea shop, and the aching beauty of the mountains, of the warmth of Yasher next to her on a chilly night.

As the memories passed, she was filled with a sense of quiet purpose. Emari was worth fighting for. Her people, her friends, even the broken systems she had once obeyed —each deserved a future free from the darkness that had infiltrated the Mashyana's power. Her heart clenched at the thought of Yasher's face, his cautious smile, the look he gave her that told her he saw the depths of her struggles, the hidden strengths she didn't always recognize in herself.

In the midst of her reverie, she heard a soft rustling, the faintest echo of wings. Startled, she looked back, but

Rashnu was gone. The bridge, too, was fading, dissolving into thin air as her surroundings began to change. Colors bled into view—the rich amber of early dawn, the cool blue of shadowed stone, the soft greens of distant trees. She was returning.

The mist parted, and Farah blinked, her eyes adjusting to the dim glow of torchlight reflected off cold stone walls. She was back, no longer on the bridge but in a cavern, the faint scent of earth and rock filling her senses.

Beside her, Yasher lay slumped against the wall of the bridge, his face pale, blood seeping from his leg, the rough bandage on his hand curling away. He looked up as she appeared, relief flooding his expression even as pain tightened the lines around his eyes.

"Farah..." he murmured, his voice weak but laced with a quiet joy. "You... you came back. I was wondering if you were choosing to run off with my lucky charm for a life of crime."

Her lips curved into a faint, tired smile.

"I was... somewhere else." She didn't know how to explain it, how to tell him she had crossed into a realm of gods and truth, of choices and revelations that could shatter everything she had believed. "How did you get off of the bridge?"

"I don't rightly know," he said, looking around. "I'd resigned myself to you telling me 'I told you so' on the other side of the bridge in the afterlife... Closed my eyes, and then I opened them here, with you next to me."

She dropped to her knees beside him, ripping the hem of his tunic and tightening the bandage with quick, sure movements.

"I wouldn't leave you, Yasher," she replied, her voice

thick with emotion. "Look at you — you'd only get into more trouble."

He managed a small, strained smile, his eyes soft as he looked at her.

"Good. I seem to have lost this game when I lost my luck." He waved at his leg.

"I don't think you've lost your luck just yet, gharib." She stood, then helped him to stand, wrapping her arm around him to act as a crutch. She glanced up, hearing the faint sound of fighting echoing from further down the cavern—the clash of weapons, the shouts of men locked in battle.

"Rostam..." she whispered. "The Beloveds will slaughter them. They need to know what I saw, what I know."

"Farah," Yasher began, then winced as he tried to put weight on his injured leg. She adjusted her hold on him to have him lean a little more on her.

"I walked the Chinvat Bridge. The godly one," she began. "I returned the Eye to Rashnu."

"And the relic?" he said, trying to readjust.

"There is no relic here," she almost sobbed. "The people, us, are needed to fight to restore balance."

His face, his beautiful face, fell at the news, mirroring her own.

"Well, that puts a damper on our survival."

"He told me," she said after a long breath, "about a Darkness. It's ancient, insatiable, feeding off the gods through the Mashyana. She believes she's gaining power, but it's a lie. She's... she's helping to destroy them, Yasher. And the Darkness will take their place."

He let out a shaky breath, running his good hand through his hair.

"So, she's not just a tyrant," he murmured, his voice

taut with tension. "She's a puppet for something far worse."

Farah nodded, feeling a bitter taste rise in her throat.

"I was given a choice. The choice to join the House of Song, to die, or to continue the fight. I chose to remember, to come back. To carry this knowledge and fight."

A silence fell between them, weighted by the enormity of what she had just confessed. Yasher's gaze held hers, his expression unreadable. But then, in the midst of that stillness, he softly cupped her chin, pulling her face to his.

"You are so much more than all your scars, Phoenix," he said softly. "Never doubt that. I would follow you anywhere." He kissed her briefly. "Anywhere."

He leaned back against the wall so she could tighten his bandages as best she could, her hands moving quickly but gently. His leg wound had worsened, the blood had soaked through the cloth, staining it a deep, ominous red. She met his gaze, worry etched into her features, but he gave her a faint, reassuring smile, as if to say he was fine—even though she could see the strain in his eyes.

"I need to get you somewhere safe," she murmured, leaning in close so her voice wouldn't carry down the cavern, so Arash wouldn't know that she was back.

He shook his head, his hand reaching up to rest on her arm, stopping her from moving just yet.

"We don't have time to run." He struggled a little to steady his breath. "They're here because of us. I won't... I won't leave Rostam and the scouts to fight alone."

A wave of conflicting emotions surged through her. She knew he was right, knew that they couldn't just abandon their allies, but seeing him like this—injured, exhausted— made her want to protect him, to shield him from the danger. The memory of her encounter with Rashnu, the choice she had made to return, to fight, burned brightly within her, urging her to push forward.

But if she was going to do that, she couldn't leave him vulnerable. She had to trust him, to accept that he was part of this fight, just as she was.

"Then we do this together," she said finally, her voice a low whisper. "But you stay close to me, and you follow my lead. Understand?"

He nodded, his eyes hardening with determination. He tried to shift himself up off of the wall, his injured leg trembling slightly under the weight, but he steadied himself, gripping her shoulder for balance.

"Together," he agreed, his tone leaving no room for argument.

Farah took a deep breath, steeling herself as they moved deeper into the cavern, the sound of the battle growing louder with each step. It was a different route than they'd taken to get to the bridge, but Yasher pointed weakly the proper direction for them to take. She worked as his crutch, supporting his taller form as best as she could as they moved through the narrow passages, her senses on high alert. Every instinct within her screamed caution, warning her of the danger that lay ahead.

Rostam and the scouts came into view first, their figures dimly illuminated by the flickering torchlight, pushed against the tunnel entrance. It was as if no time had passed. They fought with a fierce determination, their weapons flashing as they engaged the Beloveds, whose talents surged in the dim light, casting strange shadows on the cavern walls. But the center of the storm, the one who commanded the winds themselves, stood a few feet behind them—Arash, his eyes cold and sharp, his focus deadly as he controlled the currents of air that tore through the cavern.

Her heart pounded as she took in the scene. She had sparred with Arash before, had witnessed the power he wielded with such ease. She had even bested him in the Trials so long ago. But now, with the full force of his Talent unleashed by Behnaz sharing the spoils of siphoning Talents, he was like a storm given human form, his control over wind and air absolute. He raised his arm, and a powerful gust shot forward, scattering the scouts and forcing them to stumble back.

She knew they couldn't withstand him for long, not without help.

She tightened her grip on Yasher's arm, leaning close to his ear.

"Stay back," she whispered, her voice barely audible over the chaos. "You're too injured to get in close. I need you to cover me from a distance." She handed him one of her jeweled daggers.

He hesitated, his jaw clenched, but he nodded. "Just... be careful."

A faint smile touched her lips. "I will."

Taking a steadying breath, she focused her attention on the metal in her surroundings, drawing strength from it, feeling it resonate with her Talent. The metallic elements in the destroyed boxes that held relics in antiquity, the weapons scattered across the cavern floor from the fallen scouts and Beloveds, even the faint traces of ore in the rock around her that had started to dislodge from the manipulation—all of it became a part of her, an extension of her will. She let that strength settle within her, a quiet but unyielding resolve, and stepped forward into the fray.

"Arash!" she called out, her voice carrying over the noise.

His head snapped toward her, his eyes narrowing as he registered her approach. He gave her a mocking smile, his expression twisted with disdain.

"Farah. Come back to join the fun?" he sneered, his tone dripping with contempt. "I thought you had already fled by now, like the coward you are."

She clenched her jaw, refusing to rise to his bait. Instead, she focused, drawing some of the larger bits of metal closer to her body, reinforcing it, creating a protective layer of armor against his wind. "I'm not the one running from the truth, Arash. You think you're serving the Mashyana, but you're nothing more than a tool to be thrown away when it's no longer useful to her."

His eyes flashed with anger, and the wind around him surged, swirling with a violent intensity that whipped through the cavern.

"You don't know anything," he spat, his voice laced with fury. "I am the storm. And you are nothing."

He thrust his arm forward, and the air erupted in a powerful gust, a wall of wind barreling toward her. She braced herself, extending her Talent to pull shards of metal towards her in her own spiral of a shield. The wind slammed into it, nearly driving her back, but she held her ground, her feet digging into the stone, her focus unbreakable.

With a fierce cry, she stepped forward, pushing against the wind, her determination like a shield around her.

"You can't stop me," she shouted, her voice cutting through the storm. "Not while I fight for something real."

He snarled, his control faltering as he poured more energy into his Talent, the wind growing sharper, more frenzied. But she pressed on, her gaze fixed on him, her purpose burning within her.

From the corner of her eye, she saw Yasher, his stance steady despite his injured leg. He gripped her dagger and raised it, his gaze locked on Arash. The dagger was not meant for throwing, but the look in his eyes said he was just waiting for the moment that Arash was fully locked onto her to strike.

She took another step forward, the force of the wind battering against her, and raised her arm, focusing her Talent to push her makeshift shield into a gauntlet. She extended it, forming a blade, a single, sharp edge that gleamed in the torchlight.

"Arash!" she shouted, her voice fierce, unyielding. "Your storm ends here."

For the first time, she saw hesitation flicker in his gaze as he registered the full force of her determination.

In that instant, Yasher acted. He hurled the dagger with all his remaining strength, his aim unerring, guided by his luck. It sliced through the air, cutting through Arash's wind, striking him in the shoulder.

Arash staggered, his concentration breaking as he clutched at the wound tearing into his shoulder. The storm around him faltered, the wind dissipating as he lost control, leaving him vulnerable, exposed as he yanked the blade out.

Her heart raced as she seized the opportunity. His control had slipped, and the fury of his storm faded into a few scattered gusts, leaving him defenseless, the once-deadly currents reduced to a faint rustle. Around them, Rostam and the scouts had pushed the Beloveds back, each fighting with a fierce urgency, galvanized by the sudden turn in their favor.

The respite was fragile, and if they didn't end it now, they might not get another chance.

"Rostam!" She called out, her voice steady, carrying over the echoes of the cavern. "Focus on the Beloveds! We need to break their line."

He glanced back, his eyes meeting hers. He gave a sharp nod, rallying the scouts with a quick command, and they pressed forward, cutting through the Beloveds with renewed vigor. She turned back to Arash, whose sneer had transformed into a grimace of pain as he clutched at his shoulder.

"You're outmatched," she said, her voice cold. Stepping forward, each footfall a declaration of her resolve. "It's over."

He snarled, his face twisting with hatred as he glared up at her.

"You don't know what you're dealing with," he spat, his voice low, a hint of desperation creeping into his tone. "The Mashyana's plans are beyond anything you can understand. You are the tool—a broken one at that."

She ignored his words, unwilling to let his taunts cloud her purpose. Instead, she extended her Talent, feeling the metal in the cavern around her, preparing.

"Your loyalty has blinded you," she replied, her voice quiet but laced with conviction. "You serve a force that would consume us all, and you call it loyalty."

With a defiant cry, she lifted her arm, gathering her power, and let the metal break apart and surge forward forcing all of her Talent into the push, forming a barrage of sharp, shimmering projectiles aimed directly at him. Arash staggered, trying to summon his Talent, but the currents of wind he managed were weak, scattered, no match for her assault. He stumbled back, the sharp edges of her metal finding their mark, driving him to his knees.

Around her, the scouts had managed to overwhelm the remaining Beloveds, the last of them faltering under the relentless onslaught. Rostam himself struck down one of the last opponents, his blade swift and sure, and in that moment, it looked as though victory was within their grasp.

She breathed a sigh of relief, her gaze flicking to Yasher, who had been watching her back, his small punch dagger held tightly in his hand, his stance steady despite the pain evident in his face. She felt a surge of gratitude, of fierce loyalty to him and to the others who had stood by her.

A shadow shifted in the corner of her vision, and her instincts flared, too late to react. One of the remaining Beloveds, whom she'd thought down, lunged from the shadows, his Talent—a twisting, spiraling energy that warped the air around him—crackling with deadly force towards Rostam and the scouts.

"Rostam! Get out!" she screamed, her voice desperate, the warning tearing from her throat.

His eyes wide with realization, shouted a command to the scouts. They scrambled, pulling back toward the passage they'd entered through, the wounded supporting each other as they ran. She saw him glance back one last time, his face conflicted, before he turned and disappeared into the shadows with the remaining scouts, ensuring they would make it out.

But her warning had focused the attention of the Beloved. He was upon her in an instant, his Talent surging toward her. She felt the impact, a shock of pain that shot through her, and the world spun, tilting as her vision darkened. She tried to hold on, to push back against the overwhelming force, but her strength was slipping, the edges of consciousness fraying.

The last thing she saw was Yasher's horrified expression, his shout blending with the echoes of the cavern, his voice reaching out to her as everything went black.

CHAPTER 27

FARAH WOKE to the dull ache of her body protesting every movement. The room swam as she blinked, forcing her eyes to focus on the too-familiar sight of polished cedar beams overhead. The faint scent of rosewater hung in the air, cloying, suffocating. She sat up abruptly, her heart hammering in her chest.

Her room. Her old cell in the Citadel.

The realization hit like a dagger to the gut. This was the very room where she'd grown up, a ward of the Mashyana. Every detail felt like a twisted mirror of her childhood.

How did I get here?

Her last memory was the chaos of the cavern—the sharp clash of blades, the roar of wind from Arash's Talent, and the blinding pain when something heavy struck her head. Yasher's cry as she fell. After that, only fragments: shadows, whispers, the sensation of floating. Days, it must have been days. Her muscles ached as though she'd been motionless for far too long, and her mouth was dry, her tongue heavy with the bitterness of drugs.

The fight. The relics. Yasher.

She swung her legs over the side of the bed, gripping the edge as dizziness threatened to pull her back down. Her breath came in shallow bursts. Where is Yasher? Did Rostam escape? What about the Mashya? She pressed a trembling hand to her temple, willing herself to think, to remember, but the haze in her mind offered nothing but silence.

Her gaze darted around the room, searching for anything out of place. Why bring me here? Why not throw me in the dungeons?

The sound of muffled voices on the other side of the door made her freeze. Guards, from the cadence of their speech and the occasional metallic scrape of armor shifting. She strained to listen, catching snippets of conversation—mundane topics, complaints about patrol shifts. The realization set her heart racing again. I'm being watched.

The guards' voices grew louder, and she stood, looking for anything that she could use as a weapon. Panic clawed at her chest. She needed to get out, to find Yasher, to—

The door creaked open.

Farah whirled, her fists clenched instinctively. Arash stepped into the room, his presence like a stormcloud darkening the air. His face bore the marks of their last encounter —a deep gash along his temple, small cuts and bruises blooming across his cheekbone, and his right arm hung stiffly at his side. But his eyes, sharp and unyielding, held the same malevolent glint, though she thought it could be dulled.

"You're awake," he said, his voice rough. "I was hoping you'd not wake at all, but Amma Behnaz swears that you're important to our cause. Leyla's healing has been... a little too unreliable, and you were out for over a fortnight. Come, the Mashyana awaits."

Her throat tightened. She kept her expression neutral, but her mind raced. *Why send Arash? What game is she playing now?*

"I need answers," she said, her voice steadier than she felt. "What happened? Where's Yasher?"

Arash's lip curled. "The dirty gharib? You'll find out soon enough. Move."

When she didn't comply immediately, he stepped forward and grabbed her arm. His grip was iron, and she suppressed a wince as he hauled her toward the door, even as he began coughing. The guards outside stepped aside as Arash dragged her through the halls of the Citadel.

The journey was a blur of familiar corridors, their opulence dulled by the weight of her dread. The golden tapestries and marble columns felt oppressive now, like the jaws of a beast closing around her. As they approached the throne room, the air grew colder. No courtiers, servants, or guards walked through the halls, even though she could see that it was midday through the windows.

The doors opened with a groan, revealing a scene that twisted her stomach. The throne room was almost unrecognizable. The Mashyana sat slouched on her gilded throne, her figure draped in silks that no longer hid the gauntness of her frame. Her face, once radiant, was sallow and lined with exhaustion. Around her, a handful of Beloveds lingered—frail, sickly shadows of the powerful figures she had once known. While the ones that had survived the fight in the cavern sported their own bruises and cuts, the sickness was taking more and more control over them, the stasis that they were controlled with slowly losing strength.

And yet, the Mashyana's eyes lit up when she saw

Farah, a gleam of something dangerously close to relief crossing her features.

"Farah, my dear," Behnaz said, her voice honeyed but brittle. "You've returned to me."

Arash forced her to her knees before the throne, and the motion sent a spike of pain through her legs. She gritted her teeth, refusing to bow her head. Her gaze locked on the Mashyana, sharp and unyielding.

"I didn't return," she said. "You brought me here."

The Mashyana smiled, a strained gesture that didn't reach her eyes.

"Semantics." She waved away the words. "What matters is that you're here, safe and sound. You've been through so much, my poor Hand."

Her stomach churned. The words were wrong, dripping with false sincerity. She glanced at the Beloveds flanking the throne, their hollow eyes watching her without recognition. She had known these people once, had trained beside them, fought with them. Now they were shells, drained of all their vitality, their humanity.

Her gaze snapped back to Behnaz. "Where is Yasher?"

The Mashyana tilted her head, her expression softening into a mask of pity.

"The gharib? He's nothing, Farah." A tsk escaped Behnaz. "A distraction. He's likely run off by now, onto new adventures. I wouldn't waste your concern on someone like him."

Her hands clenched into fists.

"You're lying," she said, her voice low but firm. "What did you do to him?"

Behnaz sighed, leaning forward slightly. "Farah, you've always been so loyal, so determined to do what's right. That's why I chose you to be my Hand. But lately... you've strayed. I understand why. The rebels, the chaos, that gharib, even dear Rostam —Yes, Arash told me that he still lives — they've poisoned your mind."

She glared up at her. "Don't pretend this is about my loyalty. You brought me here because you couldn't find the relics. That's all you care about."

The Mashyana's expression hardened, the mask slipping. "You misunderstand me, dear. I care deeply for Emari. Everything I've done has been for the good of this kingdom."

"By draining the life out of your own people?" she shot back. "By turning the Beloveds into—" she gestured toward the sickly figures around her, "—this?"

Behnaz's eyes flashed with anger.

"You don't understand the sacrifices I've made. The sacrifices I've had to make." Her voice grew sharper, more desperate. "The relics, Farah. Where are they? They weren't on you, and the gharib was useless. Tell me where they are, and we can fix this. Together."

She swallowed her rage, forcing herself to think clearly. *She's desperate. She's losing control. How to get her to make a mistake?*

She lowered her gaze, feigning submission.

"I... I don't remember," she said, her voice trembling just enough to sell the lie, and willing the vision of Pari's face from her thoughts. "I don't know where they are. I had them when I was in the cavern."

The Mashyana studied her, suspicion flickering in her eyes. Then she smiled again, but it was a cold, predatory thing. "You were always such a terrible liar, Farah."

Before she could react, Behnaz stood and descended the steps of the throne, her movements eerily smooth. She reached out and cupped Farah's chin, forcing her to look up.

"I wanted to give you a chance. I wanted you to see reason. But you leave me no choice. I am so disappointed in you, my Hand."

She jerked her head away, but the Mashyana's grip was like iron. A cold dread settled over her as Behnaz's other hand began to glow with a dark, pulsing light.

"You don't understand," the Mashyana whispered, her voice soft but laced with madness. "Mazdavir showed me the truth. The gods were weak, Farah. They abandoned us. But with the Darkness, with Mazdavir's power, I can make Emari strong. Stronger than ever before."

Her blood ran cold. Even Rashnu did not know what the Darkness was, but it had a name.

"You've sold your soul," she spat. "You're no better than the Darkness you claim to control."

Behnaz's eyes burned with an unnatural light. "I don't expect you to understand. But you will serve me, one way or another."

The dark light in her hand surged, and pain exploded through her body as the Mashyana's power latched onto her, pulling at something deep within her. She screamed, her mind a storm of agony and defiance.

No. I won't let her win.

With a desperate surge of will, she reached for the core of her Talent. She could feel the threads of metal in the room—the iron in the throne, the steel in the weapons surrounding them, the candelabras. She seized them, letting her anger and fear sharpen her focus.

The throne room erupted into chaos as metal screamed and twisted, responding to her call. The Mashyana's grip faltered, and she staggered to her feet, her vision swimming but her resolve unbroken.

"You won't take anything from me," she said, her voice steady despite the tremor in her limbs. "Not my power. Not my life. And not Emari."

The Mashyana's expression twisted with rage, and the dark light around her flared once more.

Her body convulsed, wracked with an agony so deep it felt as though it were tearing her apart at the seams. The Mashyana's dark, pulsing power coursed through her, threading its way into her Talent, into her very soul. She tried to resist, to push back with the metallic threads she could still sense, but they felt slippery, elusive, as if they no longer obeyed her.

"Do you feel it now?" Behnaz murmured, her voice almost tender as she knelt beside her. The Mashyana's hand, still glowing with that ominous energy, hovered just above her chest. "This is what it means to wield true power. To sacrifice everything for Emari's future."

She clenched her teeth, refusing to give the Mashyana the satisfaction of hearing her scream again. Her mind fought to rally, but the Mashyana's power was overwhelming. It wasn't just physical—it was invasive, gnawing at her thoughts, sapping her will to fight, to breathe.

"Why... are you doing this?" she choked out, her voice barely a whisper. "You said you cared about Emari. This... this isn't saving it."

Behnaz leaned closer, her once-beautiful face now twisted by a mixture of fury and desperation.

"You don't understand, Farah. None of you ever understood, not even Enayat," she hissed. 'The gods left us to rot, left this kingdom to crumble under the weight of its own mediocrity with petty squabbles over the price of grain and charity for the indignant. Mazdavir is the only one who showed me the way."

Farah's limbs grew heavy, her strength fading as the darkness coiled tighter around her. Behnaz's power felt alive, sentient even, as if it recognized her resistance and sought to crush it. Her Talent flared weakly, a trickle against a roaring inferno.

She gasped as another wave of energy surged through her, making her vision blur. Images flashed unbidden in her mind: the Citadel burning, the Beloveds lying lifeless in their chambers, Yasher's face contorted in pain. The Mashyana's voice became a distant hum, her words wrapping around Farah like chains.

"Let go," Behnaz whispered. "You can't fight this. You were always my weapon. Stop struggling and accept your place at my side again. The things I can share with you... the power. It's remarkable."

Her heart thudded painfully in her chest. Her memories felt fragmented, slipping away like sand through her fingers. She couldn't lose herself—she wouldn't—but her will faltered as the Mashyana's power reached deeper, prying at her Talent, her essence.

She thought of Yasher, his lop-sided grin shining. Of Pari's small, defiant smile. Of Rostam's stern but kind eyes. She couldn't fail them. She couldn't let herself become another pawn in the Mashyana's twisted game. But her body betrayed her, sinking further into the pull of the dark energy. Her Talent flared again, but it was weaker now, dimming as the Mashyana's power smothered it.

"I did all of this for Emari!" the Mashyana said, her voice rising, a wild, frenzied edge creeping in. "Don't you see, Farah? With Mazdavir's strength, we could rule the world. Emari will become more powerful than ever, and you will help me do it!"

Her breathing slowed, her chest heaving as she fought against the pull. Her vision darkened at the edges, and for a moment, she felt herself slipping away. But a glimmer of something deep within her flickered—a memory, sharp and clear.

The Chinvat Bridge. Rashnu's words, solemn and resonant.

"You must fight, Farah. Not just for yourself, but for the soul of Emari."

Her lips parted, her voice faint but defiant. "This... isn't... Emari."

The Mashyana's eyes widened, and for a brief moment, the dark energy faltered. Farah seized the opportunity, summoning the last dregs of her strength. Her Talent flickered weakly, her connection to the metals in the room tenuous but present. She reached out, desperately grasping for something, anything to anchor her.

But the darkness surged back, stronger this time, and Farah felt herself slipping again. Her Talent buckled under the weight of the Mashyana's power, and her body slumped forward. The cold marble of the throne room floor pressed against her cheek, and she realized dimly that her strength was nearly gone.

The Mashyana rose to her full height, her expression triumphant yet haunted.

"You were always meant to serve me, Farah," she said softly. "And now, you will with your Talent. Such a shame that you will not join me as my Hand."

Farah's vision blurred, but through the haze, she saw something unexpected. Behnaz's hands trembled. Her face, though triumphant, was pale and drawn, and the dark energy surrounding her flickered erratically. The power she wielded, the power of Mazdavir, was consuming her too.

Her mind clung to that thought, a spark of hope in the encroaching darkness. She's not invincible. If the Mashyana was succumbing to Mazdavir's influence, then maybe—just maybe—there was still a chance to stop her.

The darkness pressed down on her, dragging her into unconsciousness, and the last thing she heard was the Mashyana's voice, low and almost mournful:

"Sleep well, my Hand. When you wake, you'll see the world as I do."

<hr>

YASHER LAY on the cold stone floor, his body aching and bruised, every shallow breath scraping against his cracked ribs. The dungeon walls pressed in around him, their damp stones leaching what little warmth he had left. He had no idea how long he'd been there—days, weeks, maybe even longer. He'd given up on the slim bench they'd kept putting him back on every time they'd come to visit him. Time was a blur of pain, interrupted only by the brief, mocking reprieves when healers would come, knitting his bones and muscles just enough for him to endure another round of Arash's torment.

He tried to recall the last time he'd heard voices outside his cell, footsteps, or even the metallic scrape of the dungeon gate. Nothing. It had been quiet for too long. Maybe they'd forgotten about him. Left him to starve. Part of him hoped that was the case. The other part feared what that silence could mean for Farah. They must have brought both of them here. He reached out, hoping that his heart was still beating which meant that she was not only close by, but still alive. It would be an empty shell if she wasn't.

He shut his eyes, fighting the hopelessness that clawed at his mind. He remembered the last he'd seen of her in the Forgotten Temple, surrounded by darkness, her Talent blazing as she fought against Arash and his storm of wind. And then, everything had been blackness and despair. His stomach twisted as he remembered her eyes just before he'd been dragged into darkness, locking onto his.

He could still feel the weight of his broken body. But what had happened to her? If she was alive, they would have tortured her, tried to break her the way they had him, and if they hadn't... No. He couldn't think that way. She was stronger than him, stronger than this place, stronger than these gods who didn't swoop in and fix things.

He rolled over, wincing at the sharp pain that radiated from his ribs, and stared up at the ceiling. In the emptiness, he found himself reaching for something he hadn't felt in days—a flicker of hope, the familiar surge of his luck. He'd always been able to sense it, that strange, unexplainable force that had guided him through so many close calls, leading him to narrow escapes and last-minute fortunes. But ever since he'd given the Eye to Farah, he'd felt hollow where his luck had once been, as though he'd lost part of himself.

But maybe... maybe it was still there.

He closed his eyes, reaching out with the faintest tendrils of his mind, seeking the luck that had once been as easy to summon as breathing. There was a strange resistance at first, a gap where the Eye had once been, and his heart sank as he felt only emptiness. He'd almost given up when, suddenly, he felt something—a glimmer, faint but undeniable. A full well of something. Luck. His Luck.

His breath caught, confusion warring with a sudden surge of relief. How was it there? And yet, here it was, alive within him, even stronger than before. He hesitated, unsure, and then released it in a single, desperate wave.

Nothing happened. The seconds dragged on, and the silence of the dungeon crept back, crushing his brief flicker of hope. He sank back, feeling foolish. What did he think would happen? That Luck alone could free him?

And then, faint but unmistakable, he heard the scuff of footsteps outside his cell. His heart leapt to his throat, but he forced himself to lie still, listening intently as the footsteps paused outside his cell door. Metal scraped against metal, and the door swung open.

A dark figure slipped inside, crouching low to avoid the flickering torchlight from the hallway. His heart nearly stopped when he recognized the figure.

"Rostam?"

Rostam's face, lined and weary, broke into a faint grin. "You're not dead yet. That's something, gharib."

He let out a shaky laugh, relief flooding through him. "Not for their lack of trying."

Rostam slipped a hand under his arm, helping him to his feet. His touch was firm, steadying, and he leaned on him gratefully.

"How did you get in here?"

The Commander's expression darkened as he glanced down the hallway.

"I had help," Rostam replied. "Some of the rebels managed to follow when you were brought back to the Citadel. They're waiting outside the walls, including... the Mashya."

His mind raced, hope rekindling with fierce intensity.

"He's prepared to take back the Citadel," Rostam

continued, his voice low. "But first, we need to find Farah and make sure she's safe. And then... we deal with the Beloveds and Behnaz. The Citadel has been abandoned by all but her closest as she descends further into the Darkness, and the city is in chaos. Behnaz has been rounding up all of the Talented for months off the streets to siphon their Talents, along with public executions for any dissent to her rule."

He nodded, though dread gnawed at him. If the Mashyana had gotten to Farah, if she had somehow broken her... But no, he refused to believe it. Farah was still alive, and if he had anything to say about it, they would both walk out of this place.

Rostam led him down the shadowy corridors, their footsteps muffled by the thick layer of dust coating the stone floors. He moved with as much stealth as he could muster, leaning heavily on the older man as they navigated the labyrinthine dungeons. With every step, he reached out to that small well of Luck, letting it guide him through the dark turns, hoping it would give him the strength he needed.

The path led them up a narrow staircase, winding through the inner chambers of the Citadel. The silence was oppressive, broken only by the occasional distant murmur of voices or the faint clang of an open shutter. They paused just outside the throne room, pressing themselves against the wall. His pulse quickened as he caught the familiar hum of power, dark and foreboding, emanating from within.

"She's in there," Yasher whispered, his voice barely audible. His Luck seemed to flare up, knowing that Farah was on the other side of the doors.

Rostam nodded grimly. "I think so. Behnaz is there as well. The servants that are still here say that she rarely leaves the throne room. Whatever else the Darkness has done to her, it's made her mad."

His jaw clenched. He wanted nothing more than to storm into the room, to tear Farah free from the Mashyana's grasp, but he knew they had to be careful. They couldn't afford to alert any guards or the remaining Beloveds.

Rostam squeezed his shoulder, meeting his gaze with steely resolve. "We go in, you use whatever you can to distract her. I'll handle Arash and the Beloveds while we wait for the troops outside to join us."

He swallowed, nodding. He could feel his Luck stirring, stronger than ever, as though it sensed the urgency of the moment. He took a steadying breath and pushed open the heavy door just wide enough for them to slip inside.

The sight that greeted him in the throne room made his blood run cold. Farah was on her knees in the center of the room, her body slumped and lifeless, her skin pale and almost translucent. Detritus lay all around the room, metal forms that were once decorations and religious icons to show that she fought hard before being brought down. But none of them close enough for her to use against Behnaz.

The Mashyana stood over her, one hand resting on Farah's shoulder, a dark, swirling energy coiling around her fingers, draining the life from Farah's body.

Her face was twisted with an unnatural hunger, her eyes gleaming with a feverish intensity that sent a shiver down his spine. She looked almost monstrous, her once-regal features sunken and hollow, the lines of her face etched with cruelty and madness, dark streaks running where her veins should be.

"No," he whispered, his heart breaking at the sight of her so diminished, so close to death.

The Mashyana's voice, low and venomous, cut through

the silence. "Do you feel it now, my dear? The power of the gods themselves, flowing through me. And you... you were always meant to be my instrument."

Farah's head lolled to the side, her eyes half-closed, but he saw the faintest flicker of defiance in her gaze. She hadn't given up, not completely. She was fighting, even now, with what little strength she had left.

His Luck surged within him, fierce and insistent. He didn't fully understand it, but he didn't need to. All he had to do was trust it, let it guide him. He focused on the faint glint of metal in the room, a broken candelabra near the wall, its iron frame catching the dim light.

Move. Go to her. Give her what she needs.

The Luck responded, releasing itself in a wave that rippled through the room. The candelabra trembled, then toppled over, its metal frame already bent, breaking apart. Pieces rolled across the floor toward Farah's limp open hand slowly, as if they didn't want to have anyone take notice of them. He held his breath, willing it to reach her, praying that she would have the strength to use it.

The metal spike rolled, nudged forward as though by an unseen hand, until it came just out of reach of Farah's fingers. Her eyes flickered, her hand twitching as she tried to hum, the sound guttural instead of the soft purr he knew it to be, pulling it into her hand. She closed around the spike, her grip weak but determined.

The Mashyana froze, sensing the shift in the air, her gaze snapping down to Farah's hand. "What are you—"

But Farah moved before she could finish, lunging upward with the last of her strength and Talent to extend the metal into a long blade, driving it into the Mashyana's side. Behnaz shrieked, her dark power flaring and then sputtering as Farah's strike disrupted her concentration.

Rostam seized the moment, lunging at Arash, who had been standing near the edge of the room, his attention diverted by the unfolding chaos. With a swift, brutal efficiency, Rostam struck, disarming him and knocking him to the ground. Arash let out a strangled cry, his Talent faltering as Rostam's blow left him stunned.

As the Mashyana staggered back, clutching her wound, the dark energy surrounding her began to waver. The Beloveds, who had stood motionless around the throne, suddenly collapsed, as if whatever force had been holding them upright had been severed.

The door burst open, and a contingent of rebels poured into the throne room, led by the Mashya himself. His face was grim, his gaze locked on Behnaz with a mixture of anger and sorrow. He motioned to the guards, who rushed forward and seized the Mashyana, pulling her roughly to her feet. She froze in place, staring at the Mashya in disbelief.

"Enayat…" she whispered. "You're… you're alive."

"Behnaz," Enayat proclaimed. "It's over."

He waved at the rebels. "Remove all of her jewelry. They may be relics. Then take her away."

Yasher watched as the Mashyana was dragged away, her screams echoing through the hall as she was taken down to the dungeons—the very same place where he'd been left to rot. It felt fitting, somehow.

But his gaze quickly returned to Farah, who was slumped on the floor, her breathing shallow but steady. He crossed the room as quickly as his broken body would allow and knelt beside her, gently lifting her head, brushing a stray lock of hair from her face.

"You did it," he whispered, his voice choked with emotion.

Her eyes fluttered open, and a faint smile crossed her lips.

"It... wasn't me. I couldn't call... the metal," she murmured, her voice barely audible. "Your Luck... was it you?"

Yasher swallowed, his throat tight. "Maybe. But you were the one who held on long enough."

Farah's hand found his, her fingers cold but steady. They sat together in the ruined throne room, surrounded by the fallen. And for the first time in what felt like forever, Yasher allowed himself to just breathe.

CHAPTER 28

FARAH STIRRED, a faint breeze brushing against her face, pulling her out of the fragile haze of sleep. Her dreams faded quickly, slipping away like water through her fingers, leaving only a lingering unease in their place. She rolled onto her side, her arm reaching out for the warmth of Yasher's presence, the reassuring weight that had anchored her through so many restless nights.

But her hand found only empty sheets.

Her eyes fluttered open, adjusting to the faint silvery glow of moonlight filtering through the gauzy curtains. Yasher's side of the bed was cool to the touch. She pushed herself upright, brushing a hand through her tangled hair as her gaze swept the room.

It wasn't the first time she'd woken to find him missing. Yasher often struggled to sleep, his mind too restless, his memories too vivid. She understood it better than she cared to admit. Sleep had never come easily to her, not in the month since the battle, not with the nightmares that lingered at the edges of her thoughts, waiting to strike the moment she closed her eyes.

The memories of those dreams surfaced now, unbidden. She shivered as the vivid images washed over her—rows of the Beloveds standing around her, their faces eerily blank, their hands reaching for her. They whispered in a language she couldn't understand, but the meaning was clear. They wanted what she had. And always, at the center of those dreams, stood the Mashyana, her eyes cold and calculating, her hand gripping her shoulder as she drained the strength from her body.

To see her in those dreams—stealing her Talent, leaving her hollow and empty—was a betrayal she hadn't yet fully reconciled, even now. Waking from those nightmares left her with a suffocating weight in her chest, a feeling she couldn't shake no matter how many nights passed.

Her gaze swept the room, taking in the stark contrast between her dreams and her reality. The state room the two of them shared was fit for royalty, its gilded walls and ornate furnishings a stark contrast to the chambers she'd once called home. She had grown up in the shadow of the Mashyana's court, among the other Beloveds, where opulence surrounded them but was rarely meant for them to enjoy.

Those memories felt distant now, like a life lived by someone else. Her role had been clear. Obedience, service, devotion. She'd been taught that her life was a gift from the Mashyana, that every Talent she honed was in honor of the queen who had raised her. She was no longer that woman, though she wasn't quite sure who she was now.

This room, with its plush rugs and golden chandeliers, felt like an impossible dream. The massive bed, far larger than necessary, dominated the space, its canopy draped with crimson silk that shimmered faintly in the moonlight.

The tapestries lining the walls told stories of Emari's glory. Victories in battle, divine blessings bestowed upon Mashyas of old, the splendor of the Citadel. She wondered if any of it was true, or if it was all carefully crafted fiction, designed to obscure the cracks beneath the surface.

Slipping out of bed, she pulled on her robe, the soft fabric heavy against her skin. The cold marble floor sent a shiver through her as she padded silently across the room toward the open balcony doors. The curtains fluttered in the breeze, carrying with them the faint scent of citrus and jasmine from the gardens far below.

Her breath caught as she stepped onto the balcony as the cool night air wrapped around her. Yasher stood at the railing, his exposed back to her, scars silver in the moonlight peeking through the clouds, silhouetted against the sprawling expanse of the Citadel. His head was bowed slightly, his posture tense, and the faint metallic glint of a coin in his hand caught her eye.

She paused in the doorway, her heart aching at the sight of him. He was flipping the coin, the motion smooth and practiced, his lips moving silently as it spun through the air.

"Tails," he murmured, catching the coin and glancing at the result.

He frowned, then flipped it again. "Heads."

She watched him for a moment, her chest tightening. This had become his ritual in the nights when sleep eluded him—testing his Luck, trying to make sense of the power that had both saved and haunted him. She knew the coin was more than just a distraction. It was a way for him to wrest some control over a Talent that he had always thought was something from outside of him.

She stepped closer, her presence silent until her Talent brushed against the coin mid-flip, freezing it in midair. He blinked, startled, before turning to see her standing behind him.

"Couldn't sleep?" she asked, her voice soft but carrying enough warmth to break through the tension in the air.

A faint smile tugged at the corners of his mouth, though the shadows in his eyes remained. "Neither could you, apparently."

"I woke up and you weren't there." She moved to his back, tracing a few of his scars with her finger before slipping her arms around his waist and resting her cheek against his shoulder blade. His warmth seeped into her, a comfort against the chill of the night.

"I didn't mean to wake you," he said quietly, his voice tinged with guilt.

"You didn't," she replied. "I just missed you."

They stood there in silence for a moment, the city stretching out before them like a living tapestry. The Citadel's winding streets glowed faintly with the golden light of lanterns, their intricate patterns weaving through the darkness, a soft rain falling as if to clean the city.

From this height, the city looked peaceful, almost serene. The news of the Mashyana's betrayal ran through the city, and the country, like wildfire in the days after their victory, damaging the very soul of the kingdom. The Mashya still struggled to keep law and order in place while they found all of the hidden corners and deceptions that she had wrought, let alone the regular mobs who showed at the doors to the Citadel, crying out for Behnaz's blood. Rostam had conscripted most of the rebels that had followed them to the city, and they held their own as much as they could.

Yasher's hand brushed over hers at his waist, his fingers tracing idle patterns against her skin. He held out his other hand under the still-frozen coin and she released it to drop.

"I was testing it again," he said, his voice breaking the stillness.

"Your Luck?"

He nodded, flipping the coin once more and catching it with practiced ease. "It feels... different now. Stronger. Wilder. I'm not sure I understand it anymore."

"What feels different?" She laid a kiss gently on his shoulder.

He stared at the coin in his hand, his brow furrowed in thought.

"Before, it felt like I was just nudging things, you know? Tipping the odds a little in my favor, or letting it pick the direction I should go towards. But now..." He hesitated, his fingers rolling the coin absently. "Now it feels bigger. Like I'm not just at advantage of the game—I'm rewriting it."

She thought of the throne room, of the way his Talent had surged, guiding her to the spike that had ended the Mashyana's reign. His Luck had been more than a tool in that moment—it had been a force, raw and unyielding, bending the world around him to ensure their survival.

"Does it scare you?" she asked gently.

He let out a soft laugh, though it lacked his usual humor. He pulled her hands away from his waist and turned to face her.

"A little," he admitted. "Mostly because I don't know what to do with it. I've always trusted my Luck, but now... it feels unpredictable. Like I'm playing with something that could turn on me at any moment."

She reached out, taking the coin from his hand and holding it up to the moonlight. The simple piece of metal gleamed in the soft glow, its edges worn smooth from years of use. She hummed softly and floated it up from her palm.

"Your Luck isn't just chance," she said. "It's a part of you, and extension of your soul. And whatever it's becoming, you'll figure it out. You always do."

He smiled faintly, his eyes softening as they met hers. "You have too much faith in me."

"Someone has to," she teased, though her voice carried a gentle sincerity. She let the coin drop back into her hand, feeling the tension of her Talent pushed just to do these parlor tricks.

She exhaled softly. The lines of worry on his face mirrored her own, but his eyes held a question she hadn't been ready to face.

"How are you holding up?" he asked, his voice quiet but laced with concern. "I mean… really. You always keep too much to yourself, and I worry."

The weight of his question pressed against her chest, and for a moment, she didn't know how to answer. The memories of the past weeks felt raw, jagged edges that cut at her resolve. Her body ached from the battles she had fought, her Talent felt strained, as though it had been stretched to its limit, and her mind… Her mind was a tangle of guilt and grief.

"I'm healing," she said finally, her voice soft but steady. "Physically, at least. The wounds are closing, though some days it feels like they've just moved to places no one can see."

Yasher tilted his head, studying her. "And your Talent?"

She hesitated, glancing down at her hands. She flexed her fingers, feeling the faint hum of the metals around her, the threads of her power weaving through the room.

"It's... there," she admitted. "But it feels different as well. Like it's not as sure of itself anymore. When she tried to take it away from me... it is healing in the same way my body is."

He nodded, his hand brushing lightly over hers. "You've pushed it further than anyone ever should. It's no wonder it feels worn."

She gave a small, humorless laugh. "Worn is an understatement. It feels like it's barely holding together, like I'm barely holding together."

Yasher's expression softened, and he stepped closer, his free hand brushing her temple.

"And here?" he whispered. "Farah, you've been carrying so much. I see it in the way you move, the way you look at me sometimes. It's like you're trying to bear the weight of the entire kingdom on your shoulders."

Her throat tightened, and she looked away, her gaze falling to the worn edges of the coin still clutched in her other hand.

"It's not just the kingdom, Yasher," she said quietly. "It's everything. The Mashyana, the Beloveds, the relics, the people we lost. The choices I made. Every time I close my eyes, it's all still there, haunting me. And now, even with her gone from the throne, from power, it doesn't feel like it's over. Not really."

He was silent for a moment, his thumb brushing lightly over her knuckles. "You don't have to carry all of it alone, you know. You have me. You always have me."

Her chest tightened at his words, the sincerity in his tone threatening to unravel the fragile control she had been clinging to. She met his gaze, her voice trembling. "What if I'm not enough?"

Yasher's grip on her hand tightened, grounding her.

"You are, Phoenix. You've already done more than anyone could have asked of you. You've given people hope, a chance to rebuild. You've given me hope." His voice softened, his eyes never leaving hers. "And I'll be here, no matter how long it takes, to remind you of that."

For a moment, the weight on her chest eased, his words wrapping around her like a balm. She leaned into his touch, letting herself draw strength from him.

"Thank you," she whispered, her voice barely audible. "For not giving up on me, even though I kept pushing you away."

Yasher smiled faintly, a warmth in his eyes that chased away some of the shadows in her mind.

"Never," he said simply.

Farah hesitated, her gaze dropping to the coin still in her hand. "The Mashya has asked me to stay at court. To be his ambassador and advisor. He thinks I can help rebuild what's been broken."

"And do you think he's right?"

"I don't know," she admitted. "This place... it's complicated. There's so much pain here, so much history. But there's hope too. If I can help the people, if I can give them something to believe in again... maybe it's worth staying."

Yasher's thumb brushed lightly over her cheek, lifting her gaze to meet his. "You've already given them hope, Farah. You've given them more than they could have ever asked for. If anyone can rebuild this kingdom, it's you."

Her lips curved into a faint smile as she leaned into his touch. "And you? What's next for you?"

"I think I'll stick around," he chuckled softly, the sound warm and familiar. "Someone has to keep you from working yourself to death. Also, I need to make sure you never call another man *insufferable*."

She laughed, the sound breaking through the heaviness in her chest. She reached up, brushing a strand of hair from his face. "No one is as insufferable as you."

Their moment of quiet was interrupted by a sharp knock at the door. Both of them froze, the intimacy of the night shattered. She exchanged a glance with him before stepping back into the room and pulling the door open.

A guard stood in the hallway, his expression pale and grim. "Khānum Farah, Aqa Yasher," he said, bowing slightly. "The Mashyana has requested your presence, Khānum. It's urgent."

She felt a chill settle over her, her stomach twisting at the mention of Behnaz. She hadn't seen the Mashyana in weeks, not since her imprisonment in the dungeons. "What does she want?"

"She wouldn't say," the guard replied. "Only that she would only speak with you."

She glanced back at Yasher, who was already moving to pull on his boots. She turned back to the guard, nodding curtly. "We'll come."

The door closed, and she moved to her wardrobe, her hands trembling slightly as she fastened the clasps of her coat. He dressed quickly beside her, his movements quiet but efficient. Neither of them spoke, but the tension in the air was palpable.

Farah's mind raced as she tied her boots, her thoughts a chaotic swirl of possibilities. Behnaz had been silent for weeks, her once-imposing presence reduced to a shadow in the depths of the dungeons, not even speaking to the Mashya, who tried time and time again to attempt to speak to her, husband to wife. What could she possibly have to say?

He stepped to her side, pulling her hand to his lips softly. The gesture was small, but it steadied her.

FARAH FOLLOWED Yasher down the dim corridor of the Citadel, the guard leading them moving with measured urgency. The cold air seemed to seep through the stone walls, biting at her skin even through her coat. Each step closer to the dungeons brought an unwelcome tightness in her chest.

The Mashyana — now just Behnaz à Radan, stripped of her titles and crown, had summoned her. Why now?

The torchlight flickered on the walls, casting shadows that danced like specters. Her mind wandered, memories of her childhood in the Citadel rising unbidden. She had walked these halls as a child, following behind the Mashyana, feeling as though she belonged to something grand and unshakable. The queen had been the only thing she had resembling a mother, a figure of unwavering strength and guidance.

How wrong she had been.

She tightened her jaw, pushing the thoughts away. Now wasn't the time to dwell on the past. Yasher's steady presence ahead of her was enough to ground her, even though the tension in his shoulders told her he was just as unsettled as she was.

The dungeon door loomed before them, a heavy slab of iron that seemed to groan in protest as the guard pushed it open. The smell hit her immediately—damp stone, mildew, and the faint metallic tang of blood and rust. Farah pressed a hand to her nose instinctively, though it did little to block the stench.

Behnaz had kept Yasher, had the Beloveds beat him, and tortured him here.

As the three of them stepped into the cold, dark hallway, Her gaze swept over the cells lining the walls. Most were empty, their iron bars slick with condensation. But the silence wasn't comforting—it was heavy, oppressive.

The guard slowed as they neared the end of the corridor.

"She's in here," he said, nodding toward the final cell.

She caught a glimpse of Behnaz through the bars, her breath hitching at the sight. The woman who had once commanded armies, who had worn the title of Mashyana like a crown of fire, was unrecognizable. She sat hunched on the cot, her once-lustrous hair hanging in limp strands around her face, gray streaks running rampant throughout. Her skin was pale and waxy, her cheeks sunken.

Farah's stomach twisted, a complicated knot of anger, sorrow, and something she couldn't name. Behnaz had brought so much ruin—to the kingdom, to the Beloveds, to Farah herself. But seeing her now, broken and diminished, wasn't satisfying. It was hollow.

"Farah," Yasher said softly, his voice pulling her from her thoughts. She realized she had stopped moving, her feet rooted to the ground.

She forced herself forward, stopping just before the bars. Behnaz's head tilted slightly, her dull eyes focusing on her.

"Farahnaz, my dear," Behnaz rasped, her voice weak and cracked.

Farah swallowed hard, her hands trembling at her sides. Behnaz was dying. She turned to the guard and spoke before she could lose her resolve, holding out her hand for the keys to the cell.

"Go to the Mashya," she said. "Tell him to come immediately."

The guard hesitated, his eyes flicking between her and Behnaz as he handed over the keys.

"Now," she said sharply, her voice brooking no argument.

The guard nodded and hurried off, leaving her and Yasher alone with the Mashyana.

"Farah," Behnaz said again, her voice softer this time, almost pleading.

Farah stepped closer, her heart pounding. "Why did you call for me? The Mashya…"

Behnaz's lips twitched into something that might have been a smile, though it was so faint it looked more like a grimace.

"Because…" her voice cracked. "I needed to see you. Before it's too late."

Farah's stomach clenched. "Too late for what?"

Behnaz gestured weakly to the cot beside her. Farah opened the door before she could think.

"Sit," she said.

Farah didn't move.

"Farah," Behnaz said again, her voice trembling. "Please."

The word hung in the air, foreign and disarming. The Mashyana had never begged for anything. Not from Farah, not from anyone.

She exchanged a glance with Yasher, whose expression was unreadable. He gave her a small nod, and she stepped forward reluctantly, sitting on the edge of the cot.

Up close, the changes in the former queen were even

more jarring. The once-commanding woman who had raised her, raised a generation of Beloveds, who had shaped so much of who she was, looked fragile, like a piece of glass about to shatter.

"I failed you," Behnaz said, her voice cracking. "I failed all of you."

Farah's throat tightened, but she said nothing.

"I thought I was saving Emari," Behnaz continued, her hands trembling as they rested in her lap. "I thought if I was strong enough, if I had enough power, I could protect us all. But I... I was wrong."

Farah stared at her, anger bubbling just beneath the surface.

"You used us. You killed us," she said, her voice low and trembling. "You betrayed us."

Behnaz's eyes glistened, her head dipping forward as if the weight of Farah's words were too much to bear.

"I know," she said. "I know what I did. And I will carry that guilt to my judging. Which is not long away now."

Farah's hands clenched into fists, her nails digging into her palms. "Why call me here?"

Behnaz lifted her head slowly, her gaze locking onto Farah's.

"Because I have damned us all," she said, her voice barely above a whisper. "Mazdavir... he's coming. He has tasted the power available, and the gods cannot, will not, stand in his way."

Farah froze, the name sending a chill down her spine. "What do you mean?"

"I failed him." Behnaz's lips trembled. "I failed the darkness that gave me strength. I thought... I thought I could control everything. I thought I could control him. And now... he will come for what I couldn't deliver."

Before Farah could respond, footsteps echoed down the hallway. She turned to see the Mashya and Rostam approaching, their faces etched with worry as they adjusted their clothes that were hurriedly put on at the call.

The Mashya's gaze went immediately to Behnaz, his breath catching as he took in her frail appearance. Farah stood up and moved out of the way for him to enter the small cell.

"Behnaz," he said, his voice trembling.

Her expression softened, a flicker of warmth breaking through the haze in her eyes.

"Enayat," she whispered, her voice laced with both affection and sorrow.

He stepped forward, kneeling beside the cot.

"Why?" he asked, his voice breaking. "Why didn't you let me help you?"

Behnaz reached out weakly, her fingers brushing against his cheek, saying nothing.

Tears streamed down his face as he took her hand in his.

"I loved you," he said. "Even after everything. I still love you."

Farah felt a lump rise in her throat, the raw emotion in the room almost too much to bear.

Behnaz's lips curved into a faint smile, her eyes closing.

"I know," she whispered. "I know."

Her body went still, her chest rising and falling one last time before stopping entirely.

The Mashya let out a strangled cry, his shoulders shaking as he clung to her lifeless hand.

"Behnaz," he sobbed, his voice filled with anguish.

Farah looked away, her vision blurring with unshed

tears. She felt Yasher wrap his arms around her from behind, grounding her, but it did little to ease the ache in her chest as she leaned her head against his chest.

The Mashya's sobs filled the dungeon, a haunting reminder of what they had all lost. And as Farah stood there, silent and still, she knew the scars of this night would linger far longer than the Darkness that had brought them here.

CHAPTER 29

THE ROYAL COURTYARD WAS SILENT, save for the rustle of the wind through the cypress trees that lined its edges. Farah stood at the edge of the gathering, her emerald coat pulled tightly around her shoulders against the early morning chill. The sun had yet to rise fully, its pale light casting long shadows across the stone-paved square. A small funeral pyre stood at the center, its simplicity stark against the ornate surroundings.

Behnaz's body lay upon the pyre, wearing a plain linen shift that seemed too humble for a queen, especially a queen like her. But that had been the Mashya's wish—to strip away the grandeur and give her a farewell befitting the woman he once loved, not the title and crown she had twisted and wielded like a weapon.

Farah's chest tightened as she watched Enayat kneel beside the pyre, a basin of water at his side. His movements were slow, deliberate, as he dipped a cloth into the basin and began to cleanse Behnaz's cold form. It was a sacred act, one that symbolized the washing away of sins and preparing the soul for its journey to the Chinvat Bridge to be judged.

He murmured prayers under his breath, his voice low and steady, though it trembled at the edges. Rostam stood nearby, his imposing figure a quiet pillar of strength. Yasher lingered at Farah's side, his presence grounding even as the weight of the moment threatened to pull her under. Pari stood a little way off, holding tightly to Shirin's hand. The girl's bright eyes were unusually somber, her usual curiosity dimmed by the gravity of the occasion.

Farah's gaze drifted back to Enayat, her thoughts churning. She had seen him as many things over the years —regal, distant, measured, even weak at times—but never like this. The grief etched into his face was raw, unfiltered, a reminder that beneath the crown and the title, he was a man who had loved deeply, even if that love had been betrayed and ground into the earth.

Her throat tightened as she watched him wring out the cloth into the nearby bucket, his hands trembling. Rostam stepped forward, placing a steadying hand on his shoulder. The gesture was brief, but it was enough to keep Enayat moving, to keep him from collapsing under the weight of his sorrow.

She turned away, her eyes stinging. Behnaz's death had left a void that no amount of anger or blame could fill. It was a reminder of everything they had lost—not just the woman she had been, but the city, the country, and the dreams she had destroyed in her pursuit of power.

When the cleansing was done, Enayat rose slowly, his movements stiff. He placed the cloth back into the basin, grabbed the linen shroud to cover her, and whispered prayers to the Unnamed Gods over her form. He stepped back, the cleansing rites complete, his gaze fixed on the pyre. Rostam remained close, his presence a quiet comfort.

Farah stepped up to the pyre, leaving Yasher's comfort, gently placing the sigil that the Mashyana had pinned on her coat not so long ago on top of the shroud. Its gold and rubies still gleamed in the meager light from the rising sun. She stepped back, Yasher wrapping a comforting arm around her and kissed the top of her head.

Enayat lifted his hands, his voice breaking the stillness.

"We send her to the Bridge of Souls to be judged, Amesha Spentas," he said, his tone steady despite the grief that weighed it down. "May her soul find peace, and may the sins of this life be washed away by the light of the divine. May Rashnu in his Justice find Mercy for our lost soul Behnaz à Radan."

The words hung in the air, heavy and final. Enayat took the torch from its stand and stepped forward. For a moment, he hesitated, his hand trembling as he held the flame aloft.

Rostam moved closer, his voice low. "You don't have to do this alone."

Enayat nodded, drawing a deep, shuddering breath before lowering the torch to the pyre. The dry wood caught quickly, flames licking up around the shrouded form. The scent of burning wood filled the air, sharp and bitter, and Farah felt a knot tighten in her stomach.

The others remained silent, their faces illuminated by the flickering light. Pari pressed closer to Shirin, her small hand clutching the woman's coat. Farah's gaze lingered on the girl, her heart aching at the sight of her so subdued. Pari had seen too much already, and this was yet another weight she shouldn't have had to bear.

As the flames consumed the pyre, Rostam stepped back, his hand resting briefly on Enayat's shoulder.

"We will leave you to say your goodbyes," he said quietly.

Enayat didn't respond, his gaze fixed on the fire. Rostam motioned for the others to follow, his expression leaving no room for argument. Farah hesitated, her feet rooted to the ground, but Yasher's hand on her arm drew her back.

"Stay with me, Farah," The Mashya said quietly. "She should have those that loved her best see her away."

She looked to Yasher, and he nodded, brushing her cheek with the back of his hand before stepping away from them, silently.

Enayat stood alone, his figure outlined by the flames as she turned back to the fire, joining him. For a long moment, neither of them spoke. Then he turned, his face streaked with tears but composed.

He looked back at the pyre, his shoulders slumping.

"I loved her," he continued. "I loved her even as I saw the Darkness take her. Even as she betrayed me, betrayed the crown, betrayed this kingdom. I thought... I thought I could bring her back. That I could save her."

She swallowed hard, unsure of what to say. She had hated her, for the lies, the manipulation, the pain she had caused. But now, standing here, she couldn't summon that hatred any longer.

"We tried," she said finally, her voice soft.

His lips twisted into a bitter smile. "It wasn't enough."

The flames crackled, the sound filling the silence between them.

After a moment, he turned to her fully, his expression resolute despite the tears still shining in his eyes.

"Farah," he said, his tone shifting. "I need you."

She stiffened, caught off guard by the sudden intensity in his voice.

"I need your help," he continued. "To repair the damage Behnaz left behind. To rebuild this kingdom. To restore faith in the crown, in the gods, in everything she shattered."

She opened her mouth to respond, but he wasn't finished.

"And we need to understand this Darkness," he said, his voice dropping to a near whisper. "This Mazdavir. Whatever it is, whatever it plans."

Her chest tightened. She thought of the final moments in the dungeon, of Behnaz's last words, of the shadow that loomed over them all. The weight of the Mashya's request settled heavily on her shoulders.

She drew a deep breath, her gaze meeting his.

"I'll do what I can," she said.

He nodded, his expression softening slightly. "Thank you."

For a moment, neither of them moved. He turned back to the pyre, his head bowing as the flames began to die down.

She stepped away as the fire became low embers, leaving her king to mourn in peace, her thoughts swirling. As she reached the edge of the courtyard, she found Yasher waiting for her, his arms crossed and his expression unreadable. She stepped up to him, his arms opening and enveloping her.

"Phoenix?" he asked, his voice low with the unspoken question of whether she'd be alright.

Farah nodded, though the gesture felt hollow.

Yasher stepped back, his hand finding hers and stepping towards the hallway out to the public areas.

"Come with me," he said.

Farah frowned, her brow furrowing. "Where?"

"I think we need tea and cakes," he said simply, "created by a little girl who talks to gods."

Farah hesitated, but the warmth in his gaze was enough to break through her uncertainty. She nodded.

"Yes," she said softly. "Let's go."

EPILOGUE

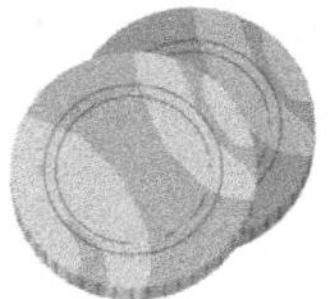

THE SAFFRON OASIS felt like a different world entirely. The air carried the warm, comforting aroma of spiced tea and freshly baked bread, mingling with the faint perfume of blooming jasmine that twined through the latticework of the shop's walls.

Yasher leaned back in his chair, letting the late afternoon sunbathe his face in soft golden light. Around him, the chatter of customers created a gentle hum, the kind of background noise that could lull a man into a sense of peace. He'd made a point of bringing Farah here every day since the funeral, just to get her away from the Citadel.

Across the table, Farah lifted her tea to her lips, her movements slow and deliberate. The soft clink of porcelain as she set the cup back on its saucer drew his attention. He studied her, letting his gaze linger on the way the light played across her features. Her hair caught the sun, shimmering with an almost bluish sheen that danced along its inky black waves, and her dark eyes had an unusual softness to them, one that had been absent in the days following Behnaz's funeral.

410

Farah wasn't smiling, not quite, but there was a quiet calm about her that Yasher wrapped himself in. She looked toward him, and for the briefest moment, her eyes lit up, as if the very sight of him brought her some small measure of joy. It was fleeting, but it was enough to make Yasher's chest tighten in a way that was both unfamiliar and entirely welcome.

He glanced down at the small plate of cakes Pari had set before them earlier, the bright colors and intricate designs a testament to the girl's growing skill. Yasher popped a piece of one into his mouth, savoring the blend of honey and spices. Across the table, Pari was bouncing slightly on her toes, watching him expectantly.

"Well?" she asked, her hands on her hips in a way that reminded Yasher far too much of Shirin.

"It's edible," Yasher said, keeping his tone deliberately casual.

Pari's eyes widened, her mouth dropping open in mock outrage. "Edible? That's all you have to say? I worked so hard on those!"

Yasher grinned, leaning back in his chair. "All right, all right. They're the best cakes I've ever had, Pari. Better than anything I've ever been lucky enough to eat."

Pari beamed, her hands clasping together. "I knew it!"

Farah chuckled softly, her hand brushing against her cup as she reached for another cake. The sound sent a pleasant warmth through Yasher, and he found himself watching her again. She hadn't laughed much lately—not since the funeral, not since the Mashya's request. But here, in this little corner of the world, she seemed lighter. Freer.

Shirin appeared at Pari's side, her hands deftly adjusting the girl's hair, which was coming undone from the ribbon Farah had tied earlier.

"Pari, dear, let them enjoy their tea," she said gently, though her smile was fond.

Pari groaned but relented, following Shirin back into the shop. He watched her retreat, then turned his attention back to Farah.

"How's it going?" Yasher asked, keeping his voice low enough not to carry. "The rebuilding. All the... damage, political and otherwise?"

Farah sighed softly, setting her cup down and tracing the rim with her finger.

"It's... slow," she admitted. "The Mashya's trying, but it's not easy. Some of the minor landholders are fighting over territories. They've lost their Talented to the wasting sickness, so their holdings are weaker than ever."

"Rostam and the Mashya are at each other's throats over it." She shook her head, her expression a mix of frustration and exhaustion. "Rostam wants to offer reparations, redistribute resources to help stabilize the regions. The Mashya thinks it'll make him look weak, like he's admitting fault for something he didn't cause. They argue like an old married couple, and meanwhile, nothing gets done."

"Rostam and the Mashya? Now that's an image. " Yasher raised an eyebrow, leaning forward slightly. "Didn't know they were that close."

Farah hesitated, glancing around as if to make sure no one was listening. Her voice lowered, a flicker of something like curiosity mixed with unease crossing her face. "They were close. Once. Before Enayat married Behnaz. They grew up together, you know. Court friends. Training partners. Some say they were... more."

His eyebrows lifted in surprise. He didn't think that the old warhorse Rostam did more than spar, argue, and dislike people, especially Yasher.

"No one knows for sure." Farah's lips curved into a faint, wry smile. "But the way they argue now—it's not just politics. There's... history between them. Before Enayat took the throne, the court gossip was always that the old Mashya quashed anything to do with Enayat's paramours that wouldn't bring in more money, more prestige, to the kingdom, and pushed Enayat to marry into a wealthy noble family. He fell for Behnaz, and Rostam became Commander of the guard."

She took a small sip of her tea. "I've seen the way Rostam looks at him sometimes, like he's reliving some moment from decades ago. And Enayat... he's softer when it's just the two of them. But in council meetings, it's all formal posturing, like he's afraid anyone might notice."

"That's unexpected." Yasher leaned back, processing her words. "So you think they're... what? Rekindling something? Think it'll get the stick out of Rostam's ass and remember he's a human being?"

Farah rolled her eyes at his commentary, ignoring his last question.

"I don't know. Maybe. Rostam's loyalty to him is absolute, even when they're arguing. And Enayat," she said, "he trusts Rostam more than anyone else. It's like they're circling each other, trying to figure out if there's still a bridge they can cross."

Yasher tilted his head, a faint smirk playing on his lips. "Sounds like you've been watching them pretty closely."

Farah rolled her eyes again, though her cheeks warmed slightly. "It's hard not to notice when they're squabbling like children in the yard one moment and exchanging these... looks the next. I just wish they'd focus more on the rebuilding and less on whatever unresolved feelings they're dragging into every discussion."

"They're probably trying to figure out how to balance what was and what is," Yasher said, his tone uncharacteristically thoughtful. "Not easy when you've got the weight of the world on your shoulders."

"Maybe." Her expression softened as she met his gaze. "But the stakes are too high for them to let personal history get in the way. The people need solutions, not half-baked arguments about who's right."

Yasher chuckled, shaking his head. "Sounds like someone's been biting their tongue a lot lately."

"You have no idea," Farah muttered, though her lips quirked into a faint smile. "Still, I can't ignore how much Rostam has been doing. He's everywhere, holding everything together. If anyone can get through to Enayat, it's him."

"Maybe they'll figure it out," Yasher said. "And if they don't, you'll knock some sense into them, right?"

Farah let out a quiet laugh, the sound soft and genuine. "I might have to."

Before either could speak again, Pari reappeared, bouncing on her toes as she tugged at Yasher's sleeve.

"Do a trick," she said, her voice brimming with excitement.

"You know," Pari said, her tone conspiratorial. "With your Luck."

Yasher raised an eyebrow, glancing at Farah, who gave a small, amused shrug.

"A trick, huh?" he said, turning his attention back to Pari. "All right. Let's see what we can do."

Farah looked up at that, her lips curving into a faint smile.

"You don't have to humor her," she said, though there was a hint of curiosity in her tone.

"I think I do," Yasher replied, reaching into his pocket for the coin he always kept there. It was a simple thing, tarnished and worn, but it had been with him through countless games, countless gambles, and now seemed to have taken the place of his old lucky charm.

He flipped the coin into the air, sending a silent nudge of his Luck along with it. It landed neatly on the edge of his teacup, wobbling for a moment before settling perfectly upright. Pari gasped, clapping her hands together.

"That's nothing," Yasher said, grinning as he flipped the coin again. This time, he aimed for the stack of plates on the table, willing it to land in just the right spot.

The coin sailed through the air, and for a moment, Yasher's Luck felt like a thread pulled taut between him and the world. He could sense the trajectory, the balance, the possibility of it all. But then the thread pulled tighter, slipping out of his grasp and snapping loose.

The coin struck the plates, sending them toppling in a cascade that caught the edge of the table. Yasher's eyes widened as he felt his Luck surge, redirecting the falling objects in a way that defied reason. The plates stacked themselves neatly on the edge of the table, the coin landing on top with a soft clink.

The entire tea shop fell silent, every eye turning toward their table. Pari's mouth hung open, her expression a mix of awe and delight. Shirin muttered something under her breath, moving quickly to adjust the plates before they could teeter again.

Farah stared at him, her eyebrows raised. "That was... more than I expected."

He shrugged, feigning nonchalance, though his heart was racing.

"It wasn't supposed to do that," he admitted, his voice lower.

"Do you think it's..." Farah tilted her head, her gaze thoughtful. "Changing? Your Talent?"

He hesitated, turning the coin over in his hand.

"It feels like it's... bigger than it was," he said slowly. "Like it's stretching further than I want it to. I can feel it pulling at things I don't even mean to touch."

"There are still a few of the old tutors who would help to train the Beloveds in the Oceanside District who may be able to help if you're concerned." Farah reached across the table, her fingers brushing against his.

Yasher smiled faintly, his thumb brushing over the edge of the coin.

"Maybe," he said. "But for now, I think I'll stick to tricks that don't involve collapsing tea shops."

Pari giggled, her earlier awe replaced by pure delight.

"Do it again!" she said, her eyes shining.

"Maybe later," Yasher replied, ruffling her hair.

Shirin reappeared with a fresh pot of tea, setting it down in the center of the table with a practiced grace.

"No more tricks," she said firmly, though the corner of her mouth quirked in a smile.

Farah's hand rested lightly on his, her touch warm and reassuring. He glanced at her, taking in the way her eyes softened as they met his. The last of his anxiety fled away as he tumbled into her eyes. In that moment, with the scent of tea in the air and the sun casting golden light over her, Yasher felt something he hadn't expected—peace.

It wasn't the kind of peace he'd imagined for himself, the restless itch of his Luck still tugging at him, the faint allure of a game of cards down at the docks never fully fading. But here, in this place, with Farah at his side, it felt like enough.

This, he realized, might have been what the Eye and his own Luck had been guiding him toward all along. Not just survival. Not just fortune. But this—moments of quiet joy, shared with someone who made the world feel less heavy.

Farah leaned into him slightly, her head resting against his shoulder as she reached for her tea. Yasher tightened his grip on her hand, his thumb brushing over her knuckles.

Whatever road she chose to walk next, he would follow her. He didn't need the Eye or his Luck to know that.

As Shirin poured their tea, the warm, spiced aroma filled the air once more. Yasher let out a slow breath, his gaze lingering on Farah as she lifted her cup, her movements graceful and sure.

For the first time in a long while, he felt like he was exactly where he was meant to be.

Author's Note
And Acknowledgements

I'm really so thankful for all of you who have read The Hand of Mashyana. I truly never thought that I'd get here, holding my own book in my hands, and sharing it with all of y'all. Every author will tell you that their book was a labor of love, and every single one of them is, and Hand was no exception.

As with most things in my life, The Hand of Mashyana all started with a song.

I was prepping for participation in National Novel Writing Month (Nanowrimo) in October of 2022, looking through all of my random idea snippets in my Google Doc dedicated to those sentences or sometimes paragraphs that I've collected over the years for potential writing projects. I really wasn't finding The Thing that was grabbing my attention, the story nugget that I thought was worth the 50,000 words that would get me through Nanowrimo.

Music is almost always playing in my house, and my hyper-fixation at the time was a British alt-folk duo, The Amazing Devil. My family hates it when I get into one of these modes, where I'm playing the discography of one band over and over again, but it seems to help when I'm stuck, so I keep doing it. And then what caught my attention was their song, Inkpot Gods, in particular the line "If I don't make it back from where I've gone, just know I loved you all along".

And all of a sudden, I had an image in my mind of of a couple on a bridge, one having to move on without the other.

Enter Farah and Yasher, having to separate on the Chinvat Bridge during the climax of the story, though I didn't know who they were or why they were there at that point. Things started to fall into place after that. For some reason, the bridge popped out as having to be the Chinvat Bridge from the Zoroastrian belief, probably as some kind of artifact from my old History degree hanging out in my noggin in place of something like, "Did I eat breakfast today?".

If you're familiar at all with either Farsi or Zoroastrianism, you'll easily pick up the language and some of the culture that I used as my muses, and I went into world-building mode, creating the world of Emari, finding Farah, Pari, Behnaz, and Enayat easily and realizing that this would definitely not be a standalone adventure. I wanted to stay in Emari and get to play in all of the nooks and crannies that this world provides.

I'm sure that I'm going to miss someone, even though I've been over and over this Author Note (I think more than I read all of the multiple revisions of this book), but I need to share some of the people that helped take this rough idea and turn it into what you're currently holding.

Hand would not exist in its current format without my village of support, starting with Patricia DeVarennes. Pat has put up with me and my shenanigans through my entire life (no, really) and she's always there for me with the best writing advice, whether it's just calming my anxiety about turning in workshop artifacts or just to be my first reader on so many other projects that may or may not reach the light of day. Even if you went and moved across the country, knowing I can call you up at any moment and you answer is worth its weight in gold.

A shout-out of the highest magnitude to Tammy Bulson. Sweet lady, work may have been the reason that we met and became friends, but you are always such a light, years after we stopped working together. You're always there to lift me up, be the Joy, along with not holding back on where I can make my writing better.

What really pushed Hand into place was signing up for Alessandre Torre's Writing Bootcamp in 2024. I had to step away from Nanowrimo after 20 years of participating due to their shenanigans over the last two years, and I was in search of something that would help me. This bootcamp not only got me to the finish line from an absolute mess of a first draft, but exposed me to more writers in the same place as I was, and put me in front of editors that I wasn't familiar with. I learned so much, and I'm so thankful that the Sparrow Cabin is still rocking and rolling after the bootcamp finished up. Jess Avril, Kerri Duffy, Kim Kookendoffer, Christopher Iolaire, and Melissa Patton, y'all are absolute rockstars!

Thanks to TikTok, I found an absolutely amazing editor in Brandy Gibson. I was (doom)scrolling one day, and this lovely person appeared on my fyp offering editorial services, and I took a shot to see if she had some time open in the timeline I was looking for to get this done. What started as just a transactional relationship has blossomed into a spectacular working friendship. Just know that I have screenshotted and saved every single "OMG" and "I aggressively love this person" to keep and look at when I'm feeling low. I can't wait to work with you again on this series!

I can't help but gush about some of my other favorite people, my beta readers — In this journey to publish my first book, y'all really stepped up to make a gal feel like gold, helping me see this story I'd been living with for two years with fresh eyes and making sure it was the best thing that I can create. Your feedback is invaluable, and I appreciate all of the help that you gave me. Thank you to Aaron Bentzel, Terri Boerwinkle, Hana Ghorbani, Isabella Mills, Alicia Ostrowski, Debrra Randolph, and Erik Sagen.

Liz Bock, you are all the things that I hoped you'd be and more, and yet you still put up with me as your mom. They are an amazing artist, and when I struggled to do my own book cover (because I am my own worst customer, seriously), they hopped onto this crazy bus for me and not only did my book cover, but also my maps of Emari and the Citadel that grace this book.

And thank you, Dear Reader — whoever you are, wherever you found this book, I adore you. I do hope you'll stick around for this adventure with Farah, Yasher, and Pari.

Amber Hansford - February 2025

ABOUT THE AUTHOR

Amber Hansford grew up a Navy brat, moving up and down the East and West coasts for most of her youth, finally landing in Atlanta, Georgia and working in the tech industry for many, many years. She's been a front-end developer, designer, product manager, and UX Director, working on everything from major league sports sites to supply chain software.

Throughout it all, though, she was writing.

For most of the time, her writing was really just for her, whether it was fanfic or original work, she kept it to herself. Sometime around the early 2000s, she found fanfiction.net and decided to try and share some Highlander (the TV show, not the movie) fan fiction she'd written a few years prior at the urging of some IRC folks who were all enamored with Methos. The rest, as they say, is history.

When she's not writing, her Too-Much Gene takes over, and you can find her at Dragon Con as the track director for the Filk Music Track, working on her freelance design and development work, or trying her hand at a new hobby that's struck her fancy as a potential Apocalypse Skill^{TM}. Lately, that's been embroidery, which may not be Apocalypse-worthy, but she seems to enjoy it.

Amber still lives in Atlanta with her husband, kid, and her "lab-mix" rescue pup, Belle.

Find out more about Amber and her books at amber hansford.com

facebook.com/amberhansfordauthor

instagram.com/amberhansfordauthor

threads.com/@ahansford

tiktok.com/@amberwritesthings

bsky.app/profile/amberh.bsky.social

Thank you for buying this Polymath Publishing book.

To receive bonus content, information on new releases, and see
what Amber's up to in general, sign up for her newsletter,
Ink & Ash.

amberhansford.com/mailing-list

Or visit her online at

amberhansford.com